Danforth had never se⋯
The flat, unyielding white was quivering like a curtain in a wind. Waves of cooler white or dirty gray chased each other from horizon to horizon.

"What do you think?" Stavros came up from the rear of the hold.

"I, ah . . . I'd guess some sort of instability along the interface between the dry heat down here and the cooler, moister air above that's creating the cloud."

"The Sawls say it's Valla's death throes." Stavros was struggling for some measure of calm. "Apparently it'll get fairly spectacular soon . . . fire falling from the sky, the like . . ." A wave of color surged past; the long ends of Susannah's hair lifted freely away from her body and crackled with tiny blue fire. Danforth saw terror bloom behind Stavros's steady gaze, but it was not fear of anything he could accept or understand. He looked at the pulsing sky and shrugged. "Best we be moving along, then . . ."

MARJORIE BRADLEY KELLOGG

with

WILLIAM B. ROSSOW

Reign of Fire

VGSF

with thanks to
    Antonia D. Bryan, Jane Ira Bloom,
    Karen Haas, Sheila Gilbert, Eric Golanty,
and Lynne Kemen

VGSF is an imprint of Victor Gollancz Ltd
14 Henrietta Street, London WC2E 8QJ

First published in Great Britain 1988
by Victor Gollancz Ltd

First VGSF edition 1988

British Library Cataloguing in Publication Data
Kellogg, M. Bradley (Marjorie Bradley)
Reign of fire.
I. Title   II. Rossow, William B.
III. Series
813'.54[F]

ISBN 0-575-04342-3

Printed and bound in Great Britain
by Cox & Wyman Ltd, Reading

In memory of *Challenger* and her crew

January 28, 1986

Commander Francis Scobee
Pilot Michael Smith
Gregory Jarvis
Christa McAuliffe
Ronald McNair
Ellison Onizuka
Judith Resnick

BOOK ONE

" 'Who's there, besides foul weather?'
'One minded like the weather, most unquietly.' "
KING LEAR
Act II, sc. iv

FTL HAWKING Exploration of Byrnham Cluster
(UWSA/CONPLEX Exp. 23)
Star system PT 6 (KO, 3 p?)

(continued)
large terrestrial planet for mineral potential
and possible evidence of ETI artifacts by landing science team for nine month period.
(2) Astronomical study of Pop.II late sequence
stellar system from supporting (in-orbit) SCR
BOSTON with focus on composition of primary
and nearby stars.

B. Expedition Complement
  B.1. Ship Complement
    B.1.1. System Carrier - research
           SCR BOSTON   UWSA 036A3
           Configured for: 1 Lander, 4 planetary
           orbiting satellites, 4 message drones.
    B.1.2. Lander - research
           LR 14   UWSA 0014C2

  B.2. Crew Complement
    B.2.1. Ship Crew
       Captain Maxim B. Newman   (Commander, SCR)
       Commander Weng Tsi Hua   (Commander, LR: Land.)
       Lt.Commander Jen Wilson   (Master Pilot, SCR)
       Lt. Veronica McPherson   (Pilot, LR: Landing)
       Lt. Bea Suntori   (CRI Specialist)
       En. Ro T. Gobajev   (Propulsion Engineer)
       En. Josei Pilades   (Engineer/MedicalMate)
    B.2.2. Science Team
       Dr. Taylor Danforth   (Ch.Sci., Planetology, L.)
       Dr. Jorge Sundquist   (Asst.Ch. Sci., Astronomy)
       Dr. Susannah James   (Exobiology: Landing)
       Dr. Megan Levy   (Anthropology: Landing)
       Mr. Stavros Ibia   (Linguistics: Landing)
    B.2.3. CONPLEX Team
       Dr. Emil Clausen   (VP, Expl& Dev, CONPLEX:L.)
       Dr. Rye Hobart   (Remote Sensing Specialist)

C. Star System PT 6 Schedule

        The schedule covers the following mission
phases: star system entry, planetary orbit entry, pre-landing orbital surveys, landing, and

PROLOGUE

The old people tell of a time when the sun was gentle for many cycles and the crops in the fields swayed low with fruit. But soon, they say, Lagri Fire-Sister stalked the halls of Her desert fortress, restless for new diversion.

She summoned Lightning, Her messenger, and sped him to Valla Ired, Her Sister of Water and Ice. Then She marshalled Her armies: Heat and Thunder, Tornado and Drought.

The Lightning spoke to Valla in Her palace beneath the ocean. "Fire-Sister proposes a wager."

Valla urged a red snail across Her coral gaming table. "I am well occupied here."

Lightning spun bright cartwheels around the shadowed hall. "Lagri mocks Your seclusion, Water-Sister. She calls You coward, and boasts that She will make You prisoner in Your own dwelling. The length of a DarkTime, She will hold You fast."

Valla looked the messenger up and down. "What are the stakes?"

"She offers the Plain of Dop Arek, which She took from You during the most recent engagement."

"A mere skirmish." Valla curled a pale lip. "The Dop Arek is not worth calling Snow and Rain from their rest. Let my Sister play alone."

Lightning sizzled enticingly. "She might be convinced to include the Talche Hills. . . ."

Valla crooked a finger. She flicked the red snail into a pocket at the corner of her game board.

"And the wide river Dym beyond. . . ."

Valla smiled coldly, easing back her chair. "My Sister will regret this reckless wager."

Lightning laughed, a shower of sparks. "Then let the Game begin!"

UWSA/CONPLEX Exp. 23: Star System PT 6
FTL HAWKING Exploration of Byrnham Cluster
LR 14, UWSA 0014C2, Landing Team D:

Cmdr. Weng Tsi-Hua   (UWSA)
Lt. Veronica McPherson   (UWSA)
Dr. Taylor Danforth
Dr. Megan Levy
Dr. Susannah James
Mr. Stavros Ibiá

    CONPLEX repr: Dr. Emil Clausen
027 - 2074   Earth Departure, FTL HAWKING
116 - 2074   Arrive Byrnham Cluster
139 - 2074   Arrive PT 6, HAWKING launch SCR BOSTON
142 - 2074   Orbital insertion BOSTON, 2-PT 6
145 - 2074   LANDING: Accomplished under extreme conditions, base camp established: Site 5: 24 10'N, 31
45'E. On the edge of a vast plain. LR 14 currently
sunk in 10 meters of snow and ice. Chief Science
Officer Danforth trying to reconcile existing weather
with expected desert-like conditions. Cave system in
high cliffs to southeast show signs of intelligent
habitation (stairs). Heavy snow and severe cold hamper site exploration. Unloading of light transport A-
and B-Sleds deemed unadvisable.

151 - 2074   FIRST CONTACT. Near-human inhabitants
are lightly built, on the small side, non-agressive,
strangely uncurious. Dr. Levy reports technology at
pre-industrial level. Snow continues.

153 - 2074   Linguist Ibiá reports inhabitants call
themselves 'SAWLS' and their world, 'FIIX'. Local
contact named 'Liphar'. Snow continues. Dr. Danforth
very perplexed: climate not behaving as it should.
    Addendum: *Young Ibiá will not see reason with regard to*
his dislike for Dr. Danforth. Dr. Levy only marginally better with
Mr. Clausen. Delay threatens our mood as well as our mission.

192 - 2074   Snow ceased 1600, near planetary sunset.
Hot winds brought sudden thaw followed by torential
rains. Beamed power disrupted, forcing evacuation of
Base Camp. A-Sled swept away in violent flooding. Possible damage to Landing craft. Light transport B-Sled
carrying Mr. Clausen and Dr. Danforth on prospecting
trip lost in storm. No communications with Orbiter or
with Sled due to unexplained "interference".

193 - 2074   Sawls have extended us the protection of
their Caves. Storms continue. Mr. Ibiá reports
PriestGuild predicted weather change accurately, also

that Sawls worship a pair of goddesses who are said to fight wars with weather.

201 - 2074   Storms continue. Communications and power beam still out. Sawl Ranger Guild conducting perilous searches for lost B-Sled. Crew morale low due to confinement, damp, and two and a half weeks of black planetary night. Dr. Levy investigating extensive gambling practices among Sawl population.

Addendum: Indications are that Mr. Ibiá is over-identifying with the subjects of his study — as Mr. Clausen would say — "going native." (Interference not yet called for.)

208 - 2074   Dawn at last, coinciding with end of storms. Sawls claim victory of goddess Lagri is cause of clear weather. Entire population pouring out of Caves to plant a crop in waterlogged mud. Lt. McPherson off with Master Ranger Aguidran to search for occupants of lost Sled. Initial inspection of Landing craft shows mud clogged engine ports, considerable surface damage to underside. Communications and power still out: main com dish and antenna destroyed or blown away by storm.

214 - 2074   Lt. McPherson and Master Ranger have returned with Mr. Clausen and Dr. Danforth. Former appears in good health. Latter sustained deep chest injury and fractures of both legs. Dr. James providing surgical care, in conjunction with Sawl healers' guild and Master Healer Ghirra. Mr. Clausen encouraged by a potentially rich find of lithium ore.

Addendum: Jhirra's guild library contains some intriguing old documents: evidence of lost scientific knowledge from a distant past? Could that diagram I found truly represent a periodic table??

215 - 2074   Communications, power still out. Dr. Danforth disabled but will recover. Lander com dish found, badly damaged. Mr. Clausen attempting immediate repair. Sawls packing up ENTIRE (?) population for trade caravan to neighboring settlement. Dr. Danforth now obsessed with solving climate mystery. Drs. Levy and James, Mr. Ibiá have been granted leave to accompany caravan in order to continue anthropological, biological and linguistic studies.

Addendum: Friction increasing between Mr. Clausen and other expedition members - remedy?

217 - 2074   Impressive Sawl Leave-taking ceremony nearly ruined by bizarre freak thunderstorms. Sawls claim goddess Valla Ired attacked sister goddess Lagri and was repulsed. Dr. Danforth could offer no scientific explanation.

1

"EMBRIHA LAGRI!" the young man cried, and thrust the shining banner high into the hot, still air.

Amber light played among its folds. Fine embroidery glimmered. The bright white cliff rose steeply behind. For a moment, the silken triangle of orange outshone even the sun hanging swollen against a wide green sky as opaque as polished malachite.

The exultant throng cheered, but as quickly quietened. Silence held for the length of a sigh while echoes rang along the towering wall of rock.

Among the white-clad ranks of the PriestGuild, the elders eyed the lofted wave-and-flame seal of their guild uneasily, flicking questioning glances in the direction of their guildmaster's frown. The Terran expeditionaries regarded their young colleague's gesture with equally mixed feelings.

"Look at poor old Ashimmel," Megan murmured drily. "There's Stav hailing the Goddess's victory, and the Master Priest can't decide whether to approve of him or not."

"What is he up to?" Susannah whispered. She sensed faint challenge as well as celebration in the raising of the PriestGuild banner.

Megan chuckled. "Always a flair for the dramatic, our Stavros." She gestured at the line of laden wagons. "Getting the caravan off to a rousing start."

But watching him, Susannah was unconvinced. The gleam in his eyes and the fervent thrust of his arm spoke of a deeper conviction. Without formality or prior announcement, the ancient Sawl Ritual Master Kav Daven had drawn Stavros into his strange ceremony of Leave-taking, as if it were the most natural occurrence to include off-worlders. *But only Stavros . . .* Susannah struggled to deny a creeping sensation of exclusion, but it expressed itself anyway, through prim censure. "I suspect you may be right about him getting too personally involved here."

Megan cocked a mildly satiric eyebrow. "Which the rest of us would never think of doing, is that it?"

Stavros lowered the banner suddenly, as if made self-concious by the spontaneous drama of the moment. Released, the crowd exploded into hubbub and bustle and a surging toward the wag-

17

ons. At Kav Ashimmel's impatient signal, two white-robed apprentice priests lifted the Ritual Master's canopied palanquin as easily as if it were empty, and trotted it across the dusty terrace to the cliff stairs. Kav Daven's milky blind eyes glimmered within the shadow of the ribboned hangings. The elderly and infirm of all the guilds followed in their own covered chairs and litters, ascending the steep, wide steps in a long and colorful line.

The other celebrants shed their finery where they stood. The winch ropes were loosed from their ballast. Standards and banners and neatly folded ceremonial robes were busily loaded onto the wooden pallets to be hoisted up the sheer cliff for safe storage in the guildhalls. The lean, leathery Master of the Ranger Guild strode among the hundred assembled wagons and countless carts, barking orders, receiving hurried reports from her guildsmen about final preparations for the caravan's departure. Every so often, her attention drifted skyward and she offered a fierce glare at the hot malachite sky as if daring it to show a single threat of cloud.

Susannah nudged Megan as some of Aguidran's urgency caught hold. "Hey, we've got last-minute stuff to do ourselves."

They pressed through the milling mass of people, vehicles and animals to the big yellow hard-canopied Infirmary wagon, stationed in the exact middle of the line. At its head, the Master Healer's dour assistant Ampiar consulted with a bright-faced ranger over the harnessing of the double teams of hjalk. The great golden beasts bore the sun's heavy amber heat without complaint. At the rear, the packing still progressed. Susannah reassured herself that her own medical kit had not been buried too deeply, then stood aside while the physician's apprentices scurried about under the calm direction of the Head Midwife, tying lash lines and stuffing each remaining nook and cranny with last-minute items.

The expedition's blond-haired Lander pilot wandered up to watch restlessly. "Gonna be real quiet around here," she said matter-of-factly. "Never thought I'd wish I was on a science mission."

Susannah smiled. "Want to come along?"

McPherson smoothed an envious hand across the wagon's freshly painted wooden sides. "Hah. Can you see the Commander letting me, after the hell Emil raised about Stavros going? I bet she ain't had a tongue-lashing like that since she was a cadet, with me and Tay right there, you know? And she just stood there and took it."

Because she's a tough old bird, thought Susannah, not for the

18

first time. "Good for her. I'm sure she's heard lots worse in her time." She exchanged a glance with Megan. "Not like Emil to throw his weight around in public, though."

Megan snorted. "Must have run out of his day's ration of oily charm."

"Besides," McPherson consoled herself, easily scaling the high side of the wagon to wriggle into the padded driver's seat with the testing curiosity of a professional. "She needs me to help get the com and power up again. It's no good you guys going out into nowhere without a connection to Base. We need CRI back on line."

"And then there's Taylor," Susannah added with a sly glint. "Someone's got to stick around to nurse him along."

The little pilot guffawed, then pushed off her perch with a sprightly bound that turned into a suggestive cavort as she touched ground. "Hell, yeah!" she grinned. "Well, see you guys." She turned to go, then lingered to point out the line of litters climbing the cliff. "Who'll take care of those oldies left up in the Caves?"

Megan draped her arms over the chest-high rim of the sturdy front wheel and leaned against it heavily. "Liphar says there's a maintenance crew of sorts that stays behind during trading trips— some priests and rangers for the weather watch and a bunch of FoodGuilder agriculturalists to keep an eye on the crop. It only looks like the whole world's on the move."

Susannah felt a moment of doctor's concern for the plump older woman. Megan looked heat-worn already, eager for some shade, reconsidering perhaps the wisdom of embarking on a month-long trek without the standard expedition amenities. The Sawls, though on the small side and chronically thin from a lack of abundant food, were a hardy people, more resilient than their Terran visitors and more resigned to hardship. Being a full decade younger than Megan, Susannah was less concerned about herself, and presented an adventuresome face to the idea of being out of contact with both Lander and Ship's Computer. But secretly, she prayed for the speedy repair of the storm-damaged communications and power link with the Orbiter. Gazing across the wide rugged plain that stretched from the foot of the cliffs to lavender mountains in the north and east, she worried about the kind of medicine she might have to practice out in the bush, with little more available to her than her own hands, a few drugs and the intriguing skills of Sawl Master Healer Ghirra.

Ghirra himself arrived then, leading his own small caravan. Commander Weng paced him on one side, dressed in habitual spotless white with her rank insignia glinting on her collar. On the other, the little apprentice Dwingen struggled to keep up with his guildmaster's long stride. Behind them marched four apprentices, carrying the expedition's injured planetologist on a leather stretcher. The bearers had been scavenged from various guilds at a moment when all other hands were needed for the packing. Stavros walked alongside the stretcher, a little apart, his body taut with barely contained energy, smiling at some private thought.

The bearers set the heavy stretcher down on its folding wooden legs, then stood back, shaking the cramps out of their arms. Susannah moved to Danforth's side to check his pulse and temperature. The big man lay like a black Gulliver fallen among the Lilliputians. The odd ceremony and the odder bout of weather that followed had exhausted his meagre strength. He grasped Susannah's hand weakly.

"Did you see all that?" he demanded. "What did *you* see?"

"Just some weird-looking clouds, Tay." She lied gently to soothe him. "A storm that didn't happen."

McPherson hovered solicitously. "He's okay, hunh?"

"This sun is not the best thing for him." Susannah adjusted her stance so that her shadow fell across his sweat-beaded face. Danforth breathed his thanks and let his eyes droop shut.

"So much damn work to do . . ." he murmured.

" . . . and so, GuildMaster," Weng was explaining to Ghirra with gracious precision while one thin hand tucked wisps of silver hair back into her neat bun. "According to our ship's clock, it is the end of a very long day for my personnel. Though I understand that it is near the beginning of a cycle for you, I'm sure you can appreciate how hard it would be on the three who will accompany the caravan if your sister begins with a full twelve hours of travel."

The Master Healer nodded, his long, handsome head inclined in patient, respectful sympathy. He looked taller and leaner without his linen physician's smock, his brown curls gathered at the nape of his neck, more like the Master Ranger, his sister, Susannah thought. Like the rangers, he now wore his blousy cloth trousers tucked into the tops of loose-fitting calf-high leather boots, softened at the ankles with long, hard wear.

"The second and third work shifts haven't had their sleep round, either, Commander," Stavros pointed out from his slight remove. "Doing their best to make up the delay. Everyone's going to be tired."

"I think my sister asks only one half throw this time," Ghirra offered consolingly. "But already we are late. We must travel many throws by Darkfall."

Megan's attention was caught. "But so long as we're into

night travel anyway in a week or so, why not rest now and then start refreshed?''

Ghirra smiled politely. ''Rest *after* a Leave-taking, Meghan?''

''Oh, right. No. Of course not.'' The anthropologist was plainly embarrassed, but Susannah sympathized. Many Sawls had learned some English after two months of the Terran presence on Fiix. But Ghirra was exceptionally fluent, and an astute observer of Terran manners besides. Talking to Ghirra, it was often easy to forget you were talking to a Sawl, until you indulged in some particularly Terran reasoning and received his oh-so-courteous but astonished response.

Stavros laughed softly. He had stopped with the others but remained a bit apart, smiling at them with uncharacteristic benevolence.

Like he has nothing to do with the rest of us, Susannah mused. She had seen that distanced look many times on Sawl faces. The Terran linguist stood calmly, but his angular features were still flushed with the excitement of the Leave-taking ceremony and his unexpected participation in it. His usual glowering intensity was transformed into a kind of glow. When McPherson joined him to discuss a strategy of repair for the comlink, his expression hardly changed. He answered her questions with benign attention and kept smiling his odd, half-wondering smile.

Kav Daven's special attentions really affected him, Susannah decided, and wondered how long this seeming change would last.

A pair of rangers came by on a last-minute inspection tour, dressed in soft road leathers and boots. Their dark faces were shaded by wide-brimmed hats of waxed cane woven on a bent reed frame, resembling the traditional headgear of Commander Weng's farming countrymen, but noticeably more rigid and heavier. With them was the Head Herdsman, a short, energetic woman with bared muscular arms and thick braids of auburn hair shot with silver. She bustled over to take the Master Healer aside. He excused himself and disappeared with her around the front of the wagon while her lively hands sketched out an explanation of the slight limp on one of the hjalk she had assigned to his teams.

Weng made a small shrugging gesture that was confined mostly to her chin. She turned to Susannah. ''I trust, Dr. James, that you three will fare well enough out there. We will assume that this more settled weather will favor our repairs here so that you will not have to remain incommunicado for too long.''

Susannah dug for the insulated desert hat that had languished for two months at the very bottom of her field pack. She held it up and shook out the wrinkles. "Guess we're going to need our hot-weather gear after all." She patted Danforth's shoulder. "See, Tay, you weren't so off base as you thought."

The leather stretcher creaked as the planetologist stirred from the fringes of a doze. "Even *more* than I thought," he mumbled, but did not elaborate.

A phalanx of ranger runners trotted along the line of wagons, their long curls bouncing around their eager brown faces as they called out the final ready signal. The stretcher bearers exchanged covert looks and shifted restlessly.

"Go on, take him down," Susannah told them, pointing toward the tilted silver cone of the Lander hulking among the terraced fields a half-mile away. "We won't leave without you."

Stavros' quick translation brought relief to the young Sawls' worried faces. They hefted Danforth's bulk willingly and started off at the fastest pace they could muster. McPherson waved her shipmates a cheerful farewell and sprinted after them. Weng nodded soberly and followed at the more disciplined pace of the able but elderly.

"You notice Emil hasn't condescended to come around and say good-bye," observed Megan, not without satisfaction.

Susannah shouldered her pack. "He'll work out his irritation on the repairs. One day we'll be trudging along out there on foot and he'll come whizzing by in the fixed-up Sled, hot on the trail of a billion-dollar lithium lode."

"Exactly what I'm afraid of," Megan replied seriously.

A sharp cry rang out from the distant head of the caravan. The lead wagons jolted into motion, a dark brown wagon with the carved guild seal of the RangerGuild gleaming on its side, the first of twenty giant red-and-blue FoodGuild wagons that were interspersed throughout the train, the Master Potter's wagon, a smaller graceful wagon from Woodworkers'. The rattle and creak of wheel and harness rose in a rumble with a spreading cloud of yellow dust. Ghirra reappeared at the side of the Infirmary wagon with the Head Midwife, Xifa. The two youngest apprentices danced around them like excited puppies. Smiling gravely, the Master Healer explained to Susannah that little Dwingen was facing his first trade journey away from his family wagon.

Megan did not object to Ghirra's suggestion that she might prefer to ride. She hauled herself up into the driver's seat beside Ampiar, groaning comically with the effort. Ampiar took up the reins. The double hjalk teams bent into their harness. When the wagons just ahead began to move, Stavros broke his silence as if suddenly recalling where he was.

"I'll be further up with Liphar's family," he announced. He

gave Susannah his same odd smile and loped toward the head of the train.

Walking alongside the wagon, Susannah asked Megan, "What's *with* him, do you think?"

"Stav? Oh, he's okay."

Susannah frowned faintly. "But that's just it, Meg. You don't think it's a little odd? I mean, he actually looks happy."

2

The wide cart track headed eastward along the stony ledge at the base of the cliffs. The long train of wagons and guildsmen walking with their families moved at a snail's pace at first, carefully skirting the acres of planted fields where the new amber shoots reached skyward with astonishing speed. The still-flooded terraces mirrored hard, green sky between neat rows of slim yellow stalks unfolding their first true leaves.

Passing under the sentinel shadow of the tall rock spindle she had dubbed the Red Pawn, Susannah conjured visions of white-topped Conestogas sailing the ancient North American wilderness, and felt her excitement quicken. As the caravan rattled down a long, stony incline to the level of the plain, a gang of FoodGuild apprentices began a song-chant that spread down the line until the refrain was picked up by the herdsmen escorting the dairy herd through the dust clouds at the rear.

Beyond the Red Pawn, the cliffs veered to the right, as the mountains behind swung south to join the rugged Grigar Range, then curved around in a deep arc to fill the distant eastern horizon with the gentle foothills called the Talche, or "the Knees." The caravan moved due east onto the plain, which opened up like a vast expanse of water. Far to the northeast waited the Vallegar, its sharp peaks a deeper, bluer green against the green sky.

Susannah found herself breathing deeply, not from exertion but in response to the sudden sense of endless space, after so many weeks of confinement in the lamp-lit caves that had become her temporary home. "Dop Arek," the Sawls called the plain—"the Goddesses' Gaming Board." Susannah found the name ominous, considering the violent nature of the sister-goddesses' games. The Sawls' eagerness to forsake the shelter

23

of their caves and brave the open ground for so long seemed reckless at best, but was the truest measure of how crucial the trade with other settlements was to their long-range survival. Ten throws, Ghirra said it would take, two weeks by the Terran clock, to reach their destination, a town on a leg of the northern ocean, called Ogo Dul.

Progress across the Dop Arek was slow. The ground was storm-ravaged, broken by deep ravines and muddy washes. Here and there, signs of a roadway showed in mounded depressions flanked with wheel ruts softened by the recent flooding to the dangerous consistency of glue. The big hjalk strained against the constant pull of the mud, and Susannah's field boots and khakis were soon caked with drying ocher. The Master Ranger was forced into frequent circular detours around steep-sided gullies and arroyos choked with rock and flood debris. The detours often required further detours, seeming to lead the caravan ever farther away from their eastward route.

The noon air was windless and thick with humidity, as the hot sun sucked water from the sodden ground. The Dop Arek was utterly treeless, either by natural habit or, as Susannah judged from the twisted nests of unidentifiable vegetable matter clogging the ravines and stream beds, due to the extreme violence of the flood. But despite the mud and devastation, new plant growth furred every surface offering moisture and nourishment. Susannah broke open a new pack of specimen bags and eagerly began her biological survey.

She took her first samples along a section of visible roadway: delicate yellow coils uncurling into fernlike brachts. They grew in soft spreading patches, the tallest reaching to her waist. On sandier ground, she found clusters of a broader, thicker leaf set in whorls about clusters of tiny scarlet flowers. She gathered several of these, of differing maturity, intrigued by the early development of prominent seed pods. It was thirsty work, bending and cutting and hurrying to catch up with the Infirmary wagon as it repeatedly passed her by. Susannah was very aware that after only two hours, the canteen on her belt was already two-thirds empty. Her ship's issue clothing, though intended for hot climates, was overly tailored and binding. Already, she missed a working therm-suit, and regretted her part in helping Stavros to convince Megan of the greater integrity, diplomatic as well as scientific, of travelling as the Sawls travelled, to experience each hardship exactly as they did.

The golden-curled hjalk, as well as the hakra, their diminutive cousins hitched to the smaller carts, pulled their loads uncomplainingly, as if they required no rest or water to maintain their

24

steady pace. Taking a break from the exertions of her survey, Susannah walked on the shade side of the Infirmary wagon. For many miles, she was haunted by the oddness of Stavros's parting smile, then set herself the more useful task of reviewing her store of knowledge about camels, reminded of them by the hjalks' broad fleshy feet, equally well suited to the mud of the Dop Arek as they would be to sand. She wondered if the hjalk and hakra stored water like the camel, or possessed the camel's incredible stamina.

Ahead of her, the Master Healer had fallen into a shambling gait as steady as the hjalks'. It was a practiced travelling pace that propelled him along with the least expenditure of effort. A ceramic jug rested in a sling across his back, but Susannah saw him uncork it only once or twice. The singing and chanting were more sporadic now, occasionally inspired into resurgence by the pipers who walked with the ranger wagons, playing the rhythm of the pace.

Megan remained in the wagon, at Ghirra's insistence. Dwingen currently occupied the other half of the driver's seat, while Ampiar took her turn on her feet with the rest of the medical staff. Dwingen was a frail but brilliant boy. Susannah guessed he was Ghirra's favorite apprentice. She grinned up at him as he tried to look serious and in control, with the great bundle of reins bulging out of his small hands to lie slack across the hjalks' backs. Fortunately for Dwingen, the hjalk knew better than he which way to go.

As the caravan wound down into a shallow valley, Susannah spotted new specimens for cutting and ran ahead armed with her sample bags. She took sprigs of low-lying scrub covered with minute yellow leaves that were thick and oblate, like tiny pea pods, and crisp with moisture when broken open. In the damp bottom of a wash, she discovered a scattering of waxy orange blossoms with sharp red spikes at the end of each petal.

The Sawl physicians eyed her with varying degrees of suspicion and concern as she rushed about taking her samples. Ghirra eventually felt compelled to assure himself that she did not try to eat any of her cuttings or use them as herbs.

"But there must be all sorts of edible plants out here," Susannah protested. "With your own supplies so short, I'd think you'd take advantage of any available foodstuffs."

Ghirra flicked a warning finger at the bagged sprigs and leaves. "These is not food. These make you sick, Suzhannah."

"All of them? Every one?"

"Yes," he replied, and from beside him, sturdy Xifa added her nod of agreement.

But more astonishing to Susannah was the stupendous growth rate exhibited by all the native flora. Several ship's days earlier, at the end of two nightside weeks of continuous rain and wind-storm, the entire landscape had been a barren sea of mud. Now it was rich with plant life in full leaf and bloom, already showing signs of rapid seed development.

"The plants grow so fast!" she marvelled to Ghirra from the Infirmary wagon's shadow, when the caravan finally halted at the bottom of a brush-lined sandy ravine, for a rest and a mid-throw meal. Master Ranger Aguidran stalked by on her routine inspection tour, nodding to her brother as she passed. The FoodGuild wagon nearest them was bustling with senior guildsmen loading bread and cheeses and dried meats into wide baskets for distribution down the line.

"It is fast?" Ghirra was interested. "Do the plants grow much slowly in your caves?"

Susannah decided not to do as Stavros would do, that is, explain to the Master Healer that the Sawl phrase meaning home translated poorly into English if rendered literally. "They grow much slower than here," she replied, turning a full sample bag in her hands. "We're always trying to make them grow faster, to mature and fruit quickly so that our very limited agricultural space can be replanted as soon as possible. The mechanism that allows such rapid growth would be well worth discovering."

Ghirra said, "You must ask this of Ard when we come to DulElesi again."

The idea of asking anything at all of the irascible Head Herbalist Ard was an intimidating prospect. Susannah was glad he had remained at home with his cave-grown medicinals and his freshly planted herb plots, sparing her the ordeal, for the time being at least.

Ghirra considered further. "I think it is that if the plants do not grow fast, they die before the seed comes to grow again after the rains."

"That's evolutionarily sound, for sure, but it's still amazing. If our computer were working, I'd cross-check in her files, but I'd bet on my guess that your plants, especially the cultivated varieties, grow faster than anything else on record. It's positively uncanny."

His interest quickened. He tried out a word he had recently learned. "You name this growth *abnormal*?"

"We think your weather's abnormal, too." Susannah shrugged thoughtfully and reached for chunks of bread and cheese as a FoodGuildsman offered his laden basket. "But growth rate is relative, isn't it—it depends on an organism's needs in a given situation. Who can judge what 'too fast' is, relative to the universe as a whole?'' She leaned back against the tall rear wheel and nibbled her cheese, happy to be out in the open air, pondering the mysterious details of her work. Megan dozed on a blanket beneath the front axel, snoring gently, too tired even to eat. A small stream wandering the flat ravine bottom played gentle music to accompany the meal. An insect, or something that sounded like an insect, buzzed out in the sunlight. Susannah looked for it, but it had passed too quickly.

"What means this word 'evolu-tion'?" asked the Master Healer.

Susannah sat up. "You could say it means changing to suit a changing environment. An organism adapting itself in order to survive."

"And your or-ganims can do this change if they wish?"

She laughed gently. "Only over many thousands of years, Ghirra. It's not a thing you do consciously, like changing your clothes. For instance, in the analyses I ran of the dried plant specimens I was given during the snows, I found a substance very like the sugar trehalose, which some Earth organisms produce to allow them to survive drought. Trehalose replaces the water that maintains the spacing between molecules on the surfaces of cell membranes. Only a few Earth organisms manufacture it, but here on Fiix, every plant I have tested so far contains an analogue for it. This is a perfect example of evolutionary adaption to a changeable environment." She recalled Danforth's pre-landing predictions of desert conditions, now confounded by the empirical evidence of two months of snow and rain. "Do you sometimes have long periods without much rain?"

Ghirra nodded as if this were grimly obvious. "When Lagri fights well her battles, the dry times is long, and the same is after a long gist, when the Sisters are tired and also their armies. It is very hot, then, as if Lagri herself breathed on us, for many cycles."

That sounds more like the desert Taylor expected to find here, Susannah mused.

He continued doggedly, as if even to speak of such things was to risk bringing them about. "But if a Sister wins in the Arrah, this is most bad of all. Many die then, in the Wet Death or the Death by Fire, and then will come Atoph Phenar, when the Sisters rest from sunrise to sunrise and the air does not move."

The air does not move? Susannah tried to imagine what he might mean by this and failed. "And that's what you call a Great Devastation?"

"This is, yes."

"But so long as Valla Ired and Lagri are fighting, which is

most of the time, you get this freakish weather? If Lagri's strong, it's hot and dry; if Valla, it's cold and wet. There's no pattern, no way to tell what the weather's going to be until it's practically on top of you?"

"There are the signs," he replied, as a hint of reproof drew down the corners of his habitual smile. "My sister's guild watches well for these, and tells them to the PriestGuild with most speed so the predictions can be given."

Susannah dusted crumbs off her hands and took up one of her sample bags. "But there's no one to warn the plants, is there . . . I think you're right. It would account for why the growth hormones are turned up off the scale." Tiny blunt thorns like ridges of little teeth poked at the resisting clear plastic in her hand. She realized that weather had not been much discussed during her time in the Physician's Hall, but when it was, it was never expressed in terms of natural phenomena. There was no "weather" or "climate": there was only the Arrah, the Goddesses' endless struggles to best each other.

"You see," she continued, "on Earth, weather patterns are more easily predictable by scientific means. They follow the dictates of season and geography with some reasonable consistency. It's never freezing one morning and tropical by noon."

"Your goddesses perhaps are kinder than ours," Ghirra murmured.

Megan had woken up and was listening from under the wagon. "When is the weather worse, when the Sisters are fighting or when they're not?"

"With no gist, the air will not move," he repeated patiently. "This is very bad. When one Sister grows too strong, this is very bad." He pushed one flattened palm against the other. "When the strengths is same, this is best for us."

"Like a balance between non-weather and too much weather," said Megan.

"Yes. This is the time of Otoph." He considered the Sawl word, nodding. "Balance is a possible translation."

"Is it Otoph now?" asked Susannah.

Ghirra spread his hands, a Sawl shrug. "It seems this, but the signs . . ." He squinted furtively at the hot, green sky. "There are other signs."

He never looks quite comfortable when speaking of the Goddesses, Susannah noted. *Not like Liphar, for example.* But then she had to admit to some discomfort herself in discussing the sister-deities as if they were the actual living beings that Stavros claimed the Sawls believed they were.

28

Ghirra sucked his cheek. " 'TavrosIbia says you do not have these Goddesses in the world you live."

"There are some who would dispute that," offered Megan into the pause that followed. "But you won't get any argument here."

"Perhaps your caves do not need the Arrah to move the air."

"You're saying the fighting is necessary, then?" Susannah asked.

His shoulders hunched as an eagerness flared in his eyes. He lowered his voice cautiously. "The Priests do not teach this but my sister shows me from her own guild books that it is so. The Priests teach that the Darkness brought the fighting, which can end only when the Darkness goes."

Susannah awaited Megan's favorite question, 'What Darkness?', leading to a discussion of the apparent lack of savior mythology and why the Sawls gambled over the weather instead of praying for it to change.

But Megan leaned forward intently, also whispering, her compass swinging loose around her neck like her own sort of talisman bead. "Do you think worlds only have gods when they need them, GuildMaster?"

Ghirra hesitated, frowning slightly as if caught by this thought.

"If a world has no gods," Megan pursued, hot on the trail of anthropological paydirt, "then who created it?"

"The creators," the healer replied with only slightly more conviction than before. "Who created all, the First Books say. If the night lanterns are worlds, as Ibi says, the creators made these also."

"Valla Ired and Lagri are not creators?"

His expression was a subtle mix of offense and amusement, and Susannah could not tell if it was with them or with what he was about to say. "I will tell you what the Priests teach to us from the First Books: that the Sisters were born as we were born." He found a sharp stone and scratched the familiar symbol of interlocking circles in the dirt. "They teach we are all three daughters of the creators."

"Not quite the supreme beings, then, these Sisters," observed Megan.

"Wow," Susannah breathed. "Meg, remember the Dance of Origins, how you complained that there wasn't a creator mentioned in it?"

The older woman nodded with enormous satisfaction. "Turns out it's our mythical king figure. Wait until I tell Stav. He's found his Sawl Book of Genesis after all."

*　　*　　*

The rangers passed the starting call down the line and the caravan continued along the marshy ravine. The gravel bottom of the streambed offered a damp but firmer base for the wagon wheels than the choppy mud of the upper plains. An occasional lavender-pinkish streak showed among the striations of earth and rock, but the tall crumbling banks of the ravine were increasingly crowded with vegetation. Susannah was forced to become more selective in her sampling so as not to use up her supply of bags too early in the journey.

After the sixth hour of travel, Ghirra asked Dwingen to surrender his place to Susannah, who was showing signs of wear. Instead, Megan offered to walk, and Susannah climbed into the high driver's seat without protest. The harsh din of wheel rattle and harness was amplified by the ravine walls into a rhythmic roar that made her dream of an ocean after a storm. Rocked by the sway of the wagon, Susannah dozed.

Later, the rhythm was broken by a jolt and she woke clutching the worn leather of the seat. The ravine had deepened further, widening and curling back on itself like the coils of a snake. The streambed gravel was roughened by larger stones and the occasional boulder. The hjalk labored under their loads and the pace slowed as Aguidran sent a contingent of her rangers ahead to clear the worst of the obstacles.

Susannah stretched and called to the girl apprentice Phea, who she noted had not yet taken a turn in the shade of the wagon's yellow canopy. Phea climbed up gratefully, and Susannah grabbed her field pack to go clambering among the rocks for samples of a fleshy orange plant growing in spiny clusters, like a vegetable porcupine.

Upturning a stone by accident, she had her first confirmed sighting of local fauna: a long, whiplike body that slithered quickly away to hide under the next boulder. Briefly glimpsed, its eyes were yellow and bulging. The shape of its limbs seemed blurred as if still forming themselves.

Amphibian, she guessed. *Like a frog tad*. But the creature's movements and its smooth-scaled skin were more like a land animal's, a snake or a lizard. Instinctively, she grabbed for the disappearing tail.

"NO!" Ghirra barked, and she heard him running across the gravel. It was as hard-edged a syllable as she had ever heard him utter. She jerked her hand away and stared back at him in astonishment.

He slowed in relief as he saw her straighten up empty-handed. "You must not touch these," he said sternly, as if to a child.

"Are they poisonous?"

30

He nodded, his long hands gesturing an awkward apology. "Lagri's Messengers, they are called. Touching brings fire on the skin. If they bite, the fire is inside."

"I see." Abashed, she tucked her spiny cuttings into her pack and climbed down from the rocks. *What the hell's the matter with me? I wouldn't go around grabbing at strange animals on Earth . . . of course, there are no strange animals left on Earth. Not any more.* She walked back to the wagon at Ghirra's side. "Are there many poisonous creatures around?"

He hesitated and once again, she recognized his look of gentle perplexity. *I've said something he considers stupid,* she guessed.

"All are poisonous," he said finally, "for their safety. If not, the larger ones would eat them and they would be gone."

He possessed an empirical understanding of evolution after all. "If they're so poisonous, would that be bad?" she prodded.

His puzzlement deepened into a frown. "You are a doctor, Suzhannah. Do you cut away your arm if it pains? All of the parts are necessary to the whole."

"Yes," she agreed, eager to disprove Megan's contention that Sawl religious views did not include a system of ethics. "Is this what the Priests teach?"

"This is what I teach," he replied softly. He excused himself and moved ahead to speak soothing words into the small ears of the hjalk as they struggled to haul the heavy wagon along the obstructed ravine.

Susannah tramped behind in silence, feeling obscurely rebuked. She decided that the new tone she had detected in Ghirra's manner since the incident with Clausen's rocks was not so much distance as subtly implied moral superiority. Contemplating it further, she found it all too reminiscent of a certain young linguist of her acquaintance.

Damn, she worried. *Now what's he been telling them about us?*

The caravan rattled around a narrow, stony bend. Ahead, the leafy banks fell away and the ravine joined a wide sand wash, which then curved and dropped to meet a deep, flat-bottomed canyon. The far rock wall was steep and sharply corrugated, with layers of rose veined with ocher and white. A thin yellow river snaked across the canyon floor. A faint stir in the humid air cooled Susannah's damp cheek and set the dairy herd, straggling at the rear, to bellowing with unrestrained enthusiam.

Tall lemon and amber grasses grew in the marshy areas between the river's tight curves. Where the water wound close to the steep eastern face, tumbles of rock were overgrown with

31

thick palmate fronds and the bristles of tall stalks resembling giant aloe. A few hard-trunked succulents with long muscular roots clung stubbornly to the stone. They were mud-caked and scarred, but Susannah found them particularly beautiful. They were the first plants she had discovered that had clearly been around since well before the recent storms.

Several dark oval creatures waddled tortoiselike to the water as the rangers led the caravan down into the canyon and halted along a gentle curl of the river. Susannah watched after them hungrily, taking quick snapshots in her mind for later translation into her sketchbook.

The herdsmen hurried to oversee the unhitching of the teams. The freed hakra and the hjalk were sent downstream to splash and roll among the dairy herd, under the watchful eye of rotating shifts of apprentices. TiNiamar, the aging Master of the FoodGuild, trudged the full length of the line, from one blue-and-red wagon to the next, hastening preparations for the cooking of the dinner meal. Water casks were unshipped. Fire pits were begun.

The first throw was over.

Susannah drained her canteen, no longer concerned if it ran empty, then kicked off her boots and walked to the water's edge. The stream was shallow and lazy, deeper along the inside of each bend where the current was busy cutting a more comfortable channel into the sand and the sparkling bottom was barely visible through several feet of golden water.

She rolled up her stained pantlegs and waded in up to her calves, then crouched to dip water with cupped hands, splashing the sweat and grime from her face, letting a handful or two dribble down the back of her neck. The water was not cold, having travelled too many miles over hot sand to retain much of its mountain temperature. But it was cooling, and Susannah lingered in her crouch, face dripping, hands trailing in the gentle current, mind dazed blank from eight hours in the Fiixian sun.

"Thank the lord for state-of-the-art sun blocks." Megan padded across the sand to join her. "Aren't you going for a swim? It looks like everyone else is."

Susannah rose blinking from her reverie. For half a kilometer in either direction, Sawls were shedding their clothes and hurrying for the water. Small children ran ahead naked and squealing with delight. Infants barely learning to walk waddled intently after their siblings. Older children carried babies in harness on their backs. The adults were no less eager, and soon the riverbank teemed with brown naked bodies easing themselves gratefully into the depths of the stream. Even paunchy TiNiamar and iron haired Ashimmel forsook their duties long enough for a cooling thigh-high wade.

Megan and Susannah exchanged glances.

"When in Rome . . ." grinned Megan.

The two women dropped their muddy clothes on the bank and threw themselves into the deepest part of the water. Susannah dove and came up for air refreshed and laughing.

On the bank, still in their sweat-stained trail gear, Ghirra and Master Ranger Aguidran walked along the row of wagons, deep in conversation.

3

The silvery landing vehicle was a surreal addition to the pastoral landscape of white rock and cultivated fields. The sheer cliff face, crisscrossed with carved stairs and ledges, pierced with neat, dark rows of arching cave mouths, was solemn, majestic. The Lander seemed almost clownish, resting at an incongruous tilt since being nearly toppled by the flooding.

A clearing surrounded the cone-shaped tower, a barren no-man's-land separating alien metal from the burgeoning red-leafed vegetation in the fields. To one side, a large dish antenna lay on its back in the drying mud, its battered spokes and torn golden mesh glinting with amber sunlight. McPherson stood next to it, a fist pressed to her jaw in sober contemplation. In the four-meter-high space between the Lander's underside and the mud-swept ground, a base camp had been reestablished.

"I assume we're all in an experimental mood tonight?" Emil Clausen wiped the wide blade of his oak-handled cleaver on a towel hitched to his belt, then surveyed the ingredients laid out on the squared horseshoe of crates. He chose a handful of brown golfball-sized spheres and set them on his cutting board. The knife made a comforting thunk against the resealable plastic as he chopped. "Rock fungus," he explained to whoever was listening. "Should do nicely. And this . . ." He lifted a bunch of vermilion leaves sprouting from broad yellow stalks. "A trifle garish, I know, but they had such a marvelous pungence, cooking up in the Caves, I couldn't resist. Still and all, you know, Sawlian cuisine will attain no great heights without the introduction of a few crucial ingredients, like garlic."

33

"You mean you didn't bring your own?" Danforth shifted his cast-bound legs with effort to the far side of his paper-littered bed. The orange sun, beginning its ever-so-slow descent, was invading his precious shade. He gasped softly as his right knee bumped the worktable that McPherson had just rigged up out of one of the smaller hatchcovers torn from the Underbelly during the storm. She had supported it on either side of the bed with upended sections of utility rack, part of which also held a small computer hooked up to an emergency battery. The concavity of the hatch and its various shallow protuberances were minor inconveniences compared to everything else that was bothering Danforth.

"By the way," Clausen continued cheerfully, "I did a few basic field tests. The ore samples turn out to have an exceptionally high lithium content for plain old lepidolite."

"I'm glad for you," Danforth muttered.

"But I'm thinking, since lithium cools last out of a melt, we can expect fairly pure veins, so maybe I'll wait the claim a bit until I find one."

"Ummm. Say, Weng, have you got a moment?" Danforth pulled himself upright by his arms, the one part of his body that remained strong and whole. The thickly humid air was like weight in his lungs. His chest wound had begun to itch as it healed, encouraging but destructive to his concentration. He settled more comfortably against his pillows and spread a sequence of photos across his work table. Commander Weng came over to stand at his shoulder, hands clasped behind her waist in an attitude of deep attention. "Okay," he said, "now tell me what you think of this."

Behind them, Clausen continued to chat as he expertly sectioned the spherical mushrooms. "You know, I seem to have stumbled inadvertently on a handy way to extort food out of these little fellows."

Danforth drew a red diagonal line across the center of a hemispheric photo of the planet. "That storm activity was confined largely to this narrow band."

"Equatorial," Weng noted.

"More or less, but inclined, as you can see, northwest to southeast." He pointed to top and bottom of the planetary disk. "Here are the rotational poles. But the axis of symmetry for the recent activity runs this way, northeast to southwest, some twenty-eight degrees off the rotational poles."

Weng gave a nod that managed to imply both encouragement and vague disassociation with the matters of planets.

Clausen's voice rose to edge out Danforth's lecture. "I simply hang around the Caves looking like I'm trying to get in without anyone noticing. The clever little buggers have psyched out my weakness: they know they can distract me with groceries."

Danforth glanced over his shoulder in annoyance. "And the wind direction is northeast to southwest and vice versa, moving in both directions along the axis of symmetry."

Weng said, "Ah?"

The planetologist's eyes rolled and his pencil beat a rhythm of frustration on the metal hatchcover. "Under *normal* circumstances, Commander, the winds should move west to east, zonally, and perpendicular to the rotational poles. A nice simple system. Not like this nonsense."

"Ah." Weng leaned in for a closer study of the photos.

"So every day," said Clausen, scraping the chopped fungus into a plastic bowl, "up I go. And every day, they trot out some new Sawlian delicacy to tempt me with. Must keep them working overtime, with so few of them left at home." He left his horseshoe counter, rubbing his hands, and went to the edge of the shade to turn the four little carcasses browning on skewers above a glowing dung fire. He chuckled, wagging his head in falsetto mimicry. "Oh me, oh my, what shall we put that dude off with tomorrow?" He poked the fire. "They've even learned to surrender the goods uncooked. Food for the imagination as well as for the stomach." He straightened and called out into the sun, "What's the verdict, McP?"

McPherson returned an unintelligible reply from her crouch beside the broken dish.

At Danforth's worktable, Weng picked up a photo between delicate fingers to squint at the dateline, then replaced it beside the others in the same sequence.

"The snow clouds breaking up," said Danforth.

"Extraordinarily rapid change," she murmured. "But then, we saw that with the naked eye, Dr. Danforth. And later . . ."

He knew she referred to the most recent and bizarre of meteorological events, the storm that didn't happen during the Leavetaking. "An anomaly due to extremes of heat and cold," he replied brusquely. "Has to be. I'll get to that later. Right now, I'm just dealing with the data we had before we lost CRI. When I woke up after Susannah sewed me back together again, I promised myself I'd approach this problem from a completely different direction: tabula rasa. I spent too much time trying to blame seemingly inexplicable data on inaccuracies in the instruments. Then I lost confidence in my circulation model. But plugging some proven Venus data into it came out fine. So after that, I started altering this term or that, tinkering with the Venus measurements, pushing them more towards this Fiixian data, and then the snow stopped and I . . ."

He riffled the corners of a stack of mud-stained printout. "Well, whatever. I never got to finish that process, and now I can't do any complicated model runs until we get CRI back anyway."

Weng offered no comment, but Danforth did not require one, only her patient, listening ear.

"So I'm thinking about it this way: A does not equal B. What does B lack to make it A? It lacks C. C is the term missing from the equation, not just poor resolution of data or some minor imbalance, but a whole term. Some X factor, some anomalous something, some force that's unique to this planet, that makes the weather behave the way it does but that the probe instruments somehow missed, so it never got into the model. That's what I have to look for now, the ad hoc that will make the model start churning out the right results."

"What are the possibilities?" Weng searched briefly for an empty crate, then slid a stack of papers aside and sat.

"Weng, don't get him started," Clausen warned, testing the heat on his portable stove with a dampened finger. "I'll have to hold supper, it'll be cold, not to say ruined."

Danforth's ebony jaw tightened stubbornly. "I started with the snow data, since that's what's available. In that case, we had a classic winter warm-front snowstorm: warm, moist air coming in from the northeast to meet cold, dry air from the southwest."

"And the moisture was precipitated out as snow," she offered.

Danforth nodded approvingly.

"Why do I get the feeling I'm being ignored?" Clausen complained.

"That was another anomaly," Danforth persisted. "On a slow rotater like Fiix, I expected large-scale wave motions, so any weather should be due to mechanical instabilities in the wind flow, not to temperature differences and these compact front phenomena."

Clausen cut a corner from a square brick of white Sawl butter and dropped it into a skillet. "Hey, don't you people talk to the help around here? Don't you know good cooks are hard to come by?"

"For Christ's sake, Emil!" roared Danforth suddenly.

Clausen hunched his shoulders and shuffled mockingly. "Beg pardon, massa, beg pardon." He danced an exaggerated tiptoe back to his cutting board as McPherson trotted in from the sun.

"Whole receiver's gone from that center shaft, Emil," she reported.

"Shhhh!" he hissed exaggeratedly.

McPherson stopped short in concern. "Why? What's the matter?"

"*He's* the matter," Danforth growled over his shoulder.

Clausen lined up yellow leafstalks with the flat of his knife. "The point is," he resumed in a normal voice, "that the Sawls are going to great lengths to keep me out of those caves. I think they're hiding something."

McPherson wrinkled her nose at the bubbling skillet. "What?"

The prospector shrugged as he chopped. "How do I know until I get in there to find out?"

"They let *me* in," said the pilot.

"Way in, McP. Way in. Beyond the beaten path."

"Oh."

"And why is that the point, Emil?" muttered Danforth irritably.

Clausen glanced up, grinning in mild surprise. "What?"

"I mean, what do you think is in there, for god's sake, dragons and treasure?"

Clausen stopped chopping. "I beg your pardon?"

"I mean, haven't we got more important things to worry about than what the goddamned natives might be hiding in their goddamned caves?"

"Hey, you guys . . ." McPherson protested.

Clausen's smile jelled, a winter stream suddenly icing over. He looked down at the leaves neatly diced on the cutting slab and nudged them around with the sharp tip of his knife. "Forget it, Tay. Go back to work."

Weng's chin lifted in silent disapproval. McPherson took a step toward Danforth, then glanced back as the prospector returned to his food preparation in chilly silence. She threw up her hands in exasperation.

"You guys . . ." she muttered, and stalked out into the heavy sunlight.

4

The FoodGuilders cut their swim short. While the other travellers lolled about in the shadows, debating the weather and trade strategies for Ogo Dul, the twenty red-and-blue wagons were turned inside out to produce a dinner meal to fill five thousand hungry stomachs. A dozen emptied two-carts, their hakra still hitched and waiting patiently, were sent off to gather the drying flood debris, the thick root skeletons and the matted brush. Long cooking pits were dug in the sand in front of each hard-canopied FoodGuild wagon. Huge fires were built. River water was set to boil in ceramic cauldrons that managed the rough journey packed among the sacks of grain. Into the bubbling water went entire bags of reddish triangular seed. Baskets of crooked tubers were buried among the coals to roast. Flatbread dough was mixed and shaped and set to bake on rocks near the flames. Milk was brought up from the dairy herd to be churned.

Megan rested in the shadow of the Infirmary wagon, fluffing her gray curls dry after her swim. She watched Kav Ashimmel consult with her senior priests, her pants legs still rolled up and damp from her wading. The priests' apprentices who were not in the water hung around listening for hints of a weather prediction.

In an earlier time, they would have called Ashimmel "a battleship." Megan smirked privately, thinking that the Master Priest was an imposing figure even without her white robes and wave-and-flame tabbard, but that her impressiveness was more political than spiritual.

The population was in a mellow mood, resting after their long day. Megan saw very few wagers laid as Ashimmel's conference dispersed and the apprentice priests wandered among the relaxing families and guild cliques with their lists and pouches.

Susannah joined her with a handful of plant specimens and her portable chemical analyzer. She sat cross-legged on the sand, her long, dark hair falling loose about her shoulders to shade her oval face. "Won't tell me much," she said, wagging the gray plastic box depreciatingly, "but at least I'll get a jump on it."

Megan nodded, leaning against a tall yellow wheel. Sometimes she thought of Susannah as a lovely, earnest child, naive, often self-righteous in the way of children.

That's the real reason we can't let her in on it all, she mused, thinking of Stavros and their plan to thwart Clausen's claiming of the planet's mineral resources for his megacorporate employers. *She still thinks everything should be open and aboveboard, as if all parties really* were *equal before the law.*

"Seen Stav anywhere?" Susannah asked suddenly.

Megan started guiltily. "Huh? No. Why?"

Susannah smiled, shrugged. "Just thinking about him."

"I'll tell him. He'll be delighted."

"Oh, Meg . . ."

*   *   *

When the caravan had cooled and napped for a few hours, rekindling their heat-dulled appetites, a wooden horn blew a tenor version of the priesthorns' basso boom. It was a less impressive call, but it sent the loungers scurrying for their platters and utensils. Susannah packed up her samples and analyzer and woke Megan from her doze.

The apprentice Dwingen reappeared, stripped to the waist, his curls still dripping wet and pale sand clinging to his thin brown legs. He dug in the back of the wagon and produced a stack of oval eating trays. He presented one each to Susannah and Megan, then scampered off with one of his own to join the long line piling up at the nearest FoodGuild wagon. The queues were noisy, an encouragement to singing and wagering debates, but there was little impatience. The accepted order seemed to be that the children be served first and sent out of the line, so the adults could help themselves in relative calm.

Susannah and Megan hung back in the Infirmary wagon's shade until Megan could no longer repress her anxiety that the food might be gone when they got there. Susannah trailed after her with less dispatch. Food lines reminded her all too unpleasantly of home.

But there was food enough when they got there, and they carried well-laden trays back to the medical wagon to find Dwingen and Phea already finished eating, and Xifa, Ampiar and the two older apprentices just settling down to their meals. Phea giggled as Megan attacked her food with a spoon and fork retrieved from her field pack. The Sawls used fingers or made neat scoops out of strips of flatbread. Susannah judged the hot grain mash bland but filling, and the stringy pinkish flesh of the roasted tubers delicious. They drank the golden river water and fresh hekker milk brought around by a FoodGuilder in jugs stacked in a brightly painted two-cart. A grateful munching silence prevailed and Susannah observed privately that the only time the Sawls were truely quiet was when they were eating.

Ghirra and Aguidran joined them as they were finishing. The Master Ranger ate on her feet, leaning against the rear wheel, her eyes flicking constantly from her food to the river, down the line of wagons and diners, to the sky above the canyon walls. Ghirra sat cross-legged at her feet, eating with slow care.

Susannah was full of questions about food and eating. Ghirra's statement about the wild creatures being part of the whole and venom as a guard against extinction had set her thinking about the issues of ecological systems. She perceived an odd duality within the Fiixian food chain.

"We eat what we grow only," Ghirra had said to her once,

after the planting of the fields at DulElesi. She had taken this as an expression of his pride in the Sawls' self-sufficiency, but now she heard his words differently: 'We only eat what we grow,' was perhaps what he meant, missing the proper English syntax, or alternately, 'we *can* only eat what we grow.'

There was no guild of hunters within the Sawlian social structure. The only flesh eaten was that of domestically raised animals. According to Ghirra, no human went out foraging among the wild plants, though the four-legged creatures were certainly encouraged to graze, without apparent ill effect.

I must note specifically what the animals eat and do not eat, Susannah decided. *And I must try to isolate this toxin of Ghirra's from my samples.*

This restricted eating pattern was not a luxury due to abundance. The Sawls survived only through careful management of limited food resources. From her own observations, Susannah knew that all vegetable scraps and the rare leftovers were collected and mixed back into the hakra feed. Human and animal waste went back into the fields. There was no such thing as a trash dump in the Caves, only storage awaiting recycling.

She extended her inquiry beyond the realm of edibles. The leathers, wool and skins used for clothing, bedding, parchment, boots, harness and countless other articles were all derived from the domestic beasts. She had learned that every other planting cycle, a portion of the cultivated acres was given over to fiber plants for paper and a cottonlike thread. The fine woven linen used in the Physicians' Hall was traded for in Ogo Dul, as was the reed and cane and rush for basketry.

Susannah ate automatically, now hardly tasting the sweet chewy tubers. Had Ghirra actually meant to say, "We *consume* only what we grow," as in "use" as well as "eat"? Could it be that the Sawls, except for the air that they breathed and the water that they drank, lived in their own perfectly closed system, coexisting with but apart from the rest of the Fiixian ecology?

Was this odd arrangement choice or necessity? Philosophy or survival?

The Sawls' birth, death and survival rates would have to be minutely well adjusted to their production capabilities in order to allow for such autonomy. If it was isolation by philosophy, say the ethics of a religion, she wondered, were they not tempted during the hardest of times, even forced, to raid the resources outside their own system? Or were these resources truely unavailable to them by cause of natural defenses they had been unable yet to penetrate?

"Ghirra," she ventured at last, "there's something I don't

40

understand." But she stopped, confounded. There was so much she did not understand, too much in fact to be able to shape the questions she needed to ask. She recalled Megan's earlier tantrums of frustration over too much data and too little insight, and finally empathized, several weeks too late. Taylor Danforth had questioned the validity of his data, Megan her own competence, but both had the right idea.

There is something odd going on here, something . . . special.

Ghirra awaited her question, a bread scoop full of grain mash poised between tray and mouth. The patience in his dark eyes could be interpreted as sympathy with her own expression of sun-baked confusion. But her mind was in a mode that questioned the easy intrepretation, and she could pinpoint exactly the moment when she had lost confidence in her ability to read him accurately.

Damn Emil and his rocks!

But she smiled as she shook her head. "It's not important."

He finished his mouthful, chewing thoughtfully.

The older apprentices gathered the empty trays and trotted off to the river to wash them.

"There's *lots* I don't understand," Megan chuckled, applying yet another layer of sun-block to her freckled skin. "But aren't you the one in favor of not worrying about it until insight sits down with you at breakfast?"

"I guess," said Susannah with scant conviction.

Xifa and Ampiar excused themselves to go visiting down the line. Megan yawned, looking at the high, fat sun and then at her wrist chronometer. "Jeez, it's six A.M. No wonder I can barely see straight. I'm turning in."

But before she could lay her blankets out under the wagon, Stavros arrived, his black hair sleek and wet, his dark eyes surveying them with restless interest. Young Liphar trailed along behind, curling a strip of bread to mop the last bits of mash from his tray as he walked. His wagering pouch bounced heavily on his hip. Stavros had shed his smart ship's whites and was back in his Sawl clothing, though like most of the Sawls he was wearing very little, just the loose light-colored pants that tied at the waist. Evidently he had gone this way for most of the day, for his olive skin was already sun-darkened. He had always favored an air of secrecy, which Susannah admitted was one of the things she found attractive about him. Now he seemed bursting to share his secret, whatever it was.

He greeted Aguidran with a hint of ceremony. The Ranger's look was more intently speculative than a mere return of civilities. Susannah noticed a new deference in her usually curt nod, and Ghirra's smile held honest welcome. Stavros lowered himself to the sand between Ghirra and Megan. His arrival was like a bolt of energy shot into their languid dinner circle. He settled among them as if he had great news to impart, yet he sat without speaking, his legs pulled up to his chest, arms wrapped boyishly about his knees.

He and Susannah regarded each other covertly.

"Don't see how it's going to be possible to get a good night's sleep in all this heat and sunlight," complained Megan idly, though she did not look particularly uncomfortable.

"Be grateful while we still have light to see by," Stavros returned, and Susannah was perversely relieved to see a trace of his old glower.

"The night lanterns will give light during the darkness," Ghirra offered, then corrected himself with a smile at the linguist. "I mean, Ibi, the *stars*."

Liphar's tray was finally scrubbed as clean as he could get it. He set it aside in the sand, unfastened the cloth pouch from his belt, then emptied its load of colored wood and stone disks into his lap and began to count them back into the sack. Only little Dwingen paid this much heed, eyeing the bright lapful enviously from his perch on the driver's seat. Finally, as if reminded of more childish playthings left at home, he asked Ghirra's permission to visit his family's campsite.

When the child had trotted off, taking Phea with him, Megan stretched her thick legs with a sigh as if some restraint had been lifted. Aguidran set her empty food tray on the lowered tailgate and hunkered down beside her brother so that their shoulders nearly touched. Ghirra sketched absently in the sand. Stavros rested his head on his knees. Liphar counted busily under his breath. Somewhere nearby, a single piper blew a sweet melancholy air, joined by a few murmuring sleepy voices. The scene was all very relaxed and casual, yet to Susannah, the sensation of being odd man out was suddenly undeniable. She sat apart from the circle, though not physically, waiting for someone to tell her what was going on.

The silence stretched uncomfortably until Stavros raised his head to gaze directly at her. The straight line of his mouth softened with an expectant smile.

And then the moment was gone. The tableau broke, all five moving simultaneously. Megan resumed the laying out of her bedroll. Aguidran rose, grasped her twin's shoulder with brief affection and departed to give orders to the weather watch. Stavros drew the healer into a discussion of the next day's route.

The two of them sat side by side in identical postures, chatting like old cronies.

But Susannah knew she had witnessed a true moment, though she could not tell what it meant. She began to suspect that however she tried to plot this five-way relationship, it would always take Stavros as its center. She pictured him among the cheering throng, raising the embroidered banner of the PriestGuild like a young warrior from another age, and she wondered once again, *What the hell is he up to?*

. . . and if Meg's in on it, why didn't she tell me?

It was clear that they did not trust her with their secret. The realization made her defensive and instantly lonely. It was one thing to remain aloof and objective within the constant company of a shipload of colleagues, but out here in a wilderness inhabited by lethal flora and fauna as well as hostile weather, she needed to know she had friends around her.

But no, that was not really it. She knew they would be there if she needed them. She simply did not like feeling excluded, and yet could not bring herself to confront them and force them to lie to her.

She waited until Megan had stretched out on her blankets and fallen asleep. Liphar finished counting and joined the two men in their discussion, which had fallen into Sawlish as it became more complicated. Susannah regretted that because Ghirra had acquired sufficient English so quickly, she had let her learning of his language slide. She rose casually, making an elaborate show of combing out her long hair, and wandered around to the far side of the Infirmary wagon.

As soon as she was away from their sight, she struck out across the sand, heading south at random, along the river, having no purpose in mind but to escape that unspoken comradery that did not include her. She broke into a trot, her stride lengthening as the release of running on the hard-packed river sand took over. She passed wagon after wagon, each sporting its painted or carved guild plaques. She passed clusters of smaller, slat-sided wagons and the single-family two-carts with freshly laundered clothing drying on their traces. Some families relaxed in quiet conversation, the children digging in the sand or playing stones, but most had laid out their blankets and rugs and fallen into a well-deserved sleep.

Beyond the last wagon, she slowed to pass through the dairy herd, and, already out of breath and sweating in the humid afternoon sun, she continued walking after she had left the placid hekkers behind to continue their destruction of a certain variety of yellow brush growing up the side of the canyon.

Well, there's one place where the two food chains meet. It was a small satisfaction, but she found totally separate ecosystems too neat for comfort.

The river slipped lazily around a wide bend. Out of sight of the caravan, away from the dust and noise and the constant jostling, Susannah's paranoia eased and she began to feel foolish that she had let it carry her even this far. As she was turning to go back, she noticed a section of the canyon wall ahead that had collapsed and spread itself in a jumble of ocher and white across half the canyon floor. The river curled languidly to one side of the obstruction, leaving some of itself behind in a deep pool held within the arms of the fallen rock. Clumps of the thick-trunked succulents sprang from between the boulders. The tallest leaned out over the pool to dip spiny amber leaves toward the water.

Susannah approached the bank, coveting the small shade of the golden trees across the water. She was hot again and sticky from her run. She wondered if Ghirra's rule about small creatures being dangerous extended to whatever might be living in the brown depths of the pool, then reflected that she and everyone else had already thrown themselves into the river without mishap. She stripped and waded in.

She felt cautiously among the sand and pebbles with her toes. When she stirred up nothing ferocious, she ducked into the water and swam a rapid nervous crawl across the pool to the rockfall. Nothing rose from the shadows to grab at her. She treaded water, holding on to a low, jutting ledge, then pushed off again to swim in slow, luxurious circles. The water cooled her as it slipped across her bare skin. The busy caravan was reduced to mere echoes sliding along the canyon walls, the hekkers bleating, a piper's sweet trill, parents calling their children to bed. Susannah's loneliness mellowed as she savored her first true moment of solitude in many months. The magnificence of the landscape was company enough, golden trees, towering walls of pink and amber rock. She lay back in the water and smiled up at the cloudless turquoise sky.

In that water-lapped stillness, she heard approaching steps, Stavros picking his way slowly along the stream, intent on the ground as his bare feet chose a careful path among the broken stones.

She thought, *perhaps I had this planned all along*, and made no move to retrieve her clothes.

He halted when he reached the pool's edge, and considered her for a moment in silence as she floated in the center, gazing back at him with as neutral as stare as she could muster. Finally, he loosened the tie at his waist with a quick defiant gesture, let the soft trousers fall and stepped out of them. He dove and came up swimming, his body slicing neatly through the water, speeding past her as she floated expectantly, heading toward the rockpile and its welcoming trees. He pulled himself up on the rock ledge, dripping, as sleek as a water animal, and stretched flat on his stomach across the warm stone.

Isolated still, treading water in the middle of the pool, Susannah could not repress a crooked smile.

Why is nothing ever simple, ever as you imagine it will be?

She considered swimming back to shore and leaving him to bake in the sun alone. It would serve him right. But he was decidedly beautiful, lying on the rock like an unwitting, handsome shepherd from a Greek myth. She did not feel very much like the proverbial goddess and he was hardly unwitting, but she decided suddenly that the game between them had gone on long enough. She swam toward him and hoisted herself up to rest by her arms on the overhanging rock. Her eyes were level with the back of his head. The smooth muscles of his back were within easy reach. Susannah did not reach. She waited.

"The most remarkable thing happened to me," he muttered at last, his face turned into the rock. He raised his head to stare abstractedly at his open palm, stroking a forefinger across it in wonder. He looked at her then, seeming to discover her nearness, and reached to touch her cheek with some of the same wonder.

"You are so beautiful," he said.

When she smiled and did not back away, he moved impulsively, arching his body across the rock to catch her behind the neck and pull her mouth up to his.

What has taken us so long? she asked herself when they drew apart.

Stavros laid his head on her folded arms and murmured, "Will you come up on this rock with me?"

"Gladly," she replied, for her body could not have refused him.

Later, she stroked his drying hair and asked, "What remarkable thing happened to you?"

But his answer was to kiss her with gentle passion and whisper, "You, I meant. Only you."

As Megan had predicted, Stavros was not to be a casual lover. During the next twelve hours of travel, he did not leave her side. He walked beside her in the sun, matching his stride to hers, helping her cut samples from the spined and needled plants along the way. Now and then, he caught her hand and held it until the damp heat or the roughness of the road forced them apart. When the caravan stopped for the mid-throw meal, he flopped down in the shade of the yellow wagon, and drew her into the crook of his arm while she laughed self-consciously and the others looked on like indulgent parents. Ghirra seemed oddly relieved and Liphar grinned as proudly as if he'd made the match himself.

Susannah was overwhelmed. Stavros seemed determined to focus on her with the same single-minded intensity he gave to his work. He said little, content to be with her, acknowledged as her lover. She thought it all a bit impulsive but, enormously flattered and instantly addicted to his impassioned lovemaking, she put it down to his youth, as she had his other excesses.

For the first part of the throw, the caravan pursued the winding canyon bottom, travelling upstream and more or less eastward toward the foothills of the Talche. After the mid-throw rest, the river narrowed as its bed was increasingly lined with rocks. The white spittle of rapids broke the surface as the current picked up speed. The canyon walls closed in around them until there was little more than a boulder-choked gorge ahead, thick with broad-leafed clusters and tangles of the yellow brush.

Aguidran turned the lead wagons into an upward-sloping dry wash, and with much urging and swearing and shouting, the lathered draft animals hauled the train of wagons back to plains level.

The Dop Arek was gentler here, the ground less ravaged by flooding. Soft brush-covered undulations flowed like waves into hills to the east. The old road appeared again, offering a decent surface over which they could at last make good time. The brush soon gave way to tall, sharp-edged grasses that bent before the wagon's passage like a mango-colored wheat field. The dairy herd as well as their drivers perked up at the sight of the hills and the rounded peaks of the Talche beyond them, but Stavros slipped his arm around Susannah's waist and pulled her close as they walked.

Aguidran pushed past the usual twelve-hour travel period in order to reach her intended campsite. Appearing suddenly out of the sea of orange grass was another river, broad and fast-moving but very shallow, full of sandbars and reddish reeds.

After dinner, Stavros led Susannah off to find a bed with him among the concealing grasses.

"When all this is over . . ." He waved an arm at the sky as they lay entwined on her blanket. The nearby clatter of the caravan was settling down for the sleep round.

Misunderstanding him, she said, "But I thought you liked it here."

He dropped his arm to stroke the curve of her belly. "Oh, I do. I do."

She fell asleep in his arms. Later, his kisses woke her. He smelled of strange grasses and desire. Sleepily, she pressed herself against him.

"I love you," he said.

She laughed softly, to lighten his mood.

"I do. Just remember that."

But when her chronometer's alarm beeped at her hours later, it lay beside her on an empty blanket. Stavros was gone.

"He'll steal the working antenna from the wrecked Sled, contact CRI in secret and send a message drone home before Clausen can file his claim." Megan was sympathetic but unrepentant. "We agreed I could tell you once he was on his way. He was afraid you'd try to talk him out of it."

Susannah stared at the ground. To her surprise, she missed him already.

"He didn't want a fight. The lad loves you, Susannah."

Susannah's voice was flat. "If you'd told me about all this before . . ."

Megan's gentle shrug held no apology. "We just couldn't be sure how far you'd carry your insistence on neutrality. Two partisan souls such as Stav and myself were sure you'd turn us in, on the admittedly sound principle that politics have no place in the practice of science. But out here, we're safely out of contact, and by the time we get back to DulElesi, Emil'll have figured out what Stav's up to anyway, so the only additional risk in telling you is to me."

"And to Ghirra and Liphar and Aguidran . . ."

Megan raised an innocent brow and Susannah's anger blossomed.

"Come on, Meg. I may be untrustworthy as a conspirator, but I'm not stupid! My own work depends on good powers of observation!" She spun away, pacing in short lengths of frustration, feeling unjustly taken to task for her loyalty to the ideal of objective observation. It did not mean that when the time came, she would not commit herself. It was just that the definition of the proper time depended so on your point of view. "Meg, if I thought there was a legal way to stop CONPLEX from ruining the planet . . ."

"Then my point is well taken. Our strategy is semilegal at best, and that's only if everything works out the way we've planned."

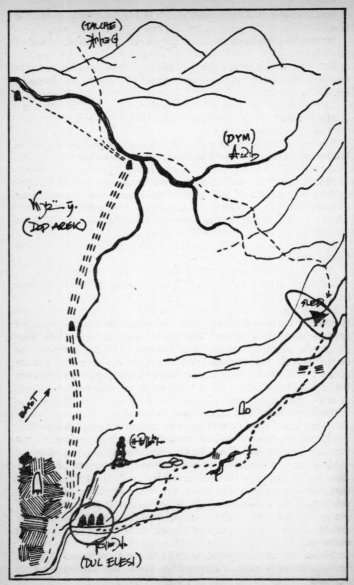

48

The fear that had stayed latent while her anger ran its course finally surfaced. She said dully, "Emil will kill him, Meg."

Megan smiled mirthlessly. "Funny you should see that as quickly as I did. It took Stav having a laser put to his head to realize that possibility." She nodded as Susannah glanced up at her sharply. "Oh yes, our man from CONPLEX came armed."

"But that's against . . ."

"Regulations? Regulations mean nothing to a man like that. And we're not safe in this either, you know. Or at least I'm not. You still have the choice."

Susannah's eyes burned with tears she did not want to shed. She was angry with Stavros for rendering her suddenly vulnerable. "Choice? It's not a real choice if you're forced into making it. I wish he'd . . ." She stopped, shaking her head in loss and confusion.

And Megan noted soberly to herself, *what sure instincts the boy has, to bind each of us to him with a different chain.*

5

Clausen bounded up the last flight of steps, ignoring the twinges in his ankle. He was glad he hadn't broken bones in the Sled wreck, as Danforth had. He still thought of his body as the well-honed tool he had made of it, but the reluctance of a mere sprain to heal forced on him another of those irritating reminders that he wasn't as young as he used to be.

He turned past the entry to the FoodGuild's main storage cave and headed along the ledge toward the stable entry. It was one of the oldest caves. The opening was ragged, shaped like a wide mouth caught in an awkward smile. The old stone shelter for the weather watch hunched to one side like a single blunted tooth.

He paused in the shade of the overhang, seeming to brush dust from his impeccably fitting khakis. No one waited on the inner stair, or hurried down to meet him with the usual armload of produce. Clausen adjusted the fit of his soft, fingerless suede gloves, pulled the straps tight around his tanned wrists. He flexed his left hand gingerly to assure himself that the tiny air-powered hypodermic lay comfortably in its sheath against the pad of his thumb. He lounged about, alert to the possibility that he was being watched. He made a show of standing back to study the guardian frieze in its high niche in the rock. The ancient frieze held no aura of mystery for him. He saw it as just one more artifact of a culture that did not impress him as particularly distinguished. He could admire the boldness of the carved representations of the Goddesses, or the crude expressiveness of the many tiny figures lamenting at their feet, but he'd seen far better in his time. Even so, he would take a few crates worth with him when he left, to make up for the regrettable fact that Sawl pottery was too sophisticated to bring much of a price on the primitive arts black market. Clausen's income was nicely supplemented by his connection to certain wealthy art patrons and dealers back home.

He edged toward the upward stair. His eyes restlessly skimmed the inner walls, tracing the smooth striations of the rock with the frustration of a compulsive reader who has been allowed only one book to read over and over. If the lithium strike on Fiix was as big as he expected it to be, he considered making it his last. He would go out in a blaze of glory, retiring to the seclusion of his colony planet estates and the company of his priceless collection of orchids. Clausen was tired of waiting, waiting for the comlink to be fixed, waiting for the Sawl rangers to return to haul the broken Sled back to base, waiting to be able to begin the task he had travelled two hundred and twenty parsecs to accomplish. But he knew the dangers of letting frustration sour into rage, and so channelled it into his fanatical cooking, into tinkering with McPherson, into disputing subtle points of astrophysics with Weng. The one near-truthful expression of his feelings that he allowed himself was to needle Danforth with relentless cheer, knowing the other's frustration to be as near the boiling point as his own. He thought it an amusing game to see who would erupt first, though he didn't consider it much of a contest.

His most serious amusement, and the one which took the greatest concentration of his effort and resources, was getting past the Sawls into the secret depths of the Caves.

The guardian frieze glared at him with unblinking obsidian eyes. He gave it a mocking salute from the bottom of the inner stairs and started up. To his disgust, a welcoming party awaited him at the top: two elderly women, bent and smiling, and a young man with a limp, well known by now to Clausen, who understood his name to be Leb. The invalid leg had been crushed in a rockslide, and the fellow supported himself with a knobby wooden cane. But Clausen noted that he moved with surprising agility when the need arose. He regarded the boy as his principal watchdog and longed to kick away the cane in order to discover just how much of Leb it actually supported.

But he could not yet afford overt acts of hostility. He needed the Sawls' help to retrieve the Sled. He flexed his left hand once more and mounted the stone steps with a hearty greeting in the beginner's Sawlish that he had finally decided would be advantageous to learn.

McPherson unloaded the last boulder into the appropriate pile. She slumped comically and let her tongue loll like a dog's. "Heavy sumbitch."

Beside their emptied two-cart, the three FoodGuilders looked on with dubious curiosity.

"Thanks for the loan of the wagon," she said, not adding that it would have been even nicer of them to have offered to help with the stones. She took a swig from her canteen and bent back to her task.

She hefted a square, flat rock and staggered gamely through the hot sun to an open area beside the Lander which she had already cleared of flood debris and raked crudely. Two neat circles of plastic stakes stuck out of the ground like concentric teeth. McPherson set her rock down between the first pair of stakes. She stood back, then nodded, satisfied with the fit, and went back for the next stone.

The three Sawls spread palms to one another. They pulled down the brims of their sun hats, reloaded their sacks of compost onto the cart and trundled off into the fields.

When she had laid the first circle of stones, McPherson paused for breath, brushing sweat from her eyes. Her hair was quickly bleaching to near white from the constant sun, and her round face was turning golden brown. Danforth said she was starting to look like a beach bum. McPherson decided to take this as a compliment.

She walked to the edge of the Lander's shade. "This is gonna work just fine, Commander."

Weng's charts rattled briefly as she leaned over to make a brief calculation on a crumpled data sheet. "Excellent work, Lieutenant."

"Then all we gotta do is scrounge enough cable to hook the damn thing up." McPherson eyed the wounded high-gain dish, flat on its back, as useless as an upside-down tortoise. " 'Course, without the omni, we'll be in deep shit if the Orbiter ain't where she's supposed to be. I mean, I can get the angle right but this contraption won't be real adjustable."

"She'll be there," Danforth rumbled from the depths of his own ruminations. "Why would she be anywhere else? Those guys up there are going to be glued to their consoles until they finally hear from us again."

"Captain Newman won't really start worrying for another week or two," Weng observed, as McPherson did an about-face and tromped back to her growing circle of stone. The Commander wore her top collar button unfastened, her only concession to the heat. She bent gracefully to a large transparent star chart that lay unrolled across her newly set-up desk of crates. Sinuous red tracings wove like the parallel lines of a contour map around and among the dark blots of stars. Weng figured an angle, drew a faint slash tipped with a spidery arrow. She sat back, considering, then folded her pale hands across her lapful of printout and well-thumbed astronavigation manuals.

"Dr. Danforth," she began carefully. "Perhaps it is presumptuous of me, but I do wonder if enough weight has been given in our thinking to the astronomical situation of this system. I have been trying to shape the navigators' approach data into a more complete and up-to-date map of this sector, and unless I am very much mistaken, the whole of Byrnham's Cluster is migrating slowly into the Coal Sack, in fact has been for some hundred-odd thousand years. It is even now approaching the regions of highest concentration of nebular materials."

Danforth looked up in wonder. This was the longest sustained sentence he had heard out of Weng's mouth since he had boarded the mothership *Hawking* in near-Earth orbit. He waited for her to make her point.

"Well, surely this could be expected to have some effect on the planet's climatic mechanisms?"

He nodded slowly. His usual response would have been to dismiss such information as the red herring he was sure it was. But Weng had clearly worked hard to derive it and he suddenly found himself without the heart to dump on the woman he had seen as a rival authority for the entire outward trip. He wondered if the heat and humidity were sapping his resistance.

"It might over an enormous time scale," he temporized. "But I doubt it could cause the freakish variability we've observed here. Unless . . ." His own word choice sparked a further possibility.

"Unless the primary itself has become variable," Weng finished for him.

Danforth rubbed his jaw thoughtfully. "Yah. Due to interaction with the increased concentrations of dust." He frowned, then shook his big head. "Scale's still too big—maybe we'd see some effect over the course of several hundreds of days, but between one hour and the next? . . . Well, what the hell. Do we have any decent stellar output figures in that stuff you rescued?"

"Some." Weng fanned a stack of water-stained papers and

spread them across the star chart. "For the twenty-two days of approach, between dropping out of jump and orbital insertion. The data since then are in CRI's files."

Danforth decided that Weng was not as pleased with this part of the evidence. "And . . . ?"

"The star's output seems steady over that period," she conceded.

His headshake was definitive this time. "With further data, we could tell better, but my guess is that collision with the Coal Sack will effect the situation only over a scale of tens of thousands of years. Let's agree, though, that the nebula is at least partly responsible for the current condition of the primary. If dust interaction is causing it to heat up, then the planet will also . . . well, we *can* be sure that the planet is not what it was before the collision began. Let me see the numbers on the dust concentration."

He stored the graphs he had been toying with on the crippled terminal at his side. Referring to the sheet she handed him, he did some hurried figuring, his frown deepening unconsciously as he worked.

"It's little better than a guess when you have to do it this way," he complained with disproportionate bitterness, letting his own frustration bleed into the task at hand. "But anyway, following your first line of reasoning: before collision, the average planetary temperature could have been a nice comfy seventy degrees, probably fairly constant, due to the negligible axial tilt. A pretty nice place to live, in other words.

"Then, as the system rolls into the center of the nebula, the temps could be working themselves up to a potential average of one thirty to one fifty Farenheit, a not-so-nice place. All very interesting, but useless for the moment, since here we are, pretty much into the middle and the temps aren't even near those levels . . . though the probe data did lead me to expect at least one fifteen . . ." He gazed musingly at the screen as his own dilemma resurfaced in Weng's figures. His hand returned to worry his jaw. "This heat business, Weng . . . it *is* a fundamental conundrum. There is heat missing from this system."

Weng's thoughtful expression did not change. She traced a thin finger around the curlicues of braid on her white cuff and stubbornly pursued her own line of inquiry. "Accepting, then, that the Coal Sack has its effect only over the long run, would the climate here be expected to revert to normal once the passage through the nebula is complete?"

Danforth winced at the word "normal," which he had taken recent care to exile from his vocabulary. He wondered what she was getting at. "Well, yes, if there's anything left of the atmosphere after another . . . how long did you figure?"

"Approximately eighty-five thousand years until the system exits the Coal Sack."

"Right. After eighty-five thousand years of heating and dust interaction. Christ, you know, come to think of it . . ." He slumped into his many pillows with a woeful grimace. "A lot of my original assumptions about this star's evolution may be totally dog-faced if the nebula's interacting enough to make the star look older than it really is."

Weng was for once more interested in the fate of planets. "Is the atmosphere really endangered?"

"It's a possibility, if the star swells up enough."

"What has our average surface temperature been?"

"Hell, you're the one who's been reading the thermometer to me these days," Danforth grumped, distracted by this new threat to his preliminary theorizing. "Locally, it's been around eighty degrees, but averages don't mean much when you leap from zero to seventy in an hour and a half, then back to forty in twenty minutes. Globally, it's been . . . Holy shit!" He sat up so suddenly that his chest wound protested with a lancing arc of fire that took his breath away.

"Dr. Danforth, please . . ." Weng reached to steady him.

"No, I'm okay, I'm okay." His hand grasped for his keypad and though his face was rigid with pain, he began tapping at it frantically. "Damn it, CRI," he rasped, "where are you when I need you!"

Weng waited in silent concern.

Danforth stared at the figures evolving on the screen. "*Global* averages, that's the key . . . well, I'll be . . . that heat's still here, all of it." He squinted out past the shading trusswork of the landing strut, through hard amber sunlight and dust, to the russet and gold wall of stalks and giant leaves ringing the clearing. "Somewhere."

"Dr. Danforth?" Weng prodded gently.

"I was stuck on the time averaging, the variability, but the *spatial* average is correct for the model!" he explained, waving an arm in emphasis until his pain stopped him. He wiped his hand across his mouth. "I kept looking for the extra heat! Well, it's still goddamned here, only something's out there moving it around!"

Weng's chin lifted. She gazed down her nose at him in restrained surprise. "Something out there, Dr. Danforth?"

He flicked a dark wrist. "I mean, some redistributing mechanism, you know? The missing term to my equation, my X-factor."

54

He glared at her to cover his embarrassment. "What'd you think I meant, some old guy with a wand?"

Weng pursed her lips noncommittally. "It strikes me that the Sawls would say very much the same thing: that something's moving the weather around. But they have, as it happens, given that something names and personalities."

"Oh, no you don't, Weng. Leave that goddess crap to Ibiá, eh?"

She let the impish smile she'd been hiding surface. "My apologies, Dr. Danforth." She gathered up her lapful of papers and dumped them on her worktable. "I must concentrate now on trying to extract from the Master Healer's library a reasonable estimate of this civilization's age."

"You must?" he asked, thinking that Weng made the most bizarre connections sometimes, as if cause and effect followed different rules in her spacer's mind. But it was his stated new policy to remain open to every possibility, every path of inquiry.

"Well, think, Dr. Danforth," she replied with calm intensity. "If the collision with the Coal Sack has altered the planet's climate, imagine what it might have done to something as fragile as a human civilization on that planet. Worse still, if the planet continues to heat up."

At the top of the steps, Clausen smiled at the old women, giving them his courtly half-bow. The ladies dipped their heads and laughed, rearranging the wrap of their shawls like young girls. The prospector inquired after their health and crouched to admire the spotted eggs gathered in a basket on the stone floor. The young man Leb stood in the middle of the tunnel, leaning on his cane. He returned Clausen's smile pleasantly.

Chatting his way toward the limit of his command of the language, Clausen straightened and backed up casually as if to include Leb within the circle of his attention. He draped his left arm genially around the boy's thin shoulders, palm down against the soft muscle behind the neck. Leb's shoulder twitched and his eyes flicked to Clausen, briefly puzzled. The prospector drew his arm away to reinforce a further compliment to the ladies, and bent to pick up the egg basket offering. Leb's knobby stick clattered to the floor. The boy sighed once, staggered to the wall and collapsed. The women gasped and scurried to his aid. Clausen was beside them one minute, checking the boy's pulse. In the next, he was gone up the passageway, shouting back that he would bring help.

* * *

The clinking in the clearing, as McPherson built her wall, was as disrupting to Danforth's concentration as the heat. A further uneasy counterpoint to the irregular rhythm of stone on stone was the reedy chanting from the fields, as the home guard continued its round-the-clock care of the precious food crops.

Muttering into the privacy of his pocket recorder, Danforth tried not to think about how much he would dearly love to be able to get up and pace about.

"Concentrating on the snow data. Normal circumstances that would give rise to such activity within the observed semi-equatorial band: One, winds blowing northeast to southwest and southwest to northeast, converging on the band. Two, strong heat flux away from the band. Three, strong moisture flux into the band.

"Now, at these low latitudes, we would expect the radiative heating of the surface, plus the small-scale dynamic heating of the atmosphere to balance the large-scale dynamic cooling."

He paused, let the recorder drop to his lap and sighed, rubbing his eyes. Sighing was not something Danforth had done much of in his life. He was well aware of fighting a sense of hopelessness. He picked up the recorder with weary resolve.

"What we seem to have in fact is strong radiative cooling plus large-scale dynamic cooling balancing the latent heating."

He paused again and let his attention wander, distracted by McPherson's bright shape moving about in the sun. The distant singing rose and fell. McPherson had achieved a fieldstone circle as high as her chest, intended as a base for the high-gain antenna. She had planned carefully and laid the widest stones in the lowest layers. The wall tapered upward in neat overlapping tiers of pale, dusty rock. Danforth smiled faintly as he watched her set the first of the partial layers that would allow the dish to rest at its proper receiving angle. He was impressed by her careful craftsmanship and the structure's apparent stability. He found her wisecracking persistence comforting. She was one of the things that was keeping him sane.

At one side of the clearing, several sun-hatted FoodGuilders took a break from hauling water to observe the mysterious stone circle taking shape. They stood in the shade of their own tall crop, chatting among themselves with the arm-waving, measuring gestures of a building crew assessing the problems of the site or the quality of a competitor's work.

Danforth wrenched his attention back to his recording.

"In addition, the movement of the snow to the northeast, toward the great northern ocean, was observed throughout the entire band of activity. Thus, in relation to my X-factor, we cannot assume spatial dependence only. Frontal movement indicates that the missing term is also time dependent, and is, we will assume for the moment, global in scale.''

He took a breath and reached under his worktable to haul one useless leg into a more comfortable position.

"Now. Must-do's for when we finally get CRI back: detailed mapping of heat and water distributions, horizontal and vertical profiles.'' He touched the recorder to his lips pensively, then set it aside and lay back against his pillows.

"Right through the goddamn Coal Sack,'' he muttered, then closed his eyes and surrendered to his exhaustion and the heat.

Clausen jogged lightly through the stable caverns. He slowed at each turning or tunnel crossing, watching his footing carefully in the half-dark, hugging the walls, ready to leap back into shadow at the slightest sound.

He knew the layout of the stables well. The Sawls had not bothered to curtail his explorations there. But for all their size, these caves did not extend deeply into the rock. Instead, they spread laterally across the cliff face, several large entrances joined by interior corridors. The caverns were high and wide, and Clausen liked their smell of dry hay and manure, reminiscent of his own small stable at home, the home he rarely saw. But these caves were by now familiar. The prospector did not linger. He headed for the nearest ramp to the upper levels.

The ramp was empty but pitch dark. The pragmatic Sawls did not waste good lamp oil on unused corridors. The darkness heightened the sound of his own footsteps, even with the soft-soled shoes he had worn for the specific purpose of stealth. He paused, weighing his minute flashbeam on his gloved palm as he debated the disadvantage of feeling his way in blackness against that of giving his presence away with light. He stowed the beam in his pocket and put a hand to the wall, remarking to himself, not for the first time, that no deep-cave rock surface had a right to be so warm and dry.

The wide main thoroughfare at the top of the ramp was lighted again, though only one lamp in five had been left burning, and those had their flames turned as low as possible. Clausen looked around cautiously. The alternating light and shadow was further punctuated by the dark half-moon entrances to living enclaves. Several paces to the left was the back entry to the MeetingHall, impressive but again, familiar. Beyond it were more dwellings and other guildhall entries, Woodworkers' and Keth-Toph. Clausen had no fondness for wood or its related technologies, only for fine objects into which it had already been made, preferably long enough ago to add to the objects' value.

57

He glided to the right and slipped into the first tall archway he came to. He listened to the darkness, then palmed his light and nosed the beam around the room. Tall wooden rug looms lined the walls, each with its attendant well-worn bench and great wood skeins suspended above the frames like bunches of multi-colored fruit. The storage racks for the finished rugs were picked clean but for one or two tightly bound rolls lingering like rejected suitors in the isolated upper reaches of the shelves.

The prospector shrugged and turned away down the outer corridor, dipping in and out of dwelling entries until he found what he had hoped for, a wider tunnel that did not dead-end in the usual trio or quartet of living caverns, but continued inward, sparsely lit but passable. Single-unit dwellings opened to either side. Bachelor quarters, thought Clausen, amused. His pace quickened. He was into unexplored territory at last, heading deeper into the rock.

He passed dwelling after dwelling, and side corridors and cul-de-sacs that led to multi-unit complexes. He allowed that Ibiá was right to say the Caves were like a small city. A good half mile of cliff face had been hollowed out into a giant apartment megalith. Even this deep inside, the air remained temperate and sweet-smelling. Clausen looked for vents and shaftways, and finding none, concluded from the constant slight draft against his face that the tunnels themselves comprised the ventilation system. He had also noted from the first something he had not seen fit to pass on to his colleagues, particularly the bleeding-heart anthropologist Levy: some of the tunnels appeared to be extremely ancient, easily many thousands of years old, yet none were natural formations. Clausen could not help but admire the Sawls' determination, digging a city out of solid rock with what must have amounted to their bare hands, due to the scarcity of decent tool-making metals. Idly, he speculated about the heights their civilization might have achieved, had they been gifted with the planetary resources that he considered essential for bootstrapping a society out of its initial stone age.

A noise ahead alerted him. His inward-leading corridor intersected with another, running perpendicular. Voices raised in cheerful debate floated around the corner. Laughter was followed by a chorus of heavy groans, as if a weight was being lifted, unsuccessfully, for the groans broke off and the laughter increased. Clausen crept forward to peer around the corner. A large cart with a broken axle filled the passageway. Four sturdy Sawls milled about exchanging jocular repair suggestions. In the opposite direction, the intersecting tunnel ended after several hundred paces in a blank wall.

Clausen flattened himself against the rock, considering his next move. When, almost simultaneously, he heard new voices proceeding toward him along his own corridor and retreat became impossible, he knew the Sawls had activated another of their seemingly endless repertoire of defense strategies. He eyed the unlit doorway of the nearest dwelling, but found that an unsatisfying option. If discovered in hiding, his hand would be forced, and he was not yet ready for open warfare. He had yet to assure himself of allies among his own party.

Carefully, he stripped off the fingerless gloves, disengaged the tiny mechanism, then slid the needle and its heavy dose of tranquillizer into a slot in the butt of his laser pistol. He folded the gloves around the little gun and shoved the wad into his deepest pocket. He took what satisfaction he could from the fact that he had gotten further in this time than any before. Then, laying an expression of urgency across his face, he launched himself into the open, calling for help.

6

For two throws, Susannah drew her anger up around her like a wall. She adopted Ghirra's habit of walking silence. At mealtimes, she buried herself in note-taking, ate mechanically and withdrew into sleep as soon as the clean-up duties were done, or went off to other wagons to gather information for her population survey. She let observation become her obsession, as if a conscious retreat into empirical practice could save her from messier, more subjective considerations.

She decided it was selfish of Stavros to take her as a lover when he knew he would be leaving so abruptly. But he had been right to think she would try to talk him out of his plan, had she known about it beforehand. Her "determined neutrality," as Megan called it, was a learned defense against the same impulsive streak that had catapulted her into the sun after the snows and nearly cost her life, as well as Liphar's. As she mistrusted this tendency in herself, she also mistrusted it in others, and resented being dragged into a dangerous scheme that she was not sure she approved of. She recalled her frustration at feeling excluded and wondered if it might have been better left that way.

Megan watched and worried and speculated, giving it time that should have gone into her own notes and observations. But Ghirra simply left Susannah alone, waiting for her to come to terms with the situation and with herself.

Meanwhile, the landscape blossomed. The rapid growth cycle progressed into full flower. The roadside was a riot of color. Tender shoots and leaves broadened and thickened, soaking in and storing the now abundant water.

In the east loomed the Talche, oddly rounded little mountains with a friendly aspect, like ranks of golden buttocks. The dairy herd had turned aside midway in the third throw to climb the curvaceous grassy slopes into the lush foothills. Several senior herdsmen remained with the caravan, shepherding two dozen prize heifers to be bred in Ogo Dul. Relieved of the drag of five hundred ambling beasts who would rather eat than walk, the caravan made better progress, for the first time accomplishing the full twenty kilometers per throw that the term implied.

A contingent of rangers went with the herd, taking two spare teams of hjalk, to guard the placid dairy animals from the increasingly active wildlife on the road to their new pastures. Afterward, they would return to DulElesi for the salvage of the Terran flying machine. As Megan explained it, while Susannah tried hard not to listen, the rangers would contrive to arrive at DulElesi about the time that Stavros and Liphar were expected to reach the site of the wreck, giving the conspirators the needed time for their own secret salvage project, yet seeming to offer Clausen the help he demanded.

The caravan followed a rough track winding among the crotches of the amber foothills. A stream accompanied them, lined with lithe river grasses. The wagons splashed across many clear, shallow rivulets rushing down from the hills to throw themselves into the silty, slower-moving water. Susannah saw entire herds of the shy tortoiselike creatures, and amphibious lizards cavorted like otters in the brown water. More than once, she spotted huge, spiked, toadish beasts who shot basilisk glares at the human intruders from the safety of midstream boulders. They did not attack, but she thought they seemed to be just waiting for an excuse.

As well as shooting up and bursting into bloom, the flora diversified geometrically in the wetter foothills. Susannah did not have to pretend to be kept busy with her notebook and sample case, though sampling became increasingly difficult as the plants' natural defenses improved along with the growing conditions. The squat clusters of bristles that had dotted the Dop Arek grew here into clumps of tall yellow swords, triangular and

60

barbed in bright red, as thick as a man's thigh. The desert brush enlarged into misshapen trees, stubby trunks caught in a mare's nest of tubular branches that twisted and curved back on each other. The branches were jointed like fingers, and brittle looking, but resistant to every blade except Ghirra's obsidian flake scalpel.

Deeper into the hills, the air smelled sweet and damp. The cart track narrowed where huge trees reclined along the stream as if blown over at an earlier time, but content to take life lying down. They sent out rows of frail shoots to stand up like soldiers at attention along their fallen trunks. Tall, waving stands of amber-plumed succulents uncurled fernlike in the shallows, offering occasional feathery shade for the sweating travellers. Tangled root systems fringed the riverbank, competing for space with the razor-edged grasses and spreads of fleshy ground cover. Broad orange pads armed with crimson thorns sprouted masses of lemon-colored blossoms iced with pollen and humidity like a lady's powder puff.

Ghirra's insistence kept Susannah to the path. Beady eyes in the underbrush followed her movements along the verge. Shiny red leaves as big as dinner plates shuddered to the passage of heavy reptilian bodies beneath. She knew that later she would have to risk trapping a sample population of wild creatures. But for now, she would concentrate on the flora, for the sake of the Master Healer's peace of mind. Her anger with Megan and Stavros did not extend to Ghirra. After all, she could hardly expect him to be objective about the fate of his own planet.

During the fourth throw, the meandering stream showed a few stony rapids. The hillsides steepened. Craggy rock broke through the yellow topsoil, and the gentle river glen roughened into a deep gorge. The wagon wheels clattered over exposed stone ledges, descending with the river toward the northeastern reaches of the Dop Arek. Stretches of the pinkish plain below appeared in brief vistas over the canyon's crumbling rim, through gaps choked with soaring amber plumage.

Picking her way along the rocky path behind Ghirra, Megan noted an unusual restlessness in the Master Healer's gait.

As if he's looking for something, she decided.

The air hung heavy and still, sluggish with moisture. Megan's trail clothes clung like a binding second skin. The hjalk snorted and shook their manes, bracing their fleshy feet against the slanting ledges to hold back the weight of the wagons. Ghirra's restlessness was evidently shared, for Xifa sent Phea and Dwingen to crowd into the driver's seat beside Ampiar, then went herself to walk beside the lead team of hjalk. Megan was not surprised when several PriestGuild apprentices came running down the line of wagons, their high voices overlapping urgently as they announced a weather alert.

Ghirra counted heads and called Susannah back to the wagon immediately. Up and down the line, guildsmen checked the fastenings of harness and canopy stays, and watched the sky. Conversation swelled as wagering and debate spread from wagon to wagon.

"A little rain might be nice," Megan remarked mordantly as Susannah drew up beside her, stuffing her notebook and samples into her field pack.

"I don't know." Susannah peered at the still-cloudless green sky, then at the enclosing walls of the gorge, her sullenness set aside for something grimmer. "Not a good place to be," she murmured. "Flash floods nearly got me once before."

Aguidran apparently had the same thought. On the heels of the PriestGuild alert came a phalanx of rangers to urge the drivers and the teams to maximum speed. Passengers piled out of the wagons to lighten the loads. The strongest lent their backs to push or pull. The brittle rock was treacherous underfoot. Thorny vegetation poked through the cracks to snatch at pant legs and the curly fetlocks of the hjalk. The beasts bent their broad high shoulders into the harness to haul valiantly against the stubborn drag of brush-bound wheels.

The clouds appeared suddenly, as if by magic. The hot sunlight flickered and dimmed. Fat cushions of mist with ominous mouse-colored bellies gathered overhead, jostling about like an expectant crowd.

Megan jerked a thumb at them darkly. "Valla's army awaits her orders."

The Master Ranger halted the caravan and ordered the wagons drawn up against the side of the gorge farthest from the riverbed, where ledges and high piles of rock offered some escape. Rope coils sprouted like a plague of snakes as wagons and carts were lashed to everything available: rock, dead tree stumps, the rigid sword plants, anything solid enough to hold a line.

Aguidran appeared in person to direct the Infirmary wagon onto a stretch of particularly high ground, helping her brother to fasten it down as best they could. Ghirra sent Megan and his four apprentices to climb the rocks in search of a safe niche to ride out the coming storm.

Megan did not argue. "I'm not so quick on my feet as you," she said, as Susannah, elected to stay with Ghirra and the others, on the canyon floor with the wagon.

The clouds closed ranks abruptly, shutting out the sun. The

ocher walls of the gorge darkened to dull shadow brown. As Megan pulled herself onto a perch at the top of a rockslide, she saw Xifa and Ampiar busying themselves at the rear of the wagon, checking the accessibility of supplies. Susannah waited with Ghirra as he soothed the anxious hjalk. Megan recalled her own more adventurous youth, envying Susannah's ability to submerge panic within her physician's emergency training.

Silence settled over the gorge. No wind or thunder threatened. Ghirra stared at the leaden brown sky, his mouth hard set, his long fingers tapping a quick rhythm against his thigh.

He's not afraid, observed Megan with some puzzlement, *he's angry.*

The first drops fell like buckets spilled from the sky, huge and scattered, exploding little dust puffs as they hit the dry rock. The ground was hardly wet when Megan was slammed against a boulder by a sudden jarring of the air, like the shock wave from an explosion.

A spasm of cold turned the rime of dust and humidity on her skin to a chill sweat. The giant raindrops froze midair into a thunderous downpouring of hail.

A mad scramble for shelter ensued. Many flattened themselves into the lee of the gorge wall or crowded beneath the overhanging ledges. Others dove under the wagons. The hjalk dropped their heads, skittering and wailing, unable to escape the merciless pounding of the ice.

Megan struggled further up her rockslide to curl into a ball beneath the brush clinging to the wall. The branches broke the fall of hail on her upper body, but left no protection for her legs. The ice balls were as big as eggs and hit with the force of a stone flung from the top of the gorge. Megan turned her face into the wall as her whimpers joined the chorus of pain and confusion rising all around her.

And then there were strong hands pulling at her roughly. A wiry ranger, her hard-brimmed hat deflecting the hail, dragged Megan from her perch and hauled her down the rockslide through the battering of ice. She was shoved under the belly of the medical wagon, where Susannah huddled with the others.

Xifa received her with soothing hands as she wept in shock and relief. The hail roared down around them, filling the cracks between the rocks, piling up in the gullies, bouncing and rolling beneath the wagon in chill cascades. Thick clots of ground fog congealed above the ice and spread to isolate each wagon in a blind cloud of mist and noise. Through the din came the sound of shredding wagon canopies and the squealing of the hjalk.

Xifa passed Megan a blanket, then helped her to wrap her

shivering body. Megan did not see Ghirra anywhere. Beyond the sheltering curve of the wheel, she saw the booted calves of the rangers and some brave bare legs race among the tethered wagons to release the beasts from the prison of their harness. At the front of their own wagon, the four moaning hjalk broke away one by one as their straps and buckles were loosed. When the last had bolted off in terror, Ghirra ducked and skidded under the wagon to hunch beside the left front wheel. His usually tranquil face was twisted with righteous rage, as if he saw in the hail storm not just ill luck or the vagaries of a capricious climate, but a genuine maliciousness, directed at innocents.

Megan was distracted from her own pain. She had thought stoic resignation to be characteristic of the Sawls' attitude toward the lethal weather of their world, the classic victim's acceptance of his lot at the hands of the gods. But Ghirra's mask of outrage was anything but accepting. She remembered then that his parents had died in a storm-triggered mudslide on a similar trading trip long ago.

No wonder he's at odds with the Goddesses . . .

The wagon vibrated with the drumming of the hail. The still-warm ground ran with melt water and grainy slush. The cold mist wrapped the canyon in a smoky shroud.

And then the roaring abruptly ceased. The silence left behind was almost as painful as the noise. A gust of wind swept through the gorge, stirring the fog into spiraling tendrils. The sky lightened.

The wailing of a child broke the silence. Ghirra levered his lean body out from under the wagon, squinted at the thinning clouds, then forward, looking for his sister's all-clear signal. Xifa and Ampiar tumbled out after him and went immediately to unpack the medical supplies. The four apprentices climbed down from the shelter of an overhang, wide-eyed, checking each other for bruises and scrapes. Susannah helped Megan to a comfortable seat on a rock. Hjalk wandered dazed among the wagons. Rangers came and went, relaying damage and injury reports, their bootheels rattling the scattered ice like stones on a beach.

The clouds vanished and the sun shone hot again. Steam rose glistening from the melting layer of hail. Megan thought of the mist burning off a summer dawn and wished for something as peaceable. The faint breeze was noticeably fresher and drier than it had been before the storm. Bringing a load of bandage from the wagon, Xifa paused, sniffed the air, then shook her head worriedly as she went back for another load.

Susannah treated minor injuries for many hours without a break. Few had escaped some light cuts and scrapes in that first mad scramble for safety, and there was a great deal of serious bruising from the hail. The elderly had fared the worst, being the least agile and the most sensitive skinned. Ghirra set one broken arm and calmed the terrors of several messy broken noses. Susannah and Ampiar wrapped sprains and swabbed and polticed and bandaged wounds, while the apprentices tended the fires, and Xifa brewed and dispensed her herbal teas as painkillers and calmatives.

The material cost was higher. With the exception of the Infirmary wagon and the FoodGuild's hard-topped giants, hardly a wagon was left with its canopy intact. Some, with tough double layers or a wicker understructure, had suffered minor puncturing. The worst were totally shredded, and the goods inside battered by the ice.

The Potter guildsmen muttered and swore as they dug out the shards of countless jugs and bowls that had been packed uncrated to fill the excess spaces in the loads of all four of their wagons. The Glassblowers gathered silently around the second of their three blue-painted wagons, afraid to even look beneath the crumpled heap of torn, ice-damp canvas. Megan's weaver friend Tyril had confided that the Glassblowers of DulElesi were considered the finest among all the nearby settlements and were always the prime attraction at the Ogo Dul market. But they would show little profit this trip. Most of what survived would be bartered for items the FoodGuild would take in trade for the standard food ration.

But the real victims of the hail were the animals. The hakra, being little and quick-minded, had generally taken care of themselves. More than one frightened Sawl had shared his shelter with a small, insistent beast. The herd of prize hekkers had their frantic herdsmen to search out trees for their protection, and keep them from mindless panic.

But the big hjalk had suffered greatly. They stood about on splayed legs, stunned and swaying. Ghirra set Dwingen to ferrying pots of infusion to the anxious herdsmen, to sponge clean the blood from the beasts' golden coats. Several of the older hjalk had been driven to their knees by the ice. They lay moaning while their drivers washed and petted them and tried to coax them to their feet.

Swabbing grit from her hundredth nasty scrape, Susannah found herself in tears. She was too busy to wonder much at this uncharacteristic display. She continued her cleaning and binding while the tears ran unchecked down her cheeks. She took comfort from the fact that she was not alone. The tears of the many

65

hurt and confused let Susannah's tears go unremarked, except by Ghirra, who watched her covertly as he worked at her side.

When the line of injured had thinned at last, and the apprentices could give their attention to repacking the wagon, turned virtually inside out to cope with the emergency, Aguidran appeared to ask her brother's prognosis in the case of a hjalk that had broken a leg in its frenzied attempt to climb the canyon wall.

Ghirra crouched beside a weeping little boy, bandaging his thorn-ripped arm, softly talking him into a smile. When Aguidran touched his shoulder, he barely raised his eyes. He asked a few murmured questions, then merely shook his head sadly and went on with his work.

Aguidran's mouth tightened regretfully. She bent to her boot and drew out a razor-edged, eight-inch sliver of metal, mounted in an handle of age-dark bone. The blade was nearly two inches wide at the handle, narrowing toward the tip and wafer thin along the cutting edge from generations of sharpenings. It glittered darkly in the returned sunlight, a tapestry of ancient etchmarks and scourings. The handle bore on its butt the carved hallmark of the RangerGuild.

The drawing of the shining metal caught everyone's attention, those who saw it and those others who heard the collective intake of breath. The child in Ghirra's arms shrank against him at the sight of it. Aguidran herself regarded it with respect tinged with distaste, though it rested in her hand with the ease of long familiarity.

None of the life-threatening events she had experienced so far aroused Susannah's sense of mortality as profoundly as Aguidran's knife. It was the longest blade she had seen on Fiix, and the first true weapon. Its impractical length, its slim profile, its demon edge, all declared without apology that it had been forged for one purpose alone, the taking of a life. Its efficiency and sophistication brought to mind a sudden vision of Emil Clausen.

"Ghirra, wait . . ." On impulse, Susannah fumbled at the bottom of her medikit. She dug out a syringe and laid it in his hand. Its plastic housing did not glitter. Ghirra frowned at it. He knew its workings. She had schooled him in its use.

Aguidran shifted, gently slapping the long blade against her thigh.

Ghirra closed his fingers around the syringe, then handed it back. He nodded to Aguidran, who strode off down the line of wagons. A crowd had gathered around the stricken hjalk. As Aguidran shouldered her way through them, a mournful chant was begun and soon spread along the entire caravan.

66

Susannah watched the Ranger kneel, then turned her head away, her tears flowing again unbidden.

Beside her, Ghirra said gravely, "The killing must not be ever easy."

"No," she agreed, shaking her head and weeping. She pictured Stavros caught in the sights of Clausen's gun. "No, it must not." And then she whispered, glancing across at Megan on her rock, "And yes, Ghirra, you are right to try to stop those who think it ever should be."

7

His eyes were open and alert but his mind dreamed of holding her in his arms. His empty hands remembered the pale silk of her skin. The pain he felt was physical. He could lay his palm against the place where it lived, deep in the soft tissue between heart and groin. Yet it was a different pain, his palms' faint heat, whose summons he followed.

"Ibi." Liphar touched his knee gently.

"I know," Stavros replied. "It's time."

They crawled out from under the low-hanging ledge, dusting dirt and crumbling twigs from their hair and clothing. The hai glistened like wet pearls on the battered grass. Steam misted the ruddy landscape with a golden haze as the sun renewed its hot glare. Stavros found the combination of debilitating heat and autumn-colored flora to be subtly disturbing to his body chemistry, sending mixed signals of Indian summer that had him anticipating the sudden cold snap that announced the advent of winter.

But there were no seasons on Fiix, only weather.

Their young ranger guide adjusted her pack and pointed across the brush-choked gully, where ground fog obscured their path. Edan was the Master Ranger's protégé, as thin, hard and energetic as Aguidran herself, but with an overbearing arrogance that Aguidran had grown out of long ago.

A thorny companion, but worth it, Stavros reflected, for despite the wild explosion of plant growth that had, to Stavros' untrained eye, rendered Aguidran's map irrelevant, Edan had found the Sled, the proverbial needle in the haystack of the Fiixian wilderness. She had kept them alive as well, the two tenderfoot adventurers, a university-bred off-worlder and a skittish apprentice priest. Stavros was not sure which task had required the greater effort.

He squinted at the steep slope ahead as it faded in and out of the shifting fog. He had spotted the Sled before the hail, a bright sun-glint on a patch of white amid the tangles of reddish vegetation. The downed craft lay on its belly at the edge of a plateau backed by the northernmost scarps of the rugged Grigar, "Lagri's Wall." It was impossible from this distance to judge its condition, but Stavros felt sure that the hail had not done it any good. He hoped the plastic bubble over the communications equipment had withstood the bombardment.

Edan and Liphar were not happy about the hail, either. While the young ranger strode ahead into the waist-high fog to scout out the trail, Liphar studied the skies with genuine anxiety and a tinge of priestly officiousness. He continued muttering to himself about this sign and that, long after Stavros had stopped listening. He worried the blue talisman bead on his wrist until his telling of its obscure rosary was no more than a reflex.

His complaint with the hail, Stavros finally understood, was not its abrupt violence and peril so much as its abnormality. Applying his own definition of the word, Liphar explained that "normal" for the current progress of the Sisters' conflict would be Valla Ired feinting with quick, light thrusts of rain, a mere flexing of muscles, good for the crops back home in DulElesi and not threatening enough to entice Lagri from the rest period gained by her recent successful skirmish.

But, Liphar fretted, Lagri was clearly not resting. She was engaging in active counterattack. He rolled a handful of ice through his open fingers to illustrate how Valla's soliders froze in terror as they fell, and thus brought hurt instead of moisture to the ground.

Edan called to them then, and Liphar shouldered his pack resignedly and crunched away through the rising patches of steam and the melting hailstones to descend the brittle ledges of the fog-bottomed gully. Stavros followed, adding Liphar's worries to the long list of considerations jostling around inside his head.

He had done a lot of thinking since slipping away from the caravan, leaving Susannah asleep in the yellow grasses, a lot of thinking while they searched for the wrecked Sled. Walking away from the woman he had just won had been the hardest part, but as he let himself be lost in an alien wilderness with aliens his company, he had the distinct sensation of relaxing into the arms of his destiny.

He meant nothing predetermined, nothing so melodramatic.

Stavros did not believe in fate. But he did believe that for each individual, there is a given course to follow. Such life courses are never obvious, but for the lucky few who stumble upon theirs by accident, there is no refusing it, and thus it becomes a kind of destiny.

And so it was with him, he was coming to believe, though what that destiny was to be, he was not sure. It was his scheme to foil Clausen's claim and it was his promise to the Master Healer to discover the true nature of the Sister Goddesses, and it was more, unknown as yet, or unrecognized. But at the center of the mystery was the old Ritual Master, Kav Daven, and the miracle of the guar.

Stavros considered his miracle as he crashed along the bottom of the fog-wrapped gully, ripped by finger-sized thorns and tripped up by entangling roots and undergrowth. He had felt the corrosive guar, the pure lithium from the bedrock, placed in his hands by the old priest during the Ceremony of Leave-taking. He had suffered the very real agonies of seared flesh and a touch of inexplicable Presence, yet his skin survived the ritual intact, unburned. Only a ghost of the heat remained, haunting the centers of his palms as a constant reminder of the moment of his "calling."

But Stavros had learned not to trust the evidence of his senses, so often too willing to be ruled by his imagination. To balance the strong evidence for mysticism, his personal proof of the Goddesses' power, Stavros cherished the flame of Ghirra's skepticism, far more grounding than his colleagues' knee-jerk disbelief. Unlike the other Terrans, the Master Healer had witnessed the details of the "miracle," but his response had not been to praise the goddesses as Liphar had done, but to imply that Kav Daven was somehow toying with Stavros, involving him in some private plan. He would not accept that a miracle had occured.

The healer's questioning of the Goddesses was the more compelling because it involved a moral *why* as well as a quest for the truth behind the myth. While the PriestGuild counseled acceptance of peril, suffering and even periodic extermination, Ghirra demanded an explanation for such godly negligence. It was not the goddesses' existence he questioned but their right to rule his own life so capriciously. As a true believer must, he denied the Sisters their godhead to spare himself from the crushing possibility that the gods might indeed be blind to the fate of men.

Stavros, in his willingness to blur the line between things that must be taken on faith and those possessing a confirmed reality, explored a third avenue: if something other than a freakish nature was at work in the Fiixian atmosphere, with the power of a god if not a god, could it be reasoned with like a man? Had Kav Daven's ephemeral magic, the pure intensity of his faith, somehow touched this realm of Power when he danced the Tale of Origins or later at the Leave-taking, enough to shift the balance of strength from one Sister to another? Had Stavros himself, with the guarfire searing his hands, felt that Power singing through him?

He stumbled, caught himself on an overhanging branch, then swore and jerked away a lacerated palm. The thick orange branch was armed with rows of needle teeth. Stavros stared at his own bright blood welling up from parallel punctures. What the guar had not harmed, a simple plant had shredded with ease. He was not immune.

Remember that, he advised himself, feeling again the cold shock of Clausen's pistol against his skin. He must not exaggerate the content of his miracle, even if he accepted it as such, with the ghostly fire still burning in his palms. It frightened him to imagine the recklessness it might lead him to, if he took on illusions of immortality.

And remember what's really at stake. The deity of the Goddesses, though an intriguing philosophical question, was not what mattered. Their *actuality* did. Science or magic, they must be proven to exist, for only then could they be used as an argument against the commercial development of the planet.

Liphar fussed over his bloodied hand. Edan trudged back through the brush to give it a quick glance and a shrug, then waved them onward. She had nosed out a rocky access to the plateau via the scar of an old landslide where the spiked and knife-edged vegetation found less encouragement to grow. They struggled upward, using hands and knees as well as feet. Stavros left a trail of blood-stained boulders in his wake.

Breathing hard at the top, he sluiced water from his canteen across his palm and bound it with a strip of linen that Liphar unearthed from one of his many pockets. The fog had dispersed from the open areas of the plateau. The hailstones had melted into the spongy ground. Edan waded into the dense growth enveloping the Sled. Stavros followed, wishing for a machete.

Even close up, it was impossible to assess the flier's overall condition. Broad-leafed vines already obscured most of the delta-winged body, insinuating fuzzy tendrils across the crumpled nose. The cockpit had been neatly secured with a tarp, covering the seats and control panel. A precaution of Clausen's, Stavros was sure, one he must grudgingly admire. The open cargo hold showed signs of habitation, more tarps, some clothing hastily tossed inside. Beneath the tilting wing, the damp ground was still barren, packed down from the weight of bodies seeking shelter from the storm. Stavros crouched and peered into the pocket of dank shadow, imagining them stuck there together, Clausen agile and restless, Danforth crippled, fevered, eventually delirious.

He straightened with a shudder, and pushed through the grasping vines to the rear of the Sled. The bent tail fin poked up through a tangle of prickers, looking much as Aguidran had drawn it. High on the upper curve of the hail-scarred hull was the transparent com blister that housed a high-gain grid inbuilt to receive the operating power beam transmitted from the Orbiter, plus high data rate com for navigation. It could be removed in pieces but was too much to carry and more trouble to repair. But tucked along one side of the blister was a slim metal whip, the omni-directional antenna that Stavros sought, his potential link to CRI, to the legal files stored in her memory, and eventually, to the authorities back home.

Though his instinct was to call CRI immediately, his faith in McPherson's ingenuity stayed his hand. If she or Clausen had managed to fix the antenna at the Lander and were in contact with CRI already, the computer would give away both his position and his purpose before he had time to accomplish it. He must also do his salvage hastily and be well away from the site by the time Clausen returned with the rangers to haul the Sled back to base.

He set his pack down on the hull. The omni's electronics were inside the blister. He would need them too. He had purloined a few items before he'd left with the caravan, the appropriate tools from the Lander's general repair kit, and McPherson's own well-thumbed Sled manual. He had taken a few other precautions as well, most of which would not make him popular with the remaining crew of the Lander.

He beckoned Liphar to his side, his extra, clever pair of hands, then drew out his tools and set to work.

8

Weng stood vigil at the edge of the clearing, in mute sympathy for the handful of Sawls striving to restore order to their battered fields. Sadly, the fastest growing of the plantings were the most damaged. The younger shoots were already drawing themselves upright on their own, but those closer to harvest were more brittle. The Sawls were lovingly splinting weakened and bent stalks, but entire rows had been snapped clean in two. The broad once-graceful leaves were riddled with holes and hung limp on their stems like red-gold lace. In the terraces, the succulents wept from fist-sized punctures, their precious juices evaporating into the building heat.

The Sawls sang softly as they worked, and Weng's silver head faintly acknowledged the rhythm. Her family hadn't seen the inside of a planted field for many generations, but a lingering farmer's instinct had her debating an offer of assistance.

The drumming hail had woken all of them out of restless, heat-dreaming sleep. On the far side of the clearing, McPherson yanked the silverfilm sheeting off the high-gain dish, fussing and cursing to herself over the minor damage sustained before she'd gathered the wit to cover it.

Clausen joined her, checking first his watch and then the sun, now beginning its low drift toward the horizon. "Our salvage help should have been here by now. Ibiá better be dealing straight with me on this." He glanced at the dish. "How'd she do?"

"Mother Nature sure ain't giving us much of a break." McPherson folded a tarp and tossed it brusquely to the ground. "We've got holes here and there. Could be worse, I guess. Could be like that." She jerked her thumb at the fields.

Clausen took in the frenzied activity as if he had not noticed it before. He stroked his newly bearded jaw speculatively. "Yes, I suppose this might seriously cut into their food supply."

"And ours, if we can't ever get ourselves outa here!"

"Tut, McP. Nary a discouraging word."

She tossed the last tarp on top of the others and dusted her hands. "I was kinda hoping to get some of those guys to help me lift this thing in place, now the base is finished. But I guess I'll search up the cable we need first. They're gonna be busy a while yet, I'd say."

In the darkened cave that had been home for three cold wet weeks, McPherson searched through the supplies that had not yet been hauled back down to the Lander. She found clothing, utensils, medicine and some packaged food. She stumbled over the edge of the sleeping platform and smashed a small Sawl oil lamp into smithereens. She found the utility racks that had held the back-up computer and electronics components, the extra monitors and several reels of cable. The racks were empty.

Puzzled, she flashed her battery lamp around the cavern. She knew there had been equipment left after Stavros brought a load down to the Lander for Danforth's use. She sucked her cheek. She guessed it was possible that he'd taken it all down and stowed it away in the Lander's upper levels while she was distracted with the dish.

She let the lamp beam droop. Without the cable, all her obsessive efforts to repair the dish would be useless. The power and com links would remain severed. There would be no words of reassurance from the Orbiter, no force field to restore climate control to the Underbelly, no hot water . . .

McPherson fought an upwelling of dismay.

"Emil'll be real pissed at this one," she muttered. But worst of all, Danforth would get a little angrier and more depressed, as he did each day that there were no new data coming in, and no master computer to help him solve his mysteries.

She turned from the cave resignedly and went down to search the Lander.

"Sixteen feet?" said Clausen with deadly calm. "That's all you could find?"

"Yah. And we need at least a hundred." McPherson shuffled, planted her hands on her hips in unconscious imitation of the prospector's stance. "You think the Sawls might've taken it?"

"What would they do with it, eat it?" Clausen's eyes narrowed as he contemplated subtle mayhem. "No, I'd say this is our young friend Ibiá up to his tricks again."

"Why him?"

"You tell me, McP., you tell me." He regarded her owlishly. "But no, you're fortunate enough not to be afflicted with that particular sickness of youth." When she blinked at him uncomprehendingly, he chuckled. "The disease of idealism, I mean, McP."

"Oh. No, I guess not." But McPherson found herself frowning gently.

Clausen stood utterly still, thinking hard, then shut his eyes convulsively. "Jesus! The Sled! The antennas on the Sled!"

Already moving, he grabbed her arm. McPherson hesitated, taken aback by his sudden ferocity. Clausen jerked her forward. "No more waiting for our native guides to show. We're wasting daylight. Round up your gear. We'll find the fucking Sled without them!"

9

Within a day's journey of DulElesi, distinct trail signs reappeared, old cairns and ranger blazes chipped into the sides of boulders. Stavros made Edan turn aside, to lead them across a stony rise where the harder surface would hide their tracks. The young ranger's sharp face was shadowed into obscurity by her wide-brimmed hat. She grumbled, because it was her nature, but agreed that an unused route would be wisest.

Stavros squinted down the trail they had left behind. "I'd hate to run into them on their way out here to pick up the Sled. Clausen's sure to be with them."

Liphar nodded dutifully, absorbed in his own concerns.

The nearness of their goal renewed Stavros's flagging optimism. "Don't worry that hail to death, Lifa. We haven't seen a cloud in two whole cycles."

But the hail had upset Liphar badly. He used every excuse to point out that the heat was increasing steadily, even as the afternoon sun reddened and sank between the teeth of the mountains. He straggled along at the rear, his eyes on the salmon-stained sky, muttering and stumbling until Edan threatened to abandon him in the wilderness if he did not watch where he was walking. Stavros silenced her impatience with a rare stern glance. Though Liphar's unrelenting caution was exhausting to listen to, as a priest-to-be he was trained in the details of weather prediction. Stavros lent at least half an ear to his mumblings and insisted that Edan do likewise, as well as keeping her sharper ranger's eyes open for the signs of a change.

As they trudged among the rocks and brambles, Stavros tried to pin Liphar down to a specific prediction. This was difficult, for he tended to lapse into abstraction and priestly hyperbole when approaching the subject of the weather. He quoted the PriestGuild records, his version of scripture, and unraveled long histories, couched in the quasi-archaic language of the tale-chants.

Hearing the OldWords again made Stavros think of Kav Daven and of the questions he longed to put to the old priest.

Meanwhile, Liphar muttered about impending Devastation, maintaining that the signs were right, as recorded in the oldest books. During the storm and flood, he had feared a final victory

74

for Valla. Now the building heat had him worried about Lagri's continuing domination.

Furthering his quest to prove the Goddesses real, Stavros probed the specifics of the myth. If the Sister deities were actual physical beings, and Ghirra and the priests agreed on at least this point, then they must have shapes, sizes, places to live. Liphar's chants and legends were colorful but hopelessly metaphorical on the first two counts—Lagri was as tall as the mountains, Valla's veins ran with icy sea water. Lagri's voice was the desert wind. Valla Ired's white hair trailed for a hundred throws along the sea bottom. Stavros took it all with a grain of salt.

But the chants and songs and records were unanimous and very clear on the issue of habitation. Lagri dwelt in a high-walled palace of rock that dominated the very heart of the southern desert, far beyond the three ranges of the Grigar. There her sun fires burned perpetually and nothing mortal lived.

Liphar recited the tale-chant of the Building, when Lagri's parent sent a stupendous bolt to upthrust the desert rock. The rubble fell back to earth as a magnificent cave complex, vaster than a thousand settlements, with endlessly intertwining corridors and the finest carving, and great-halls so high that the night lanterns drifted through the clerestories to light the Goddess's solitary banquets, leaving the surrounding desert in darkness.

Valla, on the other hand, as her name suggested, inhabited the bottom of the great northern ocean, called DulValla in her honor. This wonderful home was also created for her by the mysterious unnamed parent, in the same mighty gesture that housed her sister Lagri. Valla's halls were jewel-encrusted, Liphar sang, and the giant barbed fishes kept watch when she went out to war with her sibling.

The desert and the ocean, mused Stavros as he lowered himself down the sheer face of a boulder, nearly losing his grip on the rope. Edan waited at the bottom, coiling her own rope and Liphar's, impatient to move on.

It shouldn't be hard to check up on, he decided. *I'll have CRI scan her remote sensing data, see if anything shows up in either of those places. Something concrete, something real . . .*

At last, the bulbous spire of the Red Pawn appeared above the hillocks and rockslides. The travellers came down out of the mountains onto a stony plateau whose gradual slope fell away abruptly several miles ahead to form DulElesi's cliff. The plateau supported a rich garden of cacti and gorse, nothing tall enough to hide a man. But along the rubbled southern border was a scattering of hidden tunnels, entrances to the cave complex itself. Most were known only to the RangerGuild, the secrets being passed down through the generations as closely guarded guild lore.

Edan led them to a nearly invisible cleft masked by a jumbled rockfall and boasting the additional camouflage of a thicket of sword plants and brush. Though invisible from the cliff top, across the plateau, the site afforded a panoramic view. Grimly, Stavros reflected that a situation advantageous to observing the weather lent itself to detecting approaching enemies of another sort as well.

He dug his small battery lamp from his pack and showed Edan how to use it. She rewarded him with a brief, delighted grin when he gave it to her to carry. He squeezed after her into the narrow cleft, realizing once he was in its shadow how oppressive the heat outside had really become. He longed to sit down and absorb the coolness, but the tunnel was too confined even to crouch. After hairpin right and left turns, it appeared to dead-end in a confusion of crevasses and burrowings.

Edan flashed the lamp around unnecessarily. The tight directable focus of its beam fascinated her. She let it linger on a random crevice, then suddenly twisted sharply, inserted herself sideways into the wrinkled rock and vanished. Darkness descended. Stavros felt Liphar tugging at the straps of his pack, urging it off his back, pulling him toward the wall. Then the pack was gone, Liphar's hands were gone, and Liphar's thin voice was calling him through the invisible crack.

Stavros turned sideways in the darkness and eased his body into the tiny crevice. Rough rock embraced him front and back. With his head twisted, his chest presented the broadest obstacle to passage. Momentarily, he knew the horror of being pinned for life by the weight of a mountain. Then with a final skin-scraping wrench, he was delivered into the inner tunnel.

Liphar lay collapsed against a wall, mopping his sweat-drenched face with the hem of his tunic. Edan had lowered herself to the floor in what passed for a willingness to rest.

Stavros crouched with his head sunk between his shoulders like a tired horse. But letting the fact of arrival at his goal sink in meant he could not sit idle for long. He stood wearily, gazing around to orient himself, then padded down the corridor to reach into a high niche in the wall. He hauled out a thick coil of cable, stashed there by ranger allies a week before. Reclaiming his pack and lamp, he sat down on the stone floor to refit the whip antenna of the Sled's omni to a scavenged mount. He cabled it, then made up the connections to the electronics box.

Then, with the antenna in hand, he squeezed back through the entry crevice to string the cable to the outer entrance. Outside in the heat again, he scaled the rockfall, careful to keep out of the line of sight from the cliff top, just in case. He tied the antenna in a high clump of brush, buried the cable with stones and dirt and retreated into hiding.

He told Liphar and Edan they could go on to their home caves to clean up and rest, as long as they kept out of sight. Liphar looked hurt and Edan's sour smirk suggested that her guildmaster would have her head for dereliction of duty if she left him unchaperoned. Stavros was relieved. He had not relished the prospect of sudden solitude. He grinned at them, gathering the last dregs of his energy, hooked the cable coil over his shoulder and headed down the tunnel, reeling out the line as he went.

The passage was straight and low, still narrow enough to force them to proceed single file. No concessions had been made to aesthetics in these secret diggings. The rock remained as ragged as the excavators had left it, many ages ago, though the tunnel widened at intervals into larger chambers as if to relieve the claustrophobia of long travel through a constricting tube of stone.

The coil of cable lightened rapidly. It had nearly played out when the tunnel widened once again. Here, instead of a single chamber, there were several, opening off a central hall. Stavros paused at a left-hand archway to let Edan go ahead of him with the lamp.

His equipment awaited him, set up on a wooden Sawl table, ready to go as soon as he made up the cables. He sent Liphar around the low, domed room lighting oil lamps. A bedroll was revealed, a rough firepit in one corner, stoneware jugs filled with water, boxes of purloined ship's rations, tools, utensils, clothing.

He was stopped briefly by the sight of all the detailed preparations he had made in his first blind rush into commitment. With Aguidran's help, he had planned the theft of the antenna very well. But he had let the long-range consequences of his actions slide by largely unexplored. The rage from his humiliation at Clausen's hands and his heady new sense of mission had carried him this far, when in reality, it was mad recklessness to launch himself nearly single-handed against a corporate juggernaut like CONPLEX. For now he would be safe enough in his secret cave, while he did his research and framed his court case. Later, he would worry about consequences, when the message was sent and the die truly cast.

He thought of Susannah, and wished her there with him, if only to help him forget for a while. And he thought of Kav Daven, here in the Caves, near to him now, yet still inaccessible. Stavros could only guess how long this dark space and its associated caverns would be his home and his prison. He could not safely venture into the open until Clausen's hands were legally tied.

And maybe not even then.

Stavros suspected the prospector of a taste for revenge.

He slouched toward the table with a resigned sigh. Edan watched intently as he plugged the antenna cable into the scavenged system. He wondered what end results she expected from their long trek through hail and thorns and heat. What a puzzle all these cables and switches must present to one who'd never heard of domesticated electricity, never mind the entire rest of the electromagnetic universe.

He pulled up the waiting wooden bench, and sat down to activate the terminal. When the ready light glowed, he poised his fingers over the keypad, then froze, tongue-tied at the final moment.

So what do I say for openers? Hi, CRI, how ya doin', it's been a quiet month and we're all fine and dandy down here . . . ?

He grinned nervously, playing out the conversation in his head.

What? . . . Oh, no, sorry . . . No one else is available to talk right now . . . Yup, all real busy . . . real busy.

Liphar eyed him with concern. Stavros shook himself free of his paralysis and touched in CRI's call code, followed by his own. He put the call on repeater and waited.

CRI had kept a search circuit functioning round the clock. Edan jumped as the computer's tinny voice filled the room. Stavros lunged for the volume controls and hurriedly flipped on the vocal transmission toggle.

"Don't shout, CRI, I'm here."

They were not the immortal words he had imagined himself uttering, but they would have to do.

10

As travel became harder due to the heat, Susannah spent less time on her sampling and more time trudging along in the sun, deep in a muddle of thought. She started keeping a list. It contained nothing conclusive, but the illusion of cohesion it provided was somehow comforting, to see all her most burning quandaries neatly inscribed on the same back page of her notebook, as if grouping them physically might also relate them causally.

As the list grew, she began to see that new entries were often variations of questions she had already noted several items earlier. The basic issues were settling out like salts in solution.

Megan discovered the list at the end of a long cycle's march through the tall amber grasses of the northern Dop Arek. She snatched up the notebook as if hungry for something other than her own notes to read. She flipped through it, then stopped and held the last page up to the orange light of the lowering sun. She read the heading aloud as Susannah sat working with her portable analyzer.

" 'Oddnesses'?"

Susannah tossed her head diffidently. "Well, not each one so much, but maybe together . . ."

" 'Three beasts,' " read Megan.

"The hakra and the hjalk and the hekkers. I told you they seem remarkably similar, like specially tuned forms of the same animal."

"Generations of clever breeding."

Susannah nodded. "But if so, still an astonishing achievement, to breed three out of one and so perfectly adapt each to its intended specialization."

"The Sawls have had a lot of time, judging from guild records."

"But I can't think of a Terran animal that breeders were able to work *all* the kinks out of before the genetic engineers were around to lend a hand. I'm going to do a DNA match as soon as I get done with my plant chemistry and can reprogram the box here. I mean, for instance, where are these animals' other relatives? We haven't seen a single wild herbivore, not a single wild *mammal* for that matter."

"Or birds. No birds, just those hideous flying lizards." Megan shuddered only half jokingly. "Have you asked Ghirra about this?"

Hammering resounded from the Weaver wagon next to them as a wheelwright from the Woodworkers' Guild stopped by on his repair rounds. A group of Weavers patching the shredded canopies stopped work to help jack up the wagon and hold muttered debate over the significance of the heat and the long stretch without rain.

"Ghirra says such animals were not meant to run wild. Now what the hell does that mean?" Susannah understood his surface meaning, that wild animals were those who could survive in the hostile wilderness without man's care, being hard-skinned, spiny, sharp-toothed, poisonous, aggressive and omnivorous. "I mean, did he intend the subtextual implications of that remark? When he said 'meant,' was he suggesting intention and creation, and if so, by whom?"

Megan offered the anthropological interpretation. "Those mysterious creators, remember, who bore both the Goddesses and the Sawls? However much the rationalist he claims to be, Ghirra's still the product of a society steeped in religion."

Susannah made a face. "Try as I might, I do not find 'the gods made it that way' to be a very satisfying answer, Megan, and I'm surprised Ghirra does."

Megan shrugged. "I'm not sure he does. Next item . . . 'abnormal growth rate' . . . The domestic crops really grow faster?"

"Stav pointed that out to me before . . . before he left."

Megan continued reading. " 'Trehalose analogues' . . . 'poisonous'?"

"Yes. Doesn't it seem odd to you that *all* wild animals and most wild plants on Fiix should be poisonous?"

"Do you know that they are?"

"No, but Ghirra says . . . well, besides, it's the only excuse I can come up with for the split food chain."

"Ah ha. The very next item."

"I'm positing two separate ecosystems in operation here: the Sawls and their domestic plants and animals versus everything else. Normally, this would be an inelegant system, not making efficient use of the planet's resources. It would seem to work against survival, unless survival was what necessitated the split in the first place. Thus, I'd prefer it if all the wild animals do prove to be poisonous."

"Does evolution work that way? I mean, support the development of coexisting separate systems?"

"On a planetary scale? If it's a natural mechanism, it's unprecedented," Susannah admitted.

"*If* a natural . . . ? Now who's getting heavy with the subtext?"

"Well, I keep thinking about Weng's periodic table."

"Weng's so-called periodic table."

"She's only suggesting there were some people here once who knew some things the Sawls don't know now. Not unreasonable."

"Ummm. So you *are* suggesting the three H's might have been engineered?"

"No. I . . . I don't know . . . well, maybe. But that could be my Terran frame of reference asserting itself, plus a poverty of the imagination. The real explanation's probably a natural one, but just as unlikely, I'll bet."

Undisturbed by further violent weather, the caravan settled into a routine walking, eating and sleeping deeply after long hours in the heat. The hail damage was repaired little by little, injuries healed, and the wagons inched across the open plain at a measured crawl, like the sun sinking slowly at their backs.

On the sixth throw, they picked up a little stream, shallow and sluggish, but the first fresh water since leaving the canyon of the hail. An unscheduled stop was made to refill the water kegs tied to the sides of the wagons. The brush-grown track ran parallel to the distant northern mountains, the Vallegar, Valla's Wall. In the east, the turquoise sky faded into pale ambered green as it dropped to the grassy horizon.

By the seventh throw, as the sun rested its salmon disk on the western limb, the stream had widened into a small sand-bottomed river. The caravan plodded through a hot, red dusk. The sharp grasses in Susannah's path were darkened by her long, purple shadow.

She thought it a trick of the odd light that the plain no longer seemed to stretch ahead to infinity. But again, there was a restlessness building along the caravan and she found herself searching the ruddy sky for sudden clouds. She was rewarded instead with the shrill music of the pipers striking an upbeat rhythm. The hjalk jostled and picked up their pace self-importantly, as if embarrassed to have been woken from a walking doze.

From the head of the train came scattered singing, weary but cheerful. Susannah saw the lead wagons turn abruptly aside and appear to fall off the edge of the horizon. Over the rattle of harness and cartwheels, she heard a steady roaring.

Ghirra smiled as she stopped to stare in confusion. He took her arm and drew her forward to the edge, where she stood gaping like a tourist at Olympus Mons.

The plain simply ended. And then, a kilometer below, it began again, as a lowland savannah that sloped gently toward a green arm of ocean curling around the eastern extreme of the Vallegar. The northern bay shore was sharply mountainous, broken by rugged fjords. The southern shore was too distant to be clearly seen in the red dusk. At the nearer, western end, a region of tall sea cliffs and steep-sided inlets sheltered a smaller, narrow cove.

Ghirra pointed. "Ogo Dul."

Susannah squinted into the dusky distance. She saw no bustling trade city on those wave-splashed cliffs, no sign of human habitation at all. The battered yellow canopy of the Infirmary wagon passed beneath, drawing her attention downward. A road nestled into the side of the stupendous drop, descending in eight long switchbacks. It was two wagon-widths across and paved with worn octagonal stones. A knee-high stone curb ran along the drop-side edge of the road, broken in places, where dry slides of dirt and gravel had shoved across the pavement. The lead wagons, beginning the third switchback, seemed cast in miniature, already far below.

Susannah looked for the source of the roaring. To the north of the road, the little river that had accompanied them for the last few throws fell in a single red-gold ribbon off the edge of the precipice. Several hundred meters down, it smashed into a ledge and rebounded in a cloud of ruddy mist to drop again, a fan of sparkling threads cascading into a wide pool at the shadowed base of the chasm. There were clumps of trees, a level meadow flanking the river where it flowed out of the pool to resume its seaward journey, and blossoms large enough to be visible at a distance as points of vermilion glowing in the yellow grass.

"Hell of a drop," murmured Susannah inadequately.

"Um. Kinda looks like Paradise down there," Megan remarked at her side.

They missed the first sunset in two and a half weeks, by their ship's clock. The air cooled only slightly as they descended the long curl of road into premature evening and the fat red sun disappeared behind the chasm's rim.

"My ears just popped," Megan noted.

"And the humidity's back," Susannah added regretfully. She watched the lead wagons reach bottom and pull aside onto the grassy terrace beside the pool.

"Will Aguidran let us stop here?" Susannah asked.

Ghirra nodded at the russet mist. "This water we call Imvalla, but it is a favored place."

"Imvalla?"

"Valla's Tears. She left them here at this place, the tales say, and this is why Valla does not cry for the hurt she brings."

The air was warm and still in the poolside meadow, but a long collective swim in deep water and the absence of the punishing sun brought a festive air to the campsite.

Megan relaxed and stared contentedly at the distant hot gleam of sunset ocean. Ghirra rediscovered laughter, telling light stories of past trade trips. Even the laconic Master Ranger was persuaded to sip at a ration of sour beer, adding the occasional droll detail to her brother's recitations. At the twenty giant red-and-blue wagons, the FoodGuilders sang as they cleaned up after the dinner meal. The terrors of the hail seemed for the moment forgotten.

As Susannah rolled out her blanket in the red twilight, she said to Megan, "It's great without the sun, but how will we find our way in the night?"

Overhearing, Ghirra smiled like a parent on Christmas eve. "You will know this, Suzhannah, when you wake."

Singing woke her, throaty and solemn. Shadows moved through warm dim light, and Susannah was confused, mistaking it for lingering dusk.

But the light was in the east. The ocean horizon glowed in secret anticipation. The waking caravan faced the east and sang its welcome.

Dawn already? I thought . . . Susannah's entire understanding of the lengthy Fiixian light-dark cycle was abruptly thrown into question.

And then the false dawn faded as the night sky's glowing magnificence, the densely packed star globule of Byrnham's Cluster, nosed above the horizon.

Its center, perched on the sparkling rim of the ocean, was a rosy fuzz as luminous as an aurora. As darkness fell, its halo became visible, a semicircle of pointilist light that dominated half the sky, thinning gradually toward the perimeter and ending quite suddenly against velvet black. There was no familiar background star field. A profusion of nearby stars, bright as planets, were scattered across the otherwise empty night, red, gold, white and blue, like glimmering shells thrown up on the dark sands of a volcanic beach. Sooty tendrils of the surrounding black invaded the cluster's luminous arc. Susannah thought of dark, long-fingered hands grasping a glowing melon.

Ghirra crouched beside her, his expectant smile of the evening before made proud by her wondering delight. "Do you like our night lanterns?"

She nodded, unable to frame an appropriate reply.

He pointed out a huge red giant of a star halfway out from the cluster center, then a hotter blue spark caught in a dark cloud wisp. "The Rangers," he explained. "They watch the Darkness, the red light for Lagri, the blue light for Valla."

"The darkness?" she asked, thinking he meant the night. But Ghirra traced a finger in the air, outlining the tendrils of nebular dust.

"There . . . you see this? The Darkness." He sat back on his heels pensively, then murmured, "Ibi says each night lantern is another world. Do you say this also?"

"Well, yes, of course. At least, maybe not a world that supports life, but lots of stars have planets, worlds, that is. Mine has ten, but people only live on three of them, plus some of the moons."

"Mooon." He wrapped his tongue around the syllable, making it two.

"That's right, you have no moons here, do you? A moon is a smaller world that moves around a larger world."

Ghirra lowered himself to the damp grass beside her and sat like a small boy with his knees pulled up to his chin. "Ah, so many. So many worlds."

11

"The salvage party has finally left, and the two hjalk teams with them." Weng set a Sawl oil lamp down on Danforth's work table. "I thought you might appreciate some additional light."

Danforth nodded abstractedly, staring over steepled fingers at the Cluster glowing above the dark silhouette of the Talche. "I don't know. Pretty good night for stargazing."

"The Cluster must have great spiritual significance for the Sawls," noted Weng. "They sang in the fields when it rose."

"They sing all the time, Weng."

"But this time, they stopped work and sang."

Danforth squinted into the shadowy stalks walling the clearing. "They're out there working in the dark? Don't they ever quit?"

"The Fiixian night is too long for work to stop every darkfall, Dr. Danforth. And we must be grateful that the ranger salvage party had no reluctance to set out in darkness. I wish M-Clausen had seen fit to wait for them."

Danforth made a small noise of disgust. "You think Ibiá is really after the antenna?"

"I really couldn't say."

Danforth faced out into the darkness, but his gaze turned inward. "Well, if he is, I hope for his sake he gets the hell out of there before Emil finds him at it."

Stavros shoved his bench away from the makeshift console. CRI was relating a long horror story and would not be sidetracked.

The cavern was suffocating, the unrelenting heat of the night outside beginning to translate downward through the rock. Stavros's fingers were slippery on the keypad.

He stood, stretching the cramps out of his back, and went to the stone sink to splash water on his face. The water flowed by gravity from a cistern buried in the hill above his hiding place. It was tepid and tasted faintly of earth, but he gulped it gratefully from cupped hands and let it stream down his bared shoulders and chest. He decided to risk a trip to the Baths later, even if he had to overcome Edan's caution by force.

After reestablishing contact with CRI, Stavros had unburdened himself of the complicated fiction he'd invented to explain the "temporary" absence of all his colleagues, and went right to work, first to do the necessary fiddling to hide all record of his inquiry, from the Orbiter crew as well as from the landing party, when and if the comlink was fixed. Then he set CRI to search her files for all existing regulatory legislation that covered the operations of corporations exploiting extraterrestrial natural resources, with specific reference to mining companies.

It was soon clear that Megan had been right. A statutory scheme did exist, whereby the World Federal government claimed jurisdiction over the actions of corporations operating within the settled zone.

The stated intention of this body of law was both to protect a legally staked claim, and to provide for circumstances where private claim rights might be overriden by a regulatory agency. However, specific determination of such circumstances rested with the agency involved. Stavros found reference to protection of preexisting populations or unique natural wonders, but the language seemed, to his linguist's ear, to be intentionally vague. Asking for a history of past cases, he discovered that removal of a population to a reservation or even off-planet entirely, had often come under the World Court's definition of protection.

"The law would seem to lay responsibility for compliance on the corporate entity," CRI had pointed out. "And there is an admitted difficulty of enforcement over such great distances."

"And if they don't comply? Could WorldFed put the squeeze on them back home?"

CRI took a moment to review her files. "This has been done in one or two cases of blatant infraction or complaints by rival corporations. In cases where regulatory infractions are alleged by private individuals, such individuals must file an action with the World Court. In emergencies, where the allegations can be substantiated, injunctive relief may be sought."

This lawyer pal of Meg's better be a genius, he had thought glumly.

"What constitutes 'substantiated'?"

"That is obviously for the Court to decide."

And then, operating out of some mysterious prime directive, CRI had begun to tell him horror stories.

Cautionary tales was a more accurate description. The data bank's supply seemed bottomless. Tales of extortion, blackmail, bribery, mayhem and murder murmured in his ears, all acts of vengeance called down by CONPLEX and her fellow mega-corporations on the heads of those who thought to defy the mega-corporate will. Stavros wondered if this admonitory device was CRI's own invention or was somehow imbedded in her programming, to steer a user away from ill-considered action. Either way, he cursed the computer's designers, who had seen fit to program such stubbornness into a machine.

Two cycles of lost sleep later, he was able nearly to filter the recitation out of his consciousness altogether. CRI chattered on nonetheless, assuming, in her machine way, his rapt attention. Stavros had turned off the audio several times already, then back on again, made anxious by the silence. Should the com to the Lander be relinked, he needed to know it immediately, faster than CRI might think to tell him on screen.

At the sink, he dried his face on a sweat-stained shirt and raked back his damp hair. He considered taking the time to hack at it with the clippers from his tool kit, but he liked the thought of letting it grow until he could tie it back as the Sawls so often did with their dangling curls, as Ghirra did, so that with his slight, elegant body and diffident stoop, he resembled an eighteenth-century dandy, lacking only a frock coat and lace.

Stavros left his hair alone. Turning from the sink, he tuned one ear in on CRI's recitation. He judged the current tale to be in a wind-up phase.

Will she start all over again once she runs out?

The thought appalled him. He paced toward the narrow entry arch, feeling caged. Liphar was stretched on his bedroll in front of the doorway, fast asleep. Stavros stared at him, considering escape, then slouched back to the terminal. He bent reflexively to check the time elasped on his power cells, noted the oil level in his lamp, and resettled himself on the bench with a ragged sigh. He glanced at the screen, readying his notes.

While CRI lectured him on the folly of his ways, she was also searching the legal files for precedent that might help Stavros build a case. The message sent to the lawyer could not be an inarticulate call for help. Such a person needed to be wooed, to be convinced that the case had merit. Most of the cases that CRI dredged up were further indication of how sporadic the enforcement of existing regulations was.

But occasionally, there was something hopeful for Stavros to add to his notes, inscribed in tiny space-saving letters in a small sketchbook he had liberated from the ship's stores.

At the back of the same sketchbook, during the few breaks he allowed himself to do anything but eat or sleep, he recorded his recreational thinking. He worked on recalling the words that Kav Daven had spoken to him in the private language of the PriestGuild, during the time of his "miracle." He told himself he was building a vocabulary for the more complex ancestral tongue, with its hints of a technological bias. But in truth, his search was for answers to the mystery of the Ritual Master himself, for clues to what the old priest expected of him. The events of the Leave-taking had become dreamlike in his mind. The grimy task he now performed was far from his vision then, of himself as a hero of the people, raising the shining banner of the PriestGuild.

A new entry appeared at the bottom of the terminal's screen. Stavros reached for his pen. *Halloran vs. Microdyne, 2067,* he wrote, then waited, his pen poised, while CRI's other more vocal self nudged at his flagging concentration.

". . . remains in prison, WorldPen 435 at Lima, serving three consecutive life sentences." CRI paused. The speaker hissed softly, and as he had during each and every pause over the last two cycles, Stavros prayed that she had come to the end of her supply.

"*New York Times,* Thursday, December 10, 2059: The disappearance of Gabrielle Roget has been . . ."

"CRI, I'll shut you off again," he growled wearily. For reasons he was unable to comprehend without resorting to hopeless anthropomorphism, CRI did respond briefly to threats of being cut off. He failed to see how such an imperative could have been printed into mere circuitry, or for what reason, but he smiled bitter thanks into the blissful if temporary silence and bent to his note-taking.

". . . under investigation by the Department of Commerce, following allegations by several witnesses that . . ."

"CRI!!"

On his blanket by the door, Liphar stirred, shifted and went back to sleep.

CRI replied, "Yes, Mr. Ibiá?"

"This will do no good, CRI, worse torture though it may be than any that CONPLEX could dream up to put me through."

"Mr. Ibiá, Captain Newman up here is very disturbed to have remained out of contact with the Landing Party for so long."

"I'm part of the landing party. You're in contact with me now."

"Mr. Ibiá, if you would allow me to patch you through to Captain Newman, I am certain he would be able to put all of your worries concerning the fate of the inhabitants of 2-PT 6 Fiix to rest in no time."

Stavros rested his forehead on his pen hand. "CRI, I think you know better than that. Just who do you think pays Captain Newman's salary? Now why don't you try approaching this as a challenging puzzle you'd love to help me solve? Have you no curiosity for the mysteries of legal linguistics, for the intricacies of the argument?" He blotted his damp upper lip against his equally damp arm and tried blunt honesty. "CRI, please understand. The price of development here is just too high."

"Mr. Ibiá, it is my duty to inform you that . . ."

Stavros reached and cut her off.

He sat in the silence for a while, feeling the heat like an unbreathable thickening of the air. The smell of his own body sickened him. He wondered where Edan was, prowling the tunnels in search of food or just outside the door, waiting to spring if he should so much as stir from hiding.

"Lifa!" He barked suddenly, and swiveled from the bench to shake the young Sawl awake. "Lifa, come on, get up! We're going to the Baths, and I'll fight like Lagri herself if Edan tries to stop me!"

12

Megan envied the illusion of precision Susannah's list provided, but she was unable to work that way. She attempted lists on occasion, hoping that her habits had progressed, but her lists all too quickly evolved into mammoth run-on sentences whose clauses were not easily dismembered into discrete items placeable one above the other behind a neat column of numbers. She also denied herself the geometric comforts of the assorted graphs and charts employed by her younger colleagues, who held that anthropology could be pursued through statistical analysis like any other hard science.

Intuitive connections were Megan's method. Often before she had gathered what others would consider "adequate" data, the structure of a culture became visible to her. She visualized the process as an old-time photograph swimming up out of the ripples of the developing fluid, at the same time admitting that her imagery was as old-fashioned as her methodology.

But by the time you're forty-seven, you work the way you work, she mused defensively as she swished through the dark meadow grasses in Ghirra's wake. *And so far, the way I work has worked for me.*

"That's why I was feeling so frustrated," she exclaimed to Susannah, her arms spread wide to provide the emphasis her lowered voice could not. The overbearing magnificence of the night sky had the two women whispering as if in a place of worship. The light of the Cluster was, as Ghirra had promised, enough to see by, but only just. Enough to keep from stumbling into holes or bumping into a neighbor or his wagon.

"Like Tay, you know?" Megan continued. "Lots of data, no connections."

"And now? The only connection I've come up with is a bunch of items on the same piece of paper."

Megan's head bobbed, somewhere between a shrug and a nod. "Well, now, here and there. Bit by bit." She kept her eyes on the steadying image of Ghirra's back.. Walking in the half-dark was awkward. The ground was either deceptively close or too far away, and the stiff, sharp grasses snatched at the blousy fabric of the Sawl pants she had taken to wearing, stubbornly enough to break her step.

Susannah paced alongside patiently. "Meg, I sense you working yourself up to theoretical levels."

Megan blotted her brow on her bare forearm. The coming of darkness had only barely lessened the heat, a fact which made the Sawls clearly apprehensive. "Well, I was thinking about survival."

"That's been on all our minds lately, I suspect."

"But you know, we take survival too much for granted with respect to developing cultures. I mean, the pursuit of survival. We say: they work so hard to survive, or: they must do thus and such in order to survive, as if the pursuit of survival were merely one more obstacle to the real business of culture, which is to get on with expansion and development."

"Isn't it?" asked Susannah.

Watching Ghirra ahead, Megan wondered how much of their conversation he could hear, or more important, understand. "Usually we think of it as Emil does, that civilization only moves forward. But it could be considered a cultural bias to assume that expansion and development are civilization's only valid goal."

"If not expansion, then at least evolution, yes? Change?"

Megan chuckled. "Spoken from the bias of a biologist. I wonder if man's horror of stasis is a race memory of eons of evolve-or-get-eaten . . ."

"I think I shall keep my mouth shut until I hear this theory."

"Not a theory. Not yet. But change is part of it, as a matter of fact." Megan paused to glance around as if checking classroom attendance. "Sometimes I find those connections I'm looking for in the patterns of change in a society, as reflected in their history or their myth or their artifacts over a period of time. But here, I sense a pattern of *no* change.

"Look at it. If the histories have any relation to fact, we have a cycle of devastations, repeating itself for thousands of years, that more or less regularly decimates the world population. So it's built up to a certain point of development and then, wham, back to where you started. The net result is no change. Stasis."

"Therefore, the very idea of progress, as we understand the word, has never entered the Sawls' vocabulary. For instance, do you ever hear the FoodGuilders talk about developing a faster seed?"

Susannah's incredulous expression passed unnoticed in the dim light. "A *faster* seed? How much faster do you want?"

"Well, then, how about a way to grow more food indoors, or improved farming methods so they could increase the acreage under tillage?"

"There's not much of that kind of thinking," Susannah admitted. "But then, they've got their hands full just getting what they *do* have to grow."

"There! You just made the excuse. You're assuming they'd do more if they could. Okay, how about this: would you care to hazard a guess at how long it's been since the Engineers' Guild built a new winch?"

Susannah laughed. "No, but I'll bet you can tell me to the minute."

"I asked. It's been the equivalent of two hundred years, if I understand their calendar right. And though they made a few improvements at the time, the new one was mostly an exact copy of one that had been in use for the previous three hundred and fifty-odd years. I have this through Ghirra from Aguidran, who thinks it would speed up the loading at caravan times if Engineers built another winch, but she hasn't been able to talk them into it. Another one, mind you, not a *better* one!"

Self-consciously, Megan dropped her voice. "The point is, the Sawls perfect, but they do not advance. Expansion and development are not part of their cultural imperative. Why is the population contained in such regularly spaced settlements? Why do we go to Ogo Dul to trade rather than to conquer? Not because the Sawls are so peaceable, as I used to think until I heard them arguing like banshees among themselves. It's because they don't even exhibit that most basic of developmental urges, to expand territorially. They divided the available resources up amongst themselves long ago and are content to keep it that way."

"Meg, it's all they can do to hold on to what they have. There's a big enough war going on over their heads, without their starting new ones."

"Again, you make the old excuse. But that's fine, because it brings us back to the issue of survival." Megan slowed to let the Master Healer move ahead, out of earshot. But somehow the space between them remained the same.

He's listening, she decided. *But I'd bet he's always listening.*

She continued more quietly. "It would be logical of course to suggest that the Sawls have stagnated due to the harshness of the climate and the lack of metallic resources, that their growth is stunted by the extremities of their world."

She felt a soft, insistent nudge against her shoulder blade, and stepped out of the path of the lead hjalk of the wagon behind her. She saw Ghirra also move slightly aside, but was too involved in airing her thought out loud to stop the process.

"What if we turn our thinking end for end, and suggest that the stasis is not a *result* but a *goal*? A necessity. That the Sawls have survived *because* they have not changed."

"Blasphemy," accused Susannah wryly.

"I know. Antievolutionary claptrap, right? But hear me out." She tossed Susannah a sly grin. "Jews understand these things, you see. Sometimes just laying low is the better part of valor.

"Here's another little detail: how about the Sawls' obsessive record keeping? Beyond the usual religious books, the priests' First Books of the Goddesses, and their Second Books of purported history, there are all the guild ledgers, the reams of lore and records and instruction going back for hundreds of generations. There are the endless weather rolls, and the stories carved on every available surface, plus the whole oral tradition, the songs and chants, not to mention the family records and geneologies."

"And the Birth Records, and the crop inventories and the animal breeding charts," Susannah added.

91

"This represents a high degree of literacy and literary consciousness for such a technically backward culture. Well, for a while, in the Middle Ages and later, the Jewish people were doing just what these folks are doing: keeping the records, observing the old ways . . . and waiting."

Megan's tone made this last word the solid core of her thesis.

"Waiting," Susannah repeated. "What for?"

"For an end to persecution," replied Megan with unusual gentleness. "Like the Jews. For an end to the wars. The Sawls are waiting for peace."

"Meg, the entire galaxy is waiting for peace."

Megan shook her head stubbornly. "No. Everyone else, it's within the power of the participants to end the wars if they really want to. Not so here. The Sawls are victims of a war they cannot participate in, beyond offering their prayers of support to the goddess who seems to be weakest at the time. And remember what Ghirra said: they can't even hope for a victory to put an end to the struggle, because a victory of one side is supposedly what brings on a Devastation.

"They're lost in a cycle of hopelessness. The myth is quite specific on that count. Stavros found no ambiguities in his translation of that section of the Tale of Origins. The Sisters have been blinded by the Darkness and they will not see clearly again until the Darkness ends."

"And they fall into each other's arms," remarked Susannah.

Megan frowned at her. "More or less. Anyway, the Arrah will end. Why are you being so snide?"

Susannah ducked her head. "Sorry. It just smacked a bit of the Second Coming or something . . . do I detect a Judeo-Christian messianic bias here?"

"If so, it's yours," Megan returned. "There's not even a whisper of messiahs in this myth. It's far more pragmatic. The struggle will go on until the Darkness ends, or lifts or passes, whatever. Nothing will help it along, not prayer or good works or sacrifices, nothing but the passage of an unspecified length of time. *That's* why the business of this culture is survival, for the sake of that day when peace will be restored."

Megan was silent for a while, walking, chewing her lip. She gazed ahead, at Ghirra's gray silhouette outlined by the glow of the Cluster and the black of its encircling smoke. "I tell you," she added softly, "if I had this damn climate to deal with, theirs is exactly the sort of myth I'd develop, as a weapon against self-hatred and despair. A society cannot be allowed to feel responsible for this sort of random suffering."

"A culture in limbo," mused Susannah.

"Exactly. Seeing them that way answers a lot of my questions about them. It explains this dogged acceptance of theirs. Have you ever heard a Sawl rage against the injustice of his goddesses?"

Together, as she said this, their eyes went ahead to the Master Healer's back.

"Except for him," Megan whispered. "It also explains the lack of a coherent ethic tied to the religious teachings, because it shows that the Sawl religion is not an ethical system, it's a survival system. Behavioral ethics become irrelevant in religion when they aren't seen to influence the response of a deity. If prayer and good works won't end the wars, then the only true moral imperative becomes survival, or I should say, survival *until*. The day to day issues of ethics and behavior are left to the guilds within each settlement to teach and administer. The PriestGuild deals with the long-term issue of surviving the wars, with the Rangers as their active analogue. Aguidran and her guildsmen teach the practice of survival while Ashimmel teaches its philosophy. The ceremonial association of ranger and priest that puzzled me at the Leave-taking represents their dual guardianship over their people."

Her mouth dry from talking, Megan uncorked her canteen. The heat was like a weight on her brain. But there was a further thought to add.

"Now the gambling is a classic reaction to despair. Gambling elevates the power of luck—*khem*—in their lives, which are denied free will. If the Goddesses view them with such disdain, then so be it, life will be treated as an ironic game. What better response for the powerless? The philosophy of luck encourages two hopes: first, that it's your *luck* and not you that's at fault if you suffer, and two, that things might get suddenly better. You might win."

"The Darkness might end."

"Right."

Susannah walked a while, considering. The caravan ahead was a long line of gray shapes receding into steamy night. She laughed softly. "Stav would be scandalized."

"That is often his response to my ideas, yes."

"I mean, elevating gambling to such noble heights."

"Well, there's no one here getting rich off the losers. Plus it helps let off competitive steam. This society *must* work together to survive. In the long run, it's still share and share alike."

They trudged along some more, listening to the wagon wheels grind through the brittle grass. Beside them, the hjalk snorted wearily. In the driver's seat, little Phea crooned gentle encour-

93

agements. Somewhere in a wagon behind, a father sang to his fretful child. The pace music of the pipers seemed caught in a mournful key.

"You know what else he would say?" Susannah said finally. "He'd remind us once again that the Goddesses are real to the Sawls. Not a colorful metaphor . . . no mere article of faith."

Megan was acutely aware of Ghirra's rigid, listening posture. "Doesn't change my thinking one iota. Valla and Lagri could sit down to dinner with us and the theory still stands, with fact substituted for mythos. That's why I'm happy with it."

"Meg, does this mean you're leaving yourself open for the possibility?"

"It means I've decided to leave issues of faith and reality to the theologians, or to young linguists who care to act as theologians. As the poet said, 'There are more things twixt heaven and earth, Horatio . . .' "

Susannah sighed. "Amen to that."

Ghirra was silent through the mid-throw meal. He ate quickly with lowered head, then excused himself, claiming business with his sister. Megan watched him stride away through the dim starlight. She wondered if the slight jerkiness of his step was due to roughness of the ground or to anger.

"He was listening," she worried to Susannah.

"To every word."

"And understanding it?"

"Stavros said Ghirra's intellect was awe inspiring. That's a quote."

Megan shifted uneasily, setting her empty plate aside. "Even allowing for Stav's penchant for exaggeration, he's got a point. I have a feeling we'll hear about this sooner or later."

Ghirra rejoined them at supper. He brought a lantern from the back of the wagon and set it lit in front of them. He bent the stiff grass into a mat beneath his long legs, then settled himself comfortably with his laden food tray balanced across his knees.

He smiled at the two women, who had ceased even pretending to eat the moment he sat down.

"This was much interesting talk, Megan," he remarked gravely, without letting go of his smile.

"I thought you might have been listening," said Megan lightly.

Susannah said nothing, feeling that the moment was rightfully his.

The healer turned his smile to her. "It is like, I think, when

94

you lie on the stone and the doctors talk about how you are sick and how they will do for you."

Megan cleared her throat. "Ghirra, I didn't mean to offend. Only to try and understand."

"Yes," he replied, drawing out the final consonant into a faint hiss of resignation. Yet his back was straight and his manner hinted at challenge through the veil of his smile. "Do you want knowing of how I think with this?"

The two women leaned forward with an eager deference that made him laugh. His dark face relaxed with the line of his back. He set his food aside and leaned forward as well, still smiling. He folded his hands in a mimic of Megan's professorial air, his elbows resting on his knees. The yellow lamplight caught the occasional strand of silver in his curls.

"I think that you understand this right, Megan, in many matters. It is true that we wait for many generations for the ending of the Arrah." He paused, and then said, without a trace of resentment, "For many generations more than all Terrans have lived on your world."

Susannah felt a little jolt at the word 'Terran,' a term that Sawls rarely used, favoring their own 'wokind.' Ghirra's use of it seemed intended to emphasize his recognition of their differences.

"That old?" Megan prodded.

Ghirra nodded. "We counted this, Ibi and me. If I tell him a history, always he wants knowing when it was, and it is not good enough I say, a long time past. He say . . ." The healer was struggling now against the limits of his imperfect English, but slipped into a passable imitation of Stavros' edgy tones. "He say, 'but when? When *exactly* did this happen? How long? How many times?' I begin wondering that Terrans are so worried with time." He sat back and cocked his head at the women questioningly. "You take a short cycle, you need sleep very often, eat very often. A thing of work must end for you at . . . at a time that you say, instead when it is finished."

He looked aside, seeming to remember his meal cooling on the tray. He nibbled a spoonful of mashed kamad root. Megan took this as a cue and began eating with a restrained care that allowed her to keep her mouth full and her eyes glued to the Master Healer's face.

Ghirra swallowed. "How I understand now is that our time here is different. Also our animals and our plants and what you call our 'weather.' Suzhannah say, the plants grow too fast, this is 'abnormal.' But Megan say, the Sawls do not grow fast, and *this* is abnormal."

He ate another spoonful, using the moment to form his next sentence.

"What I say is, the things here are as they must be to live, so this is not abnormal for these things. Also I say, we do grow." He leaned forward again and Susannah was moved by the depth of passion he managed to express within such calm, measured phrasing. "The winch you talk of, Megan, was a better winch than the old winch." He tapped his chest in restrained emphasis. "I am a better healer than she that taught me. It is only you, Terrans, that have not these Sisters to hold you back, only you can grow so fast that it seems to you that the Sawls stand still."

Listening in creeping shame, Susannah heard Emil Clausen's bored voice repeating its lesson in her head. '. . . *these little brown folk have a brand-new view of their universe simply because we appeared in it, out of the heavens . . .*' She finally understood why he scoffed at the noninterference regulations. The only true noninterference was to stay away.

"Meghan, your talk of accepting is correct. The priests teach this and they say this is to be until the Darkness ends. They mean this is a comfort, yes, a . . ." He quoted Megan neatly. "A weapon against despair. For me, it is no comfort. Not ever.

"But," he continued, into the silence his eloquence had created, "same as you learn and watch me and ask your questions, I learn also. I learn that a box can have words and knowing inside. I learn about the other worlds, that have no Sisters. I learn also this what Ibi calls 'impatience,' that it is not wrong, Aguidran and me to ask our questions about these Sisters. I learn that accepting is not the only way of men.

"And I feel more angry at these Sisters from this learning, but I am happy at it." He regarded them both seriously, then smiled with a clear intent of irony.

"For me, Meghan, this learning is a faster growing."

13

The light was dim in the BathHall. Four of the pools had been drained. The water was low in the remaining two, and a faint soap scum floated about the tiled edges.

Stavros did not care. He tossed his pants aside at the nearest pool and dropped into the waiter's tepid embrace with a grateful sigh. Liphar dunked, washed himself hurriedly, then sat with his legs dangling over the edge, watching over his shoulder for Edan, still clearly astonished that they had managed to elude her. Stavros swam the length of the pool and back, rolling his body around and around like a playful seal.

"Lifa!" he challenged, "She comes, we'll just throw her in! She could use it!"

Liphar grinned, but nervously.

Stavros dove and surfaced, scattering water with an exuberant shake of his head. Then he noticed a small group of bathers at the shallow end of the other undrained pool. His legs drifted down and found bottom as he floated motionless in surprise.

Kav Daven hunched naked on the green tiled corner steps, his knobby thin legs soaking in the water. Two other elderly priests sat nearby in weary conversation. At Kav Daven's side, his child companion wrung out wet cloths to drape on his bent head and shoulders.

Stavros climbed slowly out of his pool. He had never laid eyes on the ancient Ritual Master outside of a ceremonial context. At ritual times, he had felt that the frail body barely contained that vibrant spirit with its aura of power and magic. Now he saw how tenuous the old priest's grip on life really was, how his withered skeleton was sadly burdened by the heat, how surely he was failing. Stavros had a moment of reluctant sympathy for the Master Priest Ashimmel, understanding why she must press Kav Daven to designate an heir to his office. Should he die without training an apprentice, ritual knowledge that he alone possessed might be lost to the guild forever. But according to Liphar, the old man resisted stubbornly, refusing all candidates that had been offered him so far.

What is he waiting for? Does he think he can go on forever? Stavros was almost ready to believe it possible, to believe anything possible, remembering the miracle of the guar.

"Lifa!" he whispered, motioning Liphar to join him. The dim fire in his palms, almost forgotten over the past cycles of concentrated brain work, flared anew as he padded across the tile.

The other priests nodded at Stavros with neutral wariness, but the blind Ritual Master did not acknowledge his approach. His bony shoulders were drawn up high about his neck as he muttered soundlessly, faintly rocking. His small attendant looked away from Stavros shyly and laid a damp cloth gently across Kav Daven's back.

Stavros crouched tentatively at his side. "Kav . . . ?"

The old man ceased rocking at Stavros' murmur. He sat up a little straighter and a smile lit his gaunt, papery face. "Raellil," he said, liquid syllables but distinct, spoken softly as if in welcome.

Stavros did not recognize the word. He glanced at Liphar.

"OldWords," the priest-to-be mouthed apologetically.

"Tell me later." Stavros stored the word in his memory but did not want to waste precious time with the Kav debating appropriate translations. He had so many questions, pounding at his mind like a crowd outside the door, and had lost confidence suddenly in his ability to express them.

"Lifa, please, tell him I need to understand better what happened at the Leave-taking."

Liphar's look was reproving, as if miracles were not meant to be questioned, but he bent respectfully and spoke beside Kav Daven's ear.

The Ritual Master nodded and smiled, but continued to murmur unintelligibly, and Stavros began to suspect that this long-awaited meeting was not going to be the clarifier of mysteries he had dreamed it would be.

"Ask him about the guar, Lifa. Why didn't it burn my hands like it burns everyone elses'?"

Liphar tried again, his thin mouth set in protest.

Kav Daven's smile widened but he continued to stare blindly ahead, his head marking the unheard music of his silent chant.

"Kav, please . . ." Stavros squeezed his eyes shut anxiously, wondering if the priest was somehow testing him. He gathered his courage and framed the next question himself.

Is there not a way, he asked, to talk to the Goddesses, and if one decided to try to reason with them, how would one go about doing it?

The Kav's answer came in whispered OldWords, sounds like water, and fabric falling in silken folds. Stavros noted that the word "raellil" fell softly among them.

"Lifa?"

Liphar's expression was as cryptic as his Ritual Master's. "This kav say you have this answers."

"What?"

"Yes. But only, Ibi, you not see this yet."

That's for damn sure, thought Stavros, frustrated into irreverence. He sat back on his heels, watching the old man chant and sway.

"What is 'raellil,' Lifa?"

"This is like me, the learning ones, that brings the words around."

"The guild messengers, you mean? The apprentices?"

"Yes. Like me. I am raellil." Liphar tapped his chest, and

then glanced up abruptly, past Stavros, toward the entrance to the hall. Stavros let his head droop, knowing what the young man saw.

"She found us already, did she?"

Liphar nodded.

"Damn, Aguidran trained that girl too well."

He leaned toward Kav Daven, opening his palms in offering though the blind man could not see them. "When I find these answers you say I have, I will ask you, Kav, if I have them truly."

Then, as Edan strode angrily across the hall, he rose regretfully, leaving the old priest to his private litany.

14

The descent across the grassy savannah to Ogo Dul took far longer than Susannah had estimated from atop Imvalla's dizzying precipice. The succession of gently rolling meadows was treeless, though not so arid as the upper plain, despite its sandy salt-rich soil. The grass grew tall and even, like a field of wheat, and stretched before them as featureless in the gray half-light as an ocean before dawn.

The caravan followed the windings of Imvalla's river for two full throws. During meal stops, lanterns glimmered along the line of wagons, like bright beads between the flickering jewels of the cookfires. But while moving, Aguidran's rule was to make eyes to adjust to the lowest level of light. At the end of a throw, Susannah's entire face ached from constant squinting.

With darkfall, the wild creatures grew bolder. The rangers patrolled the train constantly, guiding stragglers closer to their wagons, keeping up the pace. During sleep rounds, though there was never a breath of wind, the grasses rustled mysteriously beyond the light of the lanterns. Once Susannah woke to the cries of a terrified hakra and the pounding of the rangers' feet as they raced past to its rescue. Visiting her brother at dinnertime, Aguidran watched the darkness with narrowed eyes and muttered about the continuing heat.

Ahead of them always was the glow of the Cluster, a cloud-wrapped beacon that inspired their constant wonder. Susannah remarked that it felt like marching fully aware into the maw of a smoking inferno.

"The Celestial Firepit," quipped Megan.

Susannah groaned. "You'd expect to see Valla up there roasting her dinner."

"Poetry was never my long suit."

Susannah drew her long hair back and fought a comb through its mats. She felt sticky and dirty and longed for a bath, but Aguidran would allow no river swimming in the darkness. "We could use a poet on this expedition," she ventured more seriously.

"I know what you're thinking," Megan replied heavily, "but it wouldn't do a bit of good. Beauty is a recidivist sentiment. It wouldn't move the Court an inch without the legal legs to stand on, even if Stav could muster eloquence enough to bring tears to the judges' eyes. I'm resting my hopes on our boy surprising us with all the instincts of a crackerjack lawyer . . ."

"He's got CRI for a research assistant. That should help." Susannah smiled, picturing Stavros as he struggled through the baroque jungles of legal precedent under CRI's machine-patient tutelage. And picturing him, she wanted him with a sudden fierceness that startled her. She had been right, then, not to let herself dwell on him and the risks he had undertaken. At certain times, certain things just did not bear thinking about.

Early in the third throw past Invalla, faint firefly sparkles sprang to life across the savannah in the direction of Ogo Dul. A ragged cheer rose among the wagons. The hjalk pricked up their ears and snuffled.

"The welcome lamps," Ghirra explained. "Our cookfires say we come."

His smile was relieved and he ruffled Dwingen's hair as the boy trudged beside him. The child's thin face was taut from fighting exhaustion and the heat, but he perked up at his guildmaster's touch and walked a little straighter.

Sweating rangers trotted past with orders for running lanterns to be lit. A near impalpable stirring of the heat-laden air brought a scent of salt and the growling sigh of distant surf. The weary guildsmen found the energy to revive their long-discarded discussions of market strategy.

Peering ahead at the meager pinpricks of light, Susannah could discover no other sign of a city. The steep fjords to the north towered darkly visible against a darker sky. The broken sickle shape of the ocean bay tossed back a glimmering reflection of the Cluster.

"How will the people of Ogo Dul feel about offworld visitors, do you think?" she asked Ghirra.

He did not respond immediately. Then he said, "They will think as most here, that your 'other world' means a Cave more far than they have knowing."

"You mean, just another settlement here, but very distant?"

"Yes. They will think this, and none will say them no."

"Stay undercover, he's saying," Megan interposed. She tugged at her Sawlish pants. "Shouldn't be hard, so tanned, and dressed as we are."

"But why?"

"The signs is not so good to bring strangeness here," said Ghirra.

"Ashimmel was ready once before to blame Valla's strength on us," Megan reminded her. "No point taking that chance again with a whole new group."

Ghirra nodded gravely. "I am glad you see this, Meghan."

The lights of Ogo Dul did not seem to grow bigger and brighter as they neared. Susannah still waited to see the gaily lit windows of a bustling town at night. When the running lights of the lead wagons began to thread among those isolated sparkles, she realized that their seeming distance was a deception of the darkness. The sparkles were indeed just lamps, as Ghirra had said, small lanterns suspended on poles stuck into the sandy ground. A few pale streamers rustled at the base of each lamp as the wagons passed by.

The poles were set several hundred paces apart in a broad northward snaking curve. They picked out a road worn through the savannah grass to a base of fine sand that shone white in the starlight. At the end of the curve, free-moving lights bobbed among the larger flames of a double row of stationary torches. Beyond the final pair of torches was velvet darkness.

Susannah watched carefully, forewarned by her experience at the precipice, and sure enough, when the lead wagon reached the last bright torches, its running lights set like tiny moons as it passed over an invisible edge. Chanting and music rose up past the descending wagon. A faint glow from below caught on its torn and mended canopy as it disappeared. As he had at Imvalla, the Master Healer led them both forward to the rim, this time to gaze down on Ogo Dul, his birthplace.

Where the torches ended, the white sand road swerved to drop along the side of a deep ravine. The incline was steep and neatly paved, walled on the dropside by a shoulder-high stone balustrade. The railing was an arm's span wide and carved of thickly veined and polished marble. The balusters were thinner slabs cut in the design of the three interlocking circles.

Susannah leaned across the slick wide marble and saw dark water filling the ravine far below.

A dozen pairs of bridges spanned the seawater canyon, joining five tiers of shops and dwellings hollowed out of the solid rock walls. Each tier was fronted by a lamplit portico of marble columns and arches. The inner walls were pierced by half-moon doorways and round windows glazed with colored glass. The interlocking circle design was repeated in the portico railings and along the low walls of the bridges. The salt smell was sharp, and the wave sigh magnified by the reflecting rock, growling a bass accompaniment to the chatter of the crowds that filled the tiers and flowed across the bridges beneath strings of swaying lanterns.

"This is Trader's Finger," Ghirra announced, then considered his own hand, fingers outstretched. "No. How do you call the finger of a plant?"

"A leaf? A twig?" supplied Megan. "No, a branch."

"A branch. Trader's Branch, it is then." He gestured into the darkness toward the glimmering ocean bay. "Along here, there is many cuts into the cliff. This is each a branch, and the large branch has also small branch. They come by tunnel through the rock, like DulElesi. Or if Valla allow, you travel by chresin."

Ghirra pointed straight down at the black water. Narrow boats with lanterns at stern and bow poled back and forth between rows of floating docks lining the water's edge. He smiled boyishly. "By chresin is more fun."

"You were born here," Susannah recalled.

"It's like Venice was," murmured Megan in an attack of nostalgia.

Ghirra's smile saddened as he pointed into the further darkness. "In Potter's Branch, I was. Very big, with many small branch. When we come back here first time, my sister and me go there to discover which cave was ours, but we cannot. Too many, there are."

"No other family?" asked Megan.

"My three-father is too old to go that time, but he is dead when I come back to Ogo Dul. The other ones, all was dead in the mud, and many other not my family. My sister and I had luck. The mud fell not near us."

He allowed the lantern-jewelled boats on the water far below a long moment of his attention, then shook himself free of his melancholy with a soft self-scolding laugh. "This is old rememberings, not for now. Much here to see that is not sad. I will show you this." He smiled at them to prove the return of a cheerful mood and added, "We will go by chresin."

The travellers descended to the highest tier on the heels of the dawdling dairy herd. The incline was paved with rounded oblongs like cobblestones to assure secure footing, but the young hekkers chose to snort and shy about and give the herdsmen needless anxiety until they were on level ground once more, swinging their heads about in bovine curiosity as they waded through the crowds thronging the noisy columned street.

The portico was several wagons wide, from its pierced marble railing to its smoothly polished inside wall. The columns were as thick as a man's torso and skinned with shallow carvings that told the histories of the Goddesses in spiraling panels.

In the brightly lit shops that honeycombed the inner wall, the guildsmen of Ogo Dul bustled about, chatting a local patron toward a choice, moving goods around and restocking shelves in preparation for the new influx of customers.

The street was hot and stuffy, though open to the air along one side. Susannah stuck close to Ghirra, avoiding the brighter lights, but no one paid two Terran woman in Sawl clothing any particular notice. After two and a half weeks of sunshine, Megan, whose skin was naturally darker than Susannah's, was the close image of a sturdy Sawl matron. Like Ghirra and his sister, the ocean folk of Ogo Dul were generally taller and broader of frame than their cousins from DulElesi. And though Susannah had never seen a Sawl who could be considered anything but thin, the heat and the constant walking had slimmed Megan considerably, and hardened them both.

"We'll fit right in," Megan assured herself. "As long as we don't open our mouths."

"Too bad we haven't got anything to trade," said Susannah wistfully, her eye caught by the colorful clothing hanging in the shop windows.

The columned street twisted right, conforming to the natural shape of the ravine, which soon opened out to admit a narrow side branch. The portico wrapped around into the branch and a wide bridge carried the major traffic across the cut. A muffled racket of snorts and bleats and conversational lowing rose out of the side branch. The herdsmen turned the hekkers aside with loud whistling and mock gruffness. As Ghirra led his companions across the bridge, the rich animal smells from five tiers of stabling joined the pervasive tang of salt air and iodine.

They caught up with the end of the caravan where it was stalled on the far side of the bridge, a jumble of small wagons and two-carts and tired families. The street was wide enough for a wagon to be drawn up against the inner wall and still allow passage along the outside. In place of the shops were many smaller rooms and suites of rooms to serve as temporary dwellings and trade stalls. Susannah poked her head into one where a single lamp burned in a corner niche. The arrangement was familiar from the domestic caverns of DulElesi: a stone sink with ceramic piping, a raised hearth surrounding a sunken firepit, a neatly swept stone floor and no furniture or decoration.

Further down the line, they found the Infirmary wagon, its dented yellow canopy grazing the vaulted ceiling. Xifa explained the delay as a problem with the assignment of quarters, since the population was larger than on past trips. She noted with good-natured disapproval that the crowd was unusually impatient and disagreeable in the heat and congestion, while Susannah pondered questions of population growth and the straining of psychological as well as biological resources.

The FoodGuild began passing out sour beer rations by hand to hand relay, unable to squeeze their little delivery two-carts through the press. Ghirra disappeared into the sweating throng and returned a while later with a tray piled with bread ends and bits of cheese, all that the FoodGuild could manage until their giant wagons could be maneuvered into the larger halls intended for their use.

Megan was uncommonly grateful for stale bread and cheese. "Is it always this bad?"

Ghirra laughed, sipping his beer, and repeated the query to Xifa and Ampiar as if it were a modest sort of joke. Xifa joined his laugh but Ampiar nodded darkly.

"Not so much heat, most time before," Ghirra admitted. "Also, this time we are too many."

Eventually, the crush eased, just when Megan thought that the last molecule of hot salty air had been exhaled as waste. Proper quarters were found, with much doubling up among related families. The carts and wagons were lined up in tight formation against the wall.

The medical staff was assigned two large adjoining rooms on the second tier. The wagon was driven down and unloaded as Ghirra set them immediately to converting the larger one into a mini-infirmary to deal with the sickness and minor injuries already accumulated during the confusion of their arrival.

Hours later the FoodGuild brought them dinner, lukewarm and soggy, and still the parents were turning up at the door with wailing infants and snuffling older siblings. Susannah worked hard to maintain her patience with the endless apparently psychosomatic complaints. The elderly in particular were finding the unrelenting heat a difficulty. She kept at it doggedly until Ghirra took pity. He came over and gently removed the cloth and bowl of herbal disinfectant from her trembling hands, and sent her into the other room to sleep. Megan had long since found her bed.

The smaller room was close and humid. The single window was draped with a torn tunic to muffle the noise from the street. Dwingen and Phea had crowded into the back of the room with the older apprentices. Megan lay crossways at their feet, head to the wall, breathing thickly. Susannah laid out her bedroll next to Megan and collapsed.

She woke later to the soft clink of a lantern being set down nearby. Ghirra rolled out his pad, pulled off his loose shirt and made a pillow of it. He lay down on his back with a tired sigh, giving himself a moment of comtemplative stillness before he doused the lantern.

Susannah feigned sleep, watching him through lidded eyes. She enjoyed watching men when they were unaware of being observed and unwittingly offering clues to their inner selves.

Where does Ghirra go in his head? she wondered.

His face was delicately orchestrated, a harmony of elements tuned like a fine instrument, color and line flowing together without one feature standing out, unless it was his wide gentle mouth, and that only because it so often smiled.

Though not so much of late, she reflected.

Age had hardly lined his brown skin, but for the weary crinkles at the corners of his eyes. She guessed him to be over forty in Earth years. He looked ten years younger.

He turned his head, reaching for the lamp, and found her watching him.

Susannah smiled and raised herself up on one elbow. "You look exhausted. What a night! Did they keep coming in at that rate?"

Ghirra mirrored her pose. "My sister needs my talking with the priests and the Kethed and the Kethed of Ogo Dul."

"What was the matter? Ashimmel up on her high horse again?"

He gave a soft chuckle that turned into a yawn. "Suzhannah, you must talk English at least to me."

"What, a horse? It's like a . . . never mind. What's Ashimmel's problem?"

"The word comes not good from other far settlements. The PriestGuild worry that it is so hot now everywhere. The FoodGuild worry about the plantings. All want to go back very soon."

"Early, you mean? Poor Aguidran, always getting caught in the middle."

Ghirra shook his head. "This time she speaks not for the Kethed. She worries also, talking to her guildsmen from south on DulValla. Everywhere it is not good."

"Aguidran agreeing with the priests? Wow." Susannah was surprised that this small bit of information should have the power to chill her so. She had come to rest total confidence in the Master Ranger's judgment, as did her brother. "We'll go back early then?"

"Yes." He rubbed his eyes and forehead, holding back another yawn. "When the FoodGuild wagons is full for the return, and the broken parts is made again. This is two, three cycles." He focused on her and managed a smile. "This is small time for you here, to see Ogo Dul."

"And you promised me a chresin ride," she teased.

His laugh was a hoarse tired whisper. He leaned to blow out the lamp. "This promise I keep, Suzhannah."

Susannah lay in the stuffy darkness, listening first to his breathing as it evened into sleep, then to the sounds of the alien city, the muted lapping of the sea canals three tiers below, the cries of the boatmen ferrying across the dark water, the steady murmur from the upper tier as the traders got underway a half cycle early to make up for time that would be lost to a premature departure.

She decided that if Aguidran was worried, then so was she, and she fell asleep to dream fitfully of broiling on the slow spit of the planet's unnatural heat..

15

". . . Suit was brought by the heirs of Michael J. Halloran . . ."

Stavros muttered as he wrote but his next glance at the screen stopped him cold. Not only did this case involve CONPLEX, but among the names listed by the complainants in the suit was one Emil Friedrich Clausen.

It was like dropping anchor after a long drift at sea. A chill of remembered humiliation and fear dispelled the dream-like aura of recent cycles. The threat of Clausen and CONPLEX became real again.

He asked CRI for press reports on the Halloran incident. They were scanty, suspiciously inconclusive. Halloran had been the staff anthropologist on a CONPLEX-funded expedition into the Perseus sector. He had advised a hold on mining activities to allow for the exploration and cataloguing of certain extensive ruins on a small world that CONPLEX later developed into a colossal source of titanium. When Halloran died in a landslide on that world, his heirs sued for negligence. The company prospector with the expedition was Emil Clausen.

Stavros felt sure that poor Halloran had been good and dead long before this convenient landslide had occurred.

Noises in the outer hall spooked him. He sprang up, knocking over his bench, and shrank into the darkness at the back of the room.

Liphar pattered around the corner. He halted in dismay at the sight of the deserted console, the toppled bench and the single oil lamp burning low. Feeling foolish, Stavros moved back into the light.

Liphar jumped, clearly on edge himself.

Edan arrived at her more measured pace, appearing silently in the arch behind him. Stavros waited. The pair came empty-handed and brimming with what looked to be bad news.

"Clazzan," Edan hissed.

Stavros was amazed to discover that one's heart really can react with sudden thunder to such announcements. "Here? Now?"

Liphar nodded. "He come now, with Furzon, from the Grigar."

Stavros breathed a little easier. *Not* here *then. Not in the Caves.*

"McPherson," he corrected automatically, thinking that Liphar would never make it as a Scot.

"Yeah," Liphar replied. His best ear was for the colloquial. "Very mad, him."

"I'll bet," said Stavros grimly. "He's down at the Lander? Have they got the Sled?"

"Come soon, they say."

Stavros pressed his eyes shut. A desperate urge to run was expanding like a bubble inside his chest. The cavern was hot and dark and close, too much like a trap. Only the knowledge that it was hotter outside than in sobered him out of this seizure of the old panic.

"Our grace time has ended," he murmured. "Now the battle begins in earnest."

He knew activity would distract him from his creeping sense of helplessness against the corporate juggernaut Clausen represented. Such fears only played into the prospector's hand, and here on Fiix, Clausen was still only one man, however skilled, well-armed and ruthless he might be.

107

Stavros asked Edan to post an all-cycle watch to report on goings-on at the Lander. He described the antenna, emphasizing the need to observe and report all changes in it carefully, so that he could assess the progress being made toward reestablishing contact with CRI. He also asked for a tail on Clausen.

After listening at length, Edan threw him one of her odd looks that mixed a growing deference with her own edgy reminder that he was not after all her real boss, then turned and strode off down the tunnel.

Only after she had left did Stavros begin to pace. Liphar stood watching with solemn concern while the linguist wore out his surprise burst of adrenalin.

"Gotta get the case together now," Stavros said. "Gotta send the damn thing out, fast! You hear that, CRI? Clausen's back from the hills! You know, the man who pays for your juice?"

He felt immediately guilty. CRI had been designed to be all things to all users. It was unfair to accuse her of taking sides.

"Shall I expect to hear from Mr. Clausen shortly, then?" the computer asked neutrally.

"Maybe so," he replied, thinking, *By the Goddesses, I hope not!*

Weng and Danforth were sleeping when Clausen stormed into the Underbelly, dragging an exhausted McPherson in tow. He shoved her in the direction of the Commander's curtained cubicle of crates. Bleary eyed, she stood outside the curtain, knocking on the crates and calling softly, glaring sidelong at Clausen as he shook Danforth roughly until the black man stirred, grumbling, out of deep, sweated sleep.

Weng drew the curtain aside dazedly. "What . . . ah, Lieutenant. You're back." She was wrapped in a wrinkled silk robe. Blinking into the glare of Clausen's searchbeam, she looked pale and unusually disheveled from the heat.

McPherson sagged against the crates. "It's Stavros, Commander . . ."

Weng stiffened. "Hurt?"

McPherson frowned, confused. "No, he's . . ."

"The omni's missing from the Sled," Clausen snapped. He unbuckled his laden pack and stood with it slung across one shoulder, awaiting Weng's response.

"During the storm . . . ?"

"Removed, Weng, as with tools." He advanced on Weng's worktable, swept her precisely ordered papers to the floor with a vehement arm and swung his pack into the middle of the cleared

108

space. "Ibiá's stolen it, as I suspected. McP, bring in that other gear."

He began to unload bits of wiring and circuitry from the pack's side pockets, spreading them out on the table.

McPherson hesitated, looking to Weng for a cue. Weng's delicate chin, lifted at Clausen's destruction of her paperwork, settled stubbornly. But she gave McPherson a stiff nod, and the little pilot retreated into the darkness.

In his bed by the landing strut, Danforth struggled into sitting position. He exchanged a groggily covert glance with Weng over the prospector's back. "What the hell's going on?"

"However, the kid's not as clever as he thinks." From the center of the pack, Clausen lifted a large chunk of electronics. He set it down carefully in front of him and smiled at it as if it were a newly won prize. "Hook this up to the dish and we'll be in business."

Danforth could not restrain his interest. "To replace the receiver?"

"Right. Didn't think of that, did he."

Weng bent to retrieve her papers from the ground. She held them to her chest for a moment, watching Clausen fuss over his trophy. "What makes you so confident of Mr. Ibiá's responsibility in this matter?"

Clausen glanced up with a feral grin. "Experience, Commander. Plus a little gift I have for knowing who's on my ass. You need that in my business."

Weng sucked her cheek and stared back at him silently, tucking a strand of silver hair back into her disordered bun.

"What I can't figure is why, Commander," said McPherson, returning with a second bulging pack.

"Doesn't really matter why, does it, Weng?" Clausen grabbed the pack from McPherson's listless grasp. "We have ourselves a saboteur and the only thing that matters is stopping him."

On a calmer, cooler evening, Clausen's grin might have seemed unnaturally fevered, but Danforth found it frighteningly in tune with the sweltering, suffocating dark.

"Gotta find him first," McPherson remarked, slumping onto a crate.

Weng seemed to discover anew the clutter of papers clasped in her arms. "Go to bed, Lieutenant," she said with pointed kindness.

"No way," countered Clausen. "I need her artful little fingers right here."

"Mr. Clausen, such tired fingers can hardly be artful."

Clausen leaned over his assortment of parts. "We're both

109

tired, Weng. What do you think this is, kindergarten, we should all go take a nap?"

"I think it is an expedition of which I am still in command."

Clausen's eyes flicked up from his work, a reflex checking for the weapon he considered to be the only possible backup for such bravado. He smiled mockingly at Weng's empty hands.

"And I will not allow mistreatment of my crew," she continued icily. "Lieutenant, you have your orders."

"Yessir!" McPherson saluted gratefully and escaped, offering Danforth a wanly affectionate pat of greeting as she slipped by him into a farther corner of the Underbelly.

Weng approached her appropriated work table and began collecting her papers into a single thick sheaf. "Now, Mr. Clausen. If you will grant me the favor of allowing me to get dressed, I myself will assist you with this assembly."

Clausen ended his heavy-lidded stare with an insouciant shrug. "I would welcome your assistance, Commander."

Weng neatened the edges of her stack of papers, gathering it to her like a shield as she retired behind her curtain.

Danforth watched from his bed while Clausen went to work, his stubby fingers probing the central chunk of circuitry with careful confidence.

"Crazy motherfucker," he commented finally. "Probably hasn't a clue what he's getting himself into."

"Taking on CONPLEX is never wise," Clausen agreed.

"Actually, I meant taking you on," Danforth replied casually. "I notice it's never occurred to you that he may be aiming this at me."

Clausen chuckled nastily. "Professional jealousy, I suppose?" He held a small bit of wire and plastic into the beam of his lamp for closer study. "You 'pure' scientist types have such grand ideas about your place in the scheme of things."

"But I have you around to ride herd on my illusions. I'm grateful for that, Emil, I truly am." Danforth kept his tone light, hoping that in the darkness, the prospector would be unable to read the real depths of the ambivalence he felt showing on his face even as he worked to erase it from his voice.

He wanted the comlink restored as desperately as he wanted to stand up and walk again, but his dismay at the disappearance of the omni was tempered with curiosity and a touch of reluctant admiration. He longed to know what was in Ibiá's mind that could drive him into open sabotage. It was too easy to dismiss his actions as merely crazy. Danforth knew there was more to it.

He wondered if Ibiá realized, so fresh from the womb of the university, that this single gesture of defiance had most likely

110

earned him permanent exile. He might find a safe port in the Colonies and work enough to keep himself fed, but Earth belonged to the corporations, and as Clausen had said, crossing them was never wise, or healthy.

But that, Danforth decided, *is Ibiá's problem.*

"Send the drone out as soon as I complete transmission of the text." Stavros yawned convulsively. He wished he had not turned his nose up at the instant coffee when he had raided the ship's stores in preparation for his siege. The equivalent Sawlish brew, even in Liphar's long-simmered version, just did not pack the same caffeine wallop. He shook his head, doglike, blinking at the scribbled and madly annotated mess of notes confronting him and the hopefully more coherent message on the screen.

He had given up trying to perfect the legal case himself when word of Clausen's premature return was brought to him. It seemed to him finally that legal language was beyond even a linguist's interpretation, and he was running out of time rapidly.

In the end, he opted for a straightforward description of Fiix and its inhabitants, including an outline of CONPLEX's intentions as he saw them. He ended the statement with a desperate plea for help. He would have to leave the lawyering to the lawyers, and hope that Megan was justified in her assertion that there was at least one lawyer left with morality enough to react to his report with indignation and outrage, plus a willingness to take on the case. He found it frustrating and anticlimactic to have struggled this far only to be forced to hand over his efforts into some distant stranger's hands. He could not repress a nagging sense of futility.

Too little, too late, too small, too weak . . .

He had to take some more immediate action.

Once again, he let thoughts of murdering Clausen mill about in his brain, wondering how he could even manage it. He had no weapon, and Clausen had already proven himself superior in a hand-to-hand situation.

The next transmission completed, Stavros blanked the screen.

"You are requesting a court injunction against CONPLEX?" The computer sounded incredulous but Stavros put that down to intervening static and ignored it.

"The message is top priority, with the seal to be broken only upon proper voice-print identification of the recipient."

"Authorization?"

Is that real resentment I'm hearing? Stavros felt a lingering guilt that he was forcing CRI to bow to the imperatives of her basic programming. No matter if the computer's ephemeral sentience preferred otherwise, his instructions must be obeyed. "My authorization," he replied dully. "As Communications Officer, I am authorizing the sending of a message drone."

"Without Captain Newman's prior knowledge or approval?"

"Yes, CRI. I *do* have that authority."

"Of course, Mr. Ibiá."

"Signal me when the drone is off."

Stavros laid his head among his scattered papers.

Officer . . . , he mused, yawning.

How far removed by time and distance that responsibility to Earth and her authorities now seemed. How illusory the formal rank had been, always a fiction in his mind till now, when it had become real in a way he could not have predicted, at its most useful when it meant the least to him, a tool against all it stood for.

He argued the case in his mind. Could the lawyer really know, never having set foot on Fiix, never having talked to a Sawl or watched the Sisters battle from the safety of a cave mouth?

In the waking dream of his exhaustion, Valla Ired and Lagri appeared in court as witnesses for the complainants.

Stavros sat up suddenly. "CRI!"

"Mr. Ibiá?"

"There's something else! I want you to run through the re-mote sensing data to see if you pick up any geographical features of interest in either the desert highlands in the southern hemisphere, or the northern ocean."

CRI was silent a moment, as if puzzling over this sudden shift of emphasis. "Could you be more specific, Mr. Ibiá?"

"No." He was reluctant to admit the purpose of his request. "It's a long shot and I don't know exactly what I'm looking for. Anything anomalous, I guess."

"I will see what I can do, Mr. Ibiá, though I might suggest that you consult with Dr. Danforth . . . or is this inquiry also to be entered in a coded file?"

"No, leave it open."

It'll do as a cover, he thought, as his eyes drooped. Besides, Danforth might have something useful to offer.

"I'll wait for your signal."

"Yes, Mr. Ibiá."

The heat made him overpoweringly drowsy. "CRI?"

"Yes?"

"Thanks."

The computer did not reply.

16

Megan slouched in the doorway of the empty infirmary.

"This leaving early is a disaster. All my craft guild contacts are too busy at the market to help me gain access to the local records."

"Too busy to get sick, too . . . a little peace at last!" Susannah transcribed figures from the tiny screen into her notebook and slipped a new blood sample into the analyzer. "What about Tyril?"

Megan grunted. "Problem with her is, she doesn't understand the statistical need for a broadened data base. She claims I won't learn anything here that I can't learn when we get back to DulElesi. History, I said, history! Says she, it's the same where ever you go. Listen to the chants."

"Surely you can make her understand the difference between myth and history."

"Nothing sure about it," Megan replied. "All this doomsday talk going around is no public exercise in metaphor. Here's an interesting point, though—Tyril also claims, as if it were no way unusual, that all the known settlements on Fiix are the same age, which we are, of course, as yet unable to determine."

"All of them?"

"So she says. What brought it up was my remarking on the seeming lack of dialect differences between DulElesi and Ogo Dul. Stav would have a proper theory for this, but normally, geographically isolated settlements develop as distinct linguistic units."

"So they aren't so isolated."

"Or haven't *always* been isolated . . . keeping in mind Weng's theory about a former, more advanced civilization."

Ghirra came yawning from the inner room. He noted with relief the wrinkled but empty field cots, and padded up to look over Susannah's shoulder at the glowing numbers on the analyzer screen.

"Got quiet all of sudden," she reported, smiling up at him. "Xifa said to let you sleep."

"What is this you do now?" he asked.

"Blood and tissue analysis, for my population survey. I asked anyone who came in to be treated if they'd mind a few extra tests. Well, actually, sometimes it was simpler not to ask, just do the tests. Back home, they'd have my license for that.''

"I've been trying to get her to take a tour of the market with me," Megan complained. "All she wants to do is work, work, work."

Susannah laughed. "Not true. Now that Ghirra's up, I declare myself off-duty . . ." She glanced at the Master Healer. "If that's all right?"

"This is my insis-tence, Suzhannah," he replied, his grand tone undercut by a mischievous smile.

Megan unearthed a small camera from her pack to record their explorations. She took her pictures unobtrusively and hid the silver rectangle in the folds of her sash.

"To tell you the truth," she excused as they fought their way through the throng around the Glassblowers' stall, "I don't think the Ogo Dulers would notice it unless we offered it for sale."

The market was in full bloom. In the visitors sector of Traders' Branch, the goods of DulElesi were laid out across four brightly lit tiers: soft rugs and knobby woven wools, dyed leathers and embroidered bolts of linen, delicate eating and sewing implements of bone and wood, polished buttons and flutes, sturdy unbleached papers with lacy edges, inks and hand-colored picture books. Even the Potters had managed, despite the hail damage, to mount an impressive showing of their richly glazed stoneware. The Glassblowers looked on with saddened pride as the remains of their own depleted wares sold like hotcakes.

The congestion along the columned streets thickened to near immovability as the craftsmen of Ogo Dul jammed in to finger and compare, bringing samples from their shops, offering their openings in the intricate game of bargaining. The street lanterns flared above the crowds with a daylight brightness that reinforced the sweated excitement of the market, reducing the dark sky and darker water to zones of forboding mystery.

"The haggling is done in great good humor," Megan observed, "but does the hilarity seem maybe a little desperate to you?" She thought the boisterous joking hid an impatient edge, that the milling sea of heat-damp faces glistened with unnatural emphasis.

"I do notice onlookers laying bets on some of the bigger trades," said Susannah under her breath. "I don't blame them for being edgy, with all this heat and worrying what's going to be left of their fields when they get home."

"Mmm." Megan wished the message drone to Earth could wait

114

for picture evidence of the vitality of Fiixian civilization. "How do you think the Sawls will do in the interstellar market place?"

"I guess that sort of opening up is inevitable, isn't it."

"Eventually, sure—if they don't get their planet taken from them first." She watched the traders' quick hands and sharp eyes. "A little regulated commerce isn't always a bad influence, and I think with the right merchandising guidance, the Sawls'd learn to hold their own in no time, with very little effect on their present way of life, which is already heavily influenced by notions of exchange."

Susannah smiled sideways. "Is that *you* advocating change and progress?"

"At this point," the anthropologist replied grimly, "I'm for anything that might help them to survive."

They crossed a bridge into a sector of local shops. The dark canals were choked with loaded chresin, lanterns bobbing at bow and stern. The smooth marble railing of the bridge was warm to the touch. Shoppers taking a break hung over the balustrade in search of a stray breeze.

Beyond the bridge, the portico was lined with food stalls, stocked with smoked and salted fish, cured seaweeds and other edibles unrecognizable in such wizened form. The DulElesi FoodGuilders crowded around offering baskets of their mountain herbs and dried mushrooms. Beyond the fish market, local curd cheeses were being weighed against the hard cloth-bound wheels of cheese from across the plain, and a lively debate progressed over open sacks of grain and seed and crates of dessicated berries.

"Let's head up top," Susannah urged. She had brought her last unused spiral-bound sketchbook, some soft drawing pencils and a new gum eraser, determined to trade them for some new and exotic bit of apparel.

Megan followed, insisting that she find someone from Dul-Elesi who knew them, to carry out the bartering. Miraculously, they met Tyril in front of a fabric stall on the fourth tier, with her baby asleep in a sling across her back. She was deep in conversation with the proprietor about the finer points of a certain weaving technique, but waved when she saw Megan and put aside her shop talk to join their tour of the market.

And the women went shopping, thought Megan with a private chuckle.

They jostled through the crowd, pointing and admiring. Megan fingered the silky rugs longingly. Her long-ago first paycheck, brought home to a rented room devoid of furniture, had gone as down payment for a fine rug.

The jostling and noise finally woke the baby, who whimpered at finding herself still bathed in heat. The child's only covering was the sling itself, yet her little body was slippery with perspiration. Tyril dried her with her tunic and put her to her breast as they moved on through the crowd.

She readily agreed to act as Susannah's proxy at the clothing stall. She studied the sketchbook and pencils with a trader's assaying eye, and led the way to the shops that displayed ready-made clothing. When she asked what piece of clothing was needed, Susannah had to admit that she did not need anything, except to sooth an irritation with her perfectly serviceable but travel-stained ship's pants and Sawl overblouse.

"Something . . . happier," she shrugged.

The idea of dressing up for festivities struck a truer chord with the weaver than the multiplication of wardrobe for the sheer sake of variety. With the baby still at her breast, she ushered them through the hot bustling shops, advising on the best workmanship and materials.

Megan put away her camera to rely on first-hand observation. She noticed many of the young guildsmen from DulElesi milling about, the first-season journeymen, each with a glazed pot or leather pouch or bolt of bright cloth under one arm, their ration from the work of their guild, theirs to barter for some item of personal desire. They chatted and giggled, fingering the finer embroideries, but more often than not, shrugged wistfully and moved on.

Susannah's fancy fell at last on a long, sleeveless robe exiled to the back of a tiny stall stuffed with drab, more practical overshirts and tunics. The pale yellow fabric draped across her hand like watered silk.

"This one," she said.

Tyril took the sketchbook and pencils and went to work on the thin, sweating woman in charge of the stall. As she bargained, Megan heard a similar negotiation in the next shop rise into unusual acrimony. It ended abruptly when an older Basketmaker threw down the knitted jacket he had been bidding for and stalked out of the stall. The proprietor was left with his jaw sagging open, the multicolored basket that the other had offered dangling loose in his hand.

Onlookers exchanged nervous glances. One of the offender's fellow guildsmen stepped forward with shamed excuses and apologies, and a promise to return the basket to the guild himself. The crowds and the demands of business closed over the incident like the tide, but Megan wondered if she was the only one left pondering the unfortunate coincidence of heat and bad temper.

Meanwhile, Tyril's success had been nearly instantaneous. Though the thin shopkeeper had examined the sketchbook dubiously at first, her enthusiasm had increased geometrically as she smoothed a practiced hand across its snow-white pages, admired its laser-cut edges and marvelled over the springy plastic spiral binding that allowed the leaves to lie so flat when the book was opened. Tyril was clearly disappointed that the bargaining was over before she had a chance to enjoy it. She did not even have to offer the pencils and eraser.

The shopkeeper folded the robe carefully and handed it over with a smile that suggested congratulations to Tyril for having produced so clever a book, while barely concealing worry that the weaver might change her mind and demand more than a simple robe in trade for this paper treasure.

"Actually the papers they make in DulElesi are much more remarkable," said Susannah, clutching her new acquisition to her chest as they rejoined the milling crowd.

"Novelty value," replied Megan, as usual taking the comment more seriously than it was intended. "She'd never seen a binding like that but she recognized the efficiency of its design. They adore efficiency, these Sawls. They see their ideal selves reflected in an efficient instrument. Efficiency is central to their survival."

"Whew! All that from a little sketchbook!"

"Mock, mock," said Megan, trying for a rueful smile. But the display of temper at the neighboring stall still haunted her, dampening her mood as they headed back toward the infirmary.

They found the food wagons along the way nearly deserted, the available fare limited to bread, hard cheese, the ubiquitous kamad root mash and a tepid milk pudding. The FoodGuilders were at market reprovisioning for the return trip, as well as gathering supplies to replenish diminishing food stores at home.

A young apprentice cut them bread and cheese, and nodded in conspiratorial agreement when they turned down the milk pudding.

The infirmary was as they had left it, the lamps turned low, pervaded by a tired silence. Ampiar waited beside a fretful old man, patting his scrawny hand and murmuring soothing nonsense as if to an infant. Xifa lay curled in a corner, asleep where she had sat down for a minute to rest.

Ghirra motioned the women in from the portico and poured water into the stone sink for them.

"I know a place that is not hot," he offered.

"That would be a miracle," said Megan, dousing her face gratefully.

Ghirra smiled. "It is."

He led them to the lowest level, along the waterline, where there were no shops, only the wide columned walkways, open to the water. The narrow snub-nosed chresin bobbed in long rows, moored to blunt marble posts. Oil lamps threw hard light among the shadows of the beamed ceiling. The briny dark water stirred with oily ripples from the rocking of the boats as cargo was loaded in and out.

Ghirra wove familiarly through the noisy dockside maze, between the precarious towers of waiting goods and the anxious boatmen vying for space along the quay. The change in schedule had made them frantic and none were willing to take the time to ferry passengers about on nonessential business.

But near the end of the quay, he found an old man napping in the bow of an empty boat tied stern first to the last mooring. Even in the dim light, Megan could see that the craft was in sore need of a scraping and a new coat of varnish. At least two inches of murky water washed beneath the grating that spanned the curved wooden ribs. But the boatman smiled as he snored, and Ghirra called to him and crouched to rock the boat gently until he woke with a start, blinking.

He grabbed the bow lantern from its post and thrust it forward to squint at the rude folk who had summoned him from sleep. But when he saw Ghirra, he grinned and cackled, then stood up unsteadily and waved the lantern gleefully before he dropped it back on its peg. With spraddle-legged steps, he jerked his way to the stern while the little boat tossed wildly. He grasped Ghirra's hand heartily and scrambled onto the quay with surprising agility, chattering like a gossip, herding the women into the boat without a pause for breath. When all were settled, he cast off and launched himself into the stern seat just as the chresin shot forward into darkness.

Out on the water, the boatman unshipped his long pole. He stood up in the stern, clutching the damp shaft under one arm and gesturing with the other to illustrate his continuing stream of chatter. The waterway was crowded. The dark hulks of loaded boats dwarfed them, passing like sea dragons with hooded lanterns for eyes. The old boatman hardly seemed to notice, consistently waiting until the last possible moment to avoid impact.

The lighted tiers rising sheer to either side reminded Megan of the decks of a glittering cruise vessel. Caught in a romantic reverie of lamp-lit water and the echoes under bridges, memories of another canal city, she was about to trail her hand in the black water when Ghirra stopped her.

"This is not safe," he advised.

"Ah." Megan was obscurely disappointed, but Susannah leaned over eagerly to peer down at the schools of phosphorescence sliding through the depths.

"I wondered why I'd seen nobody swimming. These are not the domestic fish, then? These are poisonous?"

Ghirra nodded. "The eating fish is growed in the branch where the wild fish cannot go."

Megan hunched in the bow as an overladen chresin bore down on them from the darkness dead ahead.

"There is also things with hard skin that live in mud," Ghirra continued calmly. "Also the water plants."

"Ah . . . ?" Megan clutched the gunwales, white-knuckled.

"This is very healthy," said Ghirra. "The FoodGuild brings to home most that they can trade for."

Just as Megan was considering prayer, the old boatman deftly swerved away from their collision course. He exchanged greetings of maniacal cheer with the poleman in the other boat as it skimmed past with mere inches to spare, its lanterns and towering cargo swaying like drunken companions.

The little craft gained the first intersection without being rammed, and slowed in the crossroads traffic. The old man snaked through the congestion into a wider darker canyon. A steady stream of loaded boats poled up from the open bay, moving slowly against the tide with sails furled around cross-rigged masts.

The boatman let the chresin drift, carried seaward with the current, then a moment later, dug his pole into the invisible bottom and swerved the boat about with a grunting shove to send it gliding up another steeply narrow waterway.

The raucous market noises gave way to scattered domestic sounds softened by distance, a child's laugh or wail, a woman calling to a neighbor. Ghirra studied each glowing window and doorway with a sober questing eye until Susannah was moved to inquire gently, "Where are we now?"

He drew himself away from his private study and smiled, and Susannah understood finally that this easy smile, his accepted public manner, was a conscious camouflage. He could not be said to be moody; he did not let his disquiet come and go, but kept it always with him, beneath his smiling surface, visible only when he let the mask slip.

She thought he was letting it slip more often lately.

But now he brought out the smile and slid into the role of tour guide, pointing out the finely wrought balustrades lining the tiers, the intricate column capitals and the tales of the Goddesses wrapping the sturdy shafts.

The steep canyon narrowed further. The chresin slipped past a final street lamp, past the last window glowing amber and lavender through tiny round panes. Beyond the bow lantern, the darkness was impenetrable. No one spoke. The boatman steered with nonchalant confidence into the void. He began a little singsong count, swaying the craft to his rhythm. He built to a murmured crescendo and plunged his pole into the water on the final note. Ghirra laughed gladly as the boat skewed into a breathtaking right angle turn. The old man let it glide a while in darkness, then dug into the bottom with renewed vigor to swerve the boat again, returning to its former course. The void parted in front of them like a velvet curtain, sweeping aside to reveal a broad rock-walled arena.

The water canyon dead-ended ahead. A giant, glowing cave mouth perched like a rising moon at the top of a wide lamp-lit flight of stairs. Sheer walls towered all around, covered with intricate carvings. Layers of incised geometric designs alternated with shallow friezework where the vengeful figures of the Sisters faced each other repeatedly over the heads of the suffering multitude.

On either side of the cave mouth, a long path twisted down among the friezes from the high rim of the canyon to the paved stone quay at the bottom. The stair to the cave ascended in waves of curved steps, flanked by graceful railings and matched pairs of carved stone lanterns.

The chresin's bow nudged the worn edge of the quay. Megan grabbed for a mooring post. The boatman swung the stern around and Ghirra leaped out to tie the bow. Other boats rocked gently against their moorings. A young couple sat in a pool of lamplight midway up the stair, talking in quiet, worried tones while their baby slept in the father's lap. Ghirra handed the two women out of the boat and led the way up the steps. The old boatman resettled himself in the stern and closed his eyes.

At the top, the monumental curl of the entry opened into a shining square corridor that burrowed straight and tall into the rock. White marble as smooth as new ice sheathed its sides, broken only by glittering wall sconces of porcelain and blown glass. The end of the corridor dissolved into a golden infinity. While Susannah floated along like a pilgrim in a foreign cathedral, Megan felt for the camera still stashed in her waistband.

They walked in silence for several minutes before the seamless white was broken by intersecting corridors, all cloaked in the

120

same shining stone, bejeweled with glass and lamplight, but otherwise unadorned. The largest exuded odors of steam and dampness, and Megan heard the faint drip and trickle of running water mingling with a chanting voice or two.

The narrower corridors were lit only by slim blue flames burning in shallow wall niches. Here and there, Sawls sat opposite the flames on low benches set against the wall. Megan noted familiar faces from the Priestguild, Kav Ashimmel among others, deep in solemn contemplation.

The golden infinity ahead grew a dark spot at its center. As they neared, it swelled into a shadowed archway. The arch was a simple half-moon shape cut into the glistening white marble. The smoothness and plainness and whiteness of the walls rendered them insubstantial, as if walls of pure light gathered around a darkness that drew all things inward toward its center. A profound silence emanated from that darkness, together with a hint of blessed coolness. Ghirra's pace quickened.

They entered a vast dome of rock.

The center was unlit, a pocket of deep night. The curving sides were defined by successive circles of light from tall free-standing stone lanterns spaced around the perimeter. The familiar pattern of interlocking circles traced giant salmon-colored loops across dark green marble paving. The lamplight faded with distance as if the central darkness were physical, like a mist or a thin black drape.

Megan's impression was of infinite space. The air was in motion. A cool upward spiral brought damp relief from the outer heat. Ghirra pointed straight up. An impossible distance above, the dome opened a small circle to the sky. Stars sparkled against a velvet background of night, less dark than the enclosed void beneath them.

Ghirra offered another of his carefully considered translations. "Your words name this cave SkyHall." He crouched and pressed his palm to the floor, smiling and beckoning.

The stone tile was chill and beaded with a thin film of moisture that reformed the instant it was wiped away. Megan would have been content to flatten herself face-down on the cold stone, but the dignity of the place, as well as her own, restrained her.

"There is water under," Ghirra explained. "From the rock. Here it is never hot."

Megan laid her chilled palms against her cheeks. "I'd live down here if I were them."

"It's not always this hot," Susannah reminded her, slipping off her sandals to soak up the coolness through her feet.

They moved through the darkness into the light of the first lantern. It stood in splendid isolation, like a giant chesspiece, as tall as they and carved of rozy quartz, in the shape of a slim woman hugging a hekker calf between arm and hip and balancing a loaded food basket on the opposite shoulder.

The lamp flame burned within the lattice of the basket, the translucent smoke of the quartz diffusing the light so that the lithe figure glowed from within. The carving was startlingly lifelike, unlike the sad grotesques of the friezes or the stylized likenesses of the Goddesses.

Megan traced the graceful line of the back tentatively, as if she expected the statue to move beneath her hand. "A Sawlian Ceres. Isn't she lovely!"

The second lantern was a seated male figure whose muscular knees embraced a crystalline potter's wheel. The pot he was turning formed the lamp, shaped by complex curves and mysterious inner spaces. The stone of his body was opaque, so that his intent face was lit from without, by the light of the work beneath his large, capable hands.

The third was an old woman, spinning finely wrought handfuls of quartzite wool into a glowing skein that imprisoned a small bright flame. The next was a young man tanning translucent leather, the next a weaver, then a joiner, then a stonecarver who chiseled away at a glimmering lantern that was a miniature of himself.

"Are all the guilds represented?" Susannah guessed.

Ghirra nodded, looking proud and satisfied.

Megan lagged behind, caught by odd markings on the perimeter wall. She moved closer to touch the dark rock. An incised pattern of lines and circles textured the surface, smoothed to near-invisibility by age and the wear of hands tracking their shape just as she was doing. Above her reach, the lines were sharper, but it was only the sharp, shadowing angle of the lantern light that had caused her to notice them. She stood back to take in the pattern as a whole.

"Klee," suggested Susannah at her shoulder.

"Or more recently, Michaelmas, but even more abstract . . . This is very interesting," she added to Ghirra as he joined them.

"Yes," he noted pleasantly. "Old drawing."

"What does it mean?"

He spread his palms. "This is nothing, I think. Old drawing," he repeated, but less securely.

"Just decoration?" Megan was unconvinced.

"Why not?" Susannah asked.

It was Megan's turn to shrug. "Instinct, I guess."

Ghirra stepped closer to frown up at the wall as if he had never seen it before. "You say this drawing has meanings?"

He drew them along the curve, in and out of darkness, to the next pool of light. Again, faint lines and circles enlivened the wall, these slightly less worn, some intersecting, curling about one another.

Susannah backed away to stand beside the lantern. "You can see it best from here, actually. This pattern's pretty much the same as the other?"

Ghirra dogged Megan's shoulder. "Why do you say this has meanings?"

"Wait," said Susannah, moving to the next pattern. "It's not the same. It's changing, very slowly." She hurried on to the next, her bare feet slapping eagerly against the damp floor. "Some parts of it are coming together, others drifting apart. See that section of dense markings? See how it moves downward and to the right?" Her pace increased with her curiosity. "It intersects with that strong right-left diagonal by this panel here. And then . .. damn! Stavros should see this!"

"But this is not language," Ghirra objected, following hastily.

"Art is always language," said Megan. "These could be like pictographs, for instance. Symbols that do not represent words but ideas and emotions."

By the fifteenth panel, the lines were strong and deep, the pattern clear even without benefit of shadow.

Susannah waved her empty hands in frustration. "I should know better than to go anywhere without my sketchbook! Ghirra, will we have time to come back here?"

His shoulders hunched uneasily. He was clearly caught between not wanting to deny her and thinking her interest a waste of time.

Megan offered a cheesy grin and pulled the tiny camera from her belt.

"Technology to the rescue."

Ghirra handled the silvery little box with reverent care, twisting it repeatedly in his hands. He set it to his eye as he had seen Megan do.

"This will give a picture out of the air?"

"Out of the light," corrected Susannah. She hitched the oil lamp closer to the sketchbook, blotting at her sweat as it dampened the page. The Infirmary wagon's tail gate was too low for a proper drawing table. Her back ached and she longed for the miraculous coolness of the SkyHall.

Ghirra lowered the camera to stare soberly into the lens.

"It doesn't give an image right away," Susannah continued. "Meg's old-fashioned that way. Has to be computer processed, so we won't know what we have till we get back to DulElesi, and that's only if CRI's back on line. Meanwhile . . ." She erased energetically, redrew a line or two, then straightened, stretching the cramp out of her spine. "Does this look accurate to you?"

Ghirra watched two boatloads of priests pole by on the water below, then slouched away from the balustrade, the camera cradled in both hands. He set it down on the tailgate with infinite care.

"You draw this well, Suzannah." He tapped the pencilled lines and circles with an emphatic finger. "But this is not language."

His stubborn mood matched her own. "Why are you so sure?"

"Old drawing," he said again. "Priests' drawing. This is nothing."

"Ghirra, the pattern shows a consistent change from beginning to end. That can't be accidental!"

He twisted away gracelessly, heading for the infirmary door. "This is nothing, Suzhannah."

"The artist had *something* in mind!" she called after him, but he tossed back a gesture of dismissal and ducked into the entry.

"I suppose there is such a thing as *l'art pour l'art*," Megan commented, plunking a loaded dinner tray down on the tail gate.

"Here?" replied Susannah rudely.

"Well, probably not. The Sawls are neither primitive nor sophisticated enough for that sort of decoration, but maybe in the past . . ."

"Why is he being so obstinate about it?" Susannah fussed. "It's like he doesn't *want* it to mean anything!"

"Why are *you* pushing him so hard about it? Maybe the idea is new to him. Maybe he'd have preferred to have thought of it himself." Megan handed her a warm ball wrapped in russet leaves. "Here, eat this. It's like cooked sushi."

Susannah closed her sketchbook and shoved it aside.

"Or maybe," Megan offered, chewing placidly, "he doesn't like us constantly telling him what goes on in his own turf. He's touchy enough as it is about the PriestGuild having any claim to the truth. Wasn't it you who once admitted that doctors get so into their power over life and death that they end up sure they know it all?"

"Yeah, but Ghirra . . ."

"What, but Ghirra? Because he's bright and gentle and dedicated, and an alien, he shouldn't have an ego? Those are the guys that usually have the biggest, because they're smart enough to *know* they're better than most."

"But he's been so openly curious all along."

"Sure. He has a good scientist's instincts. But Ghirra's a pretty big fish in this particular pond. Hard to have a bunch of strangers show up to tell him all he knows is still not nearly enough."

"I've never said . . ."

"Of course not. But you have all this equipment and methods and ideas . . ." Megan hoisted the little camera guiltily and stowed it back in her sash. "We're talking self-image here, not racial—the way Ghirra pictures himself in relation to his own world. That has to have changed radically since our arrival. No matter how eager he is to learn and share knowledge, all this has probably left him a little sensitive to challenge."

"Challenge? I didn't . . ." Susannah's denial faltered. She turned away to lean over the outer railing and stare down at the boatmen still hard at work on the water. "Ah, hell. I guess I haven't been the most tactful about this. I keep forgetting he's . . ."

"I know." Megan spoke in italics. *"Not one of us."*

"Yeah."

"You'd do him more honor," she finished slowly, "if you remembered."

Susannah retired to a dark corner of the inner room to try on her new robe. The apprentices came in to hang up their smocks while she was stripped to the waist, washing.

Privacy, she reflected, *is of little value in this society.*

Xifa joined her at the sink with a weary smile and the information that a special invocation to Valla Ired was to be performed after the dinner meal by Ogo Dul's PriestGuild, led by their young Ritual Master, who had only recently inherited her post. Susannah promised to attend.

When she was alone again, she undressed fully and slipped the robe over her head. It was not too small, as she had feared, but draped gracefully along her body. Even in the stifling heat, the silken fabric felt cool to the touch. The pale yellow was luminous against her tanned skin.

Susannah felt beautiful, but could not be sure. For the first time she wished the Sawls used mirrors.

She turned to find Ghirra in the doorway.

"You will come to see Kav Larma dance?" he inquired formally.

"Of course." She felt intruded upon, but ashamed of the

125

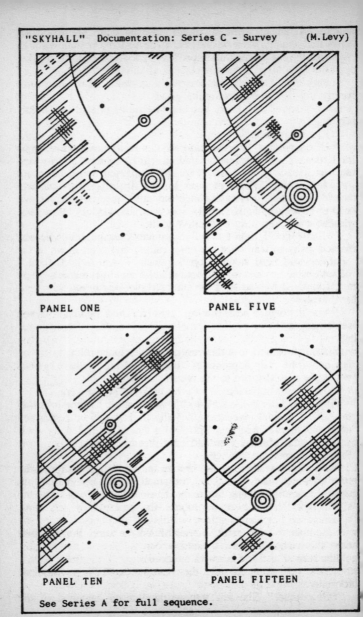

PANEL ONE

PANEL FIVE

PANEL TEN

PANEL FIFTEEN

See Series A for full sequence.

moment of temper that had passed between them. She made an awkward, apologetic pirouette. "Do you like my new gown?"

"This is very beautiful," he acknowledged. "Ibi will like seeing you in this."

Some demon of heat and exhaustion made her press him further. "Do you like seeing me in it?"

His head tilted, as if he was not sure he had heard her right, and his surprise made Susannah laugh.

"Of course, it never even occurred to you, did it," she said, rueful with relief. She went to him abjectly and leaned her forehead against his shoulder like a friendly animal. "Forgive me. Do you understand any of this?"

"I think, yes." He slid a paternal arm across her back, taking instinctive charge and reminding her that his own practice of healing extended to the mind as well as the body. "You feel without him."

"And the heat," she murmured, already comforted. "Making me a little crazy."

"This is its other danger," he agreed.

"Ghirra, I hope you do know how much I respect your methods, that I've learned as much from you as you say you have from me."

He let his arm drape over her shoulder in a companionable fashion, a smile curving the corners of his mouth. "This is good hearing, Suzhannah," he replied with gentle irony. "Maybe with this, we will find some true knowing together."

17

Clausen straightened from his crouch and slid the cooling laser gun into the holster on his belt. He wiped sweating palms on his thighs, frowning irritably at the damage done to his trousers.

"All right, that should do it. Let's run the cable."

"Done that, while you were welding." McPherson gestured with the battery lamp and the beam sliced randomly through the heated darkness. Clausen's shadow lunged across the fragile golden span of the dish antenna suspended in its slanting ring of stones. "With the extra from the Sled, it'll reach just inside, a little past the first landing strut. Least we'll be undercover."

"From what?" Clausen fastened the flap on his holster and

kicked at the ground with a booted toe. Dust rose up like smoke in the lamp beam. "Not even a goddamn dew fall here to worry about."

"The sun," she replied earnestly. "When it comes back."

He shook his head. "McP, you're losing your ear for irony . . . if in fact you ever had one."

He grabbed the lamp and strode across the dark clearing to the Lander, elbowing past Weng who watched from beside the landing strut, fanning herself with a plastic container lid. McPherson followed reluctantly, with a glance into the rustling blackness of the encircling fields, where the Sawls were hard at work on some project of their own.

Clausen moved in on Danforth's bedside work station without ceremony. The planetologist howled as his keypad went dead beneath his fingers. He returned McPherson's weary look of apology with a glare as she unplugged his monitor.

"Get your own equipment down from the Caves, for Christ's sake!"

The pilot shook her head. "Gone. Like the cable."

"All of it? Jeez, the kid's serious."

"No shit."

The monitor was not heavy, but McPherson sagged under it as if it weighed a ton. She looked pale and heat-worn in the glare of the emergency lamp that served as Danforth's work light.

"Pushing you hard, isn't he, babe?" he muttered with a sidelong glower as Clausen carried off his terminal and keypad. Clausen was now flaunting his armaments by wearing the laser openly, and Danforth considered this a challenge and an insult to them all, especially to Weng. Still, beneath his resentment, he allowed a flicker of gratitude that *someone* was seeing to the repair of the comlink.

McPherson nodded, brightening a little to his show of concern. "Listen, don't worry about this, huh? I got an idea for a kind of chair we can rig up, let you move around a little so's you can use the stuff too."

"I need that box *today*, McP," Clausen barked from the far side of the Underbelly.

"Yessir, right away, sir!" She mugged a giant tiger snarl at Danforth and went off lugging the monitor so that it bounced against her hip with every step.

Danforth switched off his lamp and sat in darkness, pretending it was cooler that way, laying out his own sequence of priorities for the reestablished link. He had developed theory and planning into a sublime art to pass the time, but cherished the hope that real answers would now be forthcoming, with CRI back on line.

New data were his primary concern. He needed new data badly, global data for the freak monsoon that had wrecked his Sled, and then for the recent lack of rainfall as well. He needed to know where they had come from, and if those activities were restricted to the same narrow band as the snowstorm seemed to have been.

Then some proper *modeling to get a lock on my X-factor.*

He was distracted by the mysterious clinkings and soft chatter from the Sawls working in the dark fields. He could see by faint Cluster light that the broad leaves hung limp with thirst and heat fatigue.

And we're no different, he mused. He couldn't recall what had caused him to start hoarding water. Even before Weng had declared the practice official in the Underbelly, each had been doing it privately. He wondered when they might be forced to begin rationing as well.

And he worried that the prolonged darkness and unrelenting heat might at last be nibbling at the fringes of his reason, just as the tides work patiently to erode even the rockiest shore.

Nothing so extreme as panic or madness, Danforth consoled himself. *We'll leave all the melodrama to young Ibiá, who has obviously gone over that edge he's been teetering on for so long.*

But Danforth had caught himself of late replaying the strange weather events at the time of the Leave-taking, events he preferred to forget as he stared up at the panoply of burning stars, listening hard into the night silences as if there were something out there in the dark that might offer a more satisfactory answer to his questions than the data chattering across his computer screen. He mentioned these lapses to no one. Clausen, he suspected, would mockingly blame some animistic African gene for his recent tendency to ascribe intent to the windless suffocating heat. McPherson would look at him with incomprehension, maybe even pity. And he himself felt that anthropomorphizing was a sign of desperation, of grasping for the easy, sloppy answer.

So he fought off his seizures of what he lightly diagnosed as intellectual dehydration, and renewed his commitment to the search for Factor X, determined to make measurable sense out of weather that was thus far as adequately explained the way the Sawls explained it as by any other more rational and "scientific" means.

"Need another foot or so!" Clausen called out from the newly arranged console. "Grab that other end!"

Danforth twisted his disabled body sideways on the bed and eased over the edge the leg that was cast-bound only below the knee. The weight of the cast pulled at his unused muscles. The healing gash in his chest was no longer so painful, but sitting upright unsupported in the heat made him reel with weakness.

"Damn!" he rasped, craning his neck to watch as Clausen bent to plug the cable run from the antenna. McPherson hovered and Weng stood back, still fanning herself with the slow, detached dignity of a fairy tale empress. "Damn, I'm tired of these legs!"

The console looked like it was a million miles away.

Damn you, Clausen! he raged more silently, while part of him noted with interest that it was not Ibiá the saboteur who was the focus of his impotent wrath. Still another part wondered how his colleagues would react if he broke down and wept out of sheer frustration.

"I have completed that data search you requested, Mr. Ibiá."

Stavros shuddered awake from dreams of talking to a towering pillar of fire. CRI's tinny summons reverberated in the darkened cavern. He felt for his oil lamp and shook it gently.

Empty. Must have fallen asleep and left it burning.

He let his head sag back to the table.

"Mr. Ibiá?"

"Just a moment, CRI." His voice creaked. Fumbling, he located his little battery lamp and switched it on, then gazed about, groggy and stiff from his long, exhausted collapse at the makeshift console. Liphar lay naked on his pad against the wall, frowning through his sleep. Discarded clothing lurked in the corners like corpses. There was no sign of Edan.

"What day is it?"

"L plus 84," responded CRI briskly.

Stavros pinpointed the urgency nagging at him the most, beside the desperate need to relieve himself. "Did the drone get off?"

"Exactly according to your orders, Mr. Ibiá." The computer managed to sound insulted by his worried tone.

Stavros closed his eyes, then roused himself with effort and shuffled to the sink. The water was no longer merely tepid, it was warm, and flowed slowly from the tap. He regarded the thinning trickle with foreboding and shut the tap down tightly as soon as he had splashed his face and chest and drunk his fill. He nosed around among his supplies and dug out a packet of freeze-dried apricots to dull an unreasoning hunger, then slouched past the console, dripping from face and hands, heading for the lavatory at the far end of the outer hall.

Back in the cavern, he stripped off his loose linen pants, offended by their griminess and by the pungence of his own unwashed smell. He sat down at the console, feeling oddly vulnerable as he faced the sophisticated machinery in his sweating nakedness.

"Okay, CRI, I'm in one piece now. What did you find?"

"A preliminary scan of the remote sensing data, together with the hemispheric photos from the polar orbiters, has turned up a few items that might be of interest to you. First, in the northern hemisphere, Mr. Clausen's deep sensors indicate a sizable gravitational anomaly near the center of the great ocean, suggesting the presence of a buried mass."

"A mass of what?"

CRI hesitated, as if recalling that it was not Danforth she was reporting to. "A solid body, Mr. Ibiá. Its composition is impossible to determine at the moment, but the ocean is roughly circular and could be interpreted as a water-filled impact basin."

"Oh. One hell of a crater."

"Is this the sort of anomaly you were hoping to discover?"

Stavros rubbed his eyes. "Not precisely, but it's interesting. Go on."

"It is particularly interesting in light of the specifics of your request," CRI encouraged. "In the southern hemisphere, at a point exactly opposite to this gravitational blip, is a large but clearly defined area of severe upthrust. Very broken terrain. This would also be expected in the case of a major impact. It is the only feature in the southern desert highlands that could be considered anomalous."

"Hmm." Stavros ran through the words of the tale-chant describing the creation of Lagri's mountain fortress. It did not seem impossible that the "bolt of the creator's might" could have been inspired by some race memory of an ancient meteor strike.

"Can you get me a picture of that area, CRI? Some kind of close-up?"

"The polar orbiters are equipped for hemispheric resolution only, Mr. Ibiá. As for the radar imaging . . ."

"Come on, Clausen must be flying something that'll produce high-resolution pictures?"

"I am not at liberty to divulge . . ."

"Okay, okay. Tit for tat. How about this: don't tell me anything 'sensitive', just get me the photo. Can you do that?"

"At the present low-transmission rate, it will take some time, even supposing I can locate such data."

"Sounds like I damn well gotta go there myself!"

Stavros fumed. Were he dealing with a human, this kind of foot-dragging would be preparatory to the suggestion that a

131

certain sum might unlock sticky doors. However, he had not yet heard of anyone successfully bribing a computer.

Go there myself, he thought ironically. *If I only had wings.*

But the notion had its attractions, despite its current impossibility. It was so obvious and simple that he could not understand why he hadn't thought of it before. He shoved his stool away from the console and, despite the heat, began to pace excitedly.

What better way to prove the Goddesses exist than to go find one?

He wondered how Kav Daven would look on such an idea.

"May I ask a question?" ventured CRI after a few moments. "What?"

"If you were not looking for evidence of an impact, what led you to request information about an anomaly precisely where one seems to be?"

Stavros remembered his hunger and ripped at the packet of apricots. "You really want to know?"

"I am not programmed to make insincere requests, Mr. Ibiá."

"Well, your input might be useful, so I'll play you a tape." He heard Edan's quiet trot speeding along the outer corridor and decided not to care that he had discarded all his clothing. A Sawl wouldn't give it a moment's thought. "Run the tape through my translator program, store it and tell me what you think."

He took the battery lamp to the rear of the cavern and unearthed a metal box from beneath a pile of silverfilm blankets, his cache of precious hours of singing and chanting and story telling.

"In fact," he called back to the console, "I really should upload *all* my tapes, before the heat gets to them, or . . ."

Or something gets to me. Something like a convenient landslide.

He located the cartridge he wanted, Liphar's throaty rendition of the Fortress of Lagri tale-chant. He brought it back to the console and fed it into the slot. "Chew on that for a while."

Edan materialized at the entrance, sweat-drenched and eager. As he'd predicted, she paid his nakedness no heed but announced breathlessly that the ranger salvage party was on its way in with the wrecked Sled. Liphar stirred on his bedroll and sat up groggily. Edan delivered her second piece of news to him. A ceremony was planned, an attempt to sing strength to Valla so that the crops might have a little rain.

Stavros's attention caught on the Sled. He thought it remarkable that the vehicle should reappear coincident with his notion of going in search of a physical Goddess.

"Mr. Ibiá, I seem to be receiving . . ."

"Just a minute, CRI." He pressed Edan for a report on the apparent condition of the Sled and the progress of the antenna repairs. Liphar woke up enough to clamor for further information about the ceremony.

"Mr. Ibiá, there is a signal . . ."

"CRI, Lifa, please!" Stavros pumped the younger ranger patiently, for she was having understandable difficulty describing objects for which she lacked the appropriate vocabulary.

"I am patching it in now," CRI continued, oblivious.

The speaker snapped and hissed warningly. Stavros whirled in horror as Clausen's voice invaded the room, transmitting his call code from the Lander. Liphar scrambled up in confusion. Edan flinched into a fighting posture and scanned the darkened corners for the man she knew the voice belonged to.

Forcing himself to exhale, Stavros lunged at the console and shut down all but the listening mode.

"The Orbiter is receiving you, Mr. Clausen," came CRI's welcoming reply. "Captain Newman will be relieved to have you back in contact. You have had a successful trip, I hope?"

"Trip?" Clausen's voice was as clear as if it came from the next room.

"Across the plain, with the traders? Mr. Ibiá has kept us well informed of . . ."

"IBIÁ? WHERE IS HE?"

"Oh, Christ, he's fixed the link." Stavros slapped off the audio and sat in numbed silence for the approximately thirty seconds required for him to realize that CRI would be able to supply the prospector with an exact fix on the location of his hiding place.

Suddenly the air in the cavern was too hot to breathe.

"We've got to get out of here, we're sitting ducks." He whispered when what he really wanted to do was shout and run. Instead, he grabbed his pants for some small sense of security, then began to explain to his shaken companions the new depths of their predicament.

Clausen summoned a deadly calm in place of his first explosive rage.

"Where is he, CRI?"

"I was unaware that you were ignorant of Mr. Ibiá's whereabouts," the computer replied peevishly. "I will supply those coordinates."

"I'd appreciate that, CRI." Clausen curled into a predatory slouch. He watched hawklike as the figures appeared, pointedly placed dead center in the screen. His eyes slitted. "That little shit! He's right on top of us!"

Weng stood blocking him by the time he came erect.

"Out of my way, Commander."

Weng's hand shot out and unsnapped the flap on Clausen's hip holster. "Perhaps you would rather leave your . . . tools here, Mr. Clausen?"

Clausen knocked her hand away, with more force than was necessary. Behind him, McPherson tensed but remained immobile with indecision. He glanced at her, then chuckled and drew the little pistol.

"How right you are, Commander. I won't be needing this, will I?"

He handed the laser to Weng butt-first and snatched up his searchbeam instead.

Weng stared after him stonily as he loped up the dark path toward the Caves. Then, impulsively, she stooped to the console.

"CRI, kindly inform Mr. Ibiá that Mr. Clausen is on his way."

McPherson stared. "Commander, why did you do that?"

Weng backed slowly away from the console as if it had made an indecent proposal. Her powder-soft brow creased with unease. "I don't precisely know, Lieutenant. To save Mr. Ibiá's life, I suppose."

Later, as they nervously awaited Clausen's return, Weng filed a month's worth of status reports with her superiors in the Orbiter and began the downloading of recent instrument data for Danforth.

McPherson trudged up to the small work encampment at the foot of the cliffs to borrow an idled water wagon. She met one of the returned rangers trotting down the path, on his way to announce the arrival of the salvaged Sled. She greeted him gladly in her fledgling Sawlish and paced after him to the encampment, where the battered vehicle lay just outside the circle of firelight on its hastily assembled sledge.

She walked around the winged hulk. The nose and tail hung precipitously off either end of the sledge. A thick coating of dust turned the smooth white plastic to ochre. The hjalk team that had hauled it blew heavily into their water buckets, their lathered ribs heaving. McPherson guessed that the lashed and pegged wooden sledge itself weighed more than the Sled, and pitied the Sawls for their lack of lightweight construction materials.

The salvage party had collapsed in scattered twos and threes out of range of the fire's heat. As McPherson approached, they glared dully as if daring her to demand the Sled's immediate delivery to the Lander clearing.

Instead, she thanked them and made arrangements with the

party leader to haul it down at the start of the next work cycle. The tired Sawls were relieved enough to assent immediately to the loan of an empty two-cart. McPherson placed herself between the shafts and trundled off to the Lander to make a movable bed-chair for Danforth.

She took advantage of Clausen's absence to raise the new computer desk so that her invention could slide underneath and Danforth could face the terminal as if seated at a standard console. Weng agreed to use it standing up. When he had been painfully levered into the adapted cart, Danforth greeted CRI like a long-lost lover, and was beyond reach for the better part of an hour. Eventually, he sat back from the console with a frown.

"That's odd." He turned to Weng and McPherson, the first sign that he was aware of their constant presence at his shoulder. "Want to know what Ibiá's been up to all this time?"

Weng leaned into the screen. "I see."

"That's weird, all right," McPherson remarked.

"What possible interest could a linguist have in the sensing data?"

Weng pointed a slim, dry finger. "Just with reference to those two areas, it would seem."

"If I may, Commander," offered the computer. "I believe Mr. Ibiá was attempting to draw some connection between locations figuring prominently in the Sawlish mythos and actual geographical features of the planet."

"What locations?"

"The homes of the Goddesses, Commander."

This silenced them a moment. Then Danforth noticed the angle that would result if a line were drawn between the two points of Stavros' interest: the now familiar northeast-southwest diagonal slash across the face of the planet.

Coincidence? he wondered. *Or the beginning of a pattern?*

He soothed his chill with the reminder that mythological locations were often inspired by some extraordinary feature of local geography.

Still . . .

"Weng, how good is your Sawlish?"

"Nearly nonexistent, I fear."

"Yeah. Me too. How about you, Ron?"

McPherson shrugged. "I get along."

"Mr. Clausen has been giving it some attention of late," said Weng.

Danforth bared his teeth, then sighed. "Think he's good enough to get a Sawl talking about the weather?"

"I wouldn't know, Dr. Danforth." Weng permitted herself the ghost of an ironic smile. "If he could, *would* he?"

Danforth cursed softly. "I've been a damned fool, passing up data that's been right under my nose!" He shifted awkwardly in the wheeled chair. "Listen, Weng, we've got to get Ibiá down here. Can we offer him amnesty or something? I really need him here to translate."

"Mr. Clausen may be doing us that favor as we speak," Weng reminded him. "CRI says she was unable to contact Mr. Ibiá again to warn him."

Danforth's eyes flicked over the dark fields, toward the towering bulk of the cliff kissed by pale Cluster light. "Damn! I sure hope the kid's in one piece when he gets here."

BOOK TWO

"Look, here comes a walking fire."
KING LEAR
Act III, sc. iv

18

Once again the wagons were being loaded, but this time the waiting stacks of goods bore the guild stamps of Ogo Dul. A more solemn frenzy prevailed along the columned streets of Traders' Branch than had enlivened the joyous departure from DulElesi three weeks earlier. The street lanterns seemed to burn unbearably bright. No songs of celebration rose above the clatter of crate and wheel and harness. After Megan had provided what little help she could with the reloading of the Infirmary wagon, she wandered the bustling crowd, taking its temperature.

She missed the music. She had grown used to a sung or chanted accompaniment to almost every Sawlish activity. She thought of music as a calmative, a matrix on which to weave human passions into a more coherent order. But singing required effort, even if minimal, and in this great heat and hurry, not a soul was willing to squander even an ounce of energy on a nonessential pursuit.

The children were another telling barometer. The youngest instinctively stayed out from underfoot. Their older siblings raced around laden with sacks and baskets and armloads of cloth-wrapped merchandise bigger than they were. Their small faces were serious with purpose. They were eager to prove their adulthood in the face of an impending crisis whose nature they did not quite comprehend but whose aura radiated from their harried, grim-faced elders.

In the crowd, disputes flared easily and the talk was of Devastation. The wagering was fast and reckless, though the Priest-Guild hung close to its own wagons, offering nothing more than predictions of continuing heat. The rangers circulated constantly, calming tempers, arbitrating difficulties and encouraging a rapid, efficient pace. Megan overheard them spreading Aguidran's directive that space be found in each big wagon for two extra water kegs.

When the heat seems to be emanating from within as well as from without, she decided, *that's when you start to get frightened.*

She worried about the long return trek across the Dop Arek. As hot as it had been on the way out, water had been plentiful, left over from the storms. But she expected that the three and a half rainless weeks since had seared the arid plain into virtual desert. Worse still, sunrise was due within the week, when the caravan would be well into the most open stretches of the plain.

Normally, I'd welcome dawn with joy and relief after two weeks of darkness.

Now the very thought of it filled her with dread.

Along the railing outside the infirmary, Ghirra and Aguidran leaned shoulder to shoulder in gloomy conference with a lanky balding man who Megan recognized as the head of Ogo Dul's RangerGuild. Susannah and Xifa sat on the yellow wagon's lowered tail gate, little Dwingen sandwiched between them. Three pairs of legs swung back and forth to the same nervous rhythm.

"All packed?" Megan rubbed her hands in a manic attempt to break out of her own doomsday mood.

Susannah nodded. "The herdsmen are bringing the hjalk around now."

"Be better when we're moving again, making actual progress toward home."

"Home?" Susannah echoed.

Megan listened for bitterness but heard only rueful confusion.

When the hjalk arrived, they were restive and grouchy about being laced into their harness. Ghirra came over from the rail to draw the great curly head of the team leader down to his, holding it gently by its undersized ears for a murmured chat. Aguidran went on her way, her fellow ranger beside her, to hurry along the rest of the harnessing and start the long wagon train moving up the steep ramps to the savannah.

At the top of the ramps, the tall torches blazed against the blackness. The smoke rose past the smoke and light of the Cluster, fading the dimmer stars. The shining worried faces of Ogo Dul lined the white roadway to bid friends and guild-mates a safe journey. Relatives embraced. Last minute wagers were offered and exchanged, to be collected at the next market. Ogo Dul's PriestGuild stood apart in the darkness, chanting ringing choruses that were answered antiphonally by Kav Ashimmel's retinue at the front of the caravan.

"Khe khem!" Megan heard over and over, called fervently and often followed by a whispered "ValEmbriha!"

A faint breath tinged the air with the salt pungence of DulValla. The tall torch flames leaped. The hjalk danced with flared nostrils while their drivers struggled with the reins.

"I am not meant to live in a cave!" Susannah breathed in

140

grateful release, the only one among them welcoming the dark emptiness of the rolling savannah.

Megan, who had discovered that she was perfectly at home in the deepest of caves, wondered how it was possible to feel safer out in the open.

The first two throws brought the caravan up the gradual slope from the sea, through the long, brittle grasses to the cooling depths of Imvalla's pool. The great waterfall cried out in a tumbling roar of phosphorescence. The incredible precipice loomed above the camp, visible only as a darker darkness devoid of stars.

When the wagons were settled, Aguidran ordered all the water kegs to be emptied, then sent the entire caravan to the pool's edge for a last long bath.

At the beginning of the next throw, the wagons' loads were further lightened by the amount that each person could carry on his back. The arduous slow climb up the eight long switchbacks began.

What had required a mere matter of hours in the descent took the better part of a full throw to accomplish in the ascent. The halk balked and complained. Even the reliable little hakra showed a more goatish nature. The herdsmen swore and pulled and finally resorted to occasional blows. When the last panting hakra had heaved its burden over the top, and the dark expanse of the Dop Arek stretched before them, Aguidran declared an early camp, set careful perimeter watches and called a conference of the guild leaders.

The conference was interrupted by a child screaming among the herd of hakra and hjalk gathered to drink at the river. Rangers pounded past the wagons and a scuffle exploded in the darkness, more screams, not the child, but a dying angry beast.

The terrified child was rushed to the Infirmary wagon. Xifa searched hurriedly for teeth marks while Ampiar ran for the antivenom poultices. But the boy was found to be uninjured and was soon grinning with pride at having evaded his attacker's lethal jaws.

Ghirra returned later from the conference to find his staff drawn in a close circle around a low-burning lantern. He settled himself cross-legged among them, smiling at Susannah over his tray of cold food.

"I have ask my sister give you some of this lechrall that is kill by her guildsmen."

"An animal sample!" Susannah cheered softly. "Thank you!"

"I know you need this thing, Suzhannah."

"And he'd rather you didn't go after a live one yourself," said Megan.

Ghirra swallowed several quick bites of food, then slowed to explain Aguidran's plan.

"We'd call that a shortcut," said Megan, when he had finished scratching maps in the dust. "But I'd think it'd be worth the two extra throws it'd take to go back via the Talche. Won't there be more water available?"

Ghirra nodded pensively, and Megan decided that he was not totally in favor of his sister's strategy, but did not think it right to speak out against it. "Every throw longer, the crop is dying," he excused. "And the FoodGuild keeps the food of two cycles if we go as my sister says."

"What about the herds waiting in the hills?" asked Susannah.

"My sister send some guildsmen, bring food to the herdsmen, tell them stay in the hills where the more water is."

Megan set her food tray aside and leaned back against the hard rim of a wagon wheel while Ghirra questioned Xifa about the refilling of the water kegs. It seemed to her now that she had lived this way all her life, heat-drenched, striding through dust, eating bland food, sleeping on the dry ground. It was a hard life, and she marvelled that the Sawls, after centuries of it, retained the energy to go on.

"So," she mused aloud. "One hundred-odd nasty kilometers straight across the Dop Arek, eh? Five throws, if we can really manage the twenty klicks a throw like we did coming out."

"Five throws in this heat is better than seven," Susannah pointed out.

"Only if the water holds out."

Ghirra nodded. "Dop Arek gives no shelter to hide from the Sisters."

The rangers brought Susannah the tail of the animal that had attacked the child. They had wrapped it in heavy cloth and helped her transfer the bloody tendril of flesh and scales into a plastic bag with great care to avoid touching it. Susannah packed it away according to Aguidran's express order, though she longed to feed a chunk of it into her analyzer. When the rangers had gone, she sat by the wagon, staring up at the Cluster. Megan snored between the wheels with the apprentices.

"Show me your world," murmured Ghirra, appearing silently at her side.

Susannah gazed blankly at the spectacle of stars. "I can't," she admitted with a small laugh. "I can't even tell you which direction to look in. Probably you can't even see our sun from here. Ask Taylor when we get back, or Weng."

"TaylorDanforth, he studies about this things, worlds, stars?"

"Worlds, mostly. What they're made of and how they got that way."

"He comes also from your world?"

Susannah smiled. "Tay? Of course. Why?"

Ghirra held up his hand. "He is like I am, more dark even."

"Yes. Black, he would call it, and it comes in many shades. There's lots of people on Earth with skin the exact color of yours."

"I could be there, and they not see me different?"

Susannah's smile warmed. "A haircut and a change of clothes, nobody'd be the wiser."

Ghirra considered this for a moment, then nodded. "I will have talk with TaylorDanforth about this thing of worlds."

Aguidran drove the caravan hard for the two throws of remaining darkness but received few complaints. The hjalk were reasonably fresh and the travellers eager to cover as much ground as possible before the return of the burning sun. Megan estimated that they made twenty-five kilometers the first leg and a whopping twenty-eight on the second by shortening the dinner rest period and extending the period of travel from twelve hours to fifteen.

By the beginning of the third throw, the velvet black sky had softened to dark gray. The Cluster fire dimmed with its attendant stars and the broken horizon ghosted into view.

"Amazingly, the darkness hardly slows their growth rate," said Susannah over breakfast, sorting through the few plant samples she had been able to collect in the dark, under the wary eyes of the ranger perimeter watch. "It helps answer one of my questions, though. With flora already evolved to survive this protracted light-dark cycle, some clever selective breeding *might* produce the fully dark-adapted varieties they grow in the Caves."

"You mean genetic engineering isn't the only explanation?" Megan shook her head, grinning. "Sometimes I think you biologists have forgotten about the good old-fashioned farmer." Her eyes followed a ranger scouting party as they loped past in search of their guildmaster.

Susannah held up a thick, prickled knob. "Farmers didn't create lush tropical bushes that metamorphize into this when a dry spell arrives."

"You're sure it's the same plant?"

"Same name. Ghirra said so. He was quite surprised when he

realized that I expected to find separate plants filling the various ecological niches. The way he explained it, more or less, since the Sisters can produce any possible weather in any possible location, all living things must be able to adapt quickly and completely in order to survive the whims of the Goddesses.''

"Makes sense—the freakish environment selecting for flexibility?"

Aguidran came pacing down the line with her brother and one of the scouts. Ghirra carried his breakfast tray, spooning grain mash into his mouth as he walked, as if determined that at least once a cycle, he would eat a meal while it was still warm.

Aguidran crouched before the two women and waved the young scout closer. He gave a shy nod of greeting but remained standing, thin and eager, leaning on the stout wooden club he carried during his watch.

"The guildsmen has find a thing," Ghirra explained. He gestured to the southeast. "Away some way."

"A thing?" asked Megan.

"A thing not our making. Your making, he think."

Megan and Susannah exchanged glances.

"What sort of thing?" asked Megan. "How big?"

Ghirra conferred with the scout. "More big than a hjalk wagon."

"Maybe he could draw it?"

But the young man's willing scratches in the dust only mystified them further.

Susannah shrugged. "So we ought to go take a look."

Ghirra murmured with Aguidran, talking her indecisive frown into a reluctant nod. "We must take water," he noted finally.

Megan and Susannah refilled their field canteens from the kegs strapped to the side of the wagon. Ampiar grew more solemn than usual and Xifa fidgeted, her cheery round face tight with worry as she watched them prepare, gently clasping Dwingen's shoulder to keep him from asking to go along. Ghirra smiled at their concern and slung his water jug gaily across his back. They fell in behind the waiting scout and moved out into the greying night.

The walking was hot and dry but not arduous. Past floods seemed to have neglected this central portion of the Dop Arek. The ground was flat and hard as baked ceramic, marred only by the fine-lined cracking of its dull glaze of dust and sand.

"Damn, it's desolate out here," said Megan nervously.

"A proper surface for a gameboard." Susannah imagined giant dice rolling like tumbleweed across the hardpan. The odd half-light was a woolly limbo between the realities of day and night. She would not have been too surprised to see the pale reflective ground fade into the angular black-and-white of a checkerboard.

The scout led them southeast of the caravan route, miraculously steering a certain path across the featureless landscape. Eventually, the rim of a wide ravine appeared suddenly out of the pearly gloom, part of the branching system of a dry watercourse. The drop was short but steep, the boulder strewn bank as black as pitch. The scout pointed, then shyly touched Susannah's elbow and pointed again, eager to prove that the mysterious object of his report was not imagined.

Deep in the shadow of the far bank, a lighter colored, triangular shape nestled among piles of rock and uprooted brush.

"Well, well, well," exclaimed Susannah softly.

"Where?" Megan scanned the semidarkness unsuccessfully. "What?"

"I think it's A-Sled. Or what's left of it. Let's take a look."

She scrambled down the rubbled bank, the scout keeping anxious pace with her. His eyes raked the rocks and ravine bottom for signs of reptilian motion.

"It is!" she called back from the far side. She approached the pale hulk and laid her hand on its mud-encrusted skin as if it were a sleeping animal that might stir to her touch. She traced the neatly stenciled registry numbers. The Sled's machined familiarity was like a shock of cold water waking her from a dream where mankind hurried along the ground but gave no thought to flying. She wondered how McPherson was, ashamed to realize that she had hardly thought about her in the last three weeks, and not much more about Taylor or Weng or Clausen.

Emil. Oh, lord. She wished Megan hadn't told her that Clausen had a gun.

"How is it?" Megan called breathlessly, hurrying across the ravine in Ghirra's wake.

"Okay, I guess. Hard to tell in this light." Susannah walked the Sled's full length. The nose was badly misshapen, but the wings showed only fine-line cracks and the tail mostly intact. "It's real dirty but seems to have ridden the waters fairly bravely."

Ghirra ticked at the smoothly resistant hull with a thumbnail. "This is not like glass," he commented.

"Plastic," said Megan.

"How is it here if Ibi . . . ?"

"Oh. We brought two Sleds. This is the one the flood washed away." Megan reached to feel around the edges of the transparent blister in front of the tail. "Wonder if the com still works."

"You know how to fly one of these things?" asked Susannah.

Megan laughed. "No. You? They don't want us scientist types knowing how to get around by ourselves."

When Ghirra had walked away toward the nose to peer into the dusty cockpit, Susannah said quietly, "We've got to get it back to the Lander somehow."

"Do you think they'll object?"

"In this heat? The extra load and effort?"

"Well, why don't you go to work convincing Ghirra while I clean off the com and try to raise CRI."

The open compartment was littered with flood debris. A cracking layer of dried mud roughened the flooring. Megan heaved herself onto the wing, then over the edge of the cargo hold, and clambered forward through matted brush and water-shaped mounds of gravel.

The upholstery was brittle from weathering. It crackled in complaint as she sat down in front of the instrument panel. She tapped at the once transparent housings. Dessicated yellow scum flaked away to reveal a more stubborn layer of mud beneath.

Megan dug at it with a thumbnail. The mud had hardened around the switches. "Might as well be set in concrete," she muttered.

She spat on her fingertip and tried to soften the coating, then searched among the scatterings on the cockpit floor for a rock to chip it away. She decided it was really not much different from freeing a shard of ancient pottery from its prison of sediment, but hoped it would not take as long.

She was struggling with an immobilized pressure switch when Susannah sauntered back, victorious from her conference.

"He's sent the scout back to request a tow for the Sled," she reported. "He has a bet on with him that Aguidran says no, but I think that's to get the boy working harder to convince her. They both figure it'll cost nearly a throw if the caravan waits for us, so we'll have to play catch-up. Any luck with CRI?"

Megan sat back in disgust. "I think the insides are solid mud."

Susannah scratched at the yellow film rimming the windscreen. "Needs a wash all right."

"So what now?"

"Ghirra says we sit tight and watch out for the creepy-crawlies."

The young scout returned several hours later with two hjalk and a driver. Aguidran had agreed to the tow, but promised to abandon the Sled without question the moment it became too much of a burden. Ghirra paid off his bet with a satisfied nod. He set them to digging out the Sled, marveling particularly over the hard rubber of the wheels as he and the scout freed the landing gear from the encasing debris.

Once loose and hitched to the hjalk, the lightweight craft bumped along quite willingly on its own wheels.

"Well, that was easy," commented Megan as the team hauled the Sled up out of the ravine.

Susannah made light of Meg's suspicious frown, but her laugh rang too loudly in the pale half-light. Ghirra was somber, too, as the scout pointed out that with the approach of dawn, the heated air had assumed a sluggish sort of motion, too fitful for a breeze but enough to send occasional dust devils scurrying across the dry ground.

Susannah coughed and took a long gulp from her canteen, then stoppered it tightly. She noticed that the scout's worried eye scanned the full circle of the horizon in more than a casual search. The driver, a weathered older man, sucked on his blue talisman bead and urged the hjalk along as fast as they could manage.

19

"Amnesty?" Clausen laughed harshly. "You've got to be kidding."

Danforth settled his head on his forearms while McPherson massaged his bed-stiff back. She was an efficient masseuse but ungentle, and her hands were hot and damp against his skin. "Well, what's he done, Emil, really? Ripped off some equipment, caused a little inconvenience. Nothing lethal."

Clausen swiveled away from the computer table. "Tay," he said with sour disbelief, "a month ago you were ready to strangle the kid if he so much as looked at you. Now when he's really fucking us over, you want to forgive and forget?"

Danforth shrugged beneath McPherson's busy hands. "I need him down here to translate."

"Fine. He can translate from the brig."

"The *brig*, Mr. Clausen?" Beyond the edge of the lamplight, Weng's head inclined to the reedy sound of chanting, now drifting almost perpetually from the Sawl encampment at the cliff base. The darkness over the fields was lightening into gray.

"Figuratively speaking, of course, Commander."

"Are you suggesting that we actually incarcerate Mr. Ibiá?"

Clausen turned back to the console. "Christ. You people."

"Well," said McPherson, "I wouldn't mind you spending less time on Stav and more time fixing the Sled with me."

"The kid's crazy, Emil," Danforth rumbled reasonably, as McPherson pummeled the small of his back. "He's not responsible."

The prospector tapped the keypad impatiently. "He's responsible enough to plan and carry off a well-organized theft, then cover his tracks fairly skillfully, electronically and otherwise. You think he's just fooling around, Tay? Playing little kid's tricks on us? You're the fool if you do." Clausen shook his head. "He's deep into something and I damn well want to know what it is!"

McPherson nodded toward the wilting fields, where the meager Sawl home guard were still hard at work laying irrigation pipes. "I think they're helping him."

"Of course they're helping him!" Clausen fumed.

"They?" said Danforth.

"The Sawls." McPherson dug into the muscles knotting around his spine. "They're real helpful bringing in the Sled and all, but I'm sure they're hiding him. I went up there with Emil, you know? There's a whole new rock slide just where CRI said Stav was supposed to be. Now, how could he do a rock slide by himself?"

Clausen raised a briefly ironic brow but let her query go by. He returned his concentration to the keypad and a screen full of sensing data.

Danforth stirred irritably. McPherson gave him a final slap and helped him as he struggled to turn over and sit up.

"Those little Sawls seem to be hiding just everything up there," he murmured, while reminding himself privately that Clausen's obsession with the hunt for Ibiá conveniently occupied the prospector away from the Underbelly. CRI was then left free to help Danforth pursue his scientific quarry.

"There's a bit of a breeze coming up," Weng noted, coming in from the half-light.

"Breeze?" Danforth sniffed the air like an eager dog.

Weng moved about with distracted purpose, collecting dirty dishes left from the dinner meal. "I will need some power for the sonic, Mr. Clausen. We can't afford to use water to wash up anymore."

"Maybe when the Sawls get their pipes laid, we can borrow from them," McPherson proposed.

"Emil, have CRI check wind speeds," Danforth interrupted. "We haven't had real air movement in weeks!"

Weng scraped drying food out of compartmented plates. "Such waste."

"This food tastes pretty yucky now," regretted McPherson.

"A pity Mr. Clausen won't stoop to applying his culinary talents to ship's rations."

"Nothing can come of nothing," Clausen replied tartly.

"Anything on those wind speeds?" Danforth grunted at the pain in his chest wound as he levered his rangy body into his makeshift wheelchair by the strength of his arms alone.

"How about magnetic and gravity field data?" Clausen replied. "Got some interesting fluctuations there."

The computer spoke up of her own accord. "Local winds are from the northeast, Dr. Danforth, building slowly. Now intermittent at four to seven mph. Current local temperature is ninety-three degrees."

"Thank you, CRI. Keep an eye on it for me, will you?" With effort, Danforth hand-wheeled the two-cart into the work area, refusing all help as had become his habit. He did allow Weng to adjust his position at her worktable and push his papers within reach. She perched on a crate opposite him, and he thought of a tall and steady-eyed heron.

"How are you coming with the water mapping?" She turned over a heavily annotated data sheet to scribble on the unused side.

"CRI's done prelims so far, vertical profiles for each weather station. I'd hoped the new data would answer the questions, not just confirm them, but I'm afraid the results were what I'm coming to expect: they don't fit my model and they don't make sense."

Weng made encouraging listening noises while slowly covering her sheet of paper with numerical jottings that might have been formulae, or something else entirely.

"For instance," Danforth continued, "Global Theta's stationed over the northern ocean. You'd expect to find a lot of water there, at all altitudes. But the instruments say it's confined to near the surface.

"Also, you'd expect to find *less* water as you move away from the ocean into the drier areas, water vapor being drawn there from the ocean to support global equilibrium. Instead, we've got water moving all over the place, apparently at random, apparently as isolated local phenomena." He settled back against his cushion of blankets, finding a kind of wondering calm within the depths of his frustration. "Now ain't that the

149

damnedest? A system refusing to move toward equilibrium, I mean, *refusing*. It's the same thing we noticed with the temperature, with the heat often moving away from cooler areas instead of toward them.''

"Heat moving toward heat, water moving around at random."

He nodded, grimacing at the illogic of it. "Like that damned freak thunderstorm, in apparent violation of dynamical laws, of basic physics." He nodded again, pensively, like an old man praying. "Something's got to be pouring a hell of a lot of energy into holding this system away from equilibrium."

"Your X-factor again?"

"Yeah, for lack of a better culprit." He drummed his fingers on the table. "I promised myself to look for naturally occurring patterns. Well, here's one I can no longer deny: if you combine all the dynamical data, a clear trajectory asserts itself. Except for the dry period between the flooding and the hail, when some east-to-west zonal movement actually occurred, all the movement is along that northeast-southwest axis."

"Yes?" Weng waited while he mused over a notion he was reluctant to express out loud. She hummed three dissonant notes under her breath, her head cocked as if still listening to the distant chanting, then crossed out one of her scribbles.

"Thing is, Commander," Danforth admitted finally with an uncomfortable grin, "I can't escape the fact that, in putting the back data together with the new to pinpoint a consistent locus of action for the snow, rain, hail and now this rising heat, I keep landing right on top of Ibiá's damn god houses or whatever the hell CRI calls them."

"Godhomes," Weng supplied, withholding all editorial comment.

"Whatever. The ocean and the desert. That's where it's all coming from or going to. It meets in the middle, within what just happens to be the planet's narrow zone of habitability, and all hell breaks loose."

He buried his fingertips in his tight curls, squeezing his head as if to keep it from flying apart. He heard a muttered exclamation from Clausen that sounded like a curse and lowered his voice. "Maybe we could get some Sawl to sneak a message to Ibiá. You think they really know where he is?"

Weng's pen point paused. "I expect they do, Dr. Danforth."

He studied her carefully. "Do you know?"

"No, Dr. Danforth. I would not want to."

He smiled, relieved but vaguely disappointed. "You know, Commander, I had you pegged for one of those discipline-at-all-costs types."

She regarded him mildly. "I doubt that I'd have survived this long had that been the case. One must always consider the costs."

"A lesson I learned the hard way," he remarked, patting his cast-bound thigh.

"One always does, Dr. Danforth."

"Well. Now this is very interesting." Clausen's voice was raised for all to hear. "CRI, let me see the original cargo and equipment manifest." He leaned forward eagerly. "Good. Now give me the updated launch roster."

McPherson slotted the last dishes into the sonic and wandered up to read over the prospector's shoulder as he scanned the listing of satellites in orbit, each followed by a brief notation as to equipment, location and purpose. Several offered no information other than the CONPLEX log and a launch date.

"Look!" McPherson exclaimed. "A drone!"

"Precisely." Hunched over the keypad, Clausen wore his hunter's grin of anticipation. "CRI, get me Captain Newman on the line."

"Captain Newman is in his sleep period. Is it an emergency?"

"No, never mind. CRI, tell me, did the Captain authorize a drone launch recently?"

"No, Mr. Clausen."

"But I see here on the schedule that a drone has been launched."

"That is correct."

"The launch coordinates would seem to indicate a trajectory toward Earth."

"I quite agree, Mr. Clausen."

Clausen straightened slowly, like a cobra uncurling. "CRI, I'd like to know the contents of that drone."

"I am not at liberty to divulge that information."

He nodded. "That's what you think."

"How're you gonna break open a confidential file?" McPherson demanded.

"Well, now, McP., if I told you, then we'd both know." He smiled nastily. "You really expect me to give up my advantage?"

McPherson blinked. "Jeez. 'Scuse me for asking."

"I have updated wind and temperature readings for Dr. Danforth," said the computer.

"By all means, speak up." Clausen sat back, smugly accommodating.

"Local temperature has risen to ninety-six degrees. Winds up five mph, gusting from nine to twelve mph."

"Still rising." Danforth shook his head.

"And so will the sun," added Weng. She switched off the

work light and turned her back to Clausen's searchbeam. Danforth turned in his chair. Beyond the shadowed belly of the Lander, the fading Cluster hung in the east like a spattered drop of bleach on a pearl-gray satin sky. Danforth thought if there was ever a time to pray for rain, this was it.

"So what do you say to that?" Clausen faced them from the hot glare of his lamp.

"To the sun?" Desert visions filled Danforth's head.

"To a drone that's been sent to Earth, but not by Captain Newman. Or by yourself, I assume, Commander?"

Weng shook her head.

Clausen stretched out his legs, his feral smile broadening. "Now, who else has that authority. Well, my, my. The Communications Officer. What a coincidence."

"You're saying Stav sent it?" McPherson asked.

Clausen laughed. "So, Tay, you still think he's just a harmless loony?"

Danforth tried to read Weng's impassive face, and failing that, looked for a hint of her reaction in the angle of her stance. *Maybe we have let Ibiá get out of hand? It is possible to be loony and still be dangerous.* He tried to imagine circumstances short of insanity that might cause himself to go renegade and fire off secret messages to Earth.

Perhaps if I made some momentous discovery that I didn't want anyone here to know about . . .

"Commander," he murmured. "I'd like to know what's in that drone, too."

In the half-dark, Weng nodded her assent. The chanting from the Sawl encampment swelled on the rising breeze and ceased suddenly. A runner was coming down the path from the cliff, his rapid footfalls softened by the thickening dust.

"Furzon!" he called. "Furzon!"

McPherson looked up. "That's me." She went out into the clearing to usher in the leader of the ranger salvage party. He was a sturdy middle-aged man with a seamy worried face. He eyed Clausen warily as he passed and continued to expostulate at McPherson's back as she led him to Weng's worktable.

"I can't quite get what he wants, Commander, but it's something about that old priest and the sky, and you know what that could mean!"

Danforth suffered a jolt of déjà vu, seeing in the ranger's stubborn agitation a memory of Stavros Ibiá, damp-haired and on the edge of panic, pleading that a priestly warning be heeded. He bit back hard on his first impulse to dismiss the man's obvious

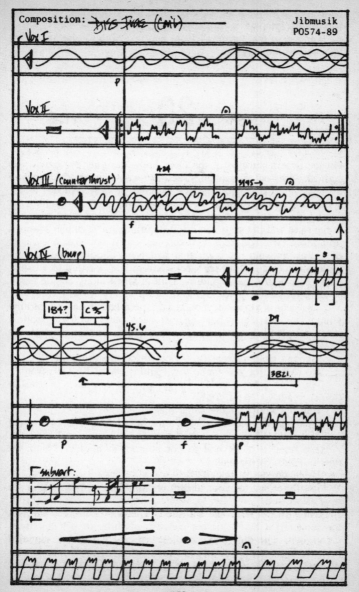

concern and shoved his wheeled chair away from the worktable, waving McPherson to him abruptly.

"Get me to that terminal, Ron, and fast! Ten to one we've got weather on the way!"

20

On the desert hardpan of the Dop Arek, the gray pre-dawn was stained with red. Susannah slitted her eyes against the swirling dust, struggling to keep the young scout in view. Ahead, to the south, the toothy profile of the Grigar wavered miragelike, its narrow peaks salmon tipped and glowing. The hot wind snatched at the sand and the scattered dry tufts of brush. Susannah scooped up a loose twig and bent it. It snapped easily and spat out a puff of yellow powder. A plant that had been budding and spongy with moisture a scant three weeks before was reduced to a brittle husk. She held it out to Ghirra as he trudged along beside her.

"It didn't even have time to develop its dry form, did it?"

"The heat is too soon. You hear?" he asked, listening into the wind. The dry stems beat against each other with the hollow rattle of pebbles cast across stone. "The Sisters prepare the game."

Susannah smiled uneasily. "You sound like Aguidran."

"No. My sister will name this fighting, what Ibi call 'war'."

"Ah. War." She nodded. He grasped the subtleties of translation so readily. "And you?"

"I do not know what I name this."

A sharp gust whipped sand against her cheeks. Her eyes stung and watered. "And are we the Sisters' gaming pieces?"

He offered a bleak nod to her attempt at humor. "You see now our life, Suzhannah."

"Understand, you mean?"

"I will not say for your understanding," he replied. "You see now as we see."

Living as you live, she reflected. The wind billowed through the loose light layers of her Sawlish clothing to dry her heat-damp skin. The dust and gravel crunched beneath her sandaled feet. *A direct and sympathetic methodology. So obvious. Stav's instinct from the beginning.* She matched Ghirra's measured stride and felt marginally less weary. The scout moved ahead, barely visible through the dawn-colored dust. Behind, the hjalk curled their strong necks into the wind, their wide nostrils opening and shutting with the labored rhythm of their step. The Sled rattled in their wake, collecting the extra weight of the sand blown into its seams and open hold. Megan struggled along in its lee, one hand grasping the wing as if the Sled itself were her guide to safety.

"What game will they play this time?" Susannah played out the metaphor like a fishing lure, to snare Ghirra's less guarded thoughts. The wind built shifting singing walls around their tiny caravan but the sky above the gusted sand was clear, shell-pink and limitless.

Ghirra dug in his pockets and held out a half-dozen black stone counters. "Do you offer a wager?"

She glanced at him, surprised. A deeper creasing at the corners of his mouth was his only hint of a smile. "That far I would not presume."

He fingered the counters thoughtfully, then put them away. "Sometime, is better to lose the stones."

"You mean you'd rather be wrong about what you think is coming?"

All trace of a smile evaporated. "This is correct, Suzhannah."

The scout called back hoarsely, urging speed. Susannah swallowed as sand grains grated between her teeth. Megan's slitted eyes were fixed on the swirling ground. She had not spoken for over an hour, a more eloquent expression of her exhaustion than any litany of complaint.

A maverick windburst momentarily thinned the veil of sand. The scout called out again. Ghirra waved back and pointed. Below the ruddy crenelations of the Grigar, still sunk in predawn shadow, the distant cliffs of DulElesi were briefly visible.

"Thank god," Susannah breathed, then as the sand closed around them again, she asked, "How long?"

Ghirra spread his hands. "Two throws, it could be."

Susannah squinted crestfallen at the vanishing rockform. "That far? Shouldn't we have met up with the other wagons by now?" she worried, clearing sand from her throat with a strangled cough.

"Not talk now," advised the physician. "See, I do this way." He unwrapped his wide cloth waistsash and wound it loosely around his head, Berber-style, to shield his eyes and mouth from the flying sand. "No worry, Suzhannah. My sister hurries, but also we hurry and there is few of us."

They crossed a shallow gravelled wash snaking up from the

south. Susannah's impulse, had she been wandering alone in this polished waste, would have been to follow its dry meanderings, if only for the suggestion of shelter in its crumbling banks, for the relief it offered from unrelieved flatness.

The Sled's wheels jolted into the wash and balked at the rise, spinning in the dusted gravel. As the hjalk strained, it lurched up over the edge. The driver alternately cooed to his beasts and berated them, as his patience waxed and ebbed. When the wheels rolled free once again, Ghirra whistled ahead to the scout to declare a brief rest stop. The canteens and the clay water jugs were unslung in the lee of the Sled. The hjalk, standing lathered and panting in their harness, sucked warm water from the driver's cupped hands. He had few words for his human companions but an endless stream of chat for his animals. The larger nuzzled him repeatedly, bleating indignantly when he stoppered his jug and reslung it across his back. Murmuring fond negatives, the old man grasped the beast's curly head apologetically to brush encrusted sand away from its long-lashed eyes.

Watching, Ghirra shared an unreadable glance with the anxious scout. "The hjalk are restless," he offered cryptically. He rose from his crouch beside the aft landing gear. "We must hurry."

The scout stayed close by as they started up again. The wind continued to rise. The thickening sand stole back the feeble light won from the coming dawn. Clumps of brush rolled loose, ripped from their moorings. Susannah rewound her sash around her face to filter the sand-choked air, suffering waking visions of being buried alive.

"Susannah!" Megan shouted suddenly. In the shelter of the Sled, she had pulled out her pocket compass and was staring at it oddly. Susannah dropped back to join her. Within its plastic case, the needle was shuddering like a live thing as it wavered wildly from point to point. Abruptly, it swung to the southwest and hovered quaking, as if fighting a pull to which it must inevitably give in.

The hair rose on the back of Susannah's neck. "Broken, huh?"

"Compasses don't break. Not like this."

"The magnetic field must be different here."

"Thing worked fine before."

Susannah's head jerked around at a sound that was not quite a sound, rather as if a tiny explosion had occurred just outside her ear. But Ghirra halted several paces ahead, alert and listening. The scout frowned, then shouted a tense query back at the older men. Ghirra answered grimly.

"What *was* that?" Susannah's words were lost to the wind.

The hjalk danced in their traces. The smaller animal skittered to one side against the larger's momentum, uttering small bleats of dismay. It was brought up sharp by the limit of its harness. It squealed and bucked. The driver growled and slapped its wooly flank to urge it forward again. The wind sighed and wound itself into tighter eddies, sucking up funnels of yellow dust to chase among the tumbling bundles of brush. Overhead, the flamingo sky grew luminous as silk.

Megan gasped. "Look! Your hair!"

Susannah's long dark hair, dangling loose from beneath her improvised mask and turban, was denying the wind's command. It floated upward as if of its own volition. She grabbed at it and shoved it under her collar. She felt an urgent need to sneeze or shout out loud, to release the tension rising through her body.

The sound came again, sharper, like a blow to the midriff. The larger hjalk shied and lunged ahead. The driver bellowed his alarm. The Sled lurched, then skewed about wildly. Susannah jerked Megan away from the tail as it swung around toward her head.

Ghirra was beside them instantly, hauling on the driver's arm as he grabbed frantically at the tow ropes. The physician's greater height was no advantage over a man who had spent a lifetime managing giant beasts. The driver tossed him off roughly and continued to yank at the ties. The Sled careened from side to side as the hjalk leaped and fought the harness. The scout screamed at the driver over the hum of the wind, waving ahead and then up at the sky. The wind wound its eddies tighter and spat spirals of razor-edged gravel. The grinding hum coiled into a whine.

Susannah snared Ghirra's arm as he readied himself for a second assault. "Let him! We'll leave it behind!"

"No!" he shouted.

His insistence confused her, his uncharacteristic sudden fury.

"We need this now!" He slammed his weight against the driver's shoulder, throwing him off balance. The scout grabbed the driver from the other side and hauled him away from the Sled. Ghirra planted himself in front of it before the old man recovered his balance.

The sand sang in Susannah's ears. *This is more than heat madness.*

The driver regarded Ghirra in bewilderment and disgust. The master Healer glared back and spat a terse command, suddenly so like his sister that the scout seconded him automatically, as if backing up his own guildmaster. The old man dismissed them both with a gesture. He flung an arm up at the sky and stalked ahead to his animals. They moaned at him but his coming settled their struggles down to frantic head tossing and shifting from one broad padded foot to the other.

Susannah hovered uncertainly, fighting the gusts. Ghirra's mouth was so tight that his lips were pale. He nodded calmly to her as he readjusted his head cloth, but his eyes, squinting into the sky, showed more than their usual white.

"This is a *chukka* of the oldest legends," he declared flatly.

"A what?"

"A plan of the Sisters, in the Game. This we never see yet in my life, or of my two-father or even my five-father."

Not rage at all, then, Susannah realized. *It's fear. He's afraid. Ghirra is afraid.*

Chilled, she grasped his arm as the wind snatched at her clothing. "We don't really *need* the Sled!"

"You do not understand, Suzhannah! Now to go fast does not help. Where do we run?" He spread his arms to the sky. "We need this thing to be inside it!"

"Inside? Ghirra, it's an open cockpit. You can't get inside it!"

Doubt and a moment of true panic flickered in his eyes. Then he set his jaw determinedly. "No matter. It is better than nothing."

"What is happening? What's coming?"

The scout read her bewilderment. "Ph'nar khem!" he offered breathlessly.

Ghirra translated. "He says these Sisters are most angry, so it is our worse than bad luck to be here where they chose to make their game."

He refused to say more and hurried them onward. The driver got the Sled moving again, his gnarled hand wrapped tightly in the lead hjalk's head rein. He yelled at the frightened scout to grab the other, and the beasts danced forward reluctantly, their small round ears flat against their heads as they listened to their driver's soothing patter. The weathered hostler snorted at the young scout's fear and held up four fingers to offer a wager.

Suddenly, the hjalk came alert.

The wind shifted, forsaking its whirligig habit. Hot and sand-laden, it charged straight at their faces. The hjalks' ears swiveled. Susannah braced herself for the next onslaught of panic-inducing non-sound. Instead she heard faint shouts carried on the wind. The scout cheered and danced about, still grasping the head rein, then held out a boyish demanding palm to the driver, who grudgingly paid over four shiny black counters.

Ghirra's stride lengthened with relief. "There! They are there!"

Susannah linked her arm through Megan's to keep her from falling behind. The stinging wind eased for an instant. In the near distance, she heard the bleats and bellows of frightened hjalk. Then the wind rose again, building until its engine whine drowned out all other sound except the one she feared.

It hit with a jolt and the pressure impact of a thunderclap. Susannah's ears rang and a blue-green afterimage flared inside her eyes. The unheard sound came in a blaze of invisible light.

"Incredible!" exclaimed Danforth from the terminal.

Wind gusts growled through the underbelly, sweeping loose papers and plastic cups off the crate tops to skitter across the hard ground.

Out in the clearing, Clausen and McPherson scrambled about in the dim pink dawn, throwing silver tarps around the base of the high-gain antenna and over the half repaired B-Sled. The Sawl ranger who had rushed down to warn them strung tie ropes and helped to weigh the tarps down with stones.

"Cover the dish last!" Clausen yelled over the wind. In the terraced fields, the tall red stalks rattled like dice in a cup. A few frantic and sweating Sawls rushed among them drawing the stalks together into conical bunches and tying them gently with strips of cloth.

"The music has stopped," Weng noted from Danforth's side. "Up in the Caves."

Danforth was oblivious. "Christ, here we go again! Look at this!"

The terminal displayed the local weather map.

"Discrete packages of turbulence charging around like goddamn bumper cars! Without a cloud in sight! It's dry as a bone out there and hotter than blazes! And look at this! CRI, show the Commander what's happening elsewhere in the so-called habitable zone!"

Weng leaned in closer as the glowing image shifted. The wind loosed silver tendrils from her neatly bound hair.

"This damned nonsense is planet-wide!" the planetologist fumed. "But only within that narrow band. Return us to local, CRI."

Weng's fingertip followed a phosphor-green packet as it sped across the map of the plain toward a larger frontal indication. "Would you say that was random movement, Dr. Danforth?"

"Random? Weather's never random. I . . . ." Danforth stopped, looked at Weng sideways. "But that's not what you meant, is it?"

"No, Dr. Danforth, it's not." She glanced around as Clausen snapped a string of orders at the Sawl ranger in very passable and hitherto undemonstrated Sawlish. She tucked hair back into her bun and continued. "We have seen this behavior before."

"I know. That damned thunderstorm."

Weng nodded. "According to Mr. Ibiá's files, the Sawls would say there was a battle being waged out there on the plain. Don't you find that description rather appropriate, Dr. Danforth?"

Danforth watched the storm pockets march across the screen like little legions, unable to bring himself to voice the affirmative. *Not yet. Not out loud.* But Weng's faint smile, as she steadied her slight body against the rising gusts, was like an invitation to join in some wonderful secret. Weng, a complication of hidden strengths, whose moral support had kept him sane during the recent weeks of his confinement, whose command he had resented enough to nearly kill himself in the process of insubordination. Danforth hoped there were a few corners of his soul that the Commander's bright black eyes could not see into.

And I called Ibiá a punk . . . he thought ruefully.

"Well, Dr. Danforth?"

"Appropriate, yes," he conceded. On the screen, the wind packets halted briefly as if awaiting orders, then altered course in phalanx. "But intent is in the eye of the beholder."

Weng's mildly raised eyebrow did not hide her satisfaction. "It was yourself who first ascribed intent, Dr. Danforth, as much as two weeks ago. 'Something's out there moving it around.' I believe I am quoting you correctly?"

"Metaphorically speaking, I meant," Danforth hedged.

"Ah. Metaphors." Weng eyed him sternly. "I thought perhaps you had more in mind. Well, then, let me tell you of a little metaphor that I have been playing with lately." She frowned slightly as Clausen's harsh shouts, aimed this time at McPherson, nibbled at her concentration.

"Noisy, isn't he," muttered Danforth. "What ever became of the velvet glove? Never thought I'd miss it."

Weng closed her eyes, opened them. "As you know, Dr. Danforth, I often exploit the principle of game theory in my musical compositions. Recently, I thought to apply those principles to your problem as well."

"My problem?" Danforth was momentarily distracted by ominous flickerings of the weather map. He touched a pleading hand to the screen. "Gods, CRI, don't crap out now."

"The x-factor. Your ad hoc."

"And?"

"Game theory is really number theory, yes? The analysis of coincidence. But if you think of the theory as being primarily about relationships, you can examine a given series of events as moves in a game, in order to detect patterns of motion among these events and with an eye to discovering what the object of those motions might be.''

"As I recall," Danforth countered, "Game theory does not postulate intent in that objective."

"No." Weng's smile was a forest of possibilities and her calm a steady island within the rising storm. "It is an analytical way of describing something that is happening—as in, 'here is a list of numbers, what do they have in common?'—and thus, speaking of the given series of events in terms of a game, of understanding what constitutes winning that game." She paused, but only for effect. "In light of the Sawls' own explanation for these events, I thought the metaphor particularly appropriate."

"What constitutes *winning*?" Danforth repeated, as if the idea had never occurred to him but had an increasingly reasonable currency.

"Do you know what the Sawls think constitutes winning?"

"Keep those tarps ready, McP!" Clausen stormed from the clearing. "Out, Tay. I need my console back."

"*Your* console?" Danforth grabbed the prospector's wrist as it reached for the keypad. "Hold on, man, look at what's going on out there!"

"Enough of your simulation games, Tay. I've got to worm the contents of that drone out of this computer before we lose her to the weather again."

Danforth's grip tightened. "That's what I mean! Look!"

Clausen snarled and levered his arm free of the bigger man's fist. "Move your crippled butt, Taylor, or I'll move it for you!" He grasped the wheels of Danforth's cart-chair, threatening to tip it. Danforth clung to the sideboards in mute outrage.

"You stop that!" McPherson flung herself at the cart to steady it. The Sawl ranger pulled up warily behind her.

"What the hell's your problem?" Danforth roared.

"I need this terminal!" Clausen stared straight at Weng, daring her to challenge him, then jerked his thumb at Danforth. "Get him out of here, McP. And stay ready to cover that dish!"

"In a pig's eye, Emil! Cover your own fuckin' dish!" McPherson pulled Danforth's chair out of Clausen's range and planted herself between them.

"That will do, Lieutenant," Weng advised, barely audible over the wind.

Clausen let his hand fall to the holstered gun on his belt, then swiveled back to his captured terminal with a mocking laugh. The three glared helplessly at his back while the hot wind leaned its weight against the Lander's hull. The metal trusswork groaned. The waiting Sawl ranger broke their deadlock with a shout. He pointed over the swaying fields toward the plain. The silhouette of the Vallegar was a distant darkness against the rosy sky, but a ruddy swirling mist hung over the plain.

"Jesus!" McPherson exclaimed.

"Dust storm," said Danforth. "A real mother. Batten the hatches."

Weng was silent for a moment, then said, a trace unsteadily, "Has it occurred to anyone to wonder where the market caravan is just now?"

At the terminal, Clausen exploded. "Sonofabitch! So that's his game!"

He flung the stool aside, and was racing across the clearing before anyone could think of trying to stop him.

Stavros pounded through the fourth-level tunnels at a dead run, with Edan a long step behind him and gaining. Liphar struggled to keep up, wasting needed breath on futile high-pitched remonstrance. The tunnels were deserted, the stone floor barely lit. One lamp in ten burned in the niches along the walls. The updraft was hot and smelled of dust. Edan made a grab for Stavros's back-pumping arm and missed.

"No go out, you!" Liphar yelled breathlessly.

"The Kav is dancing, Lifa!" Stavros shot back. The guar-heat in his palms strummed with the rhythm of his step. "And the fields! They'll need every available hand!"

Edan concentrated on gaining the extra step.

"Crazy, you!" Liphar panted.

"In this weather, they'll never even notice me!"

They sped through an empty residential district. A half-pace behind, Edan lunged for her quarry's naked shoulder. Her fingers slipped along his damp skin. She made a second grab for the loose folds of his pants.

Stavros swerved aside, beginning to enjoy the chase. He had had his fill of being cooped up in a stuffy hot cavern, and refused to miss any chance to see Kav Daven dance. He angled at an intersection, speeding toward the nearest cave mouth. The darkened entry to the Potters' Hall loomed up to one side. To the other, the tall doorway of the Glassblowers' Hall, framed by its glimmering hand-blown pilasters and arch. The tunnel slanted as the floor broke up into stairs. Stavros flew down steps too narrow for his stride, keeping his balance by a miracle. His face lit up with unholy joy as the dark walls warmed with the glow of dawn.

But he slowed at the foot of the steps when the cave mouth yawned in front of him and the full force of the dust-thick wind slammed into his face. His hesitation brought Edan down on top of him, spilling him to the floor. He rolled away to the wall but she rolled with him. Sweating body to sweating body, they grappled like wrestlers. Edan wrapped her arms around his chest and her legs around his knees, immobilizing him.

Stavros swore and struggled. Her strength took him by surprise. Her agility suggested that she had been trained for this. *Martial arts?* he wondered with a shock. *The Ranger Guild? Not just grown-up boy scouts but cops as well?* Intrigued with this new insight, he let himself be manhandled into a sitting position against the rock and regarded his captor with quizzical admiration as she eased her grip and settled herself between him and the cave mouth.

"Maybe you could teach me how to toss Clausen around like that the next time I see him." He dropped his head between his knees, glad for the chance to catch his breath.

Edan scowled, hearing Clausen's name. Her sullenness accused Stavros of making her job unnecessarily difficult. Liphar gained the bottom of the stairs and dropped to his knees at Stavros' side, his thin chest heaving. He coughed violently as he inhaled a lungful of dust.

"Ibi, please. No go, you."

"Lifa, I have to! So do you. We can't go to all this trouble and then let everyone die of starvation anyway! They need help down there in the fields. Oh my god, look at that!"

Stavros stared into the face of the yowling wind. Out on the Dop Arek, cloud-high columns were forming out of a swirling red mist. As broad as the legs of colossi, they marched across the distance, rank after rank, like an invading army, dwarfing the rocky spire of the sentinel Red Pawn, whose crown glowed with the first touch of morning sun. Overhead, the sky was pink and clear and charged with blue-white lightning.

Liphar's hand went to his talisman. He scrambled to the edge on hands and knees to stare outward in awe.

"O chukka desa!" he moaned, and raised the blue talisman to his trembling lips.

Edan heard the horror in his voice. Her head whipped around, her attention snared by the astonishing vision on the plain. Stavros seized his chance. He leaped up, evading her grasp as she whirled back and grabbed for him.

"Come on!" he shouted as he swept past Liphar and charged down the outer stairs.

On the Dop Arek, the ruddy dust thinned in a spasm of release like a gasp for breath. The tail end of the caravan ghosted

163

through the haze, tall wagons crossing a broad salt flat. A disarray of overladen hakra carts and families on foot struggled to keep up. The young scout hailed the stragglers and broke into a run.

"He goes to tell my sister," Ghirra remarked in an old man's voice, hoarse from thirst and the effort of making himself heard over the roar of the wind.

Susannah jiggled the canteen at her hip and hoped that the caravan had water enough to pass a little around. A hard salt crust crunched under their feet, glittering white stained with yellow.

Hurrying, they caught up to the line of carts. It unnerved Susannah to see the heat taking its toll so quickly. The hakra pushed forward gamely with eyes closed and tongues protruding. Some limped, leaving bloody trails across the brittle salt. Small children huddled together in the carts among piles of cloth-wrapped market goods. Adults and older children trudged alongside, their heads swaddled against the stinging sand. They greeted Ghirra and his party wordlessly, with nods and expressions of quiet fear, an occasional spasmodic cough, or a whimper from a child as the wind blew up again.

The bulk of the caravan had halted ahead. Arms waved and bodies plunged through the dust in a dreamlike chaos as the Rangers rushed to pull the wagons into tight rings around the giant FoodGuild wagons. The animals were unhitched without ceremony and hustled into the protective circles to mill about among the people and smaller carts, bleating unhappily. Guildsmen emptied their wagons, piling goods and cargo underneath.

The driver hauling the Sled drew up beside a FoodGuild wagon and immediately loosed his hjalk team from harness. The frantic caravaners took no notice of the Terran vehicle but hastened to lash it down along with everything else.

Ghirra led Megan and Susannah through the dust and noise, searching for Aguidran, for the Infirmary wagon, for the rest of his staff. They found the wagon first, just as the half-lit dawn broke open with another blast of sound and light. Susannah stumbled, momentarily blinded. The sound grew more audible as the light flashes brightened. Inside the ring, the older apprentices had finished the unloading. Ampiar, Phea and Dwingen scrambled around tying the wagon to its immediate neighbors, on one side a big Dyers' wagon, on the other the first of three from the Papermakers. Up in the driver's seat, Xifa looped rope through holes in the canvas flaps covering the opening, and drew them tight to the canopy. The contents of the wagon lay piled underneath, heavily shrouded and lashed to the wheels.

There was no time for reunion greetings. The lightning flashed again, blue-white and crackling. Ghirra sent them scurrying into the emptied wagon. They fastened the flaps and flattened themselves against the floorboards. The wind took a quantum leap as if lunging to the attack. It ran screeching among the fabric canopies to pounce on seams and mended tears and patches. The shuddering ring of wagons sang with the flap and shred of canvas.

The animals wailed. The panicked cries of men and women joined in as their shelters shredded around them. The wooden canopies squealed as aged ribs bent inward and patches of bright paint were sandblasted down to the naked grain.

Susannah huddled close to the wagon's sideboard, ears ringing, her face buried in Ghirra's hip, Dwingen shivering at her back. She clasped Megan's hand tightly. Dust blew in through every cranny.

The wagon shook as if seized by a demon fist. Outside, the wind yowled and the light blazed, leaving the tang of ozone in its wake. Wood splintered and a hjalk screamed.

Panic-stiffened fingers thrust through the split in the canvas behind the driver's seat. A woman's voice begged for help. Ghirra twisted around in the crowded interior to free the ropes fastening the flaps. A young woman shoved aside the canvas, tossed two small children into the wagon and disappeared just as Ghirra shouted to her to stay. The children were dazed and weeping. The older, a dark-haired boy, bled from a gash on his forehead. Susannah struggled to sit up, gathering a child under each arm. They clung tightly, unquestioning.

The lightning flared and flared again, burning jagged forks of heat and sound through the dust-choked air. The salt pan trembled with each hit. Shock waves shuddered through the hard ground. Susannah searched for some inner spot of calm where she might take refuge from the unrelenting roar and flash and crack. Ampiar's lips moved as she fingered her talisman bead.

Prayer? Susannah wondered, and considered the possibility herself.

A wrenching crash came with the next flash of light. With a pop and a roar, a wagon down the line burst into flame. Smoke cascaded into the Infirmary wagon. Shouts rang out, a call to action. Ghirra tore aside the flaps and leaped out. Ampiar and Xifa followed without hesitation. Little Dwingen squirmed out of Megan's grasp and vanished after them.

Susannah thrust the two children at Megan. She scrambled into the driver's seat to stare after Ghirra as he raced toward the wreckage. Loose canvas lashed at her face. The smoke and flying dust invaded her lungs. She pulled back as the lightning smashed into another wagon further off. She took a grim breath, then wrapped her sash about her face.

"No, for god's sake!" Megan clasped the weeping children.

Susannah paused, but could not sit still to the chorus of desperation building outside. She gave Megan the high sign and bolted from the wagon before she could change her mind.

She hit the ground as it was jolted by another strike. The scent of charred flesh sent her spine crawling.

A dead hjalk lay to one side of the ring. Its fellows herded along the far side, away from the smoke and leaping flames. Human injured lay scattered across the hot ground, some moaning, some not moving at all. Parents clutched their children while the merchants rushed to save their hard-won goods.

The Rangers had cut loose the precious water kegs and piled them in the center. Susannah ran toward the fire, saw Ghirra's lean form silhouetted against the bright heat, then Xifa and others, pulling burning bodies out of the flaming wagon. Guildsmen tore at the ropes fastening the wagon to its neighbors. A woman snatched up a shred of blackened canvas to beat out sparks landing on nearby wagons. A man grabbed up a water keg from the side of a Potters' Guild wagon and prepared to bash one end in with a stick.

A Ranger charged at him and caught his upraised arm. He jerked the stick away, shoving the man aside. The man screeched his outrage from the ground, then scrambled up and fled. The burning wagon was hauled from the ring, but too late. Its canopy collapsed in a wind-whirled shower of sparks. Flaming splinters spilled onto the second Papermakers' wagon. The cargo underneath burst into an instant fireball as the guildsmen ran to rescue it. The heat made it unapproachable. The Rangers ordered it left to burn while the third wagon was cleared from the ring to leave a fire break. The Infirmary wagon was next down the line.

Susannah found Ampiar kneeling beside a badly burned man. She took a quick look, then raced back to the wagon for her medikit. The wind beat at her, trying to throw her against the wheels. The third Papermakers' wagon was now aflame. Hot cinders flew in Susannah's face. She glanced upward to see sparks catching in the Infirmary wagon's canopy.

Someone brushed by her, running. The thick smoke and dust made it impossible to see. Someone small, a child, swung up on the wagon's tall rear wheel and grasped at the exterior frame of the canopy, scaling toward the top.

By the daylight brilliance of the next flash, Susannah saw Dwingen clinging like a monkey to the crossbar with a strip of canvas shoved into his belt. He grappled, his little legs scrabbling for purchase, then with an enormous effort, he hauled himself up onto the canopy's rounded crown. He lay for a moment face down among the flying sparks, panting.

Susannah screamed at him to come down, pleading into the wind and the fire roar until she thought her throat would tear and bleed. But Dwingen wrapped one end of the cloth around his small fist and struggled to his knees, swaying, fighting the gale. He beat at the burning cinders and the little nests of new flame rising from the bone dry wood. Lightning lit up the smoke billows around him, danced in hard blue threads above his head. He mistook Susannah's screaming and glanced down with a wave and a bright brave smile. Then, intent on his mission, he braced himself and rose unsteadily to his feet. The lightning crackled, a forked snake's tongue, searching. Susannah heard an anguished yell as Ghirra raced past, grasped the rim of the wheel and vaulted upward.

"Get down!" Susannah screamed at the boy. "Ghirra, tell him to lie flat!"

As Ghirra reached for the crossbar, Aguidran was there suddenly, a blur of motion out of the smoke. She threw herself at the wagon to pin her brother's legs in the vise of her arms. Ghirra clung to the framework, raging at her to let him go, but she dug in her heels and pulled, breaking his hold. Ghirra called out desperately to Dwingen, his arms flailing. As brother and sister tumbled to the ground, the next searing bolt found the child standing erect and proud at the top of the wagon.

Dwingen stiffened, frozen in light. His delicate face stretched into a mask of surprise. Blue diamonds danced in his ringleted hair. He hung spreadeagled in the air, impervious at last to the wind's buffeting, held by a power greater than the wind, suffused with its blue-white dazzle.

Then he crumpled to the canopy.

Aguidran scrambled up, leaped up on the wheel rim and stretched to grasp a limp ankle that flopped down around the curving wagon top. She hauled the boy's body into her arms and handed him down to Ghirra. The physician laid him gently on the ground. Though the boy's eyes gaped open and empty, he put his head to his chest and his hands to the thin neck, searching frantically for a pulse.

Susannah shook herself free of her shock and fumbled in her medikit for adrenaline while Ghirra began his own version of CPR. The boy's hair was singed and smoking, his skin blackened with char. As she knelt with the hypo, Susannah knew it was too late.

Crouched on the other side of the little body, Aguidran made no excuse or apology. She watched the tears wet Ghirra's face as he strove to restore some small sign of life to his dead apprentice. Her stern eyes held only sad relief, recognition of a bargain made with fate, not happily but without question, unless it could have been herself given in Dwingen's place in return for her brother's life.

At length, Ghirra slumped back, his hands fisting in exhausted frustration. As he reached to close the boy's eyes, his touch was a gentle last caress.

Susannah brushed at her own tears. "A valiant try, doctor."

Ghirra stared at his hands as if they had betrayed him.

Aguidran rose and left them without a word. The dust and smoke closed around her with weakening fury. The flicker of the flames dimmed as the softer pink of dawn penetrated the black haze.

Susannah looked up, saw clear sky, and prayed that the storm was over. But it was not. Through the blackened ribs of a burning wagon, she saw the ranks of giant dust columns advancing across the plain like Moses's pillar of fire in the wilderness.

"Oh god, Ghirra . . . what do we do now?"

21

The wind fought to smash Stavros against the cliff face as he hurtled down the outer stair. Hot dust clogged his eyes and lungs, tore mercilessly at his skin.

Surely they won't let him out to dance in this?

He risked a glance away from the treacherous sand-swept steps to gauge the dust legion's yowling approach across the infant dawn. The brief pink light was fading behind a swirl of murk. Stavros mocked the futility of his bravura gesture.

Save the crops? What'll be left of them after this?

He thought that the possibility of slow starvation in the shelter of the Caves might just be preferable to the certainty of being flayed alive out in the open, once the wind wound itself up to the strength promised by the massive towers thundering across the plain.

The guar-fire pulsed gently in his palms. He could feel but not hear the slap of his bare feet against the gritty stone. He had the sensation of falling through the storm, wind-tossed, sinking through noise and turbulence, drowning in dust. The rough cliff threatened at his side. He imagined his limbs splashed flailing against the rock like a breaking wave. He raced past the first of the third-level entries. Edan's throaty shout reached after him from above, echoed by Liphar's shriller pleas. Stavros twisted onto the next descending switchback and continued his headlong free-fall down the stair.

The tall, arching caves of the second level loomed ahead. The stable entries gaped emptily. The storm roared through every crevice, pelting Stavros with the odor of dried manure and a thousand tiny javelins of wind-driven straw. He slowed along the ledge, head lowered, running almost blind as the dust blotted out the last pale ray of dawn. He stumbled and slid several heart-freezing meters, found himself by fortunate accident at the head of the next stair.

He caught a glimpse of the fields through the haze of sand. A handful of FoodGuilders scurried about below, bravely attempting a task that would have tried the resources of the entire Guild, were they present and available. Barely a third of the tall red stalks had been bundled into protective sheafs. The terraces reflected the ruddy cast of the air as the lower-lying crops were flooded with countless precious gallons from the irrigation reservoirs. Stavros was sure the pipes had burst, then understood that a layer of water was the only available defense against the dust-laden gusts that were already ripping at the leaf stalks and tearing up roots.

He gained the first-level ledge where the widening stair took its final downward turn. A glance over his shoulder showed Edan gaining in her pursuit. But he hesitated at the head of the stair. A sound cut through the wind roar, a high-pitched reedy wail that snatched familiarly at his attention. Stavros let his ears follow it back along the ledge.

Kav Daven.

He turned, searching the first-level openings. The once-symmetrical shapes framed darkness with the ragged outlines of age and weather.

Empty, empty . . . where is he?

He followed the sound along the ledge, squinting into the murk. At the far western end, he discovered a small crowd gathered before the oldest cave mouth. From out of their midst, the wail rose and fell with the rush of the wind.

Stavros ran toward them, reaching the outer ranks of the gathering just as Edan pounded up behind him. She scowled at him furiously, but he gave her only an abstracted nod and eased himself intently among the observers. He sensed her crowding at his back, herding him toward the safety of the inner cave, but when he could see into the middle of the gathering, he stopped and would not be moved further.

Kav Daven danced in the center, his blind eyes closed. He was already well into the height of his chant-trance. His bony arms were raised high, as rigid as sticks. He whirled like a dervish in ever widening circles, chanting and wailing. A single anxious priest labored with three elderly FoodGuilders and a frantic apprentice girl to form a protective arc around the heedless ancient, keeping him from the edge and the worst of the wind's ravages.

A few of the watchers dutifully mouthed the priest's chant, their brown fingers telling blue talisman beads. But their faces held little hope. Feeling the old priest's familiar pull, Stavros edged forward. Edan's strong fingers closed hard on his arm. He let her draw him back against the wall, knowing it would not matter where in the crowd he stood.

Like iron to a magnet, he thought, *myself the raw ore and he the source.* For the first time since the Leave-taking, the ghostly heat in his palms flared into pain. He was unsurprised when the axis of the watchers shifted and the Ritual Master's whirlings flowed in his direction. Though Stavros' repeated ponderings had not yet deciphered it, there was a message in Kav Daven's "choosings," an unvoiced charge laid on him by the miracle of his unburned hands.

Kav Daven danced closer. His brown face was serene but for the fluttering of his eyelids, as rapid as bees' wings. Liphar arrived panting as the crowd backed off from the old priest's whirling approach. Edan's grip on Stavros' arm relaxed hesitantly.

Stavros stood as if rooted to the rock. His skin prickled to the faint brush of Power, come and gone as casually as if shouldering past him in the crowd. A scent of chaos remained behind, curling like smoke into his nostrils. The watchers remained silent, unmoved, and Stavros knew that this moment of mysticism was, like the last, between the old priest and himself alone.

Kav Daven drew his astonishing circles tighter and tighter until his frail, knobby body spun like a child's top, emitting a high, musical whine, his leaf-brown garments flying, his stick arms clenched to his ribs. His eyelids shivered. His lips drew back from his yellowed teeth. The dance was too frantic, too desperate. Though he knew the old man could not see him, Stavros raised his hands in front of him, palms erect, a silent ceremonial entreaty that he slow his mad revolutions.

Kav Daven stopped, and faced him squarely.

Edan's quick intake of breath was as audible as if the wind had ceased with the old priest's motion. Liphar murmured in awe. Stavros' palms burned. He sensed the storm bearing down inexorably, felt it tear at his hair and clothing. But he was wrapped in a circle of quiet with Kav Daven at its center. The fire in his hands flared until he was sweating and rigid with pain. But he kept them raised before him as he knew he must. His instinctive gesture had stopped the priest's whirlings. It was somehow correct.

He had learned on the day of his miracle, as the guar seared into his flesh, to envelop the pain, to make it a part of him, as the priests did who carried the guar bare-handed from the mines. He knew he would bear the pain gladly for the sake of an answer, to win from Kav Daven a clearer understanding of his miracle. He felt a responsibility had been laid like a cloak on his shoulders, but could not read its size or shape.

Kav Daven waited, milky blind eyes staring a clear plea into his.

What does he want of me?

His inadequacy devastated him, but he kept his hands raised, absorbing their increasing agony now as punishment, now as reward. The pain cycled through him like a feedback loop, building fire on fire but simultaneously energizing his resistance.

Kav Daven approached. He flattened his own hands against Stavros' palms. The silken scarred flesh was cooling to their heat. His pain drew back, as if in respect.

"Tell me, Kav," he murmured. "Teach me. Please."

Sudden fire seared past his cheek, a breath of pure lightning. Minute needles bit into his skin. Edan grunted. Stavros felt her shift and glance around in confusion. Suspicion nagged his brain, then wavered, as he blamed an oddity of the storm and held his stance, palm to palm with Kav Daven, willing calm and concentration to hold him fast to this long-sought moment of communion.

The fire scorched past again, closer, too discrete and silent for lightning. Rock spatter sprayed the back of his neck. He smelled hair burning, his own. The suspicion bloomed, stupidly, too slowly.

A Sawlish oath rang in his ear and the circle of silence shattered. Stavros dropped his hands and stared over Kav Daven's bony shoulder. The crowd erupted in confusion as Emil Clausen shoved his way through.

"Wait!" Stavros pushed in front of Kav Daven, his hands spread. "I'm here! Goddamnit, Clausen, you'll kill someone!"

Clausen eyed him incredulously over the laser's silver nose.

"How kind of you to oblige me, Ibiá," he drawled, and levelled the pistol at Stavros's head.

Stavros was still framing his reply when Clausen fired. Edan's arm whipped around his waist as fast as a snake strike, hauling him down and away. Falling, too startled to resist, Stavros looked for Kav Daven through the scrambling frightened crowd. The old priest's arms reached out to empty space. Stavros stumbled and the needle beam nicked his ear. He smelled ozone and the reek of charred skin. Edan dragged him to his feet with a snarl. Her quick response astonished him. He was unable to remain so cool.

"You goddamn maniac!" he raged at the prospector.

But Edan shoved his head low and pulled him behind the bewildered crowd. He lost sight of the old Ritual Master, then glimpsed Liphar fighting through the confusion. "Lifa! The Kav! Get him out of here!"

Stavros prayed that Clausen was not crazy enough to shoot through bystanders to get at him. He yelled again to Liphar and ran, ducking, for the rear of the cave, searching the darkness for a tunnel, for steps.

Shouts collided behind him, Clausen's warnings in bellowed Sawlish, a guildsman's outraged reply. Loping at his elbow, Edan hissed a direction into his wounded ear. Stavros swerved left in automatic response. The rock wall beside them exploded in a shower of grit and light.

Christ!

Clausen had lengthened the laser's pulse. Stavros ran for his life.

The next bolt laid his left shoulder open, slicing deep through layers of muscle and bone.

The force of the hit knocked him sprawling across the stone. Stavros tucked and rolled before he hit the wall and his momentum brought him staggering back to his feet, already running again, running for the dark of the stair ahead.

Edan swore and pushed madly at his back. His arm flapped uselessly at his side, threatening his balance. He feared the pain might cripple him, but the shoulder stayed mercifully numb. His guar-fire had deserted him. He felt only a creeping weakness in his legs as he pumped desperately for the stairs. A wash of terror as cold as sea water knotted his groin.

"Fucker's gonna kill me," he gasped to Edan, as if saying it made the unreal real and somehow comprehensible. "This time I'm gonna die."

The staircase was old and crumbling. The footing would have been perilous even in full light, but Stavros thanked the concealing darkness. The sounds of Clausen's pursuit were submerged in the pounding of his own feet and heart. He could not see Edan, but her hand stayed firm against his back as they scrambled up the ragged stairs.

At the top, she balked and veered aside, hauling him with her. Footsteps too frenzied to be Clausen's clattered through the rock debris on the steps behind them. Stavros hoped it was Liphar, still in one piece.

Ahead, a slash of light bled across a yawning stable cavern. It was faint but enough to illuminate them if they ventured into it, a barrier as effective as a moat. Edan drew him swiftly through the darkness along the wall. She grabbed him to point him across the cavern toward the warren of inner barns, muttering at the ominous warmth wetting his tunic. Her whisper was harsh. She put a hand to his head to be sure of his nod, then shoved him forward and bolted into the open beside him.

Laser fire lanced across the cavern, one, two deadly beams only slightly wide of their shadowy mark. Stavros ran a crooked path and gained the darkness of the warrens. The numbness was fading. Each jarring leap awoke a sharper pain. A stickiness clung to his back and ribs and pulled at his seared flesh. He wondered how much blood he was losing.

He dodged blindly through the unlit corridors lined with empty stalls. He had lost Edan in crossing the big cavern. He missed the pressure of her guiding hand on his back. He listened for her step, heard only his own and that lighter following patter, now pulling breathlessly alongside him.

"Lifa?"

Liphar's whisper was desperate. "Go fast, Ibi! No stop you!"

"Edan?"

"She wait, make surprise there for Clauzen." The young man snatched at Stavros' arm. "This way, you!"

"Lifa, I'm hurt."

It's not the pain, he thought. *Pain I can deal with. But it's too soon to feel this weak. Ah god, Susannah!*

"Who's left in Physicians'? I need a doctor."

"Yes," Liphar whimpered and hurried him along more insistently. They wound through the maze of stalls, turning finally onto a narrow upward ramp. The incline was slippery with dust, so steep that Stavros moaned through gritted teeth at the effort of climbing and slowed so as not to collapse. Liphar helped him struggle to the top, gamely supporting his weight, alarmed by the hollow rattle in his chest.

The upper corridor was lit by a single lamp in a niche beside huge double doors. Through blurring eyes, Stavros recognized the carved portal of the Woodworkers' Hall. Down the tunnel to the left, tall columns framed the entry to the PriestHall. Liphar shot across the corridor to haul on Woodworkers' giant panelled doors. He gestured Stavros to hurry.

Inside the hall, he barred the doors. Stavros leaned against them with eyes closed, resisting the blackness that reached out to him from within.

"Lifa, please, is there water?"

Liphar made a quick blind search of the darkened guildhall and returned with a half-filled jug. Stavros's hands would not work to grip the handles. Murmuring worriedly, Liphar held the jug while Stavros gratefully gulped stale water.

"Better," he lied hoarsely, but Liphar took him at his word and urged him to be moving again.

Stavros let himself be led among the empty worktables to the far end of the guildhall. Liphar eased open another carved wooden door. Dim light leaked through the crack. He stuck a cautious head into the corridor, then ventured out. Stavros followed, sliding his good hand along the wall for support. The corridor seemed suddenly wide and bright. Opposite, the doorless archway to Keth-Toph was invitingly dark.

Liphar nodded at it. Stavros returned the nod and pushed himself away from the wall.

They heard Clausen move at the end of the corridor, a stone rolling under his boot as he took aim. Liphar shouted. Stavros bolted for the darkened arch with Liphar tight at his heels. Hot lightning lanced past their ears. They ran through the entry hall and into the storehouse tunnels, past silent looming ranks of crates and shelves. At the end of a long tunnel, Liphar grabbed at Stavros's belt.

"Ibi! Wait, you!" He screeched to a halt, feeling in the dark for the upright support of a heavily laden shelf. Stavros turned back to lend what little strength he could. They heaved and grunted, and a twelve-foot block of shelves tipped and collapsed. Behind them, Clausen roared as tall jars of oil and bundles of lamp wick cascaded into the narrow aisle, shattering pottery, spilling gallons of thick lamp oil. The laser was knocked from the prospector's hand, his shot deflected.

Liphar contained his triumph to a shuddering sigh of relief and shoved Stavros down the next tunnel.

In Keth-Toph's vast RoundHall, a single dim blue flame glowed in the great wheel suspended above the central guild table. Liphar dashed ahead toward a remote corner behind the rendering cauldrons, where the smoothly sculpted curve of the

hall was broken by a series of natural rifts. He vanished into the
third in the row, then peered out again.

"Ibi! Hurry you!"

Stavros stumbled across the hall. Deep in the shadow of the
rift, a low hole pierced the rock, a hidden shaft barely the
diameter of a small man's shoulders. Liphar pointed to it eagerly.

"You go, ah? You go, then I go next."

Stavros shuddered, a moment of weakness. Breathing was an
agony. His head rang, his shoulder was on fire. He was unsure
he would fit in the narrow shaft. But the vicious clatter of broken
pottery echoed across the hall as Clausen fought to clear a path
through their impromptu barricade. It would not hold him for
long.

Stavros shook his head, willing the return of clarity. He
dropped to his knees and crawled trembling into the shaft. A
cool draft touched him with blessed moisture. The inner surface
was finely ribbed, like corduroy. Several meters inward, the
shaft turned and widened. It was faintly luminous and greenish
like glass. With his knees and his good elbow, Stavros dragged
himself forward at a snail's pace. Pain flared in his shoulder as it
knocked and scraped against the shaftway.

"How far, Lifa?" he rasped, dizzy and struggling.

"Very soon, ah?" Liphar returned urgently.

A last effort, thought Stavros. *I can manage that.*

But sensation was receding before a new tide of numbness,
spreading inward from his outer limbs. Distantly, he wondered if
he was already dying.

*Isn't this how it goes when you're bleeding to death? This
creeping chill, this weakness, this . . . fog?*

He felt himself slipping toward nonexistence as quietly as into
sleep.

Am I moving at all?

He forced a memory of motion into his legs and begged them
to respond. His body jerked forward, an inch, a precious foot,
almost by will alone. The pale glow of the shaftway framed a
round darkness ahead but he knew it could be a failure of his
vision. Not the ending of the shaftway, but his own ending. He
was sure that the corduroy glass was increasingly slippery, that it
was melting without benefit of heat, liquifying, pooling around
him. He sensed it swell and begin to turn, a vast maelstrom with
the slow patience of a galaxy, spinning him toward the dark void
at its heart.

"No stop, you!" Liphar grasped his unfeeling leg and shook
it.

Stavros nodded, or thought he did, as the slow maelstrom

spun him away. A worry for Edan slid through his brain as the last light faded, like a specter in a mist, calling for him to wake. But it was too late. He had already given himself to the relief of darkness.

Liphar felt Stavros stall and go limp.

"Ibi?"

He shook the slack leg harder, whimpering at the chill dead weight of it. He squeezed himself forward in the narrow shaft and pushed at the bulk of Stavros's body, easily twice as heavy as his own. "Ibi!"

He strained determinedly, muttering encouragements as if Stavros were listening, and bit by bit, his burden inched along the glassy curve. The circle of blackness ahead broadened into a perceptible opening, the end of the shaftway. When he could push no longer, Liphar rested, his face pressed against Stavros's still back, taking reassurance from the faint but continuing heartbeat. When his thin chest had stopped heaving, he renewed his efforts, until the opening was within reach. He grasped the outer rim and hauled himself past Stavros into the room beyond.

It was a long, domed space, its far end diffused with gentle bluish light. A pair of tall doors dominated one long wall. The cool dimness smelled of moisture and ash, and sighed with the soft plash of falling water.

Shaking with the effort, Liphar wrapped his arms around Stavros's chest and pulled him out of the shaft onto a smoothly tiled floor, dragging him in to a secluded corner away from the shaft opening. His hands came away wet as he laid the body out, gently as he could, and sat back on his heels. He tore off his tunic and folded it to pillow Stavros's head, then dashed off toward the soft blue light.

He returned with wet cloth and a lantern, which he lit as he knelt again at Stavros' side. Gingerly he touched the damp fabric to the wound. The burnt smell and the blackened weeping flesh frightened him. The elementary first aid taught to every Sawl child did not cover this nasty sort of Terran hurt that was both a burn and a slash. He knew he must above all stop the bleeding. He sacrificed his blousy pants, tearing them into strips to wrap the damaged shoulder as tightly as he dared.

One clean strip he retained to wipe a dark smear of blood from Stavros's face. Then he wiped his own, and his hands, sitting helplessly wiping and wiping at himself until the tears he had held back overtook him silently. He put his face in his hands. His thin shoulders heaved. But soon he straightened and roughly brushed his tears away, muttering apologies to Stavros, scolding himself for his weakness when what mattered was finding help. He blew out the lantern and rose. He gave Stavros a last grieving look, then loped across the room and slipped noiselessly through the huge double doors.

The outer hall was vast and silent. Ruddy dawnlight drifted from a high clerestory to settle like dust on a marble floor patterned with interlocking circles. Stern jewel-eyed figures of the Goddesses stared down from wall-sized friezes that marched the full length of the hall.

Liphar sped through the silence, pulling up at a wide ramphead to peer cautiously downward. Satisfied, he descended the long slope and dashed across the open plaza at the bottom. He paused briefly at a stone trough in the center. The spring was low but the water chill and clear. He splashed his face and his naked blood-streaked chest, then gulped several hurried handfuls. The gurgle of the water echoed loudly across the still plaza. Liphar retreated in haste past the deserted shops of the MarketHall, down a long, dim corridor, toward another descending ramp. He exchanged caution for speed as he drew further away from where he had hidden his injured fugitive. He met no one on the way but slowed again as he slipped into the tunnel to the PriestHall. Suddenly he flinched and shrank against the wall.

Lantern light bobbed around the turn at the end of the corridor. Someone was coming up from the cave mouth.

The mammoth carved doors of the Woodworkers' Hall faced him uselessly, so recently barred by himself from the inside. Liphar fled down the corridor, seeking shelter in the PriestHall archway. He did a small midair skip of elation when he heard Sawl voices accompanying the approaching light. He ran on to meet them, already chattering his urgency.

Two worried FoodGuilders rounded the corner, lanterns in hand, deep in discussion. A senior priest and the girl apprentice followed, supporting Kav Daven between them. The Kav's blind eyes were wide. He struggled fitfully against his companions' benevolent restraint. The girl crooned a low voiced chant to sooth his distraction.

Liphar called out, speeding toward them as a shadow materialized in the darkened entry to the PriestHall. Clausen lunged into the corridor, corralling the fleeing Sawl with an elbow clamped around his neck. Liphar was jerked off his feet, slammed hard against the prospector's hip and held tight. Clausen wiped his hand across the young man's damp chest and rubbed the bloodstain into his fingertips.

"So, my young friend, what mess have you been into?"

Liphar flopped about like a hooked fish, screeching for help.

177

"Where is he?" Clausen hissed at his ear.

The two FoodGuilders shouted and ran forward with their lanterns raised. The little laser flashed in Clausen's free hand, shattering the rock at their feet.

The FoodGuilders froze in terror. Kav Daven ceased his distracted struggles. His back stiffened. His high voice rang down the corridor, bell-like, a curt demand to the struggling Liphar.

Liphar blinked, gasping for breath. The Kav had spoken in ritual OldWords. He answered him with a stammering flood of the ancient words that were never used except in priestly celebrations. Clausen snarled and tightened his vice-hold on the young man's throat. Liphar gagged and cried out, and the older FoodGuilder blew out his lantern. The younger lobbed his at Clausen's head. The prospector sidestepped the fiery missile neatly. Glass flew. Burning oil splashed against the rock. Flames rose and died. The laser flashed wide in the sudden darkness. Clausen backed down the hall, dragging Liphar with him.

Silence settled in the blackened corridor. Face pressed to the floor, the elder guildsman hissed a query. The other answered breathlessly. Behind them, the senior priest groaned and stirred. The apprentice girl called to Kav Daven, softly at first, then more urgently when she received no reply. The two guildsmen listened to the rustling sounds of her searching in the darkness, then cautiously, the elder struck a spark and relit his lantern.

Clausen was gone, and Liphar with him. Smoking oil pooled among broken glass and ceramic on the floor. The senior priest struggled to sit up. His horrified exclamation brought the FoodGuilders to their feet.

In the middle of the corridor, the apprentice girl knelt stunned and empty-handed. Kav Daven had vanished.

22

The dust towers roared across the dawning Dop Arek, Lagri's legions marching out of the dry, dark southwest, advancing on Valla's mountain stronghold. The wind noise rose in the ravines like the screams of the damned. The flood courses filled with blowing sand and shards of shattered vegetation as the wind soldiers swept by in disciplined ranks.

A frail old man threaded an astonishing path through the vast moving grid of turbulence.

He followed a broken rhythm of scurry, halt, wait and scurry again, like a wise stray dog wading through speeding traffic. The heat parched his ancient wrinkles. His eyes squeezed shut against the bite of the sand. But the wind merely toyed with his leaf-brown garments, while five meters in either direction, an advancing vortex ground pebbles into gravel and brittle stems into dust.

The old man carried no food or water. His lips moved in a soundless chant. He stumbled once and kept going, as the first volleys of lightning arced above his bare head. He headed northeast, with the army as his escort, straight into the heart of the battle.

23

When the wind ceased tearing at his protective tarp, Danforth lifted a corner and squinted out past the dark trusswork of the landing strut. The hot air was still thick with dust but the rear guard of the storm had wreked its havoc among the planted terraces and passed on toward the central Dop Arek and the mountains beyond. The slow pink dawn returned as the air cleared. The sun had not yet shown above the horizon. The fields around the Lander looked like a deserted game of giants' pick-up sticks.

Danforth coughed. He raised himself on his elbows, spat out some grit, swallowed a lot more. On the other side of the strut, a tarp wrinkled and fell back in sandy folds as McPherson sat up, shaking her head like a dog.

"Tay? You okay?"

Danforth nodded, glancing around. "Commander?"

Weng unwound the silverfilm blanket she had wrapped herself in Indian-style, huddled cross-legged against the angled truss. She untied her dust mask, a scrap of Sawlish linen, and delicately blotted her face.

"Unreal," Danforth muttered inadequately.

Weng murmured her assent.

McPherson stretched. "Shit. Look at those fields."

Weng uncorked a water bottle and passed it around.

Danforth felt precariously close to a final loss of faith in the unerring logic of natural processes. He threw off the hot tarp and struggled to pull himself upright along the crossbars of the landing truss, thrusting his cast-bound leg beneath him as a lever and support. McPherson scrambled up to help him.

"Better uncover the dish," he said gruffly. "We ought to see if we can raise CRI."

"Sure." She backed off and brought him his makeshift wheel-chair without comment, then trotted away to check on the dish. Danforth lowered himself stiffly into the chair and wheeled across the sand-drifted Underbelly to the lashed and shrouded computer table. Weng helped him untie the wind-tightened knots, then drew the silvery plastic aside and stood with it awkwardly balled up in her arms as if reluctant to set it anywhere that it might not be immediately available.

"Ron, what's the word out there?" Danforth called.

"Seems okay to me," came the reply. "Give her a try."

CRI came back on line with a vengeance, inquiring after everyone's health and the condition of the equipment, demanding first-hand visual data to supplement her instrument record of the storm. She could offer no information on the welfare of the trade caravan, but reported that vast lightning-sparked brush fires were sweeping many areas of the habitable zone, among them the dry Dop Arek.

"But who won the war?" Danforth joked sourly.

"A mere battle, surely, Dr. Danforth," Weng reproved.

CRI added without hesitation, "Upon consideration of the data, matched with Mr. Ibiá's files, I would have to award the victory to Lagri."

"Lagri?"

"One of the two Sister-Goddesses," Weng reminded him. "The fiery one. You've noted the PriestGuild seal? A flame suspended over water?"

"Fire and water." Danforth pursed his lips, staring off into the distance. "Heat and moisture . . ." He shrugged helplessly. "Okay. Let's just go with this . . . this preposterousness for a moment: that would make it Lagri controlling the heat and the other, whatsisname . . ."

"Her name. Valla Ired."

"Her, then. She's got the water end of the thing. And each uses her gig as a weapon against the other. Jesus. That's one hell of an X-factor. Pretty neat, if you could believe it."

"Er, Commander . . . ?" McPherson padded back into the Underbelly. "I think maybe you oughta . . . they're doing something weird out there."

180

The little pilot pointed. A solemn crowd of Sawls was collecting along the ravaged perimeter of the Lander clearing. Their numbers swelled rapidly as one by one, the entire home guard filed down the dusty path from the Caves or appeared from out of the broken fields. Their grouping was informal, most sitting, some kneeling or crouching, others standing, but all faced the Lander with a silence that was neither grim nor threatening but, rather, bewildered.

McPherson squinted, pointed again. "Look. Over to the right."

A dark shape lay in a stretcher on the ground in front of the gathering. It was too distant to be recognizable in the still-dim dawn, but all three knew they shared the same instant worry.

Danforth grunted. "Whatever it is, doesn't look very alive."

McPherson brushed her damp brow with a forearm, wet her lips nervously. "Better go see, huh?"

Weng nodded. The two officers started across the clearing together, the tall old woman suiting her pace to the obviously somber moment.

Danforth put CRI on hold and wheeled himself to the edge of the Lander's overhang. His sweating palms were slippery on the wooden wheels.

Christ. Don't tell me the kid's actually bought it? It had to be now, when I really need him?

He wiped his hands on his damp T-shirt, more disturbed than he could make sense of. He stared up at the looming wall of the cliff, stained with the salmon blush of dawn. If this was Ibiá, brought down dead or dying by the mourning Sawls, where the hell was Clausen?

Damn, the kid didn't deserve this!

Danforth shoved the crippling bulk of his cast against the side of the chair, cursing his helplessness and vulnerability. Not only the weather, but events, too, had stopped making sense. He missed the comforting texture of reality. He imagined he could actually see it fading behind the wavering curtains of heat that were cutting them off from each other, and each from the dust-dry landscape. He sniffed, smelling distant smoke. Weng's lecture about the Coal Sack floated to mind, along with an image of the planet consumed in fire.

Perhaps when that sun finally does roll over the horizon, it'll be swelled up on us, engorged like a tick, sucking up atmospheres, cannibalizing its own system.

"This heat," he muttered. "This bitching heat!"

Weng and McPherson neared the edge of the clearing. McPherson ran the last few steps, as if in surprise. She dropped to

181

her knees beside the stretcher, her puzzled voice ringing clearly in the silence.

"It's Edan! I know this one. She's Aguidran's top tracker. I thought she went out with the caravan."

Danforth watched her bend over the still form.

"I think she's dead, Commander."

Danforth shut his eyes in guilty relief. *Not Ibiá, then. Not yet.*

But the thin veneer of civilization was crumbling, sure enough. Melting with the planet into the maddening heat.

McPherson sat back on her heels and spread her arms sadly at the nearest Sawl. "What happened?"

The seamy-faced ranger who had come down earlier to warn them about the storm thrust himself through the crowd. "Clauzen," he accused, his voice dark with outrage. Around him, the others murmured, as if his forthright anger made them uneasy.

McPherson turned to Weng. "What do we do, Commander?"

"Clearly we need to hear the full story," Weng replied steadily.

"Which you will, Commander," came Clausen's voice from behind the crowd. The Sawls drew back instinctively. He strode down the path dragging a half-naked and frightened Liphar in firm tow. "Just as soon as I take care of one little detail."

The prospector's bearded face showed no anger or passion, only a chill, almost weary determination. Weng stepped in front of him.

"I'd like to hear it now, Mr. Clausen, if you don't mind."

Clausen stopped with a shrug, as if chatting with a customs official over some questionable imports. "Sure, fine. Not at all. I'd spotted Ibiá up in the Caves and nearly had my hands on him, when that young woman jumped me in the dark. I reacted, ah, in kind."

McPherson bolted to her feet. "You broke her fucking *neck*!"

Clausen nodded soberly, looked to Weng, experience appealing to experience. "A regrettable accident, Commander."

Weng's reply was steely. "Regrettable, indeed, Mr. Clausen." She nodded at Liphar, whose eyes pleaded in misery and terror. "And what may I ask are you doing to this poor child?"

"Ah yes. Very simple." Clausen seemed to have just remembered the boy held in his iron grasp. "He's hidden Ibiá up there, and I intend to find out where."

"I don't think so, Mr. Clausen. You are under arrest for murder."

Clausen smiled tightly and jerked Liphar toward the Lander. "I'd like to see you make that one stick, Commander."

Danforth told himself he had always known killing would come easily to Clausen, and wondered why the actuality left him stunned. He watched the prospector drag his prisoner across the dusty clearing. The Sawls settled back into their eerie passive vigil beside the dead ranger's body. Weng stared after Clausen, as still and palely erect as a marble statue.

Danforth swivelled his awkward chair and wheeled back to the equipment table as fast as he could manage.

"CRI, get me Captain Newman. We've got a big problem down here," he began in a harsh whisper. His ears monitored Clausen's rapid approach at his back, but his eyes were drawn to the thick black smoke rising from the bright line of fire advancing almost as quickly from across the plain.

"A real big problem . . ."

24

Stavros heard water, falling softly, like rain or sleep.

In vain, this dying, but not alone, at least.

His first coherent thought in many hours was at once submerged in a noise of pain that drowned out thinking. He struggled to think again, to hear the thought through the noise. And there was one about a way to master pain, a Connection to be made, a Power waiting to be tapped. Sometimes he heard a voice advising him, but the words were singsong and the lesson unintelligible, lost with his thought in the din and the shimmering haze of fever and the sinking into nothingness.

Kav Daven's young apprentice girl sat at Stavros' side untiringly. The long hall glowed dimly, almost cool. At the far end, a slim, glassy cylinder shimmered in a column of water that rose from the center of a tiled pool. The cylinder enclosed an unwavering spear of pale blue light. The water soared, crested and fell back to sing its gentle falling music on the surface of the pool.

The girl rewetted the cloth pressed to the dying man's forehead and changed the iced herbal dressings on his shoulder.

His torn flesh rebelled with purulence and heat. Fever raged.

The elderly Master Herbalist Ard sat cross-legged on the cool tiles for long hours, watching, pondering new strategies to combat the infection.

Stavros floated in and out of consciousness. In his fever dreams, he was terrorized by continuous pursuit through an endless falling dark. At those times, he recoiled from the girl's gentle touch, certain he was eluding capture. And the girl pleaded desperately with him to rest but his inner voices clamored that survival was in resistence, not surrender.

He thrashed about uselessly. Hard-won strength was lost in battling nightmares. His rare instants of clarity brought only a clearer awareness of unbearable pain. Each retreat into oblivion was longer, each rise to consciousness more reluctant.

Ard cursed the inadequacy of his medicines. He wished for his guildmaster's special healing skill.

He knew he was going to lose this patient.

25

The last ranks of whirlwinds tore past the circled wagons. A single roaring tower of dust smashed straight through the center of the largest circle, grinding a FoodGuild wagon into splinters and upending four others. The spinning funnel blackened, sucking up smoke and charred debris along with several hjalk and their helpless driver.

The hjalk fell screaming to the salt pan a hundred meters further. The driver was swallowed by the storm.

Susannah stirred numbly in the tangle of bodies huddled against the cargo beneath the Infirmary wagon. Ghirra's thin, strong arm, curled around her back, relaxed and drew away as he rolled out from under the wagon and sat up, dazed and frowning.

"Is it really over this time?" Megan croaked. She blinked, palming grit and black ash from her cheeks.

"Please god," Susannah breathed fervently.

They crawled into the open. Xifa followed with the two children who had been thrust into the wagon earlier in the storm. They accepted sips of water with the touching stoic gratitude of young ones coming to grips with possible orphanhood.

Susannah scanned the ravaged caravan. Bodies lay scattered, wagons flattened and smoldering. Smoke drifted in sullen clouds across the dawning sky. Nearby, a man wept softly, holding his dead wife to his chest. A groaning hjalk struggled to right itself on blackened legs.

So many dead and injured, people and animals. So much destruction.

"If only it had waited one more throw, we'd have been in reach of shelter," she mourned.

"Where's Ampiar?" asked Megan worriedly.

Ah Lord. Not another, begged Susannah. *Another will break his heart.*

Ghirra answered her glance with wan distraction. Grief and dull rage clouded his eyes. He looked away.

"Why do not they think of us, the Sisters, when they play their stones?" he asked.

"As flies to wanton boys . . ." Susannah murmured. She shook her head, then sighed with relief as Ampiar trotted up, even more solemn than usual but unscathed, having found shelter beneath a string of lashed-together hakra carts.

Aguidran strode past, gripping her brother's shoulder briefly without stopping, urging haste as she pointed northward. Through a break in the circle, Susannah saw the long smoky curve of an advancing brushfire. The Master Healer shook himself out of his black gloom and began giving quiet orders to his reassembled staff.

When they had patched up the many injured and made the end a little easier for the dying, Susannah stood with Megan out on the salt pan as Ghirra prepared Dwingen's body for cremation.

The charred wagon remains had been piled into hollow waist-high squares, then stuffed with dry brush and ruined cargo. The dead were placed on top, two or three to a pyre, grouped by family or by guild. Gently, Ghirra laid his young apprentice next to the mother of the two little children. A guildsman of the father stood near, gripping the children's hands tightly as they bade their mother a silent goodbye.

"The father was badly burned," Susannah told Megan, "but he will recover."

The living formed concentric circles around the dozen pyres as Aguidran and her rangers put the first one to the torch. A breathless hush settled as successive columns of oily smoke rose straight into the still and lightening sky.

Megan noted Ashimmel standing quietly among the rest of the mourners. "Seems that the PriestGuild has no formal function in the marking of death," she murmured to Susannah. "I really should be taking notes, but somehow . . ."

"I know." Susannah leaned into her friend's side as the flames licked up around Dwingen's sad little corpse.

To the south, the rising sun touched the distant cliffs with its own, pinker fire. The sky glowed like hot burnished bronze. Sooty low-lying clouds obscured the plain in all directions.

Ghirra rejoined them, his shoulders slack, rage still simmering behind his tired calm.

"At DulElesi," he said, "they see our smoke now, and they wonder who is lost." He pointed toward the cliffs."But you see? We must wonder also."

Susannah studied the sun-bright line of rock. A single faint thread of black curled ominously from the cliff top. "Ah," she replied, feeling surrounded by a tightening ring of fire and death.

Still gazing south, Ghirra stiffened suddenly. He stretched to his full height to stare over the assembled heads, then left the mourners' circle abruptly. He drew his sister aside from her grim task. Aguidran glanced quickly southward, then called together several of her scouts. They listened, nodded and melted through the ranks of mourners, trotting off in the direction of the cliffs.

The tiny dark speck wavering against the dawn-lit amber of the plain could have been a mirage.

Or it could be moving toward us.

Susannah nudged Megan. "I think there's someone coming from the Caves."

The pyres flared and roared. The mourners' circle broke as the full red eye of the sun pushed free of the rounded hills of the Talche.

Later, while the pyres smoldered, the work details labored to bring the caravan back to some suggestion of order.

When the fires had died, Aguidran fidgeted, while the guild elders gathered the ashes of their dead. The circles of wagons were rejoined into a long south-facing curve. The hjalk and hakra had been rounded up and counted. The herdsmen eased them back into harness, rationing handfuls of grain and the last of the water. The undamaged cargo was restowed and reapportioned among the surviving wagons. Aguidran allowed only the fastest repairs and got little argument. The added heat of the sun was being felt already. No one wished to spend a moment longer than necessary frying on the griddle of the Dop Arek.

"Perhaps the real funeral rites are yet to come," Megan remarked as she watched a stout old Leatherworker kneel with difficulty to sweep her guildsman's final gray dust from the glittering slick of the salt pan.

Susannah continued repacking the Infirmary wagon without comment.

"We'll have a team to haul the Sled," Megan added. "There are more hjalk now than there are wagons left to pull."

"Great." Susannah bundled dirty linens into a wooden trunk and buckled the straps. "Lot of good that Sled is going to do these folks."

She wiped sweaty, sooty palms on her tunic and signalled Ampiar to grab one leather handle. With a duet of grunts, they heaved the bulky trunk toward the wagon.

"Good god!" Megan exclaimed suddenly.

The trunk clattered heavily onto the tailgate.

Susannah turned. "What is it?"

"Aguidran's scouting party's returned. Look!"

The four scouts approached through the bruising desert heat, their young brown faces blank with reserved awe. They escorted between them a scrawny old man. His clothing hung limp with a weight of dust and soot. The rag-ends of his sleeves were singed black. The young rangers neither guided nor supported him. They kept even pace with him as he moved in stiff disjointed strides, as if each muscle were being told what to do separately.

Susannah thought of a puppet or a mechanical toy.

"How did *he* get here?" asked Megan incredulously.

As the strange quintet passed down the line, the frenzy of repacking and repairing ceased in shock. A rising buzz of unbelieving whispers followed their progress. An apprentice priest gasped, dropping his bag of counters, and ran, yelling for Kav Ashimmel.

Ghirra and Xifa hurried from behind the Infirmary wagon. Ghirra moved forward instinctively as Kav Daven bore down with renewed energy, as if nearing his goal at last.

The blind priest halted directly in front of him. His cracked lips quivered, his jaw flapped, but only a dry whine pushed past his swollen tongue. He took a short jerky step and his knees gave. His joints crackled like brittle sticks as he toppled into the Master Healer's arms.

Ghirra eased him to the ground, calling urgently for water. The old man clung to him, his blind eyes blinking, his fingers digging in like claws. His lips labored to form words.

Xifa ran up with a bowl of water. Ghirra dribbled measured drops into Kav Daven's mouth, then wet the hem of his tunic to wipe the gray dust from the ancient face. Barely conscious of the water, Kav Daven continued his struggle to speak. The moisture eased the cracking in his throat enough to allow a hoarse whisper to escape.

Ghirra bent his head close to listen.

"Can you understand him?" Susannah crouched beside them. "It sounds like he's saying the same thing over and over."

Kav Ashimmel arrived looking thunderstruck, firing questions at the scouts. At Ghirra's desperate signal, she dropped to her knees and leaned in to interpret Kav Daven's broken mutterings.

"Old Words," Ghirra murmured to Susannah.

When she had listened for a while, Ashimmel took the Ritual Master's shrivelled hands and began to answer him, softly repeating as he did an indecipherable phrase again and again. Their combined whisperings settled into a regular rhythm of statement and reply, like the antiphonal work chants. Slowly, Kav Daven's hoarse music faded as he ceased his straining for speech. His eyelids fluttered shut. His body relaxed into Ghirra's embrace.

Ashimmel sat back, her face dark with incomprehension. Susannah felt worriedly for a pulse. She was astonished to find it whisper-faint but steady as a well-sprung clock.

"He'll need replacement fluids," she said automatically.

Ghirra laid the old priest gently on the ground and sent Ampiar for the stretcher. His hands hovered searchingly over the frail body. He shook his head. "I do not understand how still he lives."

"I don't understand how he made it here in the first place," Susannah returned. "What did he say?"

Ghirra handed the water bowl to Xifa so that she could continue bathing the old priest's skin. He moved aside to query Ashimmel. Her tight-lipped replies seemed to puzzle him. She repeated herself, stumbling again over a certain word and ending with an irritated shake of her iron-gray curls. Ashimmel did not appreciate being left as much in the dark as everyone else.

Ghirra translated pensively. "The Kav begs help for one who is dying. Someone he calls raellil. Kav Ashimmel says it is very old word, this."

"What does it mean?"

"Now, this is one who carries the priest's message, an apprentice. But when this Kav speaks the OldWords, this is the *old* knowings, the Ritual. Kav Ashimmel says she knows not this old raellil."

Ghirra spread his hands and stood up, turning his troubled gaze southward. The bright cliff face was fading behind a veil of smoke. "Raellil," he muttered intently, as if meaning could be induced to reveal itself spontaneously.

"Would he risk his life like this for one apprentice?"

"This does not matter. The Kav comes like this for my help. I give it. With one hjalk only, I will travel two times fast to the Caves." He turned back to stare down at the unconscious old man. "You must take most good care of him, Suzhannah."

"I will," she replied, frightened. He would be facing the sun's heat and the spreading fires all alone. *But then, so did the Kav . . .*

Ghirra sent one of the ranger scouts to liberate a fast young hjalk for the journey. The normally irrepressible Phea, who had hardly said a word since Dwingen's death, slipped away to a nearby FoodGuild wagon to beg enough water to fill a travelling jug.

"It would help to know what's wrong with this mysterious person the Kav is worried about," Susannah pursued. "I think I should give you part of my medikit to take with you. Painkillers, antibiotics . . . Ghirra, it couldn't hurt. It's always better to have more options than less."

The Master Healer acceded with gravity that expressed thanks but no commitment to use her pharmacy. Susannah tossed him a crooked smile and went to the wagon to prepare a mini-kit.

Megan had watched in thoughtful, uncharacteristic silence.

"Isn't this all a little strange?" she asked Ghirra, when Susannah was out of hearing.

"Strange, Meghan? Yes, this is."

"I mean, that old man has to have one hell of a reason to walk twenty-odd kilometers through a forest of tornados."

Ghirra regarded her seriously. "Yes, this is strange. Yet . . ."

"I have an awful feeling I know what you're thinking."

Ghirra's wide mouth tightened.

"You think it's Stavros, don't you. You think Clausen's got him."

Ghirra nodded slowly. "I do, yes. This Kav sees some purpose with him. For Ibi, he would wager his life, I think. No other one. But do not say this to Susannah."

"No. No point in that."

The Master Healer's gaze turned south again. "Live you, my friend," he whispered fervently. "Too many dead already this time."

26

The questions were over for the time being.

Clausen left Liphar bound hand and foot in the sun and stalked across the dusty clearing to harry McPherson while she worked on the Sled.

A dull, outraged chanting rose from among the shattered stalks around the perimeter. Clausen tossed back Sawlish insults and waved his laser pistol.

"Haven't laid a hand on him yet!" he yelled. "Just you wait!"

When the chanting continued, he fired a random bolt or two into the canes. The chanters scuttled for deeper cover.

"For Christ's sake," McPherson growled from the cockpit of the Sled. "The brush fires are close enough as it is, without you starting one right on top of us!"

"Less chat, more work," Clausen chided, then leaned against the Sled's hot white hull and offered companionably, "Do you realize that you and I are the only ones left who seem to recall what our job is? Relax, McP. We're on the same side."

"Yeah? So's you can break *my* neck someday too? Go fuck yourself, Emil. I've done enough of your dirty work already."

"Tut, McP. Such language from a young lady."

Danforth eavesdropped from the shade of the Underbelly, dreaming of convenient accidents and home-built fantasy weapons of wood and clay. He pondered hopeless plans to rescue Liphar, whose shallow, shocked breathing was like the painful flutter of a captured rabbit.

Yet this small and frightened creature apparently concealed a will of iron. After eleven hours without food and water, of long sessions alternately threatened or cajoled by the prospector, the young Sawl had managed either to tire Clausen out or to bore him, but had not revealed Ibiá's hiding place.

Maybe he's willed himself to forget where he left him, Danforth mused.

Silently, he cheered Liphar on. He wished he'd had someone to cheer himself on those many weeks ago, when *he* was being made the victim of Clausen's cruel amusements. He had not been surprised that the prospector mocked his helplessness as he lay crippled in the meager shelter of the downed Sled. At the time he'd thought it a habit of power, and he both admired and coveted Clausen's. He'd not even considered it deliberate that, when Clausen disappeared into the storm for hours at a stretch, water and light were left just far enough out of his reach that the effort of getting to them made him scream and faint from the pain in his chest and legs.

He never laid a hand on me, either, and I thought him merely ruthless. Danforth shook his head. *But the man is a sadist in his heart.*

Danforth sneaked a look at Weng, standing in the shade beside him. Strands of silver hair leaked from her bun. She did not bother to tuck them back. Dust and sweat stained her white uniform.

A command is meaningless without a weapon to enforce it,

Danforth told himself. *A weapon and the willingness to kill. And yet Weng is as good a ship's captain as any I've known. Should she have to kill to preserve the authority she needs, in order to do what she's good at? Should I?*

"He will have to sleep sometime," stated Weng implacably.

Danforth laughed bitterly. "Least that's the way it always goes in the pictures . . . Sorry, Commander. But this is getting to be like a bad holo. Let's call this one *Might makes Right*, what do you say? We could make a billion with it."

Weng's eyes were red-rimmed from dust and exhaustion. She stared at him unblinking.

"Evidently you don't share my loss of anchor in this reality," remarked Danforth quietly.

She returned her attention to the clearing. "I imagine it all seems real enough to Liphar."

Danforth shifted in his chair. "I didn't mean to make light of anyone's suffering, Commander. I was referring to the chaotic quality of recent events. The rules went down the drain and none of us noticed until it was too late."

Her nose crinkled, a chill unborn smile. "I think, Dr. Danforth, that you were simply unaware or unwilling to admit whose rules held precedence.

"The fact is, however, that Mr. Clausen is not as our sister-deities seem to be. There are still some natural rules that will hold precedence over *him*. He cannot stay out there in that sun forever and he *will* have to sleep sometime."

27

Stavros drifted, below the surface of awareness.

A scrap of memory slithered to the top intact, and pulled him unwilling with it.

He knelt at the feet of a brown old man who pressed both hands around his own. A teacher, teaching . . . what?

Kav . . .

The pain crowded in on his consciousness, pushing, pushing.

Stavros pushed back with the gram of will left to him, struggled to preserve the image of the old man in his heat-wracked brain. A thought lurked there somewhere, beyond the image, a hope, an answer.

A chunk of dull silver. A liquid fire in his palms.

Kav . . .

He had offered himself willingly to the guar-pain. It had repaid him with a glimpse into the Void, followed by a miracle.

Kav, I need another miracle . . .

Dying though he was, this seemed an audacious request.

Yet beyond the image, the answer. The answer had something to do with the pain . . .

With not resisting the pain . . .

With unlocking the vicious feedback loop that had kept him energized to evade pursuit but now devoured his body like fire through dry wood.

Stavros imagined his resistance as a single fist clenched around a swaying tree branch, suspended above dark, swift-flowing water, slowly weakening.

Letting go might be the same as dying. Didn't one always speak of *fighting* for life?

No Kav here this time to lead him through the mysteries.

If only the pain would leave him alone and let him think. But now, beyond its fierce internal static, he heard another roaring. The river, perhaps, rushing by beneath him.

The fist on the branch slipped ever so slightly.

No, not the black water at all. A great wind swept past at lightspeed. Life-hungry, it sucked the fire from his limbs, the breath from his lungs.

Voidwind.

Memory returned and with it, terror, as his grip slipped further. Liquid ice enveloped him.

His eyes jerked open to darkness. The girl, familiar as a fever-blurred presence leaning into his delirium, was gone. Stretched on the rack of his own body, Stavros cried out in pain and awful loneliness.

The fist let go.

Stavros fell . . .

The girl started out of thin sleep when Stavros screamed beside her. She scrambled up, fumbling for the shuttered lantern.

Ard grabbed it before she did, on his hands and knees at Stavros' side, spilling light across the pale floor. He swore harshly as the young man's breathing caught and stilled, the eyes and mouth gaping open in some final horror or surprise.

The girl sank to the tiles and began to weep. Ard put his balding head to Stavros' chest, muttering, then straightened slowly. His jaw tight with failure, he reached to close . . .

* * *

. . . into the wind and discovered he was not alone. The Void was not empty. Power danced in its howling swirl. Power sailed the swift wind currents like the white water of a mountain rapid, busy, intent on unknowable purposes.

Stavros was sucked into the stream unnoticed, a mote against vast dark nebulae lit from within by the slow birth-fire of stars and the explosive flaring of their deaths. He floated free, transfixed by his own insignificance . . .

. . . the staring eyes, and let his fingers linger. The dead man's fever sweat was already a chill rime on his brow. Ard muttered, puzzled by the body's abrupt cooling.

A low urgent knocking shuddered against the locked doors. The girl whisked away, still weeping, to answer. The old herbalist's eyes widened to see the Master Healer striding across the tiles. Disturbing scents of dust and brush smoke invaded the quiet dampness of the Hall. Ard's response to his guildmaster's desperate query was a brusque shake of his head. Ghirra bolted the last few steps to . . .

. . . as he floated, Stavros grew aware of certain tensions, certain lines of force, crisscrossing the Void like the strings of a cat's cradle, stretched taut in an invisible tug-of-war. The currents were being stretched, space distorted, his own void-self pulled in opposing directions.

He thought again of magnetism, feeling caught between two poles.

Two . . .

He could sense them now, discern the shifting loci of their immense and separate entities. They danced with the currents, playing out their force-lines with an angler's give and take, give and haul back hard again, playing with each other, tugging, feinting, rolling in the Voidwind like the surf, intent—oh, so intent—on the other alone.

Was the Voidwind born from their blind and whirling dance?

Stavros recalled another dancer's dance, and knew what he had found but could not put a name to them or determine their nature. Was one dry, one wet, one icy, the other hot? Such qualities were mere constructs in his mind, remnants of a more sensual reality. They had no existence in the Void. The quality of the Void was *force*.

Tension, then, and intention. Contention. Push and pull. Action, reaction. Force and counterforce.

No accompanying aura of emotion, no joy or rage. A simple,

burning energy. An eagerness as bright as hunger, as focused as greed, as single-minded as the beam of Clausen's laser.

And slightly mad . . .

Stavros sank into his insignificance as into a protective cloak. He floated unnoticed.

He drifted toward a taut and singing force-line. He was curious, delighted that it rose out of invisibility to glow for him in changing neon colors as he approached. It pulsed like a live thing, its beauty poignant, so brave against the darkness. It occurred to him to wonder if it was hot, if it would burn him if he touched it. But he decided that he could be no deader that he was already. He did nothing to alter his drift.

The glowing line neared, magenta shifting through salmon to vermilion. Stavros admired its bright clarity. Childlike, as if reaching for a new and fascinating toy, he grasped for it with an insubstantial hand. The line sparked and parted in green and yellow violence as his mind-fingers closed around it, a circuit shorted. The ends recoiled invisibly. The shock spun him away, tumbled him in the currents like water over rocks.

Had he felt the Void quake? Could a nothingness pause ever so briefly in its game of push and pull, release a fraction of its awareness from focusing on its opponent, and swing its great head around in search . . .

In his terror, Stravos summoned the wind

Whirl me away, lose me in the depths . . .

He must be a mote again, insignificant and invisible, safe from accounting for his unthinking, irrevocable ACT . . .

Ghirra shoved Ard aside as he skidded to his knees.

The apprentice girl caught her breath, tears suspended in shock. Ard said nothing, moved away, adjusting the lantern to shed more light as Ghirra put his fingers to the pulse point on Stavros' throat, then both hands to his temples. The dank chill of the skin forced from the healer a soft exclamation of despair. Ard began to murmur, offering details.

The ravaged shoulder precluded ordinary attempts at resuscitation. At his guildmaster's order, Ard resignedly began mouth-to-mouth respiration. Ghirra did not hesitate. He tore at the knots belting Susannah's mini-kit around his waist. He unfolded the pocketed sash, laying it out flat on the tiles. Stainless steel glinted in the lamplight, reflected in Ard's quick glance of suspicion and disapproval.

Ghirra slipped a syringe from its plastic sheath and fit the shining needle to a vial. His long fingers shook just once, then steadied as he laid the point to Stavros' chest and eased it into the skin, so accurate an imitation of Susannah's swift, clean motions that he felt for a moment in full control. He tossed the empty syringe down, then nodded Ard aside and took over the artificial respiration, determined to breathe warmth into the chill . . .

. . . in flight again. There was no shelter in the Void. The Void *was* the Power. The Powers. Them. Still obsessed by pursuit, he was sure they would find him and punish him for disrupting their game.

Desperate, Stavros imagined himself on the crest of the dark wave, sweeping past that same overhanging branch. Terror gave him breath and wings. He leaped, grabbed and . . .

. . . his fingers on Stavros' wrist, Ard gave an astonished cry. Ghirra felt the lungs swell on their own beneath his hands and threw his head back in silent, unbelieving joy.

"ValEmbriha!" old Ard breathed.

The apprentice girl eyed the Master Healer with new awe.

Stavros stirred faintly. His back arched in reawakening pain.

Ghirra murmured soothingly and laid probing fingers to either side of his patient's jaw, pressing gently until Stavros quietened. He lifted the dressings from the shoulder wound and his mouth tightened, anger mixed with dismay. He did not understand a thing that could burn flesh and bone more deeply than the pure guar fresh from the rock.

He sent the apprentice girl off to scavenge more ice and reached for the second syringe.

28

The caravan straggled homeward, pursued in the final hours of its journey by lines of fire closing in from the north, west and east. Susannah squinted up at the smoke-shrouded cliff, hoping to make her anxious scanning of the cave mouths appear merely casual. It surprised her that she waited to see him so eagerly.

"Lord, what a welcome sight!" Megan's voice sounded like some ancient version of herself cracked with thirst and muffled by the layers of her face wrappings. The masks were protection as much against the thick smoke as against flying sand. "We keep this pace up much longer and I'll drop!"

"You couldn't have kept up at all a month ago, look at it that way. Neither could I."

Megan grinned invisibly. "What *is* this absurd predilection of yours, always seeing the bright side?"

From the base of the cliff, three hjalk riders rode out through the dust and smoke to meet the head of the caravan.

"Welcoming committee," Susannah noted. "Aren't they in a hurry!"

The riders' faces were masked. Their hjalk looked thin and unkempt.

"Maybe it'll all be resolved when we get there," she continued. "This situation with CONPLEX, I mean."

Megan snorted. "That's if for some foolish reason you assume that the wheels of justice turn with miraculous speed, and that when they do, they turn in your direction."

"The case is clear-cut, surely," Susannah countered lightly. She would see Stavros soon, and the thought preoccupied her. She lacked the heart for another of Megan's weighty discussions. "With what we've seen of present Sawl culture alone, never mind what may have gone before, what court could dispute the Sawls' right to their own planet?"

"Easy for you to say, being here with the Sawls. The Courts however are on Earth, with CONPLEX." Megan hooked Susannah's elbow with a restraining hand. "Listen, it *is* crucial that you not say a word about any of this until I give you the okay."

"Or Stavros does."

". . . yeah. Or Stavros."

Megan's tone left Susannah uneasy, but she put it down to creeping paranoia. "What if he's not even here, Meg! What if he's been chased into hiding somewhere else?"

Hesitation again belied Megan's offhand reply. "Where else would he go?"

Susannah's gay mood wavered.

I want this to be over.

She watched the riders speed up as the caravan neared the outskirts of the wind-torn fields. Solemn chanting drifted with the dust. To the west, along the sickle curve where plain met cropland, small parties were digging fire breaks.

Megan measured the fire's advance behind them. "They'll never get those done in time," she predicted gloomily.

"We're all home now. We'll pitch in."

The hjalk riders met up with the lead wagon as it wound

among the partly flooded terraces. One rider left his companions and pushed his lathered beast through the dust to where Aguidran walked beside the PriestGuild wagon that carried the still-unconscious Kav Daven. Susannah recognized the rider's tired stoop even before he slid from the hjalk's back and pulled aside his mask. Ghirra let the heaving animal wander loose while he fell in close step beside his sister. After several paces, Aguidran stopped short and turned to face him. Her incredulity was unmistakable even at a distance. Ghirra nodded and put a sympathetic hand to her shoulder.

"Uh-oh," muttered Megan.

"Maybe whoever it was he came back for didn't make it," Susannah suggested.

She did not see Megan glance at her pityingly.

A ranger came running from the front of the caravan. Several others followed more slowly, converging on Aguidran. All wore the same look of bewildered shock. The Master Ranger spoke to them quietly, her back stiff. Only the sharp chop of her hands hinted at emotion. When she dismissed them, they trotted off in all directions, bearing the news. Ghirra glanced in on Kav Daven, then left his sister in conference with a quickly summoned Kav Ashimmel. He hurried back toward the Infirmary wagon. He was dirty and grim and as much without hope as Susannah had ever seen him.

"What happened?" she asked.

Ghirra met Megan's worried eyes, shook his head once, faintly. "Edan is dead. *Murdered*, Ibi says the word is."

Megan relaxed briefly at his use of the present tense, then said, "Murdered?"

"Murdered?" Susannah repeated. Astonishment made her feel stupid. "But how? Do they know who did it?"

Ghirra's tired eyes lidded. "Oh yes. This is known."

Megan tugged her dust mask aside. "I give you three guesses," she growled. "The goddamned laser."

"No, he did not use this . . . lazher . . . for this killing." Ghirra told them what he knew of Edan's death and Liphar's interrogation, leaving out any mention of Stavros' injury.

Susannah listened with growing indignation. Megan stared off in the direction of the Lander's white-and-silver cone.

"Maybe we really have him on the run," she mused when Ghirra was done. "This is clumsy, blatant stuff for a guy like Clausen."

Susannah stared at her. "Is that all you can think about? Edan dead and now he's got poor Liphar . . . ? Why didn't anyone stop him?'' she exclaimed to Ghirra. "What's the matter with them down there!"

"Maybe they want to live a little longer," Megan responded dryly.

"Well, I can't believe he'd . . ." Susannah stopped, chewing hard on her lower lip. "I know, I know. He did. With his bare hands. Jesus."

Her eyes flicked from Ghirra to Megan, then out over the broken fields. With an air of resolve, she unstrapped the canteen from her belt and shook it. "Not enough here. Meg, give me what's left in yours."

Megan put a hand on her canteen and left it there. "Why? What are you going to do?"

"I'm going to go down there and get that poor boy away from him."

"Oh. Just like that, huh? You've got to be kidding."

"Why? Somebody's got to do it."

"Suzhannah, please . . ." Ghirra said worriedly.

"Never mind. I'll make do with the water I have." Susannah paced forward a step or two, then turned back and faced them squarely. "Look, I'm tired of being the silent observer in this cat-and-mouse game of yours! When innocents like Edan and Liphar get caught in the cross fire, it's time to put a stop to it!"

"Game?" Megan threw up her hands in angry disgust. "Right! Put on your white hat and ride in to save the day!"

"What's wrong with that?"

"Nothing, if it were possible. Damnit, Susannah, you don't go facing off the enemy in his own lair!"

"Why the hell not, if that's where he is?"

"Because then you get killed for nothing and he goes right on doing what he pleases!"

"That's because you're letting him get away with it!" Susannah returned. "Meg, listen to me. Don't you see the game you're playing is *his* game? You run and he chases you, like he had you programmed. Or like the Sawls taking it for granted they can do nothing but suffer through the Goddesses' warring. This underdog self-image has you paralyzed. You won't grab the upper hand even when it's available to you!" She took a deep, indignant breath, expelled it loudly. "Megan, he's *one* man!"

"One killer," Megan amended. "Equipped with laser."

Susannah paced back to the rear of the wagon and grabbed her medikit from the open tail gate. Ghirra moved to block her path.

"Suzhannah, this is . . ."

She glared at him, surprised that she could be so angry, even at him. "It's what? Crazy? Maybe so, but then so is Emil, clearly."

Megan shook her head knowingly. "Oh, no, not crazy. Cold-blooded, maybe, but not crazy. Don't offer yourself the comfort of that diagnosis just because it's easy."

Susannah gripped the medikit and faced Ghirra stubbornly. Hurt mixed with the worry in his eyes and she guessed that he was taking her accusations of inaction more personally than she had intended.

"For instance . . ." Megan played her final card harshly. "Tell us, GuildMaster, how reasonable Emil has been with Stavros . . ."

Susannah felt herself pale under her tan. "Ghirra, what does she mean?"

He flicked Megan an ambivalent glance. "He lives," he replied.

"But it was close?" Megan prodded.

"Yes."

I will not weaken on this, Susannah resolved.

"*Very* close?" insisted Megan.

Ghirra frowned gently.

"What happened?" Susannah demanded.

"The lazher," said Ghirra. "Very bad burning."

Susannah winced. "Is he in a lot of pain? Did I give you . . ."

Ghirra nodded soothingly. "Yes. He does better now."

Megan kept trying. "But he's not out of danger? Suze, let Ghirra smuggle you up there now so you can be sure he's okay."

The thought of Stavros in pain made Susannah hesitate, but not for long. "Meg, he's had one good doctor already and there's another patient to look in on who he wouldn't want me to desert."

She gripped Ghirra's hand briefly, then shouldered the medikit and stepped around him, heading briskly for the front of the caravan and the Lander beyond.

"We'll have to go with her, of course," Megan complained.

"Yes," Ghirra agreed, already moving in Susannah's wake.

Danforth slumped in his chair in front of a dead monitor screen. He imagined himself strangling Clausen with the connecting cable the prospector had removed and currently wore looped on his belt. He glanced up at the shimmering clearing, Clausen's interrogation ring. The prospector bent over his prisoner in the dusty heat. The chanting continued from the wilting fields, adding to the atmosphere of heat-soaked gloom.

"Emil!"

Clausen started faintly at Susannah's shout, but his eyes did not leave Liphar for a second. He crouched beside him intently, a brimming cup of water held just out of reach of the young Sawl's blistering lips.

The hidden chanters fell expectantly silent. Danforth reached down to nudge Weng out of her heat doze on the ground beside him, then wheeled himself quickly to the edge of the shade.

"What are you *doing*?" Susannah marched across the clearing.

Clausen grinned into Liphar's tear-streaked face, swaying slightly on his haunches. He raised the cup to his own mouth and drank with slow torturous relish. But his other arm floated up from his side as if automatically. He aimed the silver laser pistol at Susannah without even looking.

"For god's sake, Emil!" she shouted.

Danforth held his breath.

Too late to warn her off. Might make things worse.

In her layered Sawlish clothing, her long hair flying loose around a tanned face sparked with righteous outrage, she descended like an avenging goddess upon Clausen as he hunched over his hapless victim.

For Danforth, helpless in his chair, it was like watching a sudden street corner collision happen in agonzing slow motion.

"He's wearing down," murmured Weng at his shoulder. "Reflexes gone."

"How much reflex does it take to pull a trigger?"

But Clausen did not fire. He seemed too entranced by the suffering he could arouse in Liphar's glazed eyes by tipping the cup and letting the precious water dribble in a thin, broken stream onto the dry ground.

Susannah strode up behind him. The laser pointed straight into her stomach. She swiped angrily at Clausen's outstretched arm, sending the little pistol flying. It skittered across the hard-packed dirt.

Clausen ducked immediately and rolled aside, kicking up dust as he lunged after his weapon. Susannah ignored him. She knelt to cradle Liphar in her arms and unstrapped her canteen.

Clausen snatched up the gun and rolled himself upright into a surprised crouch. He glanced warily around the clearing. Then he settled back on his heels to watch Susannah with bemused disbelief as she fed Liphar short sips of water and struggled to untie her badly chafed wrists and ankles.

To Danforth's amazement, Clausen started to laugh. He dropped his forehead to his knee. His shoulders shook silently. Then he threw his head back and rose abruptly, moving toward Susannah.

Danforth tensed in his chair, wondering how far across the clearing he could get on plastic-bound legs before the laser cut him down.

Clausen paused beside Susannah, but merely leaned over to murmur at her ear, then passed her by without a second glance. She stared after him as he stalked toward the shade of the Underbelly. His gun arm hung slack at his side, the pistol dangling from two crooked fingers. He stopped in front of Weng to grin at her mirthlessly as he shoved the laser into its holster and snapped the flap tight. He unlooped the computer cable from his belt and tossed it into Danforth's lap.

"Not as young as we used to be, eh, Commander?" he said.

Weng stared straight through him. "You see, Dr. Danforth," she remarked with icy satisfaction. "I told you he'd have to sleep sometime."

Clausen's grin twisted oddly. "Yeah," he said, and turned away. He crossed to the Sawl-made ladder leading up into the main hatch. He climbed it stiffly, then pulled it up after him.

"I'll be in my quarters if anyone needs me," he called as some inner, upper door slammed shut behind him.

Danforth told himself that now he'd seen everything. He wheeled out into the sun as Megan and Ghirra loped up to huddle around Susannah and the suffering Liphar.

"What did he say to you?" Megan demanded.

"He said, 'Thanks, I really needed a break. I wasn't getting anything out of him anyway.'"

29

Ghirra wisked Susannah and Liphar out of the Lander clearing, leaving Megan to deal with her Terran colleagues. The chanters emerged from the fields one by one to follow them, singing a gladder melody.

Liphar could not walk on his own, though he tried, insisting that he could but clinging heavily to Susannah. He asked about Stavros, and then Kav Daven, his joy at the good news offset by the shock of the bad. He stopped often along the dusty path to rest and down another another gulp of water, glancing behind him as if still expecting pursuit.

The head of the caravan had pulled to a halt on the rock

terraces at the foot of the cliff. A vanguard party from Engineers bounded up the stairs toward the cliff top to ready the winches for the off-loading of cargo. The rangers organized reinforcements for the fire brigade. Families left their carts or wagons in the charge of the younger children, unshipped their digging tools and hurried into the fields to help with the firebreaks. A billowing wall of black smoke obscured the plain to the north and west, close enough now for the bright lick of flames to be visible along its base.

Word of Liphar's ordeal spread fast among the wagons, though no one was quite sure how it had ended so suddenly or how they were supposed to understand that this strange behavior was confined to a single Terran. Liphar accepted his sudden celebrity with dazed good humor, even enjoying it a little, in a haunted sort of way, now that the ordeal had ended. But he wept when Ashimmel and a stony-face Aguidran met them at the foot of the stairs. He muttered brokenly about Edan's bravery, and would not allow himself to be taken to Physicians' without first seeing for himself that Stavros was alive and well.

He calmed under Ashimmel's stern eye, and two of his fellow apprentices were found to stretcher him up the long stairs. As they entered the cavernous dark of the stable level, the young Sawl breathed a visible sigh of relief and relaxed at last into the curl of the leather sling. Susannah absorbed the comparative coolness with a grateful sense of homecoming.

They waited at the entrance to Valla's StoryHall while Ard unlocked the huge doors from the inside. Liphar demanded to be helped out of the stretcher, and walked into the chill, dim hall on his own unsteady legs.

Stavros lay on a pallet of blankets, his back propped against a wall, dozing fitfully. The apprentice girl knitted quietly in the light of an oil lamp. She scrambled up in surprise and Ghirra beckoned her aside to announce Kav Daven's return with the caravan. Torn, she glanced back at Stavros, but Ghirra nodded reassuringly and she sped away to see to her Ritual Master's welfare.

Susannah held back as Liphar tottered into the pool of lamplight at Stravros' bedside.

"Ibi?" he whispered urgently, collapsing into a slow heap like a puppet with its strings cut. "Ibi!"

Stavros' eyes lazed open. His head moved vaguely toward the source of the voice.

Still drugged, thought Susannah, content now that he was there in front of her and alive, content just to look at him. He was pale from his weeks in hiding, and fever-thinned. He looked

202

older, she thought, the angles and hollows of his face now painfully sharp. His eyes seemed deeper set and very dark against his sallow skin. His left shoulder was thickly wrapped with herbal poultice. The long, dim hall smelled of herbs and lamp oil.

Stavros focused on Liphar and smiled. "Lifa. Rhe khem."

Liphar beamed, tears starting again in his eyes. "Khem rhe, Ibi."

Stavros seemed to gain strength as he struggled out of his drug haze. "Rho sukahakhe, Lifa. Han jela."

Liphar wiped his tears bashfully. "No, Ibi. Te ket-shim Ghirra sukaharhe, cedirhe?"

Stavros laughed, a muted escape of breath. "You saved me the *first* time," he insisted fondly.

He glanced up to share a weak grin with the Master Healer and saw Susannah waiting in the shadows. His gaunt face softened with doubting joy, "Susannah . . . ?"

Ghirra's paternal chuckle convinced him. He let his head loll back against his pillows and closed his eyes.

"At last," he whispered fervently.

Ghirra bent to murmur in Liphar's ear, then urged him to his feet. He let the young man walk to the waiting stretcher, making sure to collect Ard on the way out.

When the door clunked shut, Stavros opened his eyes again. He took in Susannah's guarded expression without comment as she came to kneel at his side.

Susannah felt suddenly awkward, vulnerable. She was unable to look him in the eye. Before, it had been always he who was at a loss with her. Something had changed. It confused her that she hurt with his hurt.

"You ought to let me look at that shoulder," she muttered lamely.

As she reached to check his bandages, he caught her hand and pressed her cupped palm to his lips with a tenderness that brought the warm threat of tears to her eyes.

"Are you really all right?"

He smiled happily, "You tell me . . . doctor."

He trailed his fingers down her cheek, then crooked his good arm around her neck to draw her close and kiss her hungrily. "Ah god, Susannah, I missed you! Lie down with me, talk to me, hold me. God, please hold me."

She eased him down on the pallet and snuggled against him gingerly, but he pulled her close with his good arm, with strength that surprised her, and held her very tight, his face buried in her

203

hair. He said nothing for a long time. Finally he let out a long breath and relaxed his desperate grip.

"I died, " he said, as if by way of explanation.

Susannah murmured sympathetically, smoothing her. fingers across his naked chest and belly, wanting him, wishing him whole.

"Really. I did," he said seriously, gently stopping her hand's wanderings. "I know it."

She pulled away to look at him. "Ghirra didn't mention this."

"Ghirra's sure it was the adrenaline or whatever he shot into me that saved me, but I tell you, Suze, it was too late for that. I was gone. I fought dying, fought until I had no strength left and had to give in. And then . . . I was gone. Or at least the body was. *I* ·was . . . somewhere else." He wrapped the one arm around her again, and Susannah felt him shudder.

"Where?" She had to ask.

He now seemed a bit embarrassed. "Oh, I don't know. Out there. Wherever it was, it scared the shit out of me. That's what brought me back . . . I think. Either that, or . . ." He cupped her chin and kissed her gently. "You think I'm nuts, Suze, like everyone else does?"

She smiled, shook her head.

He kissed her again. "You ready to have that conviction sorely tried?"

Susannah shrugged. "Try away."

He adjusted himself on the pallet, wincing faintly.

"Stav, you ought to rest."

"No. Listen. You have to listen." He gripped her hand. "I felt the Sisters when I was . . . out there."

"That's not uncommon . . ." Susannah cleared her throat softly. "To see god in near-death experiences."

"It wasn't near-death, it *was* death, and I tell you, I *felt* them out there, wherever I was, but not as goddesses, As . . . as *beings*. It was as if, by giving in to dying, I was pulled into some kind of natural connection, even though they didn't notice me. They were so . . . self-absorbed. I tried to catch their attention, then I got scared and ran. The terror was so . . . !" He let out an explosive breath. "But I lived, because I ran."

Susannah found herself monitoring the temperature of his skin for fever. "I don't know, Stav. What's all this supposed to mean?"

"It means that they're *there*, that maybe we can contact them, try to reason with them, show them the havoc they wreak with their games, maybe make them stop!"

"Contact them?" Frightened, she tried to make a joke of it. "By dying? Again?"

He smiled at her worry and hugged her close. "Christ, no! Once was enough. But there's got to be a lesson there, about resistance, maybe, or . . . once before, at the Leave-taking, I . . . the Kav . . . hey." He slipped his hand from her waist and stared with grateful satisfaction at his palm. "It's back."

"It?"

"My guar-fire," he replied, then started, as if remembering. "Suze, the Kav, how is he? I have to talk to him, tell him about this!"

"He's stable," she began seriously, restraining him gently. "But I don't think he'll be able to talk."

"He won't need to. We have our ways, that old man and I. He can't *see* either, and yet he does." He pulled away to gaze at her intently. "There's so much to tell you, so much I haven't told you, haven't been able to. We've had so little time, and I . . ." He toyed with the lacings of her tunic. ". . . I've had other things on my mind than talk."

Susannah grinned. "You're not actually considering making love to me, I hope, not in your condition."

"Well . . ." With a needy sigh, he slipped his hand between the layers of gauzy fabric. "I was hoping," he murmured, "to convince you to make love to me."

". . . *raellil?*" Stavros struggled up onto his good elbow. "Me?"

Ghirra traced absent circles on the floor tiles. "I think, yes. You know this word?"

"Yeah, I do." He let Susannah help him to sit up. "I was working on a refined translation recently, after a conversation— if you can call it that—with the Kav himself."

"Ashimmel says 'apprentice.' "

"So does Liphar. Also 'messenger' or voice.' But it's OldWords. Its roots are in the old technical vocabulary." Stavros grinned crookedly. "Plumbing, in fact. Sometimes internal plumbing, like arteries, but mostly it referred to pipes, you know, how they move stuff from place to place."

"Like messages," Susannah noted.

"Or like the word in English that carries a surprisingly similiar double meaning: 'conduit.' "

"Conduit for what?" asked Susannah.

"Or apprentice," Ghirra repeated pensively to the tiles, then raised his eyes. "This does not surprise, TavrosIbia."

205

"No?" Stavros met the Master Healer's even gaze. "No. I suppose not."

He flexed his left hand experimentally. Thanks to a harmonious combination of Sawl healing and Terran medicine, he could now move his arm from the elbow without gasping audibly. The guar-fire was like liquid warmth in his palms, pain no longer, but a promise of returning strength and a reminder that something beyond mere survival was expected of him.

"Time for me to try out these legs again," he declared. He rolled onto his knees and grasped Susannah's shoulder. "Help me up."

"Oh no. You're in no shape to go walking around."

He eyed her wickedly. "I was in shape enough to . . ."

Susannah touched a finger to his lips. "Hush. I know. But right now, you're not going anywhere."

He realized she was serious. "Susannah, please, you must understand. I have to talk to the Kav, and he's obviously not coming to me. Please. Help me up."

"This Kav cannot talk now," said Ghirra flatly.

Stavros frowned, a flash of temper reminiscent of his former petulance. Susannah put it down to exhaustion but Ghirra rose onto his haunches, contriving to look vaguely threatening.

"Ibi," he insisted. "No."

Stavros slumped, eased himself back against the wall. "The medical profession of two worlds, conspiring against me," he grumbled.

"Ket-shim Ghirra?" The soft summons came from the doorway. Phea appeared in the blue glow of Valla's fountain, and hurried across the hall to announce that the hastily set-up field hospital at the foot of the cliff was being threatened already by the encroaching brushfires.

"Lord. We'll have to get them all up to Physicians'!" Susannah gripped Ghirra's arm. "Don't worry. We'll find room somehow. Can we use the winches?"

"Yes, but we must hurry." Ghirra rose abruptly, then gazed sternly down at Stavros. "You will rest, TavrosIbia?"

Stavros nodded, faintly sullen but already too worn out to resist any further. "Go on, both of you. I promise to stay put. But the minute the Kav wakes up, I want to hear about it!"

30

A young Foodguilder gestured Megan to raise her dust mask against the smoke, then slapped a wooden shovel into her hand. Megan joined the diggers frantically working to cut off the fire's advance on the terraces. Along the westernmost edge, three fields of dry red stalks were already aflame. The Foodguild had agreed to sacrifice the next field for a fire break.

The amber sun was a hot, baleful eye in the malachite sky. The cliff face shone hard-white through the smoke. Troops of apprentices fanned out across the relinquished field to pull the crop up by the roots. The obscuring dark billows made it hard to tell what was burning and what was not.

Megan spotted Weng and McPherson, white-suited against a background of soot and fire, tossing armloads of uprooted stalks onto waiting hakra carts. The dry root clumps shed their soil as gritty dust. The fire's draft pushed hot clouds of ash into the diggers' faces. Megan coughed, eyes streaming, and put her mind to shovelling as fast as she could manage.

She was quickly winded in the suffocating heat. As she stood back for a moment, panting, to wipe away the stinging mixture of sweat and tears, a strong hand snatched the shovel from her hand.

"Not enough tools to go around, Megan. Take a break."

Megan backed off reflexively. The few Sawls who noticed him did the same. Clausen stepped up to the swath of raw earth and bent briskly to work, the holstered laser prominent on his hip.

The Sawls stared, confused, frightened, but unwilling to reject the labors of any able hand. They decided to ignore him. They left him ample room and continued digging beside him.

God help us all if Aguidran finds him here, thought Megan.

She freed her canteen from her sash and allowed herself a restrained gulp. Clausen had shaved the neat beard grown during his wilderness ordeal. He looked composed, if not relaxed. He fell immediately into an easy digging rhythm, his body no stranger to physical labor. She could only envy his machined efficiency, and hate him the more for her envy.

"Doing penance, Clausen?" she shouted over the fire's roaring. "Why not just let it all burn!"

He turned, leaning on his shovel, and nodded balefully at the improbably tilted silver tower of the Lander, wreathed in smoke. "And the Sled and the dish and the Lander, too, Meg? I still have a job to do, and though the chances of my escaping this planet with my life are slimming fast, I see no sense in cutting the odds back any further."

His bleak honesty took her aback. Tanned and freshly shaven though he was, she could see he was fighting exhaustion. She tried to revel in grim satisfaction, but when he reached out, requesting her canteen, she gave it to him. He took a swig and wiped his mouth with the back of his hand, watching Megan with his chill hawk's eyes.

"I didn't lay a hand on the boy," he offered wearily. "Just scared him. Kid has stamina."

Megan's lip curled. "And Edan?"

"The girl?" He shrugged. "Honest self-defense, Meg." He loosed his collar to show off dark parallel welts across the side of his throat. "Quite a hand with a leather thong, that one."

He drank again and handed back the canteen. Megan took it but he held on briefly, commanding her direct attention. "Don't you go playing the horrified innocent on me like the rest of them, Meg. Whatever it takes to do the job, we both know that, eh? I'd figured you were too smart to get involved in this stuff, but hey, you shove your man out there, and green or not, I have to go after him. You expected no less from the beginning, surely."

Megan snatched back the canteen, blinking into the blowing ash. Her open antagonism had not been the best cover after all. He'd detected her more experienced hand in what was supposed to appear to be conspiracy of one. She wondered what he was looking for now, companionship in his cynicism or a full confession.

Green. His insinuation stung her. Had she taken advantage of Stavros's innocence? If so, Stavros was a willing victim and she thought her cause far more justifiable than the prospector's.

Clausen rested from his digging to squint at the approaching fire.

"I don't suppose you'd care to enlighten me on one small point?" he asked lightly, then chose to take Megan's sullen grunt for assent. "What in the world has Ibiá done for these folks to make them apparently willing to die for him?"

"He loves them, Emil. Nothing more, nothing less. Something you wouldn't understand."

Clausen mimed a dagger thrust into his chest, "Is this the famous Levy wit and venom? Surely you can strike closer to the heart than that."

"Maybe yours is on the other side," she returned sourly.

"How about the drone? Your idea?" He cocked his bullet head suddenly and smiled.

Megan tensed. In this confusion of smoke and noise, she could be dead in a ditch before anyone would notice. *Like Edan* . . .

Clausen's smile died into a hollow laugh, "Not to worry, dear icon of the Left. You're safe until I get truly desperate. Punks like Ibiá can come and go invisibly, but the recidivists get too much martyr-mileage out of folks like you. Besides, who'd be left for me to talk to?" He shook his head disgustedly. "There's so much righteous indignation flowing around here, it could make you puke! Do they think this is the first world to be forcibly welcomed into the twenty-first century?"

"The legal argument is strong, Emil," countered Megan impulsively, then instantly regretted her need to justify. She told herself again how lazy it was of Susannah to think this man merely mad. *He's smarter than any of us.*

Clausen nodded benevolently, hugely satisfied. "I'm sure it is. Too bad no one will listen. So I gather from your general subtext that I do have you to thank for that clever but toothless ploy, but that I haven't yet managed to remove young Ibiá from the scene. Amazing, that. He bled all over kingdom come. Why not call him off, before it's too late?"

"He's not mine to call off, like some dumb animal!" She was angrier at herself for being so easily manipulated than at him for doing it. "Hey, do you like being paid to kill people?"

He turned and spat into the dust. "No."

"I don't believe you."

"Believe what you like, my dear Megan. I much prefer coming in, making my claim and going home to my fur-lined burrow with a nice fat bundle. Killing people usually means someone's going to try to kill me, and that gets tiresome."

He hefted the shovel to return to his digging, then paused. "And therefore, preferences aside, there'll be no more mercy misses, Meg, that I promise you."

"Bad shots, you mean?"

Clausen grinned wolfishly. "You really believe that? Don't. Or when next you chance to conspire with our brash young hero, you just give him my fond regards, and tell him from me that he's a dead man."

31

The frenzied last-minute effort paid off. The flames raged up to
the line of firebreaks, lunged like chained beasts at the fresh-dug
band of wasteland, and could not cross. The fire burned itself out
in frustration.

All motion of the air died with the flames.

A stillness settled over the fields and terraces, as suffocating
as the thick pall of smoke that hovered like smog along the cliff
face. The plain was a plate of hard-fired ceramic, blackened to
the limits of sight. The amber sun shone greenly through the
haze. The heat sucked the last trace of moisture from the fire-
cracked earth and the becalmed air. Messenger of an angry
goddess, it bore down with crushing weight.

112°. Getting hard to think.

Danforth let his hand fall limply from the keypad. "Are you
ready for this, Commander?" he called. "Along with her recent
storm data, CRI's reporting systematic disturbances in the planet's supposedly negligible magnetic field!" He pulled at his tight
curls. "I'm having her plot the pattern of those disturbances to
match against the weather patterns . . . if you can call anything
this wacko a pattern."

Weng stood in conference with McPherson over a soot-stained
electrical schematic. Dust drifted with every movement, clinging
in fine powder to every surface. Clausen waited a few paces
away, hands on hips, listening, whistling some pointedly silent
melody.

"Emil thinks the break's on this circuit here," McPherson
explained. Her forefinger traced across the diagram with elaborate care. "I'm gonna go in there and take a look. We're pretty
sure we got power enough." She tossed an ambivalent glance at
the prospector, who nodded without looking at her, still whistling to himself. "So if I can get the loop closed again, we
should be able to raise the field."

"Taylor? You alive?"

Megan's quiet summons startled him. *Where does my mind go
these days . . . ?*

"Asleep with your eyes open?" She stood over him with a

fistful of papers and tape cassettes. "Don't blame you in this heat. Listen, I've got the supply inventory for CRI and I'd like to feed her some of my trip data for photoprocessing."

"Snapshots of the ruins?" Danforth eased his chair away from the console.

"What ruins? . . . oh. A joke, Taylor? Didn't know you were into jokes."

He gave her a dark and bitter smile. "Cripple's gotta do something to amuse himself."

Megan dumped her stack of cassettes down beside the keypad. "Not much to tell by way of supplies, CRI. Food is okay for two months yet, and with proper rationing, we'll manage for water now we've got the recycler working again. We can't count on much of anything from the Sawls. In fact, I'd like to know what the Orbiter could provide by way of an emergency drop, should the need arise, so pass that request on to Newman. I'll give you my tapes to chew on while I enter the list." She fit the first tape into the feed slot.

"I am not currently able to provide hard copy," CRI reminded her.

"So you can give us a show-and-tell later, if Taylor'll grant me the screen time."

"Be my guest," Danforth rumbled. "I'm sick and tired of my own data. Maybe somebody else's will break the logjam."

Clausen and McPherson humped the mirrored entry cylinder into place, half into the shadow of the Underbelly. The giant tube was awkward to move but surprisingly light for its size. Clausen rocked it back and forth on the uneven ground, calling instructions to McPherson at the other end, until he was satisfied with its positioning. He walked through it, stood in the middle shifting his weight from side to side.

"The field'll break around it right at midpoint." He came out dusting soot from his hands. "Give her a try, Tay."

At the console, Danforth murmured to CRI. Megan put down her papers. Weng waited silently.

CRI chattered a reply. The air shimmered faintly around the Lander.

Could be just another heat mirage, Danforth warned himself.

The air thickened. The silver cylinder thrummed faintly. The view of the blackened plain shivered into a splintered dancing image. The distant wagon rattle and the cries of the winch men on the cliff died to a muffled echoing along the entry tube. McPherson let out a cheer, setting aside her grievances with

Clausen long enough to throw a victory punch at his shoulder. Clausen smiled.

"Well, thank god," Megan declared. "Now we can get a little cool air in here!"

"Our thanks, Lieutenant, Mr. Clausen," said Weng stiffly.

And wipe that smug grin off your face, asshole. Danforth ground his teeth symbolically.

"Congratulations, Emil," he said as Clausen gave the cylinder a last inspection and strode over to the console.

"Our deal, Tay!" Clausen reminded him gruffly.

"Right. You bet, massa! It's all yours." Danforth wheeled away from the console with exaggerated dispatch. Clausen hauled over a crate and sat.

"CRI: This will be a Section G, Priority One message, by my authority. I want it droned out as soon as I'm done transmitting." The prospector paused, then spoke for the benefit of all within earshot. "To follow will be a file of charges against certain expeditionary personnel on various counts of theft, both government property and private, economic subversion, conspiracy and treason."

"Economic subversion?" Megan repeated blandly. "That's rather creative, Emil."

"The first charge will name Dr. Megan Levy, Mr. Stavros Ibiá and Commander Weng Tsi-Hua . . ."

". . . for conspiring to prevent the capture of a dangerous fugitive, Commander Weng Tsi Hua." Clausen sat back from the keyboard, considering.

A hot draft stirring in the entry cylinder brought in the rolling basso call of the priesthorns. A full-throated chanting answered them. From the mouth of the cylinder, Megan counted the sad discrete plumes of smoke rising along the cliff top, so black against the hot malachite sky. The sight too easily recalled ranked columns of dust roaring across a parched salt-flat. Megan shuddered.

"Thirty-four," she sighed, and retreated into the coolness of the Underbelly. "Funerals are starting," she reported gloomily to whomever might be listening.

McPherson snored gently on a tarp-cushioned crate. Weng slept more quietly within her curtained cubicle, driven into seclusion by the outrage of Clausen's list. Danforth lay on his bed working a sheet of calculations by hand, but not so intently as to prevent him from glancing over at Clausen's back and remarking, "How about failure to pray five times daily in the direction of Company headquarters? You could get *me* on that one."

Megan eyed the planetologist speculatively. She was still sprinting to catch up with the shifts of alliance that had occurred while she was away. It did seem that Clausen hadn't an ally left to his name, though McPherson remained confirmed in her admiration for his general do-anything-well competence. She didn't approve of him shooting her friends, but her loyalties were not ideological. Spacer loyalties rarely were. Megan decided that the little pilot found Clausen's aura of menace exciting.

"Or how about conspiracy to consider science more important than corporate interests?" Danforth suggested.

"Feeling left out?" Megan ventured with a smile.

"A little." He returned her smile. Megan could not recall him smiling much in the past. But Danforth, so aloof and arrogant before, too self-involved to mingle much with his colleagues, now made a mocking face at her across Clausen's back and laughed silently, bitterly, his teeth a bright arc in his dark handsome face.

"I'm sure I could think of something for you, Tay," said Clausen without looking up.

Danforth's silent laughter blossomed into a mile-deep chuckle edged with loathing.

Clausen turned to stare at him coldly. "I could. Don't push me."

The chuckle expanded. Danforth laid his notes down, let his head roll back on his pillows, and laughed a long, booming laugh.

Megan worried for him. Was this contempt news to Clausen? She thought it unwise of Danforth to exhibit it any more than necessary. She conjured up an elaborate shrug, shook her head, even tried on a knowing grin, though the fit was tight at best.

"Round the bend at last. The climate control, you know—too much cool, breathable air all of a sudden." She moved to the console to provide further distraction. "Listen, whenever you're done crucifying the Commander and myself, I'd like to have a word with CRI."

"Done? My dear Megan, I've only just begun. However . . ."

"Hello, everybody." Susannah stopped just inside the entry cylinder, her medikit slung over her shoulder. She was soot-streaked and coated with a powder of yellow dust. She took a deep breath of cool, fresh air. "Lord, that feels good! It's like breathing molten metal out there!"

"You're not at the funerals?" Megan stepped forward guilty. "I thought at least one of us . . ."

"I couldn't, Meg. Three more died while we were moving everyone up to Physicians'. I just couldn't . . ." She lowered

213

her eyes dispiritedly and set the medikit on the ground with a tired sigh. "We've lost fifty-six in all."

Megan nodded sadly.

Susannah shook her hair back in a gesture of resignation, then went to greet Danforth, planting a light kiss on his cheek. "How's this patient doing? I'm glad *some* of them recover. You look a little thin, Tay. Aren't they feeding you?" She peered at the ragged scar along his side and ran her hands along his legs, checking the casts. "The wound's healed nicely, though I'm sorry I couldn't make it a little neater for you. Looks like someone attacked you with a chainsaw. How's it feel?"

"Fine. But Susannah . . ." He grabbed her hand and held it. "Walking cast? Please god, before my brain atrophies along with my body?"

Susannah smiled at him. "You got it, next thing on my list." Her eyes raked Clausen as he waited at the console with his back prominently turned. Her lips tightened briefly. Then she moved casually to his side and spoke in a tone of gentle admonition.

"Sorry to have caused such a scene, Emil . . . but was it absolutely necessary to be so hard on the boy?"

She really does think he's crazy, marvelled Megan.

Clausen swiveled in his seat. "Ah, the noble Susannah. Now which boy is that?"

Susannah did not miss a beat. "He was fortunately unhurt, but the harm done to our relationship with the Sawls is irreparable."

"Oh, *that* boy." Clausen crossed his legs, enjoying himself. "I'm much more interested in the other."

Susannah's frown mirrored innocent concern. "Was there another?"

Clausen sighed, disappointed. He turned back to the terminal. "CRI, add the following charge: for aiding and abetting the escape of an injured felon, Dr. Susannah James."

"It's great you got them to bring it back!" McPherson cracked her knuckles excitedly. "It's in terrific shape! The flood hardly beat it up at all! Just needs a serious bath."

"Real serious," remarked Megan from the console. The returned A-Sled sat in the clearing beside its damaged companion craft.

"Nah. I'm charging up the portable sonic now. Bet I have that Sled in the air inside of ten, twelve hours."

"I'm surprised Aguidran didn't hold it hostage, in return for Clausen's head."

"What about B-Sled?" inquired Susannah, keeping informed

214

on the progress of the Sled repairs as Stavros had requested. She fitted the last section of fiberplast around Danforth's thigh and strapped it tight. "Sit up, Tay. See how it feels."

McPherson glanced reflexively toward the clearing. The Sleds' sunbright image danced through the force field's distortions. "It'll come along faster now Emil's decided to get his hands dirty."

"Could they get any dirtier?" Megan muttered.

The pilot shrugged. "Say what you like, he knows his stuff. And he's real eager to get out there and get done, so's we can get out of here."

Danforth sat up and swung his legs off the edge of the bed. The fracture in his left shin was nearly mended. Susannah's new bindings had given him back a working knee. He flexed it gingerly. The reset break in his right thigh was healing more slowly and required continued immobility.

"No marathons," Susannah smiled. "I'd like you to keep using the chair as much as possible for a while, but Ghirra has sent you a gift."

She gestured to McPherson, who ducked behind a crate and hauled out a pair of hand-carved crutches. Danforth took them eagerly, stroking the smooth, aged wood and the leather-covered padding, softened with long use. He touched the lap-joints near the tips where the shafts had been recently lengthened.

"Tell that doctor-man thanks," he said.

"I think he'd like it better if you told him yourself."

"I think you should get right on them, come over here and take a look," said Megan. In front of her, CRI's screen was lighting up with pictures. "Commander?" she called. "You'll want to see this, too."

Danforth set the crutches under his arms and swung himself forward, awkwardly but with increasing ease as the memory of upright movement came back to him.

"Haven't done this since I wracked up my first car," he laughed. "Christ, it feels good to walk!"

McPherson paced along beside him, grinning happily, then dodged ahead to wheel his chair next to Megan at the console.

Weng emerged from her cubicle to join the others as they gathered around the terminal. She moved briskly and gave them all a gracious smile, but Susannah worried at the visible strain in her face, the skin taut at the corners of her mouth, marks of a hurt as deep as the gash in Stavros' shoulder. Clausen might be killing Weng without lifting a finger.

"Ogo Dul," Megan announced. "The nearest coastal settle-

215

ment and the one DulElesi trades with most often. It's built inside cliffs, too. This is one of the market levels."

"Boats!" exclaimed McPherson delightedly.

Danforth put aside his crutches and lowered himself into his chair. Megan continued her guided tour. The observers' patience with her detailed commentary told Susannah how starved they were not only for a change of scenery, but for the chance to relax and have a little fun, acting like the dinner guests of tourists just home from vacation.

Into the middle of their laughter walked the Master Healer, his shirt as limp as his stance, open to the waist. He stepped through the entry cylinder with slow care, touching its silvered inside curve with an interest restrained by caution. At the inner lip of the cylinder, he glanced warily back at the clearing where Clausen, up to his elbows in the guts of B-Sled, was whistling Mozart.

Susannah went to meet him, instantly worried. "Is everything all right?"

Ghirra nodded, then stopped short, at first puzzled, then amazed. He sniffed wonderingly. "How is this? How is it like a deep cave here?"

"The force field . . ." Susannah faltered. *Where to begin?*

"You can do this?" Ghirra lifted his dust-streaked arms to the cooling air. "With your machines?"

"Sure, doc. Watch." Danforth leaned over in his chair and felt for a loose pebble. He tossed it at the shifting curtain of energy that walled the Underbelly. The pebble sparked and bounced off what must have seemed to Ghirra to be wavering but insubstantial air.

His mouth sagged open. "How?" he demanded.

Danforth looked to Susannah. "Does he really want to know?"

"Later, later," said Megan. "Ghirra, come look at this. This is SkyHall. It was cool in there, too, remember? CRI, run the next, what was it, half-dozen or so frames in slow sequence, please."

Ghirra held Susannah back as she turned toward the console. He was eager as a boy in his astonishment. "The machines can do this anywhere?"

"Anywhere you have the power." She pointed upward. "And the loop." Her finger traced the circumference of the Lander's underside above their heads. She thought his look suggested that she'd been concealing some major bit of Terran magic. "It hasn't been working since the flood. Stav didn't tell you about air-conditioning?"

"Ghirra!" Megan insisted. "Need your help explaining this!"

Ghirra wrapped his damp shirt more tightly around his chest

and swallowed his awe enough to resume his dignity. Weng extended her hand to him with the first real smile Susannah had seen her manage since the transmission of Clausen's infamous List. "Good evening, GuildMaster."

Ghirra took her hand in the instinctively courtly manner he reserved for Weng alone, and held it, regarding her solicitously.

"Trying times, are they not?" said Weng lightly, and removed her hand gently from his grasp.

Ghirra smiled his sympathy and turned to Danforth, his eyes immediately drawn to the newly bound legs. "You are well, TaylorDanforth?"

Danforth patted the crutches beside him. "The better for these, doc. Sorry to hear about all your trouble out there."

"Trouble is shared always, TaylorDanforth," Ghirra replied quietly.

Danforth raised an eyebrow. "Yeah, doc. It is that, all right."

"Okay, now here we go," continued Megan. "These were etched on the stone walls all around the hall. I was caught by the quality of abstraction, but Ghirra here was rather dismissive. He called them . . ."

"Old drawing." Ghirra peered at the lines and crosshatchings on the screen with renewed mistrust. "I do not dis-miss these, Meghan. I say they have not meaning. They are drawing only."

"Art, he means," said Megan with a grin. "A mere trifle."

"How old are they, do you know?" Weng inquired.

"Very many generations, Commander."

"It was Susannah who noticed the changes,"Meg pursued. "Watch this."

CRI ran through the sequence slowly. The hatchings and lines shifted relative to each other, drifting, intersecting, moving apart in a choppy rhythm suggestive of a consecutive progression.

"Run it again, CRI. Faster, this time."

The second run brought a soft exclamation of admiration from Susannah. The changes from frame to frame smoothed into a virtually seamless moving image.

Weng leaned into the screen with sudden interest. "Again, please, CRI." She straightened when the sequence had finished. "I would swear . . . CRI, may I have the first and last frames, split screen, please."

"Certainly, Commander."

Weng stared."Now run the sequence again, please."

CRI complied. The old spacer watched intently, then stood back. "How does it strike you, Dr. Danforth?"

Danforth returned her look blankly, "How does it strike *you*, Commander?"

"You don't see it? Well, it seemed to me that . . . but perhaps I . . . wait, let me try something." She reached over Megan's arm to tap in a long command. "Complete without verbalizing, please, CRI."

"YES, Commander."

A single image from the latter part of the sequence filled the screen, the etched pattern of lines in sharp relief against the pebbled rock. Slowly, as CRI processed the command, a second underlying image began to surface. A flat gray background softened the sharpness of the rock. Paler connected blotching hovered beneath the intricate crosshatchings. Bright spots that might have been taken for random pitting of the stone were shadowed by a spatter of black dots.

"Excellent," said Weng. "A very good match. Proceed, please."

The two images shivered together for a moment. Then the SkyHall photo began to fade. It left behind a screen of grainy gray stained with lighter smoke and pinpricks of black.

"My god," Danforth murmured. "Could they possibly . . . ?"

"That looks like a star field, Commander," McPherson observed.

Weng's black eyes leaped past Danforth in triumph to settle on the mystified Master Healer. "You see, I believe you are mistaken, GuildMaster. This 'old drawing' of yours is very meaningful indeed."

"Star field? You mean . . . ?" Megan fell silent. "*Sky*Hall! Of course"

"What stars?" asked McPherson.

Weng's thin hand inscribed a graceful overhead arc. "These stars. On the screen is a photo-negative from the sky survey that Dr. Sundqvist is completing at present from the Orbiter's observatory." She outlined the lighter blotches with eager fingers. "There is the Coal Sack, invading the cluster. CRI, let's bring in Dr. Levy's photo again, please."

They watched again with wonder as the two images swam toward their astonishing correlation.

"The degree of accuracy is remarkable." Weng was almost voluble with enthusiasm, "And mind you, Dr. Danforth. This image, the closest match to our own current one, is from the middle of the sequence. The succeeding images are future prediction."

Ghirra had observed their building excitement in silence. Now, as they all fell silent to grapple with the flood of implication, he spoke up gravely. "What is this meaning, Commander?"

"It means someone *knew!*" Danforth rasped. "Someone here

a very long time ago knew Byrnham's Cluster was heading for collision with the Coal Sack! Unless . . ."

"No, Tay," Megan put in. "The drawings are not recent. I'd stake my rep on that."

"I believe the first image in the sequence will tell us *how* long ago they knew," Weng added. "What do you say to my periodic table now?"

Danforth shrugged incredulously. "No further questions, Counselor. Except maybe . . . who was it who knew?"

Ghirra spread his hands, pleading. "Commander . . . ?"

Weng turned graciously. "I will explain to you as best I can, GuildMaster."

"To him?" Megan exclaimed. "What about me?"

"And me," Susannah agreed. "What collision with the Coal Sack?"

"Dr. Danforth?"

"Be my guest, Commander. The stars are all earthly suns to me. I leave the astronomy to Jorge Sunquist . . . and you."

"You do know what a star is, GuildMaster?"

Susannah laid a protective hand on Ghirra's arm. "Stav's got him well on his way toward a galactic point of view."

"Excellent." Weng embarked, with CRI's assistance, on an illustrated mini-lecture on the history of Byrnham's Cluster, maintaining for Ghirra's benefit a strictly nontechnical approach.

As the explanation progressed, Clausen wandered in from the clearing. Looking a bit heat-dazed, he stood nearby, cooling off, listening without seeming to.

Ghirra listened intently. Now and then, he asked for clarification. The greatest obstacle to his understanding was the question of scale: he had no frame of reference for the vast distances and quantities involved, with one exception. Conceptualizing the appropriately enormous stretches of time did not faze him in the least.

"I have done some preliminary calculations on this, as Dr. Danforth knows," said Weng. "The data suggest that about a hundred and sixty-five thousand standard years ago, the Coal Sack would actually become visible in its approach."

Megan absorbed this with difficulty. "One six five?"

"It would have been, of course, detectable long before that," Weng continued. "With sophisticated sensing equipment."

"Our Egyptians, those great technocrats," offered Meg by way of comparison, "were just moving into the height of their powers a mere five thousand years ago."

Weng nodded appreciatively. "A hundred and fifty thousand years ago, the Cluster entered the outer limits of the nebula. The

Fiixian system, however was on the far side of the Cluster at the time. The affects of the collision would have grown steadily for the next forty thousand years as the system's orbit moved it around to the front of the Cluster, climaxing around fifteen thousand, then easing somewhat as the orbit returned it toward the back. The Cluster itself, however, continues to move into major intersection with an outstretched arm of the nebula, mitigating the effects of relative position.''

Weng paused for breath.

Ghirra stood in pensive silence, sucking his cheeks into hollows. Susannah worried that he would be overwhelmed by this onslaught of information. She recalled his metaphoric commentary on the beauties of the Cluster when night first fell over the Dop Arek.

''Getting a little over your head, is it, honored doctor?'' commented Clausen drily, from behind.

Ghirra did not seem to hear. He stared at the monitor from the depths of his increasingly pronounced stoop, his eyes half-lidded, barely focused.

Weng ceased her lecture, concerned. The others stilled around her, while Clausen chuckled softly to himself.

Susannah reached, then held back her hand. ''Ghirra?''

His eyes flicked up at the sound of his name. He glanced around, read the contempt in Clausen's face and waiting anxiety in the others'. He turned his back on the prospector, let his frown relax, and offered his most glowing smile to allay concern, though Susannah was unconvinced.

''I will tell you my mind on this,'' he began softly. ''Ibi asks me one time, do I believe the First Books? I say, only priests call them truth.''

He leaned forward to touch exploring fingers to the monitor screen. Wonder deepened his voice. ''But this what you tell me is very like . . . it tells the story very like our chant of the coming of the Darkness.''

Susannah's hand flew to her mouth. ''The Tale of Origins! Yes, it does!''

''. . . 'And then it happened,' '' Megan recited from memory, '' 'that the Darkness arrived and the king grew old' . . . according to myth, that was when all the trouble started and the Sisters started playing games with the weather.''

''Wait. Playing *games*?'' Danforth turned wide eyes on Megan. ''Thought they were fighting a war.''

''Depends on who you talk to.''

He noted Weng's triumphant smile, then buried his head in his hands with a theatrical moan, ''I give up. I'm surrounded.''

"Another reality crisis, Dr. Danforth?" asked Weng with great gentleness.

He nodded into his hands, then drew them abruptly across his face and sat up. "Sorry, doc, go on with your story."

Ghirra was perplexed by this outbreak. He spread his hands. "The story of the Darkness *is* the Darkness: The Sisters are blinded. They do not see the many dying they make with their wagers. But the First Books say also that the Darkness will end." He paused, sucking his cheek again, then looked to Weng. "You say how this . . . dust moves in the sky, Commander? Will it move . . . ?"

"Beyond, GuildMaster? Yes. Your ancestors knew that, and they even knew *when*."

Weng recalled to the screen the final frame of Megan's photo sequence. The area of crosshatching had moved beyond the greatest concentration of surface pitting. She made a fast calculation at the keypad. "In approximately eighty-five thousand years, Brynham's Cluster will leave the environs of the Coal Sack. If there is, as I believe, some direct connection between this occurrence and your world's deadly climate irregularities, GuildMaster, I certainly wish I could offer you more encouraging news."

Megan eyed the offending crosshatchings. "Christ, can you imagine how they felt, a hundred and sixty-five thousand years ago, when they looked up and saw *that* coming at them . . . ?"

32

When the force field was tuned to its highest frequency, even the harsh amber noon of the Fixian sun was discouraged from entering. A silverfilm tarp hung across the mouth of the entry cylinder to complete the effect. A cool and placid twilight reigned in the Underbelly.

Susannah lit a single oil lamp. She had become used to the warmth of their softer glow. The ship's battery lamps were unnecessarily bright, and she did not wish to wake any of the heat-drained sleepers who had at last found comfortable niches to retire to. She carried her chemical analyzer to the computer table and plugged in, then gathered her notes and samples, adjusted the lamp wick and powered up the terminal.

From each plant sample, she excised a careful slice of root, stem and leaf tissue, according to availability, the distinction between stem and leaf being moot for many of the succulents. Several hours later, the plants cut, fed in, labeled and filed, she moved on to her animal data. She filed blood, hair and tissue samples from the domestic beasts, from a cross-cut selection of Sawl patients she had treated, then unwrapped her precious single sample from the wild, her lizard's tail. Despite its air-tight packaging, it smelled of rot and poison. She handled it with great care and protective gloves, slipped the whole chunk into the analyzer's square maw, then stripped off her gloves and sat back, massaging her shoulder.

Preliminary analyses of the plant samples were already chattering across the screen when the tarp at the cylinder mouth rustled aside to admit a blinding slash of sunlight and a man. A gust of heat swirled in as if a furnace had been opened.

Clausen let the tarp swish back into place and stood waiting for his eyes to adjust. He surveyed the darkened Underbelly, noting each sleeper in her corner and Susannah at the terminal, then padded into the galley area. Susannah heard a quiet splashing of water, the prospector washing his hands of the clinging layer of grit and dust, and later, a hushed clatter as he fixed himself something to eat.

She had almost forgotten about him when he eased up behind her and set a steaming mug of coffee on the console.

"Hope you like it black," he remarked amiably. His hands and face were burned as dark as the Sawls, blistering here and there. "My greatest regret over the recent unfortunate incidents is the loss of my supply of fresh hekker milk. Boycotting me, you understand."

"You ought to stay out of the sun," she commented.

"Doctor's advice?" He laughed softly. "Got a tarp rigged out there now. Only problem is, the tools still get too hot to hold." He pulled up a crate and sat beside her, sipping his own coffee, studying the screen. "What've you got here?"

Tasting the coffee, she described her sample population. The coffee was delicious. He had a way even with instant. It was odd to think of drinking hot liquids when it was 115° outside, but it was just what she had wanted. Noting the laser pistol snuggled at his hip, she wondered how she could feel so easily companionable with the man who had nearly murdered her lover.

"Mmmm. Interesting." Clausen crooked a finger at the screen. "Look at your chlorophyll molecule: got a little beryllium in there subbing for some of the magnesium. Have you seen that often here?"

"This is the first detailed run I've been able to do, what with . . . ."

"I know, I know. Let's not even talk about being behind in our work." His eyes focused on the data speculatively. "This explains all the reddish foliage, though. The beryllium would absorb higher energies—green-yellow instead of red."

"Yes." It was hard not to respond to his informed interest. Susannah called up another set of data. "And look at this."

Clausen looked. "Hemoglobin?"

"Right."

He gave her an immodest grin.

"Terran blood here," she explained. "Mine, Megan's. Sawl blood, nearly identical. These here are hjalk and hakra samples."

Clausen beat her to the prize. "What the hell's that?" he exclaimed softly. "Beryllium again. Doping the hemoglobin in place of iron!"

"Yup, and worse. Aluminum."

"What *is* this?"

"The only sample I was able to obtain from a wild animal."

"Is the concentration in the flesh enough to be toxic?"

"I believe so, at least after a while, through accumulation. The Sawls claim all wild animals are poisonous and I think they mean more than just the bite. You've noticed that the Sawls eat only domestic herbivores? I think this is why."

"You think *all* the wild life is carrying aluminum around in them? Why doesn't it kill them?"

"Their bodies must manage it somehow. Maybe they excrete it, or maybe it even collects, to form the venom. I haven't been able to get a sample of that yet."

"An intriguing theory." Clausen nodded. "We'll have to get you a few more samples to broaden your data base."

"The Sawls don't want them collected. I only got this because it attacked a child on the caravan."

Clausen regarded her with mild amusement. "Susannah, you're going to have to decide very soon between diplomacy and science if you're going to get anything done around here."

"I have plenty of data to deal with," she replied edgily.

He shrugged, smiled, leaning easily on his elbow against the console. "Well, if I were you, I'd follow up the possibility that your hemoglobin trace metals are being replaced due to scarcity within the ecology. The planet is very poor in iron, among other things."

The idea interested her but the look in his heavy-lidded eyes made her suddenly nervous.

"You know, it's really very odd, Emil," she said, partly to

223

solicit his opinion but also to distract him. "There seem to be two coexisting closed systems operating on this world, instead of a single ecology. One, the sort of over-system, is very messy and dog-eat-dog. The other—revolving around the Sawls, their agriculture and husbandry—exists within it and seems so perfectly knit as to make you wonder if it wasn't designed."

Clausen laughed. "Nature's the best designer around." He confirmed her worst suspicion by reaching to trace the contours of her face with a sculptor's professional flourish. He let his palm settle around her cheek. "You have only to look in a mirror to remember that."

Her jaw hardened under his touch.

"Not in the mood?" he murmured. "A shame."

He ran his knuckle sensuously along her lower lip, then gripped her chin gently between thumb and forefinger. His blue eyes smiled. "Sure you won't change your mind? I haven't been around all these years without learning a thing or two, you know."

She did not doubt him, but crowding her mind's eye was a vision of the wreck he had made of Stavros' shoulder. She heard herself say in a voice of cold rage that she barely recognized, "I'm not into sleeping with killers."

Clausen dropped his hand and sat back. "Ah."

He sighed irritably, picked up his coffee and leaned over with his elbows on his knees, staring into the steam rising from the cup. "Like you said, dog-eat-dog. Very messy."

Unaccountably, his barren simplicity brought tears to her eyes.

"Why don't you care?" she demanded with childlike illogic, wishing that he did, so that she could have some understanding of this smooth, able man so apparently without a shred of conscience.

"But I do care," he replied reasonably. "I care about getting my job done right and living to see another day. That's pretty straightforward, isn't it? Lord, I'm tired of explaining myself! So I'm no martyr like your friend Megan. Are you going to hate me for that?"

"But Edan, and Liphar? . . . and look what you're doing to Weng," Susannah hissed, "and enjoying every minute of it!"

Clausen swirled the coffee in his cup and drank. "Look, if my methods turn you off, I've no quarrel with that. There's other dealing we can do to make things easier for each other. How about this: you bring me the boy, I'll drop all the charges against you and Weng."

"The boy?" she asked stupidly, thinking he meant Liphar.

224

He gestured impatiently. "Come on, Susannah! Ibiá. I want Ibiá."

"Boy?" she repeated, and laughed, unable to help herself.

Clausen stilled, eyeing her sideways. Then he softly clapped a hand to his forehead. "Fool, Emil! Of course!"

Susannah knew how an undercover man must feel upon realizing his cover has been blown. She had not understood the protection it offered her until it was gone.

The prospector ran his hand through his short sandy hair, chuckling. "Of course. I forget that what seems a young nuisance to me might seem a young beauty to you. And romantic as well, I've no doubt." His voice dropped in mocking intimacy. "Is he very passionate?"

Susannah stared at the keyboard.

"Ah well." He stretched, leaning back against the console. "There are other things I could offer, more in the way of career advancement, but there's not much chance of a deal here, I guess, if Ibiá's beaten me to your bed." He chuckled again, this time with a trace of weariness. "Good for him. I like this boy more and more. He's learning to protect himself."

If I were a man, Susannah raged, *I could hit him.*

Clausen straightened, his face very close to hers. He raised his hand once more to her cheek, let it trail down to curl lightly around her throat. "You do understand, don't you, that from now on you'll have to watch your back? Please tell me you understand that."

Her throat tensed within his easy grip. "Is that a threat?"

"Susannah, Susannah." His thumb caressed the skin over her carotid artery. "I don't know whether to be flattered or insulted that you persist in not taking the danger of me seriously."

"I take it seriously. I've seen the results."

"Yes. I know." He said it almost lovingly, then leaned in and kissed her, parting her lips gently with his tongue. The shot of desire that wriggled in Susannah's gut ran neck and neck with nausea.

"Are you *sure* you won't change your mind?" he murmured again, then let her go, laughing. "Let me know how you do with the trace-metal inquiry." He patted her shoulder and left her shaking, staring at the glowing screen.

Susannah ran to Stavros for absolution. He sent Liphar and Phea to make sure she had not been followed, then got up stiffly to bar the big doors.

He felt no jealousy, only worry. He prayed that rape was beneath the prospector's dignity. He held Susannah patiently

225

while she trembled against his bandaged chest and hoped she did not expect him to respond to her outrage with outrage of his own. He knew he had learned a major lesson in perspective when he could not muster rage enough to do more than stroke the smooth skin of her back and say, "What else did you expect of the man?"

Lately, passing the long, solitary hours of recovery, he had studied that place in himself where outrage, pique and righteous indignation used to flourish. He found there only burning determination, the result of a conservation of energies, of the focusing of all those angers into a single beam of intention. His quest for the Goddesses was his highest priority. He was grateful that rage was not now a weapon that the prospector could use against him.

"Stay away from him, that's all you can do, until we figure out a way to immobilize him."

"You mean kill him?"

Stavros shrugged. "Just stay away from him."

"Stay away from him?" Susannah sat upright, her outrage spilling over along with her tears. "Down there? When he's the only one getting this expedition back on its feet? With Taylor crippled and Weng obsessed with losing command? She's so evasive with Captain Newman when she calls in her status reports. Sometimes I think the only reason she hasn't aborted the mission is to avoid facing the possibility that she *can't*, that she won't be able to get the Lander off the ground or if she can, Clausen won't let her until he's damn good and ready!"

Her hands wrapped into fists. "Meanwhile, it gets hotter and hotter. So dry you can't breathe, yet he's out there all day working on the Sleds while the rest of us are holed up in the Underbelly like moles . . . Stav, can't you see how crazy this has become? Work has ground to a complete halt while you guys fight your territorial wars! One man and one gun, holding us all hostage! Can't you find a way to settle this without killing yourselves and anyone else who happens to get in the way? You've filed your protest, now let the Courts take care of it! This planet is going to be the death of *all* of us if we waste our time and energies fighting each other!"

"Whoa, whoa, hold it, easy, Susannah. Susannah!" He imprisoned her flying hands and held them tightly though his shoulder wound burned. "I didn't set the stakes. He did."

"Did Edan try to kill him?"

"Maybe she did."

"He says so!"

Stavros worked his aching shoulder beneath its wad of bandages. "Well, it was certainly not unprovoked. Susannah, this is no mere methodological disagreement among colleagues. Try to see the larger picture. Remember who and what we're fighting for.''

He raised his hands, palms out. His clear palms, scored by their invisible fire. His constant reminder, his goad. He let his voice resound with conviction. "Clausen is the mud we must fight through on our way to the real battle.''

He knew this would quiet her. He had learned that she would not debate him on the subject of his mission to save the Sawls from destruction at the whim of the Goddesses. She had not yet decided how much of his tale of voids and unscarred skin to believe, how much to call deception, how much to pity as delusion. But because she loved him, and he knew she did though she had never said it, she let his claims go unchallenged, waiting until proof one way or another presented itself.

"There's got to be a better way,'' she insisted, calming anyway.

"Hush.'' Stavros kissed her still-clenched fists, then pulled her down against him to soothe her with his hands and mouth, and spread the warmth of his quar-fire throughout her body.

Even then, as his cheek smoothed the intoxicating silk of her breast, he murmured, "So how *is* he coming with the Sled repairs?''

Slunk in the protective curl of Susannah's arm, Liphar avoided Clausen's mocking eye and sang the tale-chants that told of the coming of the Darkness. CRI recorded, simultaneously processing the chants through Stavros's translation program.

"I wish Stav was here to deal with this OldWords stuff,'' Megan complained low-voiced to Susannah. "However clever his program is, statistically based guesses can't make the same leaps of faith as good old-fashioned insight.''

Danforth frowned at Weng from the depths of his wheelchair. His arms were folded tight against his chest like a barrier against opinion. "How do you know those drawings weren't done in retrospect? One hundred and sixty five *thousand* years, Commander? You'd have a planet-wide civilization ten times over in that span!''

"Civilizations degrade, Dr. Danforth.''

"Or they are destroyed,''Megan added from the side. "There's another whole mythos to cover that. Lifa, sing us a tale of the Great Destructions.''

Liphar chewed his lower lip, still raw from his ordeal, then nodded. "This is not OldWords,'' he offered. "Children sing this.''

The melody was simple, mournfully sweet in Liphar's birdlike chant-voice. Megan was sure she had heard it sung while the pyres were burning out on the Dop Arek.

CRI had little trouble providing a translation:

A fire in the sky,
Flames like rain,
A thousand avalanches roar where no snow falls.
Like ancient paper, the dry earth tears.

The rocks cry out.

The children's weeping is not so loud.
Do they cry for the children?

There is no one left to hold them.

Phew," said Megan, to break the silence around the monitor screen.

"Liphar," Danforth encouraged softly, speaking directly to the young man for the first time. "Sing me another."

33

"So Taylor's decided to listen. About time."

"He sees many things with his sky eyes, Ibi." Ghirra pointed upward as they walked, meaning not the stone vault of the tunnel but as far beyond as his mind could conceive. "He shows me DulValla. And he is very amaze that these Sisters play only where we live."

"You mean the Arrah is confined to the habitable zone? His data agrees with that?"

Ghirra nodded eagerly. "This is very small, he say, for very much activity." Stavros heard Taylor's dogmatic tone echo through the healer's explication. "Still he finds no understanding of the Arrah, what he calls 'weather'. You do not use this word to me."

"Arrah does not mean weather. Taylor's playing fast and loose with his translations. You have no word for weather as we mean it, as far as I can tell. If I'd found one, I'd have used it."

Stavros could not help a hunted glance along the corridor ahead where it darkened into a turn. Aguidran and two of her tallest rangers paced behind them, scanning the tunnel in both directions. "I bet I find weather in the OldWords, though, weather and climate and atmosphere and all that. Tay will love the OldWords. It was spoken by guys like him."

"Science-ists," Ghirra ventured thoughtfully.

Stavros grinned, wanting to hug him. "Scientists. Goddamn, you're good." He was delighted to see the Master Healer's lean da Vinci face light with fleeting pride. He had not seen that golden smile for a while.

"You are feel better, Ibi."

"Thanks to you, GuildMaster."

But Stavros was pale and aching by the time they reached the PriestHall. He leaned against the columned portal, light-headed, returning Ghirra an offhand smile as the Master Healer reached instinctively to support him. Aguidran offered her rangers a few brisk words to settle their anxiety, then left them guarding the door as she followed Stavros and her brother into the hall.

Stavros felt her presence like a specter at his back. He carried his guilt heavily. There was no appropriate apology he could offer the Master Ranger for having refused to understand that risking his own life also risked Edan's. Though Aguidran had been witness to his guar-miracle, though she had seen Kav Daven literally walk through storm and fire for his sake, she was clearly mistrustful, not of his intentions, but of whether he was worth the ill wind of trouble that blew around him, sweeping up anyone in range. Stavros was sure it was only for the old Kav's sake, and because her brother asked it, that she paid him the honor of accompanying him herself.

Or maybe she figures she's the best equipped to deal with real trouble.

"It's time to do something about Clausen," he said, resting on a bench just inside the door. He sensed this was not the time to discuss it but his weakness made him irritable. "Sneaking around with a troop of bodyguards, prevented from using my own equipment." He recalled Susannah's words. "One man holding us, the Sleds, CRI, everything hostage. It doesn't make sense."

"No. This does not," agreed Ghirra but his shoulders hunched in a very Terran-like shrug of impotence.

"It would be hard to get the drop on him, though." Stavros leaned back against the wall. "What we really need is some kind of long-distance weapon: spear, slingshot, blowgun . . . better still, get the laser away from him. Serve him right to be wasted by his own gun."

Ghirra listened, missing the unfamiliar colloquialisms but not the ominous dreamy tone. Aguidran watched with a hint of new interest. Stavros thought he detected support in her stance, but reminded himself that he was overeager to regain her good opinion.

"What do you think to do, Ibi?"

Stavros looked a faint plea to Aguidran. "Nail him. Pay him back for what he did to Edan."

"You say, end his life?"

Ghirra's insistence forced him to face his own avoidance. Glib euphemism might soften the expression of the act but not the act itself.

"You would *kill* him?" Ghirra repeated.

Stavros forced his tongue a little closer to reality. "Execute."

"Murder, Ibi."

Stavros blinked at him. He had thought this was a translation debate until Ghirra chose to throw his own tactics back at him with such obvious intention. Aguidran shifted, muttering darkly. Ghirra flung back a terse response that made her stiffen angrily, but she held her peace.

Ghirra turned back sternly. "We want no murder, 'TavrosIbia"

Stavros glanced at Aguidran again. *Maybe YOU want no murder* . . .

"Ghirra, it may be the only . . ."

"No. It is not ever the only." His look said, *You kill an animal, not a man.*

And what if the animal IS a man? But Stavros dropped his eyes, nodded. "It's all moot anyway, as long as he's got the laser." He gathered his aching body and rose. "Enough of this. I came to see the Kav."

The PriestHall was hot and stuffy, depressingly empty compared to its usual bustle. All the able-bodied priests had put off their scholars' garb to help care for the wilting food crop. But a low sweet-voiced chanting whispered through the thick columns like a forest breeze. A few sober-faced apprentices, stripped to the waist in the oppressive heat, came and went singly on essential errands. The two long tables in the guild library were crowded with elder priests debating over stacks of ancient books.

At the head of the nearest table, Kav Ashimmel broke off an intense discussion to glare at Stavros as he passed. He heard the word "raellil" muttered in his wake, then Ashimmel's silencing growl.

I'm going to have to do something pretty remarkable to redeem myself with Ashimmel.

Stavros suffered another crisis of doubt. *Why me, old man? I*

*had no messianic leanings before you set your fire in my palms
. . . or did I? Walk on water, Ibiá? Tried that one lately?*

He tried to see himself as he had been, a suggestible young
man in search of something to believe in, with no special qualities beyond a thirst for miracles and an eagerness to confront
powers perhaps beyond his control but not, he thought, beyond
his understanding.

Before, I was that. What am I now?

"What's going on with the books?" he asked Ghirra when
they had moved beyond the aura of frenzy at the tables.

"They talk and study to remember the signs."

"There are still signs they don't know?"

"These signs must have sure knowing. They are White-Sky
and the rain that is fire."

"White sky?"

"Sign of Phena-Nar."

Phena-Nar. The Hot Death. Stavros caught Aguidran's grim
nod.

The PriestGuild was preparing itself in earnest to receive the
dire signs of their most fearsome legend: Devastation.

"It won't happen," Stavros blindly assured both Ghirra and
himself. "Not this time. The Kav has a plan. He'll make himself
heard somehow."

"I think these Sisters do not listen."

"He's done it before."

Ghirra's pursed lips denied it.

You think it was coincidence at the Leave-taking, Stavros
accused him privately. *You . . . scientist!*

But he admitted that the whole concept of getting through to
the Goddesses rested on the unevidenced assumption that they
possessed communicable consciousness. The intention implied in
the intricate strategies of the Arrah offered no proof of the
Sisters' awareness of anything but each other. But he was haunted
by that instant of bottomless terror that had driven him to flee
death's release for the agonies of continued existence. He had
sensed consciousness then, something *searching* for him.

Kav Daven lay in a cushioned alcove at the far end of the hall,
curtained with heavy embroidered draperies. He might have been
dead, embalmed already, so waxen was his finely netted skin
and so faint the rise and fall of his emaciated chest.

His young apprentice girl, knitting glumly beside the cushions, flushed with a shy smile of welcome to see Stavros on his
feet. Her dark eyes followed him doelike with adoration as he
knelt stiffly by Kav Daven's side.

Stavros took one ancient hand in his own, hoping to feel the dull fire in his palms leap with responsive heat. But the heat stayed steady, simmering. The old priest's hand was frighteningly cool and thin, bones wrapped with the merest wrinkled tissue of skin.

Ghirra lowered himself to the floor. His hands hovered inquiringly above the Kav's chest and Stavros thought a faint new life flushed the ashen cheeks.

"Susannah calls this 'coma'," said the healer sadly. "She could give him food with the tubes, she says, but the guild will not allow."

"Ashimmel won't, you mean."

"Yes. He will starve if he does not wake."

Stavros gripped Kav Daven's wrist and called on the magical fire in his own hands to flow into the cooling body.

Raellil, is it? Then prove yourself! Be good for something!

The old man lay unchanged, his breath the slightest flutter.

Fear seized Stavros, that Kav Daven might die before making it clear to him what he was supposed to do, or how he was meant to do it.

"It won't work," said Danforth. "I already tried to talk him into it before, while you were away."

Susannah watched the dust-sifted path for obstacles that might trip him up as he struggled gamely through the heat. He wore a Sawl scarf wrapped Arab-style around his head. A sleeveless Sawl robe draped his broad shoulders like an aba.

The Ethiopian Prince, indeed! Susannah grinned, impressed.

But the leather pads of the crutches were dark with his sweat, as dark as his glistening skin. He was giving up more moisture than even the parched air could absorb. She worried that he was pushing too hard, too soon, but the gift of the crutches had been the excuse he needed. If he was not hunched over CRI's terminal, he was hobbling around in the sun.

Damn deadly sun.

They passed a temporary irrigation outlet. The hastily laid ceramic piping coughed up the barest trickle into the seared fields. Water was being carried by hand to the root crops and succulents in the terraces. Susannah had heard that the FoodGuild had decided to harvest the grains early, to minimize the losses to dessication. The cost would be losing a mature seed crop for the next season's planting.

"Things didn't seem so critical before," she said. "I mean, the situation, the weather and all."

Danforth stopped, blowing air like an exhausted runner. "You heard Emil's reaction when Liphar was telling me about the Destructions?''

"Megan says Emil'd be endangering the legality of his claim if he took the Sawl or their Goddesses seriously," Susannah reminded him.

Danforth readjusted the crutches under his arms and looked down at her seriously. "You know, I'd like Stavros down here as much as you would. This approach is real new to me. I need his head. I either take things too literally or not literally enough. Like, should we really expect the ground to open, and, what do they mean, 'white sky'?"

"Ghirra's been trying so hard to . . ."

"I know, and he's amazing, but he and CRI are just not enough between them to resolve all the translation ambiguities in these wipe-out myths, and it's near impossible for Stav to work up there without CRI. There's a lot of time being wasted running back and forth in secret. I *need* that time!

"If I can break down these myths enough to find a real pattern that can be matched to some cyclic effect of the nebula, I could offer these folks some idea of what lies ahead. Maybe the past Devastations have been exaggerated, or they happened for some other reason." He stood aside for a line of Sawls bearing emptied water jugs back to the Caves. "Or maybe they didn't happen at all. I don't know yet. I don't have enough data. The control factor is still eluding me."

"Stav will just tell you it's the Goddesses," Susannah warned.

"Well, I'd like to go head to head with him on that, you know? Once you make one connection between myth and fact, you start looking for others. Maybe there's something in it. But Emil's not going to give on this, I assure you."

"He has let up on Weng a little."

"Mmmm." Danforth glanced back at the Lander, squinting into the sun. "And if I were you, I'd ask myself why."

When she discovered the ladder still in place in the main hatch, Susannah climbed it, nervous but determined. It was odd to walk the cool metal corridors after so long, where her footsteps rang and even the sinuous curve of the hull was broken by machined right angles at floor and ceiling.

His door was ajar, spilling a faint glow into the dim corridor. Susannah knocked, then eased the door open and found herself staring into the stubby nose of the laser pistol. Behind the door, Clausen rolled his eyes, lowered the gun and tossed it onto his bunk.

"Change your mind?" He straightened one arm against the

233

wall on the door side of her head, so that his wrist grazed her cheek and her only move away from him was into the cubicle.

"No. But I have to talk to you."

He pushed away from the wall. "Are you sure? Nobody else does."

She was surprised that he sounded so aggrieved, or maybe it was just his boredom speaking. He dropped onto his neatly made bunk, relaxing against the pillows and the wall. He watched her with a faint come-on smile. The laser lay like a third presence between them.

Clausen patted the taut blanket. "Come. Sit. As you can see, there's nowhere else."

Susannah could not share his relish in this new sex-charged game. The promise of pleasure in his eyes, the desire utterly without need, was disturbing in ways she did not at the moment care to analyze. She stayed by the door.

"Just tell me this," she demanded bluntly. "If he's sent off his protest and you've filed your countercharges, why do you still want to kill him?"

His smile broadened. "You've been talking to Taylor."

Susannah blinked, "I . . ."

"What a quandary for you, Susannah, to be both a romantic and a pragmatist at once. Let me guess: you think I should let the legal issues take their own course, set aside my unseemly bloodthirst for revenge and concentrate on getting us the hell out of here with our skins intact."

Left without her prepared speech, she blurted, "There's something very weird going on with this world, Emil! Aren't you the least bit curious?"

"Is that anything like why don't I care?" His eyes flicked away in irritation. "You really have been talking to Taylor."

"And Megan and Weng and Ghirra and Stavros . . ."

"Well. At least you admit to the latter. We have made some progress." He looked back at her tiredly. "What are you proposing?"

"A truce." To head off his expression of disgust, she added hurriedly, "Not even permanent. Just for a kind of . . . summit conference. We do need to sit down, all of us, to make what sense we can of all this, so we can know what to do. We were meant to work as a team, after all!" She looked down. "We'd do it without you if we could, Emil, but all of us agree there wouldn't be much point."

"How kind of you to throw me that bone," he said dryly. He patted the bunk again. "Susannah, sit down for a minute and listen. Really, for a grown woman, you are in such need of schooling.''

Pique strengthened her. She ventured in and perched on the foot of the bed, trying not to stare at the laser, so easily within her reach. *More of his games*, she realized.

Clausen's smile let go of its seductiveness. "Now tell me why I should care. I'll win in the end anyway. Even if the planet burns itself to a crisp and your precious Sawls with it, I still win. The mining robots don't need temperate weather or even an atmosphere to get their job done. Do you understand?''

"Sure, I understand," she replied briskly, refusing to look defeated. "But how do you win if the planet gets you first?" She reined in her impulse to grab the gun. "Weng's worried enough now to talk openly about aborting the mission.''·

"Over my dead body," he said, but he seemed to actually consider for a moment. "So Ibiá's agreed to your conference plan?''

"Not yet," she admitted. "And he was sure you wouldn't either." Sawl-like, she spread her hands. "But, Emil, what have you got to lose?''

"Not a goddamn thing," he replied with a smile so unreadable that Susannah wondered suddenly what she had set in motion.

34

Stavros crouched at the corner of the cave mouth, where the overhang dropped in a ragged slash to meet the ledge. There was deep shadow there, and concealment. Liphar hunkered beside him, with one ranger taking up her post behind them, another on the interior stairs and a third shading his eyes with casual watchfulness against the harsh sun flooding the far side of the entrance.

"Christ, what a mess," murmured Stavros. He lowered himself disconsolately to the floor and leaned against the rough rock. The glare hurt his eyes. Healing, his shoulder ached. The brutalized skin and tissue were struggling back to life.

What am I doing out here? he asked himself. *Easier, so much easier, to hole up in the womblike dark of the StoryHall, sleep and ponder, make love to Susannah as often as I can find the strength . . .*

He leaned forward for a better view to the west. His head edged out of the shadow and the three rangers moved as one to stop him. Liphar grabbed him and pulled him back. Stavros did not argue.

"Much worse than I expected, Lifa."

Liphar grunted his assent, his fingers telling the blue bead on his wrist.

The plain was burned dry. The russet foliage that had flourished in the flood ravines was reduced to sooty powder, mingling with the seared earth to dust the entire landscape with a single ashen tinge. The air was utterly clear, without a hint of moisture. The western horizon was a knife-edged curve against a sky like polished jade.

The grain crops stood like a multitude in trance, their wilted leaves like limp arms hanging beside bent and broken stalks. Dried mud choked the plantings in the terraces, the crust between the rows was broken by sharp radial cracking around the roots.

"There's nothing left," Stavros grieved.

Liphar wet his peeling lips. "Some there is."

"But it won't last long."

"Not long, no." He touched Stavros' arm and pointed across the plain at the flat green sky above the Vallegar. "This is what I want you look."

The baked sky-glaze changed color along a distinct line like a cloud front several degrees above the saw toothed profile of the mountains. But the change was slight, not green sky crossed by white cloud; rather, green meeting paler green, just enough to be noticeable.

"Will come here, this," said Liphar solemnly. "Get more hot, very bright. White-Sky."

Stavros looked more closely. "That's White-Sky?"

Liphar nodded faintly. Grim acceptance was his most recent defense, learned perhaps while waiting out the long, blistering hours in the sun of Clausen's interrogation pit. Stavros suspected that the young man was even indulging himself in a certain priestly satisfaction at seeing his guild's worst predictions proven true, one after the other.

Abruptly, the remote poetic beauty of the myths seemed a barrier to hope or progress. Fact or fiction, they were not specific enough to inform useful action. If Kav Daven's charge to him was to deal with the crisis of an impending Devastation, Stavros knew only that his knowledge was insufficient.

Kav! If you'd only tell me what . . . !

He wondered if it was finally time for him to learn to live with despair as a daily companion, as the Sawls did, as they had done for what would very likely prove to be eons. But there was another approach.

How would Taylor explain White-Sky?

He shifted, leaning forward again but only to the edge of the concealing shade. A mere half mile away, the Lander glinted dully through its coating of ash. Two, maybe three, figures moved about the scorched clearing. Aguidran's watch reported that Clausen was keeping himself in plain sight lately.

Hoping I'll get overconfident . . . hoping I'll show myself. Well, I may have to do just that.

The Sleds were parked side by side, two triangular hulks draped in dusty silverfilm.

Nearly ready, Susannah says. Both of them.

He wished now that he had learned to fly the touchy, awkward craft. If he was going to steal a Sled, he would also have to kidnap a pilot.

Can't count on McPherson . . . Weng? She might do it willingly at this point.

He pulled back into the shadow and slouched against the wall. Liphar met his troubled scowl with concern of his own.

"You go inside now, Ibi? No safe here."

"Yes, Lifa, we'll go in for now."

For now, he decided, *but not for long*.

35

Megan stilled the nervous tapping of her foot against the plastic crate. "Too dark in here," she muttered to Danforth. "Ought to let that damn sun pour in with all its fury, so we remember why we're doing this."

Danforth nodded, intent on the computer screen.

"The field uses less power than the coolers," replied McPherson with unempathetic logic. She perched on the wheel of Danforth's chair and leaned against his shoulder to study the screen.

Weng appeared from the galley area with a tall Sawl jug filled with water. Susannah followed with a stack of white plastic ship's mugs. Weng set the damp ceramic down on the first of a line of crates she had assembled into an impromptu conference table. She surveyed her arrangement like a society hostess, counting places.

Megan watched with a small smile. "You know," she confided to Danforth, "in China, they still serve tea to guests in little covered cups."

"Commander probably wishes she had some of those," snorted McPherson. "This is stupid, all this fuss, like it was some kind of party."

"Her response to the damn anarchy of the situation," said Megan reasonably. "Formalities impose structure. Structure promises to keep things from flying off in all directions."

"Rather a case of the barn door after the horse," commented Danforth. "But what the hell? If it makes her feel better . . ."

"You are remarkably tolerant these days, Taylor," Megan observed.

"I am remarkably tired of fighting wars that haven't been declared. Got enough problem here with the one that has."

"Does that mean you won't jump down Stav's throat the minute he arrives? Do you have any idea how much maneuvering used to go on trying to keep you two apart?"

Danforth raised his eyes from the screen. "I see things a little differently these days. And I'm willing to bet he does, too." He offered her a knowing smile. "Counting sides, Meg?"

Megan shrugged, refraining from glancing at McPherson, whose only clear commitment was her loyalty to Danforth. "I like to know these things."

Weng glided about in purposeful silence, bringing out a final folding chair, gathering up her notes. She circled the empty table once, checked the buttoning of her clean white uniform, then seated herself at the head and began laying out her papers in ordered piles. Susannah waited at the other end, watching both the entry cylinder and the ladder to the main hatch. Abstractedly, she traced the lettering on a crate top, over and over.

Megan fidgeted. No one was late. The meeting wasn't due to start for ten minutes. But the waiting had begun hours ago for all of them. *What kind of weird hopes are we resting on this?* she wondered. *It's just a meeting, not a solution.*

Danforth quietly voiced her worry. "You think he'll show?"

Megan's nod was more positive than she felt.

Clausen backed swiftly down the hatch ladder, swinging off halfway to land catlike on the balls of his feet. He had found freshly laundered khakis, crisply collared and cuffed. The laser in its neat holster seemed almost decorative on his belt. He stood pulling down his sleeves while he assessed the mood and marked out the positions of the players.

"Mr. Clausen," said Weng with the briefest of nods. "I am glad you could make it."

He dipped his head with a hint of satire. "Wouldn't miss it for the world, Commander."

He approached the table, unsnapped his holster flap and with great ceremony laid the laser in the center of the table. Instead of relaxing, everyone tensed to the laser's too visible presence.

Clausen smiled, then sauntered toward the foot of the table, clearly enjoying the unease that greeted his every move. Susannah slid away as he neared, but he pretended to take this for courtesy. He pulled out a folding chair and lounged into it, tipping back to rest his boots on the crate top.

"No sign of the Loyal Opposition, I take it?"

Susannah paced to Weng's end of the table. "He'll be here."

But even when Ghirra appeared at the mouth of the cylinder, Megan was still unsure. She craned her neck to see if he had come alone. There were other shadows blocking the entry, but she could not tell if Stavros was among them.

The Master Healer replayed Clausen's scrutiny somewhat more deliberately. He nodded to Weng, then noted Clausen with his feet on the table, the others grouped around the terminal and Susannah caught in her anxious drift between. Megan was intrigued to notice that Ghirra seemed to have dressed formally for the occasion, in softly draped tunic and pants of layered white linen that set off his brown hands and face and lent the straight planes of his body the grace of dignity.

When his caution was satisfied, he looked to Weng, his gaze skimming past the laser on the crate top without particular notice. Weng drew his attention back to it with an eloquent gesture of distaste.

"Mr. Clausen has voluntarily divested himself of his weaponry, GuildMaster. I think it is safe to begin."

Ghirra's eyes flashed to the laser and lingered. He moved to the table curiously. Clausen's feet hit the ground instantly. Ghirra froze, then spread his palms.

"I have not seen this before," he explained, and Megan realized queasily that his curiosity was genuine.

"Want to see what did the damage, is that it?" Clausen's smile was mostly teeth as he relaxed back into his chair and returned his boots to the tabletop. "Go ahead. Pick it up. It's not armed." He looked around to the others. "What do you think I am, crazy?"

Some errant hint of craft escaping from beneath the prospector's easeful mask caught Megan's wary eye.

He's lying.

She knew it for certain, but could not decide if it was more to her advantage to expose him, or to know better and say nothing.

Ghirra took another step but did not reach for the gun.

"Go ahead," urged Clausen. "I'll give you a demonstration later, if you like."

"There is no use for this here," said Ghirra.

Clausen laughed indulgently. "But there will be, my good doctor, when every mining sod on the planet is packing one. You of course will be in great demand, having gotten your experience with laser burns so early . . ."

"Ghirra."

The Master Healer did not turn at the sound of his name.

Stavros stood in the entryway framed by a flash of sun across the cylinder's mirrored arc. The rest of his Sawl entourage filed in on either side.

Megan's gasp was private but involuntary. He was thinner, yes, to be expected, but could he have grown taller? She told herself it was the unaccustomed straightness of his stance, the surprisingly authoritative lift of his sculptured chin. He was washed, shaved and combed, his black hair slicked back, perfectly manicured. The constant threat of temper had given way to clear-eyed determination. His dark eyes, riveting in his pale, angular face, demanded attention. Megan felt proud, and wondered how much pain he was in.

No more adolescent skulking about for this one. Green, Emil? Not any more. At least he's learned the value of putting on a good show.

She looked for Clausen's reaction to the well-staged entrance of this young lordling, who came flanked by white-clad Sawl advisors and backed up by a hatchet-face ranger bodyguard led by the Master Ranger herself. She was in time to see Clausen's jaw sag fleetingly, then tighten in automatic rage. The easy drape of his body did not change, but his fingers twitched like the tail of an irritated cat.

"Stavros, my boy," he crowed softly.

Will he see how hard it is for Stavros to look him so calmly in the eye? Megan tensed, then sighed. Clausen saw everything, every subtlety, but it did not matter. The show was for the others, not to fool Clausen, but to prove the depth of Stavros' claim on the hearts of Sawl and Terran alike. Not Stavros alone, but the entire planet must be shown as Clausen's adversary.

Weng stood in welcome, her lips pressed tight against a glad smile.

Stavros held Clausen's eye, almost succeeding in matching the

240

prospector's throaty casual tone. "If it's not armed, then it won't matter if someone else holds it."

He turned his head so slightly that his next word seemed more an order than a request. "Commander?"

"No," said Clausen, rising.

"Lieutenant?" Weng parried quickly.

Clausen acceded with a stiff nod and sat back. McPherson slipped out from behind Danforth and padded forward to take up the laser pistol. It was not swallowed by her smaller hand as it was by Clausen's. She held it awkwardly a moment, then shoved it into the hip pocket of her uniform.

"Sit, please, Lieutenant." Weng lifted her arms in a gathering gesture. "Can we all be seated?"

Stavros sat mid-table, Ghirra on one side, Liphar on the other. Aguidran fanned out the retinue behind him so that access to the cylinder was blocked by sturdy Sawl bodies. As the others moved toward the table, Clausen dropped his feet and leaned forward.

"How's the burn, boy? Nothing worse for pain, I know. I could show you scars . . ." He smiled at the memory. "Susannah giving you anything for it?"

Stavros eased back into the hard plastic of his chair and stretched his legs, soaking up the refreshing cool of the air. "I see you got the power link working even without me, Emil."

"I assume CRI will be monitoring this meeting," said Megan to the room in general.

"Every word," Danforth assured her. "Listening, CRI?"

"Listening and recording, Dr. Danforth."

Danforth turned his chair away from the terminal and drew up to the table opposite Stavros. "Welcome to the Club, Ibiá," he remarked cryptically. "You're looking remarkably well, considering."

Megan and Susannah took seats between Danforth and Clausen. McPherson and the laser were isolated in the more neutral space between Danforth and Weng. The bustle settled into anticipation.

Weng cleared her throat. "I have called this meeting to discuss the advisability of a Mission Abort."

Danforth jerked around. *"What?"*

"But, Commander . . ." Susannah protested.

Megan saw identical looks of wary surprise come and go in the faces of Clausen and Stavros. She almost laughed aloud. *Well played, Weng!* The Commander had hit on the single issue that could be counted on to unify her crew and put herself back into a position of authority over them.

"That is not why we called this meeting," Danforth began angrily.

"Please remain calm, Dr. Danforth. I said we are here to *discuss* the possibility."

Ghirra murmured to Stavros, then frowned at his muttered reply. Stavros laid a reassuring hand on his arm. Recognizing Weng's announcement for the power play it was, Clausen relaxed and returned his boots to the table, awaiting further development without comment.

Megan decided to get the ball rolling. "Why should we want to abort the mission, Commander?"

Weng referred to the pile of papers on her right. "I present the following concerns: first, the rapid shrinkage of food and water supplies available from local sources."

"We have enough supplies of our own to last at least another two months," Megan countered.

"God help us all," Clausen groaned softly.

Weng lifted the top sheet with delicate fingers and began to read. "Second, the consistent interruption of our vital main power source, due to apparently unpredictable local weather conditions. Without our power link, we are forced to rely on local generosity which . . ." She paused to offer her Sawl listeners a gracious glance. ". . . has been extreme but cannot help but be taxed by the worsening situation.

"Third, there is the equally consistent damage being sustained by expedition equipment. Fourth, the increasing frequency of violent disagreement between expeditionary personnel."

When this last provoked a ripple of ironic laughter, Megan knew that Weng's gambit had been marginally successful. The focus of everyone's energies was shifting to her. She was the one they had to convince.

It won't hold, Weng. Better play it for all you're worth.

"Finally," Weng continued, "all the above, together with the apparent progression toward increasingly life-threatening conditions, lead me to question this expedition's ability to fulfill its scientific mandate." She paused again, placed the paper to one side and folded her hands with the precision of a dancer. "And now, perhaps someone would care to venture a reason why we should *not* abort the mission."

Danforth pounced immediately. "Because we're not done here, damnit!"

"My point was precisely that circumstances may have rendered us incapable of getting done," Weng replied mildly.

"A few bad moments," he contested hotly, "do not invalidate the good work that *is* being done here!" His aggrieved tone said he felt personally betrayed. Megan wondered if Weng might have been wiser to warn Danforth beforehand of the tack she intended to take. His recent claims to the contrary, his habit of quick, arrogant rage was not completely discarded.

But Weng made no effort to soothe his outrage. "Please be more constructive in your arguments, Dr. Danforth."

Megan felt a pang of sympathy for the angry planetologist. *She's really going to string him along, use him to make this abort threat sound more convincing. To whom? Clausen?*

"But we're on the verge of a breakthrough here!" Danforth railed. "We can't just walk away from Fiix with the story only half told. How can you even suggest it, Commander, with so many of the crucial insights being your own? It could be the discovery of the century!"

Megan remembered CRI dutifully recording this puffed-up exchange, with Captain Newman and the Orbiter crew no doubt listening in.

Ah. She quickly reassessed the situation: Weng and Danforth were already in league, building up the scientific profile of the mission within hearing of authorities potentially higher than Clausen. The prospector evidently reached the same conclusion, for he began immediate steps to undermine their claims.

"A few scratches on the wall of some cave are the discovery of the century?" he drawled. "Would you care to lay that one out for us, Taylor?"

Which is exactly what they want to do, but better to have it drawn out of them than to make it obvious they're selling a line. Oh what a tangled web we weave . . .

Danforth contrived to look hesitant. "I really hate to . . . the thesis is still unpolished but . . . well, it was Weng's suggestion at first but it's becoming clear to me as well that this world was once home to a high-tech civilization."

"Is that so?" Clausen sucked his teeth, bored already.

"Well, look at the evidence," Danforth pursued. "Those wall carvings you dismiss so easily chart the progressive encounter of the Coal Sack Nebula with Byrnham's Cluster, past, present and future, with as much accuracy as our own observations are capable of."

"*Star*Hall is a more appropriate translation than SkyHall anyway," Stavros murmured.

"Further evidence," said Danforth. "The Toph-leta: ancient texts, preserved as guild treasures, that contain advanced mathematics and atomic theory, no longer recognized as such by the current inhabitants."

"A complete periodic table," added Weng, "preserved in the

Toph-leta of the Physicians' Guild, that includes elements numbered beyond those in our own table.''

Clausen flicked Megan an accusing eyebrow. "I don't recall that one being mentioned in Ibiá's little missive home.''

"The tip of the iceberg," gloated Megan. "What about the current sophisticated high-temperature ceramic and glass technology that is major levels beyond the rest of Sawl technology?"

Clausen nodded as if this was old hat, but of minor technical interest nonetheless. "Magnesium and aluminum silicates, yes. I have been wondering how they produce the heat to work those high-temperature clays.''

"Or the OldWords?" Stavros spoke up, and heads turned. "A lost language, preserved in ritual, that expresses these advanced technologies and much more that we can't even conceive of.''

Clausen laughed with all appearance of delight. "My, my, what a well-rehearsed presentation.'' His voice heavy with irony, he looked to Susannah, who was staring at her folded hands. "Nothing to add, lovely one?''

"Lord, maybe it's actually possible . . . ?'' Susannah glanced around the table earnestly and spoke as if posing them a remarkable mystery. "My evidence suggests the genetic engineering of an entire ecosystem, within the planet's existing natural structure.''

Into the pause, Weng urged, "For instance, Dr. James?''

"Well . . . three strains of dairy and draft animals, their DNA match nearly identical, the variation among individuals within a strain limited to aesthetic qualities, like color or hair quality, each strain so carefully profiled for specific use as to invite speculation that the ancestral stock were engineered or cloned.''

Susannah's enthusiasm built as she allowed herself to express her suspicions in public for the first time. "Or: food plants and animals designed to thrive in a dark cave environment. Domestic plant varieties that grow at nearly twice the rate of the wild flora. A Sawl food cycle, human to animal to plant to human, that functions in self-sufficient isolation and allows the Sawls to survive within a natural biosphere which is poisoned by accumulations of toxic trace metals.''

She met Ghirra's wondering glance. "It's true. I just know it is.''

"How quaint,'' Clausen uncrossed and recrossed his legs as they rested on the table. "A long-lost civilization. That and two fifty'll get you on the subway. I'm sorry I'm not convinced, but neither will the Courts be. A lot of worlds have been here and gone.''

Danforth rounded on him hotly. "Christ, isn't that the whole point? This world *should* be gone, but it isn't! It's still supporting life, in debatable fashion perhaps, but supporting it nonetheless!''

''I don't see how all this should affect . . .''

''Damnit, you can take the commercial politics of this situation and shove 'em for all I care . . . and I don't give a shit about my funding! A good scientist can always find backing! Meanwhile, before you go digging up the place and disturbing things, there's a major mystery to be solved here: by all known rules of the universe, this planet should be an airless chunk of charcoal by now due to collision with the Coal Sack!''

Clausen chose to let the slight against CONPLEX pass unremarked. He lifted his open palms in a Gallic shrug. ''Which it is well on its way to being! Check your figures again, Tay. The worst may be yet to come. That's what the Sawls think, correct me if I'm wrong. I'm not offering my support for any precipitous abort, but I think it would be wisest to just do our thing as quickly as we can and get out.''

Watch out, Weng! Megan worried. *He'll co-opt your initiative and have you on the defensive again.*

But Danforth was running with the ball. ''But don't you see the point? That old civilization is not lost! It's still here, or what's left of it, having metamorphosed as it engineered its own survival!'' He waved a hand across the table, so emphatic that Liphar cringed into his seat. ''These folks saw what was going to happen long ago and went into emergency mode. They went underground, dug out the cave systems, built a new lifestyle. They adapted food sources to the new conditions.''

''And they tried,'' said Megan, ''to assure the survival of knowledge as well, by establishing a tradition of extensive record-keeping. The only possible advantage to the Sawls of preserving a list of every birth since the year one is to encourage a memory of their long-ago past.''

''But the memory faded over the enormous stretches of time involved,'' added Weng. ''Science was forgotten. Goddesses were invented to explain vagaries of the weather that included periodic global devastations of the population. History became myth.''

Megan nodded. ''And the record-keeping merely ritual.''

''No,'' said Ghirra suddenly, then seemed surprised by how quickly he had their attention. He shook his head gravely. ''The Toph-leta is mystery, yes, but there is knowing for us in the guildbooks.''

''I didn't mean . . .'' Megan began apologetically. She won-

245

dered if there was a tactful way to tell someone they weren't as clever as their ancestors.

"The guildbooks tell the old knowing of the generations," Ghirra insisted. "A guildsman gives his knowing to his apprentice, but if he forgets a thing, the guildbooks keep the knowing to be found again."

"Or not found," said Clausen lazily. "Clearly, if Taylor is to be believed at all, there has been a major degradation of knowledge since your alleged ancestors saw the handwriting on the wall."

"They held on to what was necessary to survive," defended Susannah.

"The guildbooks hold the knowing," Ghirra repeated, as much to himself as to the others. "The guildbooks hold the *science*."

"Ghirra . . . ," On the verge of a meaningless sympathetic remark, Susannah held back at Stavros' raised hand.

"What's in your mind, GuildMaster?" he asked softly.

The healer hesitated. "If I know a . . . ilvesh . . . ?"

"Infusion," Susannah supplied.

"In-fusion. Yes. I make this one to cool a sick heat of children. I write this in the book of my guild, and this is science. You, TaylorDanforth, make the machine to take away the heat in the air." He stretched his arms wide in gratitude for the coolness inside the circle of the force field. "You write that in a book. That is science, yes?"

"Well, yeah . . . ?"

Ghirra appealed to him for understanding. "The PriestGuild have guildbooks also. These tell the playings of the Sisters, and the signs of the Arrah. This is their knowing from the generations. This is their *science*." He glanced around for a response, but focused on Danforth's perplexed scowl.

"More, more," said Danforth impatiently.

Ghirra shrugged nervously. "The PriestGuild say the Tophleta is the Sister-gifts, but I think this, TaylorDanforth, that the Toph-leta is the most old of guildbooks. This holds the most old science."

He ventured delicately into the expectant silence he had created, working hard at his limits within the alien language. "If the first PriestGuild write in a book how the Arrah, the *weather*, goes, what is the signs, all that, and this book is the Toph-leta of Priestguild, I think this book must has knowing how the ancestors make the Arrah, like Susannah say about the hakra and hjalk and all the plants, like TaylorDanforth make his machine."

"Wait—made the weather?" Megan was sure she had mistaken his line of reasoning.

Danforth's scowl flattened with disappointment. "You're saying your damn priests control the weather?"

"Not doing a great job, if that's the case," remarked Clausen but he allowed Ghirra some renewed interest.

"No, TaylorDanforth. I say *one time* my ancestors make the weather, to save the people from the Darkness . . . the too-much-heat that comes."

"Climate control?"

Megan hoped it was true. Stavros steepled his fingers on the table and leaned his head into them.

Danforth's chair rocked with his resistance. "*Climate control?*"

"You search this thing that makes the weather, Taylor-Danforth."

"The weather *now*, not a hundred fifty thousand years ago!"

"The made-plants and the made-animals are here. We are here, what the ancestors made us. Then this weather can be here also. Why not, TaylorDanforth?"

Tay will never make a teacher, mused Megan. *Too easily frustrated by the gaps in another's knowledge.*

But though the abyss of understanding between the Master Healer and himself was encouraging him to shout, Danforth struggled to remain reasonable. "First of all, the genetic engineering is still Susannah's informed guess. Second, you can't just make a climate and leave it at that. Weather doesn't just exist, man! Something has to make it work, make it move!"

"The Sisters make it move," said Ghirra easily. "Like here this machine makes the air cold."

"And there's your X-factor," said Weng with satisfaction.

Stavros looked up with a private smile. "We've been here before, GuildMaster." He flattened his palms on the crate top and sat forward, assuming his neutral translator's voice. "Ghirra is suggesting that the Sisters are not goddesses at all but man-made weather machines."

"The force field as big as the Ritz!" grinned Clausen. "I like your style, honored doctor."

Control the weather of an entire world?!

Danforth wasn't sure why the suggestion unhinged him so. Perhaps because it was the kind of fantastical explanation that he had been resisting, perhaps because it came from Ghirra.

He liked the Master Healer, had been convinced to accept him as an able doctor, but he still found it hard to allow any Sawl the respect due an equal in the realm of ideas. Even his recent delving into possible hints and parallels to be found within the Sawl mythology had been done in a spirit of desperate concession to necessity.

I don't believe this shit, he'd told himself, *but it can't hurt to look into it. Tabula rasa, eh? Any angle . . . all avenues of inquiry.*

He made an effort to pull his voice within a range of calm. "Does he have any idea what miraculous machinery it would take to control the circulation of an entire planet?"

Stavros regarded him impassively. "Perhaps he does. Why don't you ask him?"

Danforth could feel Weng's encouragement spreading like heat from the head of the table. He knew exactly what she was going to say.

"Something's moving it around, did you say, Dr. Danforth?"

Even that long ago, I must have suspected. "You buy this idea, Weng? You? Who's around to goddamn *run* these machines?"

"I certainly find it an intriguing idea in an area that has not been overpopulated with other possibilities." Weng shot a surreptitious glance at Stavros. "At least it offers a technological rather than a mystical base.

"It also explains the global nature of the phenomena, as well as the confinement of the actual weather activity to the narrow habitable zone. As to the issue of who would run them, I'm sure CRI would be the first to assert that a well-designed machine often runs better without human interference."

"To quote the Tale of Origins again," offered Megan, "the king/parent who was skilled in the ways of power—now read 'weather' as Stav's program suggested and we all pooh-poohed—died or went away. Perhaps I was wrong to assume no mention of a Creator."

Danforth fidgeted, preparing to make the leap. "Well, I suppose . . ."

Clausen sighed elaborately, "Oh go ahead, Tay, try it on for size. No worry of committing a scientific faux pas here. You're among friends."

Danforth thought of CRI recording every word and might have refused them the benefit of his wild speculations, were it not for the flattering eagerness with which the Master Healer awaited his reply.

"All right," he said hoarsely. "It's really very simple, given the assumption that the power and tech exist to do it. If you are faced with a heating up of the planet that is life-threatening to its biosphere, one way to deal with the crisis is to manage that heat,

248

pull the excess to, say, some uninhabited area, and to manage the moisture accordingly.

"Something like this would seem to be happening on Fiix: a zone of relative habitability is diagonally wrapped around the planet, caught between hemispheres dominated by extreme cold-wet and hot-dry foci. The anomalous southwest-northeast prevailing winds that cross this zone are the general mechanism for the exchange of heat and moisture necessary to keep the system in some sort of equilibrium.

"However," he reminded them emphatically. "It's not in equilibrium. Observing the Fiixian weather is like watching an aerialist teeter for balance. And the process is clearly not supporting the zone of habitability at the present moment, in fact it's beating the shit out of it!"

"One point for, one against," said Clausen. "The score is tied, honored doctor. What do you say to your machines' lethal inefficiency?"

"I ask this question for all my life," Ghirra replied steadily, "since that time I decide no goddesses could want this much deaths."

" 'Hast thou comprehended the earth in its breadth? Declare if thou knowest it all,' " Megan intoned. "At least Jehovah let Job know what the reason for his suffering was."

McPherson broke her long silence unexpectedly. "Maybe the machines are broken."

"Or breaking down," Megan added after some consideration.

"But then they've broken down before," Susannah pointed out. "And recovered before. Look at the guild records: a long history of global Devastations, followed by periods of relative calm."

Clausen glanced at his watch, then rolled his eyes upward. "You mean we should expect the repair crews any minute?"

"Maybe," she replied seriously, to challenge his reflex scorn. "Or if the guild records are true—and we did hear the same history in Ogo Dul—then maybe we have a periodic culling mechanism here. The wipe-outs are global and regular. Their coherence in space *and* time does look a bit unnatural. I know it sounds cruel, but some kind of built-in might have been necessary to keep world populations to levels that the reduced habitable zone can support. Maybe the Sawls have been proved to be too skilled at survival."

Megan shook her head. "There are plenty of strict population controls worked into the guild laws already."

"That could be a case of redundant systems," said Weng.

"Even the strictest of birth control programs couldn't stabilize the entire ecology," Susannah argued, "only the internal Sawlian one."

Danforth sensed the cascading of wild speculation toward the solid ground of accepted fact. "Wait a minute!" he cried into the face of their enthusiasm. "Wait just a goddamn minute!"

"You're worried about what drives it," guessed Clausen pleasantly.

"Among other things!" Danforth grabbed his temples, pressing inward. "A minor detail among other minor details, like the entire physics of the exchange process!"

"And what's your opinion of the good doctor's suggestion that fields are being manipulated to produce these results?"

Megan bridled at the subtle derision Clausen masked as encouragement. She pictured spectators at a suicide yelling, jump! jump! "I don't think Ghirra means force fields *specifically*," she declared.

"But an entire planet!" Danforth gestured helplessly. "The required energies are unimaginable. You'd need a substantial fraction of the solar constant!"

"Gigabuckets," Clausen chortled, then said with easy dogmatism, "But where there's energy to do the work, the work will be done." He leaned back, nodding. "Yep, it would take one hell of a power source."

Susannah searched Stavros' face for signs of pain that might explain his apparent withdrawal from the discussion. He sat with lowered eyes, listening quietly, his good arm flung protectively across the back of Liphar's chair. Aguidran shifted her weight soundlessly behind him, and the other rangers took this as permission to readjust their own stance. A ripple of movement passed around the table, Stavros stirring the last of all.

"Given that such machines could exist, Taylor," he proposed with studied deliberation, "would you be willing to say they'd explain all the weather anomalies you've observed on Fiix?"

Danforth pondered a moment, looking doubtful and a little trapped. "Now I know you're more sold on the goddess theory than the doc here is himself, and personally, I find that even harder to swallow than his machines, with or without human supervision. But no, I'd have to say in all honesty that no weather machine I'd design would behave this way. Theoretically, there are gentler, more efficient and potentially more life-sustaining ways to manage heat and water than slamming packets of one or the other around like cannonballs."

Clausen yawned and began a series of halfhearted calculations on his wrist terminal.

"Maybe Ronnie's right," said Susannah. "Maybe they're broken."

"Or maybe they're not," said Megan, "but the machines' design reflects some builders' preconceptions about the nature of weather that are lost to us through the passage of time."

"Who would ever conceive of weather as necessarily lethal?" Susannah countered.

"The Sawls are not far from that kind of thinking right now," said Megan.

Stavros shook his head. Susannah noted that when he laid his hands again on the table, they rested palm up, his fingers lightly curled as if protecting some treasure held within.

His guar-fire.

A passing stab of jealousy caught her by surprise. Not envy. Susannah had no desire to share the pain in Stavros' hands, but the accompanying mysticism had come to occupy the full center of his being. She believed that he believed it, but it made her nervous. And she could not compete with it for his attention.

"What you are all avoiding," he said with the kind of total conviction that disregarded other opinion, "is the notion of intention. The apparently conscious aspect of the Game. Because that, Taylor, is what Arrah really means, not weather at all, but 'game,' 'struggle,' 'contest.' "

Susannah thought it a true measure of the changes wrought during Danforth's convalescence that he did not respond to Stavros' irritating tone. Instead he turned a thin, ironic smile to Weng. "Commander, I think this is more in your area of expertise. Would you care to attempt a specific application?"

Weng toyed with the edges of another stack of notes. "I believe Dr. Danforth is referring to my recent efforts to use game theory as an analytical tool with regard to the dilemma of the local climate." She fixed Danforth with a neutral stare. "You hope, I assume, for mathematical proof that gamelike patterns can exist without needing to imply intention?"

"Numbers are not an answer to this question," said Stavros more gently.

Danforth rubbed his eyes. "Look, I'll admit it's been real hard lately to watch some of this shit coming down without jumping to the conclusion that there's some nasty consciousness out there having a field day at everyone's expense. But those kind of desperate conclusions are what occur to you in extremes. By the light of day, they don't satisfy."

Clausen broke off his calculating to offer slow applause. "Well, bravo. Then may I suggest that we explore a few more scientific avenues before falling down on our collective knees?"

"How much chance would CONPLEX stand in the Courts against actual living goddesses, after all?" Stavros murmured.

"Give it up, Ibiá. Even your pals won't go with you on this one."

"You were telling us about game theory, Commander?" Megan prompted.

Weng seemed pleased to be offered the gift of their whole attention. "Well. If the data were a simple list of numbers, we would ask ourselves, what do these numbers have in common, and what is the mathematical function that could have generated them? That function, once derived, would constitute the 'rules' that determine the various 'moves' of the 'game.'

"We then look at the pattern of these 'moves' in search of the 'objective.' In the case of Dr. Danforth's weather data, the patterns have indicated movement in response to one another. Thus we conclude that there are two sides, if you will, two sets of pieces. Patterns within the patterns indicate strategies, that is, relationships between moves that lead to consequences.

"Given all the various possible moves, we can calculate a large number of possible end states, that is, finishes for the game. The observed strategies order these possibilities into smaller and smaller numbers until you can deduce which end state is the actual consequence of those strategies. From this we deduce the object of the game.

"My conclusion has been that the object of this particular game is different for each of the two sides. For one, it is to neutralize an overbalance of heat within a given area of the habitable zone, for the other to cancel an overbalance of cold."

"With the violent redistribution of moisture as a strategy," said Danforth, eager again.

"Among others, such as the binding up of the opponent's potential energy so that it is untransferable to the kinetic energy he needs to move his pieces around the board, thus disabling him." Weng moved into her conclusion with relish, "These opposite objectives taken together could be seen as an attempt to achieve a balanced temperature in the zone of habitability, precisely the goal one would set if one were defending against excess heating of the atmosphere.

"Therefore, the object of the game—analyzed in terms that postulate no players or intention but deal merely with the coreacting data—the object could indeed be weather control."

Clausen fished a pen out of his pocket to jot a few numbers on the crate top.

Megan was unsatisfied. "Fine, Weng, but this puts us right

back where we started. It doesn't answer the question of why such extreme, lethal strategies are necessary."

"Or whose definition of weather control we're dealing with," added Susannah. "This current one doesn't seem to consider the Sawls' welfare one iota."

"Which in itself speaks against conscious intention," Weng agreed. "I understand that the Master Healer might refuse to credit a deity of such cruelty, so much worse even than indifference, but neither can one believe that the former inhabitants would go to the trouble to construct machines that produced climate inimical to life, particularly when the Coal Sack is about to do it for them."

"So I gotta be right," spoke up McPherson. "They *are* broken."

"If they exist at all, " reminded Clausen.

"Unless you go back to my culling theory," said Susannah.

"Or maybe there's intention, all right," offered Danforth darkly, "but the intention is every bit as nasty as my weaker moments lead me to suspect."

"Or," concluded Stavros with the implaccable serenity of a priest, "there is intention but we do not understand its nature."

Clausen drummed his pen softly on the crate top, then returned it to his pocket. "If you know something we don't, son, by all means enlighten us."

"I have seen an old man dance, and drive away the rain."

"Tut, Ibiá. Remember where you are. I doubt even the honored doctor here has much patience with such cant."

The prospector stretched and rose, shaking his legs out. He began a casual progress around the table, like the corporate chairman exhorting his board. "Myself, I care less about intent and more for the realities of climate control. Now this, Tay, could be the *real* discovery of the century."

Susannah felt the stirring of chill air as Clausen passed behind her. On the far side of the table, Aguidran detached herself from the retinue to move counter to Clausen's clockwise drift. She reached the space between Liphar and Weng and hovered, watching the prospector as she might have an approaching viper.

"Ah, but Emil," said Megan airily, "if you uncovered a viable process for climate control on Fiix, you'd lose the planet. Not even CONPLEX could steal legal title from a local population capable of that."

"*Once* capable," returned Clausen with a condescending smirk at Liphar, "maybe. I think we can safely assume the builders of such fantasy machineries to be long gone."

He laid both hands on Danforth's shoulders. The planetologist

253

tensed visibly but Clausen squeezed, patted and let him go. "But even old, broken equipment would offer clues to its manufacture. A find like that would make us rich, I mean all of us, CONPLEX, me, you, even the bloody Sawls." He grinned wolfishly at Ghirra. "What do you say, doc? Would you like to be rich?"

"What's got you so interested all of a sudden?" rumbled Danforth.

"I threw together a few rough numbers that might surprise you, Tay. A fusion technology not much more efficient than what generates our own FTL field could theoretically provide the energies required to move this atmosphere if scaled up appropriately."

"Theoretically according to who?"

"All we'd have to do, really, is learn how to generate the right kind of fields. We should be able to learn that, whether the alleged machines are working right or not."

He continued his progress around the table, passing McPherson who sat very still with her arms pressed into her lap. "Now, of course, it would also be interesting to learn what sort of fuel has kept our hypothetical machines stoked up over the course of a hundred and sixty-odd thousand years. Clearly they'd have to have access to an inexhaustible supply of something."

Stavros stared at his hands. He seemed to be hardly paying attention. Susannah tried to catch his eye, imagining him once more withdrawn into contemplation of his windswept visions.

From behind Weng, Clausen fixed him with a stare of innocent inquiry. "Perhaps there's a hint or two to be found in your precious myth with regard to that issue, my boy?"

On the crate top, Stavros' hands clenched and withdrew to his sides.

Stavros dared not move until the nauseating jolt of recognition passed through him. He feared he might let slip some further clue.

Does he know the answer? Can he really know what I am so sure of?

Stavros knew utterly, though it was instinct alone that told him.

In his mind, he saw the shadowed arching vaults of Eles-Nol, the guar cavern, crowded with its mammoth cylinders of glass. He saw the miles of thick white piping, and the lavender sparkle of the lithium ore, lifted from Clausen's pack by the Master Healer's hand. He remembered the grave accusatory look in Ghirra's eyes.

254

What does he with this? Ghirra had asked, and Stavros had answered with the truth.

The fire burned in his palms.

Raellil . . . ?

It is possible, then, to trace one's destiny from a single moment.

But only, he regretted, in retrospect.

Now the Master Healer frightened him further by leaning over to whisper in Sawlish, breaking their habit of speaking only English, wishing to know what had upset him.

"Private consultations, honored doctor?" needled Clausen.

Ghirra smiled humbly. "I did not know this word hypo-thetical."

Clausen smiled back and provided two possible Sawlish equivalents.

The man's calm terrified Stavros. He longed to jump up and run for the deepest cave he could find. The comfort of the heat in his hands could not salve the memory of an agonized dying. He'd been a fool to let Susannah talk him into this conference.

Gotta stick it out, Ibiá. Find out how much he only suspects.

"There would hardly be reference to fuel sources in a mythology built around living, breathing deities, Emil."

"Tut, more imagination, my boy. Do the goddesses eat? Any mention of food, perhaps?"

Stavros' breath stilled, as did Ghirra's beside him. He hoped the restraining hand he laid on Liphar's knee was an unnecessary precaution. He made a pretense of consulting Ghirra for the backward reassurance of seeing the same horrified comprehension lurking behind the Master Healer's helpful smile.

"There's no mention of eating in my recent research into the myths," said Danforth. "Only strategies and arsenals. Mostly the stories are concerned with the lengths one Sister will go to in order to beat the other to a pulp."

"And how badly the Sawls suffer as a result," added Megan, but she said it to Stavros with a searching squint that told him that his distress was more evident than he had realized.

"We oughta just go out there and find 'em," said McPherson. "When the sleds are finished."

"This is a big planet," scoffed Megan.

"If we respect the points of correlation between myth and sensing data, we start at the godhomes and work from there," Danforth suggested.

"No . . ." said Stavros, unable to stop himself.

"If they're machines, they can be fixed," pursued McPherson with the confidence of a confirmed technocrat. "That'd be good for the Sawls and everybody."

"Not good for the Sawls," said Stavros.

"It is not the worst idea, Mr. Ibiá." Weng's tone was puzzled.

"I thought we should try to contact them first," he blurted. The only definite part of his plan was that he had to be the first to meet the Sisters face to face.

"Contact a machine?"

A distant shout echoed faintly in the entry cylinder. The rangers nearest the opening stirred, looked around. One nodded at Aguidran's abrupt signal and slipped out into the sun.

"CRI is a machine," Stavros reminded them.

The shouting neared, a high-pitched summons. Stavros thought he heard his name called. Ghirra turned to listen.

Liphar fretted. "Ibi . . ."

"I know," he murmured.

"A thief to catch a thief?" Danforth shrugged. "It is something we haven't tried."

"What kind of signal, I wonder?" mused Weng.

The rangers rustled in the silver tunnel as the messenger arrived. She would not come in but stood breathless in the heat, repeating herself desperately.

Stavros listened very hard. He recognized the voice: Kav Daven's young apprentice girl. Aguidran backed three steps to the opening.

"Ibi," said Ghirra, rising. "Kav Daven calls you."

"GuildMaster?" Weng inquired. "Is everything all right?"

"A patient calls, Commander," he replied in urgent apology.

Stavros shoved back his chair.

"No, Stav. Don't move." McPherson's command froze Stavros halfway to his feet. She gripped the laser pistol with both hands extended like a cop, pointing at him. "Please. Sit."

Stavros sat down slowly.

McPherson flashed a desperate look at Weng. "Arrest him, Commander. For his own good."

"Weng, no," said Stavros. "Not now." He stood again, wary.

"Stav, he lied," Megan warned. "The gun is armed."

Clausen moved fast, flinging aside Liphar as the young man leaped on him, arms and legs windmilling like an angry monkey. Liphar crashed into the side of a crate with a yowl of pain. Aguidran grabbed Clausen's shoulder, jerking him backward, but he ducked and whirled to unseat her grip, then reached to twist her arm back and throw her against the side of the cylinder. Aguidran feinted as he turned and neatly stepped aside. His momentum carried him off balance until he was yanked back hard against her chest, his own arm imprisoned and her un-sheathed boot knife sharp at his throat.

"Now, McP!" he barked. "For Chrissakes, she'll kill me!"

Danforth lunged against the restraints of his chair to sweep his arm out and up, grabbing McPherson's clenched fists in one huge hand. He shoved the laser's nose into the air. The gun smashed a needle of light into the ceiling. Danforth wrenched the weapon from McPherson's grasp and levelled it at the struggling prospector.

"Tay, no!" pleaded Susannah at his side.

"Tell your sister to let him go, doc," Danforth growled. "She's in the line of fire."

"Tay . . ."

"Are you reading this, CRI?" yelled Danforth. "Are you getting it all?"

Ghirra said nothing, and Aguidran did not move. Stavros was transfixed by the darkly glimmering knife and the prospector's snarling helplessness. If Edan had been so equipped, she would have stood a better chance.

Hands pulled at him, Ghirra's, the other rangers'. He let them drag him up from his chair, though his shoulder screamed at their roughness.

Christ! he thought. *On the run again!*

But his next thought was for Kav Daven. He looked to Susannah desperately. "He might need you. Will you come?"

"Go ahead, Susannah," said Danforth soberly. "Nobody's going to get hurt, now we've disarmed him."

Susannah raced for her medikit.

Weng stood up, grasping at formality. "Mr. Ibiá, I expect you to report to me as soon as this current crisis is over. Do I have your word?"

Access to CRI tempted him. It would also be easier to influence their movements if he lived among them again. *And the Sleds are here* . . .

Stavros nodded. "My word, Commander."

He grabbed Susannah's hand as she trotted up with her kit slung over her shoulder, paused to throw Danforth a grateful glance, and hurried through the cylinder.

36

A winch platform waited at the bottom of the cliff, tended by an unexpectedly large assortment of engineers, priests and their various apprentices. Stavros stepped onto it gratefully, leaning into Ghirra's side.

The sun reflecting off the white cliff face scorched and blinded. The ache in his shoulder was a thumping bass accompaniment to every step. A winch ride would not only be quicker, but would save him the inevitable indignity of exhaustive collapse halfway up the broiling stairs.

Faces crowded around him, more than were needed to man the winch ropes, to steady the wooden pallet as Susannah and Liphar mounted, followed by two of Aguidran's rangers. Stavros wondered at the crowd, wondered at their intent serious faces, focused expectantly on his own.

Set a good example, he told himself, and stood as tall as he could manage. He wrapped his good arm around the twisted strands rising taut to meet the headknot of the rope bridle that cradled the pallet. His weaker arm rested about Susannah's waist, more for his own support than for hers. Her hip nudged softly at his groin. He slid his hand across her belly to press her against him, wanting her fiercely for the lovely simplicity of lust, so comprehensible and sure, so easily satisfied in comparison to the mysteries that pulled at him from every side, stretching him, redefining his life.

The engineers shouted, the crowd scattered awkwardly and the platform swung free and rose, swaying gently. The faces below followed its upward passage in silence. Most of the crowd headed for the stairs to make the slower, hotter ascent. Liphar edged around on the overladen pallet, calling attention to the sky. The sharp line of division had advanced further across the plain. Stavros was sure that the color contrast had increased. A pale greenish veil was being drawn toward the jade-colored zenith.

"You see, Ibi? It comes here," Liphar predicted.

Ghirra nodded tightly. "White Sky."

The cave mouth was jammed, more priests and engineers, and many from other guilds as well, all eager to grab for the ropes to help swing the pallet onto the ledge, to offer a supporting hand. The two rangers jumped off as the platform shuddered down, and began to clear a path through the throng.

Stavros and Ghirra led the way across the entry cavern and up the inner stairs. At the top of the stair, both sides of the corridor were lined with young priests and apprentices sitting cross-legged with their backs rigid against the wall. They chanted a dirgelike melody and Stavros feared he had come too late. He heard "raellil" murmured up and down the line. He felt a strange flutter of hands about his ankles, fingers reaching to brush the fabric of his pants, to touch the tops of his bare feet. He gripped Ghirra's arm.

"What are they doing?" he whispered, afraid that he already understood.

"They welcome you, 'Tavroslbia," the Master Healer replied, and Stavros thought he detected grave approval in his voice.

They hope too much of me, he worried. He could not recall even Ashimmel receiving such gestures of homage, only the Ritual Master himself. *Old man, what have you started?*

He glanced behind to be sure Susannah followed. Her serious calm smile reassured him. *My ballast, my anchor.* As long as he could call to mind the feel of her, skin against skin, heat and secret moisture, then he would remember he was a man, like other men.

Aguidran waited until her guildsman had cleared the cylinder, then shoved Clausen aside and backed herself into the entry. She held the long dark knife poised across her chest like a shield, glaring a final accusation at the remaining occupants of the Underbelly. She singled out McPherson for particularly black censure, then bent to sheath the knife in her boot, straightened and loped off across the sun-baked clearing.

Clausen picked himself up angrily. A hand touched to his throat came away bloodied. A slim scratch stained the crisp collar of his shirt. "That motherfucker's got an edge on it," he growled.

"Yes, she does, doesn't she . . ." agreed Danforth caustically. He cradled the little gun in his big hand and tuned it down, deactivating the pulse, bleeding off the power.

Weng pulled a clean handkerchief from a pocket of her uniform and handed it to Clausen, but made no move to help tend his wound. "Lieutenant McPherson, you are confined to quarters for the next twelve hours."

259

McPherson looked resentful and confused. "It was for his own good!" she protested.

"About the stupidest thing you could have done," said Danforth.

"What, it's better for him to run around getting shot up?"

"I do not require you to take such matters into your own hands, particularly at the expense of our good relations with the Sawls."

"Don't worry on that score, Commander," Megan assured her. "The Sawls know who their friends are."

"I'm sure they do," Clausen snapped. "The question is, do *you?*"

Danforth settled back into his chair with the laser cooling on his lap. Clausen's tanned face was etched with paler tension lines. His pupils seemed a brighter blue for being totally outlined in white. Danforth thought of the winter sun glinting off an iceberg.

The man's fucking furious, he gloated. *At last!*

"Fools, all of you!" the prospector spat. He held Weng's handkerchief pressed to his throat. "He's playing you all for goddamn fools!" He whirled on Weng. "Letting him waltz out of here like that? My god, he knows a soft touch when he sees one!"

Danforth thought Weng's control admirable, but reminded himself that her dignity was her only remaining weapon, her persistent calm in crisis the only parameter left with which to define her command.

"Mr. Ibiá will return when his business in the Caves is done," she replied without undue insistence. "I do not believe I have misjudged the value of his word."

"His *word!*" Clausen was incredulous. His hands clenched as if he would like to grab Weng and shake her. "What *is* it about that boy that you're all so blinded? You, Tay, what are you thinking of? Ibiá won't be back here of his own accord, not for a minute!"

"He came down willingly enough just an hour ago," commented Megan.

"He came down here to find out what we know!" Clausen shouted. He paced the length of the empty table, then swerved back to stand over the chair Stavros had occupied. His whole face narrowed as craft displaced the rage straining his eyes. "Because he knows something he's not telling us."

"Right," scoffed Megan.

"Mark me," Clausen returned ominously.

"What?" asked McPherson, ready to believe him.

"Something they've told him." Clausen continued around the table. "Something he's not even telling you, Meggies. You, his own mentor in conspiracy."

"Oh, come on," said Megan disgustedly.

Danforth did not offer his support but decided privately that the idea was not too farfetched. He'd watched Ghirra carefully. He'd seen the fear of discovery behind the Master Healer's eyes when the issue of the power source came up. But Danforth was sure that whatever secret they held among themselves, it offered them no answers, only further questions. He also guessed that Megan as well knew more than she had told him, but that he could now convince her to enlighten him further in return for a declaration of full support.

"If Ibiá knows so much," he said tiredly, "why would he risk his life down here to find out what we know?" It all began to sound like the worst of cheap spy thrillers.

"You don't want to see it," Clausen declared, "None of you! You're so stuck in your sentimental visions that you don't understand he'll sacrifice any of you, not just me, even Susannah, for the sake of his precious Sawls! I've seen them go native before and get that look in their eyes!"

He pulled the handkerchief away from his throat, screwed it up into a bloodied lump and threw it down on the table. "Fuck it. I'm tired of all this shit. Let him go on playing out his fantasies. I intend to beat him at his own game."

He strode to the computer terminal. "CRI, work up an equipment manifest for me—one Sled, one passenger, two weeks minimum duration."

"Yes, Mr. Clausen."

McPherson bolted to her feet. "You're going without me?"

Clausen smiled nastily. "You are confined to quarters, I believe."

"Commander!"

"You can't stop me, Weng. You have no legal authority to stop me from doing the job I came here to do."

Weng stared back at him blandly. "I had no such intention, Mr. Clausen. When there is a Sled working to your satisfaction, by all means be on your way. Lieutenant McPherson however will remain behind to continue repairs to the second vehicle, and to pilot it once it is functioning."

Clausen's outburst of temper seemed to have restored his good humor. He shook his head at the sullen pilot in mock sympathy. "Now, McP, you don't want Tay to be the only one left to pilot, do you? Look what happened the last time he went flying . . ."

* * *

Susannah had never been in the Priesthall before. She had expected something grander, or darker, or more austere, a further extension of the FriezeHall perhaps, something that better fit her notion of the religious. Though Megan tried continually to impress her with the secular nature of the PriestGuild, Susannah's early experience in Lagri's storyhall had formed indelible expectations to the contrary. And now there was the additional influence of Stavros and his 'miracle'.

But the PriestHall was columned and busy like any other crafthall. The tiled floor was warm and tracked with dust. Every possible lamp was burning, every double sconce on the columns, every wick in every chandelier, every individual lamp in the scholars' niches along the wall. The long hall trembled with feverish golden light and the steamy heat of bodies. Priests hovered in groups of two and three enlivened by animated debate that stilled into ambivalent silence as Stavros paced by.

Drawn along in his wake, Liphar's small hand guiding her elbow, Susannah contemplated Ghirra's image of the priests as preservers of the ancient weather science. She pictured each lamplit niche stacked high with the familiar gauges and dials, monitors, oscilloscopes, spiderwebs of cable and flatwire, graphics and holo displays, the only sort of equipment she could comprehend in relation to something so high-tech as climate control.

How did they do it and where did it go? Is technology so easily forgotten?

She thought of the SkyHall engravings, evidence of advanced science unrecognized even by Ghirra, that most sophisticated of Sawls. She peered into each brightly lit recess of the PriestHall, scoured the curve of every column and the surface of every wall for similiar signs.

It may have been here all along and we just haven't noticed it yet.

A notion had occurred to her, before the meeting at the Lander had been so abruptly interrupted, a suspicion, really, the kind of mental alarm bell she was used to noting and logging onto her mental priority list for later study: her suggestion of a genetically engineered inner ecology protecting the Sawls at its center had not caused the stir that it should have done.

I must have presented it badly.

It seemed to have settled into her colleagues' minds as just one more bit of evidence. But restructuring of living systems on a global level was far more significant than that, certainly more far-reaching than fancy ceramics or even astronomy.

Even the Druids could predict eclipses and the like.

Ghirra's weather machines had fired everyone's imagination, and rightfully so, but Susannah's own intellectual knees weakened in awe of the brilliant genetic achievements she had proposed. Clausen apparently could imagine conquering climate control within his lifetime and with minimal advances in technology. Susannah could not credit a parallel accessibility to her hypothetical genetic miracles.

It broke her heart that such genius might be lost in the mists of time. She wondered what guild's dusty, crumbling volumes preserved those secrets, in a form and language the guildsmen themselves no longer understood. Physicians'? The FoodGuild? How and where to begin the search?

The bustle in the PriestHall thickened, slowing their progress as they approached the farthest corner. Here the murmuring groups included men and women from other guilds, relatives of the old priest, Susannah surmised, his children and their children.

Stravos edged through the waiting crowd, his head low in unconscious imitation of Ghirra's self-effacing stoop. Susannah watched the many questioning eyes follow him. She saw reflected in them an image she did not recognize, never could recognize until she had sunk herself into the Sawl gestalt as deeply as Stav had. To identify with Ghirra, she realized, was not enough. The Master Healer was atypical. His mind ranged freely in ways that had allowed her to gloss over some of the most fundamental differences between Sawl and Terran.

It's this notion of no border existing between the real and the mystical. That's what's alien to me at its very base.

Her intellect would stretch to encompass any scientific possibility. Her heart would admit to the possibility of a miracle. A commingling of the two derailed both her rational and irrational processes, as in the case of the subtle healing in Ghirra's hands. It was nothing flashy. He could not cure fatal disease or bring life where there was none, but there was undeniable power there, consistent, real, inexplicable.

She knew Stavros would call it a "connection," and liken it to his own. How did Ghirra explain it, if he thought his goddesses were machines?

The Stavros that Susannah observed through the eyes around her was likewise an unsettling mixture. For all the brilliance and Goya-esque beauty she saw in him, to them he was overlarge, fleshy and pale, a little clumsy, clever but vulnerable, something precious to be protected, like an overgrown child in danger from its own earnest impulsiveness. But the child could grow into its potential, and it was that expectation the Sawls protected, an expectation that even Stavros himself could not define.

The crowd cleared for them around a deep alcove in the back wall. Heavy curtains were drawn to either side around a raised bed of cushions. The Master Herbalist Ard crouched over a oil-fired portable steamer by the foot of the bed, each circle of his spoon sending up clouds of rose and cinnamon scented dampness. Ampiar waited at the head with a scowling Kav Ashimmel. Xifa stood behind them, holding Kav Daven's youngest great-grandchild. Others, his sons and daughter, his grandchildren, sat in solemn observance. There was little hope in their eyes, but few tears either.

They're wept out, with all that's happened lately, Susannah told herself. *And the Kav has had a long and vital life.*

Ashimmel seemed more disturbed than anyone, but when she glanced up at Stavros' arrival, Susannah saw her distress was less sorrowing than confused and disapproving, and a tinge resentful.

Stavros moved to the Kav's bedside like a sleepwalker.

"What's with Ashimmel?" Susannah whispered to Ghirra.

"This Kav has no apprentice to follow," he said. An odd note of private speculation distanced his reply.

"What about the child, the girl who takes care of him? Isn't she . . . ?"

Ghirra shook his head gravely. "She is his daughter's daughter. The master's apprentice cannot be of his family."

"Oh." She watched Stavros lower himself stiffly at the head of the bed. Ashimmel offered only the slightest withdrawal to make room for him. Susannah bent her head closer to Ghirra's. "And Ashimmel thinks this fixation with Stavros is less important that the Kav naming his successor."

"She is GuildMaster," said Ghirra tolerantly. "She must think of the business of the guild. They argue about this always, yet the Kav has not teach one to be his apprentice. Ashimmel does not like that she will have to make the choosing."

Stavros knelt, with eyes for no one but the old man on the bed.

Kav Daven lay nearly invisible among his pillows, a fragile brown skeleton cushioned in deep mounds of russet and tan. Between protruding ribs, Susannah could see the flutter of a strained heartbeat. His eyes stared open, blind white eyes whose small unseeing movements searched the shadowed vaults and seemed to follow the ascending billows of steam from Ard's medicinal. His lips quivered in a soundless spasmodic chanting.

Stavros took the priest's papery hand between his own.

"Kav. Kho jelrho." He leaned forward, kissed the hand and bent his head into the pillows beside it.

Kav Daven's lips ceased their convulsive movement. His eyes

264

drooped shut. The hand that Stavros held lifted free of his gentle grasp to feel along his cheek and settle on his bowed head. The knotted brown fingers buried themselves possessively in Stavros' hair. The ancient lips shivered with more deliberate purpose.

"Raellil khe," Kav Daven muttered.

A rustle ran through the attendant crowd. Susannah guessed that Kav Daven had only spoken out of his coma to summon Stavros, and now to greet him with this mysterious word. She felt the chill that too-perfect coincidences arouse. She tried to read Ghirra's bemused frown as he studied Ashimmel. The Master Priest shook with unconscious negation. Susannah wondered if Ghirra worried for her health.

"Raellil khe." Kav Daven spoke more clearly than before, his fingers gripping Stavros' skull. Stavros remained motionless, though a soft moan escaped him, like a sigh.

He's hurting, Susannah fretted, *bending like that with his injury.* But she knew he would not be thinking of his pain.

"Lij, raellil," said the Kav. "Rho lijet."

Ashimmel shot to her feet in dismay. Her fellow priests gaped and murmured in surprise. Stavros stirred, as if wishing to rise but loathe to disturb the priest's hand, resting on his head in benediction.

"Kho *lije?*" he mumbled incredulously.

Susannah edged closer to the Master Healer. "What's he saying?"

Ghirra touched her arm, bidding silence. Liphar leaned against her for comfort, enrapt by the drama unfolding in front of him.

Ashimmel turned and paced away. The crowd cleared a path for her. She fell into muttered conference with three of her most senior priests, who looked equally as dumbfounded and outraged as she.

"Rho lijet. . .rho lijet. . .rho lijet . . ." murmured Kav Daven. Each repetition of the phrase grew fainter until it was an escape of breath barely sculpted into sound and meaning.

Stavros lifted his head and the priest's hand slid limply along his neck. His eyes were wet. His voice pleaded. "Kav, I don't know how!"

The withered hand closed tightly on Stavros' bandaged shoulder. Stavros' back stiffened against the pain. His eyes clenched shut, his jaw jerked in a quiet gasp. Then, as his mouth stretched wide in agonized joy, he extended his hands as if in supplication, palms up.

Susannah's chill rippled through her again. She, who had seen his face suffused with the ecstasy of orgasm, understood less the nature of his transport than his Catholic ancestors would have at a glance.

"Rho lijet, raellil!" Kav Daven commanded with sudden strength. The stringy sinews of his torso bunched as if he might sit up. Stavros laid restraining hands on the old man's chest.

"Kav, I will," he answered hoarsely.

The grip on his shoulder eased. The crooked fingers, hardly more than naked bones, unbent as if in sleep. The hand slid slowly along Stavros' arm to rest in the curl of his elbow, limp as a rain-sodden leaf.

Susannah glanced reflexively at the skin drawn tight across the old man's ribs. The drumming flutter of his heart had stilled.

"Suzhannah!" Ghirra moved quickly forward, drawing her with him. They crowded in to either side of Stavros, their professional urgency violating the peaceful spell of the moment.

Susannah knew there was little hope of reanimating the faint life spark that had already burned far beyond expectation. She gave up before Ghirra did, but at last he too sat back, with the universal head shake of a doctor admitting that final failure. At the foot of the bed, Ard sighed and capped the little oil flame of his steamer.

Ghirra rose, signaling Ard and Susannah away from the bedside. Susannah heard no weeping. She saw many faces as curious as they were solemn, as they watched to see what Ashimmel would do next.

Stavros waited, slumped back on his heels, his eyes inwardly fixed. His hands rested palm up on his thighs. In the silence, Liphar crept forward to kneel beside him.

Slowly, others of the PriestGuild apprentices, including the Kav's young grandaughter, slipped out from the crowd to join them. Susannah had the sense of an ancient tradition reasserting itself.

"Ghirra, what is going on?" she whispered urgently.

"He says to Ibi many times, you must dance, you must dance."

"I don't understand."

She thought he looked back at her rather sadly, not for the event or the death, but for her. "This means, Susannah, that Kav Daven names 'TavrosIbia his apprentice."

Susannah stared down at the kneeling linguist.

Ghirra added gently, "And Ibi says to this, yes."

BOOK THREE

"As flies to wanton boys are we to the gods;
They kill us for their sport."

KING LEAR
Act IV, sc. i

37

Stavros held Susannah close in the blue dimness of the StoryHall, wishing only to soothe her. But she was full of questions and the need for answers.

"It's a sweet gesture of ecumenicism on the old man's part," she declared hopefully, "but Ashimmel will never buy it."

Sweet? Swallowing his protest, Stavros smoothed her long hair down the length of her back. "Because Kav Daven's choice was so . . . irregular, the guildmaster will submit it to a guild vote. If it passes, she must accept it."

"But the guild would never agree to this. You're no priest. You're not even . . ."

Raellil.

Apprentice.

What else . . . ?

He touched his fingertips to her lips, then kissed her lightly. "The old Kav was well-loved, and I am not without support within the guild."

She seemed to understand something for the first time. The querulous edge in her voice expressed the one fear he could not dispel for her. "Then you want this."

"There are many in the guild who feel that in a time of crisis, extraordinary measures are required . . ."

Susannah pulled away from him and sat up. "Stav, I asked, do you want this?"

"At the moment all I want is you." He tried to deflect her with an amorous smile.

"No." She drew her tunic tight about her and her knees up to her chest. For the first time since he had won her, Stavros worried that he would lose her.

"Ah, Susannah, don't stare at me like I was some kind of stranger."

"I don't understand what you're doing!"

"Well, neither do I, really, if that makes you feel any better. But I do know it's what I have to do, and that I will do it without you, but it would be so much better to have your support. Ghirra once said the Kav had a plan for me, and he was right. Problem is, the old man died before telling me what it was."

He wanted to reach for her but feared that if she pulled away again, the distance might grow too great to bridge. The fire in his palms, his mystic goad, had burned fiercely since the old priest's death. He needed the distraction of her, her reality, to keep himself centered. "Susannah, I love you. Believe that. Believe in me. Believe that I know what I'm doing is right."

Susannah's brow wrinkled anxiously. "It's not right to agree to this, then leave them hanging when the time comes to leave!"

"Leave?" he asked gently, prompting her to admit what she knew already but was refusing to believe.

"To go home!"

"I am home."

Susannah glanced away quickly, then dropped her chin to her knees with a forlorn sigh. Stavros suppressed a grunt of pain as he pulled himself up to fold her in the crook of his good arm.

"You knew long before I did," he whispered. "You remember? The Planting Feast?" He laughed softly, his lips brushing her ear. "I'm there lost in erotic panic, trying to figure how to get you close to me, and you're playing the Delphic oracle, telling me how I don't want to leave. You scared the shit out of me."

Susannah said nothing, only shook her head. Stavros felt one, then two warm tears slide past his wrist where it rested against her cheek.

"Beloved," he pleaded huskily, trying to pull her closer. "They would welcome you too, you know they would. And I would consider myself the luckiest of men . . ."

"You'll break Weng's heart," she murmured.

"Susannah . . ."

But as she bent her head sadly against his neck, curling into the comfort of his eager body, an urgent knocking rang out at the entrance of the hall. Stavros swore in earnest, but rose, drawing on his pants, and padded across the tiles to unbar the doors.

Megan stood outside, her mouth a tight line of frustrated disbelief.

Stavros glanced behind her quickly, and in both directions up and down the FriezeHall. "You came up here with . . . ?"

She waved a dismissive hand and shouldered past him through the door. "Security be damned. It doesn't matter. He's gone."

"Gone?"

"Took off early this morning, while we were all dead to the world in our little air-conditioned cocoon. The sonofabitch was lying about how ready A-Sled was! And he took McPherson with him."

"By force?"

"Who knows?"

"And B-Sled?"

"Weng's checking it out now."

"Can she fly it?"

"She says not. Never had occasion to. I think she doesn't want to."

"Taylor, then."

Megan shrugged. "I suppose."

Susannah came out of the shadow, tying the sash of her tunic. "Will CRI say where he's headed?"

"Oh, there's no mystery about that. He's not covering his tracks. He's making a beeline for the southern desert."

"Nolagri," murmured Stavros, deadly calm. "He could be there in three or four days, if he really pushes. But it's a big desert. Does he really know where to go or what he's looking for?"

"If it's there, he'll find it, you can be sure of that."

"Wouldn't it be the crowning irony if he did manage to make us all rich," said Susannah dispiritedly.

Megan folded her arms dubiously. "What's he going to find down there, Stav?"

"How should I know?" he replied, faintly sullen. "I have no private information except the stuff none of you will believe."

"Emil seemed to think you did."

He spread his hands. "I have nothing more than a guess."

"You think there's people? A pocket of the old race left down there?"

"No. That would show up somewhere in the myths." He paced away and back again, unconsciously bringing his palms together to press one fiery center against the other. "But I do think I know the power source he was so interested in. I think it's his goddamn lithium!"

"Why do you think that?"

Stavros grabbed her arm and propelled her to the raised edge of Valla's fountain. He pointed through the arching threads of water to the blue flame burning within its central glass tube. "That."

"Not natural gas?" remarked Susannah. "Up in Physicians', I wondered."

"What, then?" demanded Megan.

Stavros' finger straightened toward the floor. "Some several hundred meters below us is a remarkable secret that the Sawls have been keeping."

"From everyone but you."

"With good reason. It's a huge power plant, built mostly of

glass. It makes the gas to fuel that flame, as a byproduct of a reaction involving nearly pure lithium dug from mines deep under the cliffs. But the Sawls don't see it as technology anymore. The whole process is heavily shrouded in myth and euphemism. The priests call it 'feeding the Goddesses.' "

Megan gaped at him, "Why didn't you tell me?"

He returned her gaze steadily. "I didn't want him to be able to beat it out of you, Meg."

She sighed, nodded reluctantly. "Good thinking."

"Lithium," said Susannah. "No wonder Ghirra was so upset when Emil came back with a pack load of it. Lithium." She made a further connection. "Your guar rock."

"Yes."

"Oh boy." It was Megan's turn to pace as her mind ranged forward. "According to CRI, he's taken a case of his atomic mining charges with him, among other things."

Stavros could do nothing more articulate than moan.

Megan spoke his thought for him. "If your goddesses exist, Clausen's not going to want them around and functioning enough to compete with him for the planet's mineral resources."

"He seemed pretty interested in stealing the technology," Susannah interposed soothingly. "He's not going to blow up something that'll make him rich."

"Unless the lithium'll make him richer faster."

Stavros paced into the darkness at the far end of the hall and came back pulling on a sleeveless tunic to cover his bandaged shoulder. "We've got, what, another shipweek till sunset? Where's the damn laser?"

" Tay's brooding over it like a mother hen."

"Good. I have to get Ghirra and Liphar to make a few explanations for me. Get back to the Lander. Tell Weng to keep working on that Sled!"

Megan blinked at his sudden speed.

"Well, come on!" he urged impatiently. "The bastard's got enough of a head start as it is!"

Susannah came through the cylinder shaking her head. "She should not be out there so long in this heat."

"She's the only one left who really knows how the Sleds work," Megan replied but she endured a private stab of guilt that she was sitting inside in the cool while out in the cruel sun a much older woman struggled to recall her long-unused mechanic's skills.

Even Taylor has the grace to keep her company. Megan roused herself and went outside.

272

Passing through the cylinder was like stepping into a blast furnace. Megan lingered within the silvered arc, shielding her cheeks with her hands. She felt as though her skin might shrivel and flake away.

She saw Stavros striding down the path from the Caves, Liphar beside him, Ghirra and Aguidran at his heels. Fine, pale dust danced around them like slow smoke. Some trick of the hot light caused their bodies to shimmer darkly against the too-white background.

Megan frowned and glanced involuntarily at the sky. It too had gone white. The sun was a hot white spot behind a glowing veil of cloud that stretched across the entire bowl of the sky. Plain and cliffs and sky blended into a single burning white-on-white vista. The fearsome glare pinched at Megan's eyes. She thought of the irony of going snow-blind without snow. A thrill coursed through her, a jolt of irrational fear at the way the sand flew up on its own to cling to her shoes and pant legs like a swarm of hungry parasites, refusing to be shaken off. She ducked back into the Underbelly to retrieve her sunlenses.

"Stav's coming down," she called to Susannah on her way out.

She hurried across the torrid clearing to join Weng and Danforth under the protection of the tarp Clausen had rigged to shade the repair work. Danforth leaned against the Sled's smooth white hull, one arm clutching his crutches, the other draped over the edge of the cockpit. Weng sat in the pilot's seat, disheveled and dust-streaked, a wet towel draped around her neck. She was touching contact switches on the control panel and conversing in mutters with CRI's tinny Sled voice.

"How's it going, Commander?" asked Megan without much hope.

The tip of Weng's tongue worked its way further into the corner of her mouth. Danforth turned aside slightly, as if to give her efforts privacy from the distractions of conversation. He wore the laser pistol stuck casually into the belt of his cut-off trousers. His dark features were nearly invisible, lost in shadow, back lit by glare.

"She's running an instrument check now," he reported. "We do have power at least."

Megan was unable to shake the unease that had settled over her along with the hot white pervasive light. "Have you looked at the *sky*?"

Danforth nodded. "A thin cloud nearly planet-wide, except where we're going, over the desert. According to CRI, it's some

273

bit of moisture being injected at higher altitudes. According to legend, Valla Ired's last gasp of defense: White Sky."

"Spooky," Megan admitted with an exaggerated shiver.

Danforth's grin was a bright relief in his shadowed face. "Just them ol' positive ions, Meg. Don't let 'em get to you."

Stavros ducked under the canopy. "Reporting for duty as ordered, Commander."

Weng did not look up from her instruments. "Ah. Mr. Ibiá."

Stavros exchanged a careful nod of greeting with Danforth, his eyes flicking from one cast-bound leg to the other. "How are you feeling?"

Danforth laughed harshly. "*Me?* How about you?"

Stavros allowed him a rueful half-smile. "Yeah. How 'bout that sonofabitch?"

Megan snorted. "If you two are going to compare war wounds, I'm leaving." But she rejoiced for anything they could find in common. They would dearly need mutual respect, if not friendship, in the days to come. She headed back to the cool of the Underbelly and found Susannah remonstrating with Ghirra, while Aguidran and Liphar looked on, the one stone-faced, the other acutely uncomfortable.

"But Ghirra, do you think it's *right* for him to accept?" Susannah was demanding. She fell silent with a gesture of despair when she saw Megan at the cylinder.

"So I was right about this planet being a good source of lithium," Danforth probed.

"A guess, Taylor. I told Megan that."

"I'm inclined to trust your guesses a little more than I used to, Ibiá." He looked down, jiggled his crutches. "I'd sure like to see that plant, but I don't suppose . . . ?"

Stavros shook his head with genuine regret. "Stairs all the way down. If we had more time . . ."

"No problem," said Danforth amiably. "I've been giving the chemistry some thought, though, since Megan told me. If the lithium the Sawls mine is as pure as you suggest, it could be combined with water to produce lithium oxide, heat and hydrogen gas."

"The blue flames."

"And the high-temperature ceramic technology. Hydrogen burns hot."

"Also, the cooling system for the reaction vessel provides heat and hot water for the Caves." Stavros was sorry to have lacked the benefit of Danforth's knowledge for so long. Ghirra was right to welcome him so readily. *Still . . .*

274

"Taylor, what's your interest in this? Sorry, I have to ask that."

"You mean, whose side am I on? Sure you have to ask. I would too, in your shoes, maybe a lot less politely." Danforth eased himself onto his crutches and stumped to the edge of the shade to stare out into the sun. "On my own side, if hearing that helps you to believe me. I'm glad to know I was right, that the lithium is here, but I think we're onto something much more remarkable and I'd be a fool to let that go down the drain. I think Emil will lose this case if it goes to court, and I think he's reached the same conclusion. If there's something out there he can use, he will. If not, he'll destroy it. He has to be stopped."

"Dr. Danforth?" Weng's voice wavered with exhaustion. "I believe it is time to clear the canopy and test the fans. The instruments do seem to be in working order."

"Congratulations, Commander. I'm on my way."

Stavros glanced at the crippled planetologist. "You're flying this thing?"

"I'm not as incompetent at the stick as Emil always made out."

"By yourself, I meant. All twenty-five thousand klicks?"

"You bet. Don't need my legs to do that." Danforth let a slow grin build.

Stavros grinned back with less certainty. "Hell of a good thing, eh?"

Behind him, he heard Weng say, very quietly, "Damn," followed by a wheezing sigh and a long, sliding thud. Stavros sprang back to the Sled.

"Commander?"

Weng lay in a heap on the floor of the cockpit. One-armed, Stavros could not haul himself up to help her.

Danforth swung helplessly to his side. "What happened?"

"Heat, exhaustion, I don't know," Stavros muttered. "Fuckin' useless, both of us." He lunged into the sun and tore across the clearing at a clumsy pain-jarred run, shouting for help.

Susannah met him at the cylinder mouth.

"Weng just collapsed," he panted.

She whirled to call Ghirra and Aguidran, but they were behind her already. They raced across the clearing to the Sled. Aguidran bent, interlacing her fingers to receive her brother's foot, and vaulted him into the cockpit. Susannah had followed him by the time Stavros regained the shelter of the canopy. Ghirra knelt and untangled Weng's crumpled limbs. He cleared tools and loose test equipment with a sweep of his arm and stretched

275

her out between the front seats. He fumbled with the unfamiliar buttons at her throat until Susannah arrived to relieve him.

"She breathes," he reported with relief, "but the heart . . ." His hands hovered, cupped around but not touching her jaw.

"Racing," supplied Susannah. "Heat prostration, I hope, not a stroke. We'll have to get her where it's cool."

Ghirra slipped his arms beneath Weng's thighs and shoulders, and lifted her with surprising ease. "She has no weight," he noted.

He carried her to the lip of the cockpit and handed her down to Aguidran. Susannah scrambled to the ground and led the way to the Underbelly. Stavros started after them, but Danforth stayed him with a big hand laid quietly on his arm.

"She's in good hands, right? Nothing further we could do."

Stavros nodded slowly, waiting.

Danforth jerked his head at the Sled. "So, want to give it a try?"

Stavros regarded the seemingly inaccessible cockpit dubiously.

Danforth swung jauntily to the midsection and patted the hull. "I think I can hoist myself in through the cargo hatch underneath . . . with a little help. You game?"

Stavros wondered in what way Danforth was testing him. "Taylor, I need a pilot. I'm game for anything that gets us in the air."

Megan ventured once more into the heat to help Stavros clear away the canopy. The silverfilm tarp flashed dully as they floated it aside into loose folds. It reflected only white. White light flooded the cockpit. Stavros swung himself up one-handed through the open cargo hatch, slammed it shut behind him, then clattered across the empty hold to drop heavily into the seat beside Danforth. The planetologist was already strapped in, his rigid right leg stretched out in front of him under the dashboard, the other crooked beneath it.

Megan peered over the pilot's side of the cockpit. "Heat prostration, like Susannah said. Most spacers have trouble after this long on the ground. She'll be fine if she takes it easy for a while."

Danforth shook his head admiringly. "The woman is a rock."

One less passenger to weigh us down, Stavros calculated guiltily. *No, two. Someone will have to stay with her.*

"You have command, Taylor, until she wakes up," Megan reminded him.

Danforth clearly had forgotten, and even more clearly worried instantly that this new responsibility might hamper his freedom to chase after Clausen. Barely giving it time for thought, he replied, "You're next in line after me, Meg. You take over."

Stavros laughed. *A month ago, he would have given his firstborn for such a chance.*

"Meaning you want me to stay behind?" Megan did not sound altogether resistant to the idea.

"Somebody ought to run CRI's first contact procedures, broadcast the usual messages."

Megan looked doubtful.

"It can't hurt to try it, Meg. Besides," he added more gently. "We can't leave Weng here alone."

"Well, it's true I'm not much good in this heat," she admitted quietly.

"Done, then," declared Danforth. "Commander Levy, please inform our colleagues that we're ready to power this baby up!"

"Forward fan, check."

Stavros envied the deep steadiness of Danforth's voice over the comset in his ear.

"Forward fan nominal," acknowledge CRI.

"Aft right fan, check."

"Aft right nominal."

As each fan spun up to quarter-speed, the haze of dust around the Sled thickened. The white silence of the clearing was invaded by machine whines. The observers drew back to the edge of the clearing, eyes slitted against the glare and flying grit. In the open cockpit, Stavros coughed convulsively.

"Aft left fan, check," said Danforth hoarsely.

"Aft left nominal. I have no reading on the cockpit shield, Dr. Danforth. Is that an instrument malfunction?"

"Shit," muttered Danforth. Stavros saw him squint uncertainly at the control panel, then touch a switch. Within a matter of seconds, the noise of the fans abated to a mildly deafening level. The hard white light eased as a small protective force field enclosed the cockpit area. Danforth flipped a toggle, touched another contact. Air flowed into the static heat already building up inside the little shield.

"It won't keep us cool, Ibiá, but it'll keep us breathing," Danforth apologized into his comset. "My mistake, CRI." He flipped three more toggles, hit the first of three switches. "Aft engine check: One?"

Stavros felt the Sled shudder and begin to vibrate. He wondered why he was not more concerned about Danforth's untested pilot's skills.

"One," agreed CRI.

"Two? Three?" Danforth touched the last contacts in rapid sequence.

He's just as eager as I am. Stavros welcomed back his sense of high adventure and the surge of elation that came with it. He laughed aloud, forgetting the comset hugging his jaw, and Danforth swiveled in his seat to stare at him. His voice in Stavros' ear was silky with amusement.

"Off to see the wizard, eh, Ibiá? Then let's do it!"

His fingers went to work, and the Sled jerked and lifted, seesawing sloppily within its dust cloud. Danforth whooped softly and closed his hand around the stick. The craft rose sharply. Danforth's whoop died into a tight-lipped gulp as he steadied the rise.

"Sorry 'bout that." He grinned sickly, then eased the stick forward. The Sled dipped, wavering from side to side, then shuddered off above the fields, banking gracelessly toward the open plain.

38

Liphar did not intend to be left behind. He ran about tirelessly in the staggering heat, hauling supplies to the Sled, carrying messages back and forth between Susannah and Danforth in the cargo hold, Weng in her sickbed in the Underbelly and Megan in the Lander's storage bays above. He assigned himself a slot on one of the two padded benches at the forward end of the Sled. Climbing in to run a final provisions count, Stavros found the young Sawl half strapped in, struggling with the buckles, ready to go.

Stavros looked down at him sternly but Liphar returned a sly smile.

"You are new 'prentice now, Ibi. You listen now what I say, more big 'prentice than you."

"Lifa, I don't think . . ."

The young man folded his arms across his thin chest with stubborn dignity. "I teach you be kav first, ah? Then I listen you again."

Stavros crouched in front of him, nonplussed. It had not occurred to him that any other priest could teach him what Kav Daven had failed to. "All right. Then what do you say to me now?"

"I say, I must go with you, help talk this angry Sister."

Stavros frowned at the dust-powdered plastic floor grating. He could think of no reason to refuse him but concern for his safety.

An agile figure in white swung up through the cargo hatch and edged forward through the maze of equipment and supplies. Stavros glanced up, then rose in slow astonishment.

Weng's therm-suit fit the Master Healer as if it were made for him. He wore it as if he had worn it all his life, as if he savored the close, slick feel of it against his body, as if he shared some of Weng's pride in what it meant. He had tied his brown curls at the nape of his neck and abandoned his characteristic stoop. Weng's gold command bars glinted on the open collar. He looked like a slim, able spacer, fully at home in the Sled's smooth, plastic environment. Only his faint self-conscious smile gave him away.

"Ghirra, what the . . . ?"

Stavros' stare stopped him mid-hold. His eyes accepted Stavros' surprise but not his reflex disapproval. "Suzhannah say wear this for best safety," he explained coolly.

"Yeah." It frightened Stavros that Ghirra could seem so at ease in Terran uniform, embracing the very image he himself had cast off for the Sawls' sake. But he understood that the neat white uniform bore a compelling significance for the Master Healer, of the brave new universe out there beyond the dome of his own familiar sky, a universe he was increasingly curious about.

Startled into self-doubt, Stavros fingered his own Sawlish clothing. He questioned his fear of the modern world intruding upon the Sawls. Was he fighting it for their future good, or was it, as Clausen always implied, for romantic reasons of his own, to find and preserve a backwater kingdom where he could live and work in peace?

Relax, Ibiá, it's only the clothing he's put on, not the entire value structure!

"Looks pretty good on you," he offered lamely.

Ghirra's defensiveness eased.

Stavros plucked at his gauzy tunic, limp with sweat. His bandages itched. The therm-suit would keep him cool and dry. It was absurd to resist it. "Better get mine on, too, I guess."

To cover his discomfort, he cuffed Liphar lightly on the head. "You too, Lifa. Untangle yourself from those straps and go tell Susannah to issue you one of McPherson's suits. That'll be the smallest we have."

Liphar was out of the harness within seconds, disappearing through the cargo hatch wearing a grin as wide as his jaw.

Aguidran refused to wear a therm-suit and was nearly as unwilling to buckle herself into the flight harness. Like a great dark bird, she half crouched, half perched on the edge of the bench behind Stavros, the plastic strapping draped over one leather-clad shoulder, gripped tightly in one hand but not fastened.

Stavros had claimed the copilot's chair. He muttered intently into his comset, pressing CRI for an update on Clausen's location. His white therm-suit was unzipped to his navel, as if in rakish refusal to submit to total uniformity, but actually to ease the fit around his bandaged shoulder. Fully secured behind Danforth, Ghirra lounged into the padded bench with anticipatory relish, watching carefully as the planetologist punched through his final engine check. Liphar pressed close to Susannah on the rear bench. Arms stiffened, his hands grasped the forward edge of his seat. He anxiously monitored the three Terrans' actions as if to be sure that everything was proceeding as expected. Occasionally he threw a guilty glance up at the white cliff. The black cave mouths and the hot bright ledges were crowded with faces, too distant to be recognizable but eloquent in their waiting torpor.

Susannah tried to summon a brisker sort of energy with which to face her second trek into the wilderness, but her sense of adventure was blunted by the crushing white heat. The merest movement was like swimming through shimmering will-sapping glue. The best she could do was to keep from drifting into daydreams of rain showers and cool forest glades.

Dust stirred in the clearing as Megan retreated into the shadow of the cylinder. She hovered behind a stubbornly erect Weng, who moved another step into the sun as the Sled's fans hummed to life.

Susannah waved, partly in salutation, partly to shoo Weng inside, away from the heat and roar and the whirling sand. She realized sadly that when the expedition was, if ever, over, her medical report would have to recommend no further landing missions for the aging spacer. But she was not sure Weng would mind that. *She's got plenty of service years left on FTL craft and orbiters, if she takes care of herself.*

She leaned forward to Ghirra. "Did you have a chance to ask Ampiar to check on the Commander every so often?"

He nodded without taking his eyes from Danforth's work at the controls.

"He's got a ten-hour, thirteen-hundred-kilometer start on us," Stavros was saying, raising his voice over the noise of the fans for the benefit of the others.

"But he seems to be taking his time so far," Danforth replied. "I'd guess he's feeling his way and doesn't expect immediate pursuit."

"He didn't think we'd get her fixed so fast."

Danforth grinned. "Or come up with a pilot. Underestimated both the Commander and me . . . and it'll cost him. We'll pick up time if I push her hard, plus we may be able to cut some corners off his route."

"CRI says the type of charge he's using is hand-activated, but she can pick up telemetry the moment he arms them."

Danforth nodded and raised his arm in a warning signal, then touched a switch to lift the windscreen extensions. A meter-high shield of clear plastic rose out of the hull to either side of the passenger area. As the fan and engine noise increased, he activated the force shield. The surrounding glare of cliff and sky dulled to a cooler dancing shade, cut at eye level by the hot white slicing through the narrow arc of the windscreens.

Danforth signalled again, thumb up. The Sled shivered and rose. Then, rocking on its cushion of air like a boat in choppy seas, it rose again and surged forward clumsily. Aguidran snarled as she was thrown off balance into the padded curve of the bench. Liphar strained against his harness to huddle closer to Susannah.

Stavros spoke to Danforth over the com, circling his hand in the air. Danforth made a dubious face but nodded. The Sled wavered out over the blackened fields beyond the fire breaks, then banked sharply and circled back around the Lander to skim recklessly past the thronged cliffs in a parting salute. Ghirra's head was pressed into his back rest, but his eyes were eager. Susannah wished she had a full-face view of his reaction to his maiden voyage.

What is it like to have never flown before? To have never even thought of flying?

Liphar answered her question by burying his head in her side with a trailing squeal as the Sled tilted into its sickening turn and the white cliff face filled the windscreens. On the crowded ledges, mouths gaped. Heads withdrew in fear and surprise.

Danforth laughed and veered the Sled toward the plain again. Stavros turned in his seat with an encouraging smile.

"Everyone with us so far?" he called over the steady hum of the fans.

When he received no replies to the contrary, he nudged Danforth's arm and jerked his head southward.

* * *

They flew due southwest for the first several hours. Danforth hugged the ground, building his confidence at the stick. He followed the margin of the Dop Arek until the steep rise of the perimeter cliff was jumbled by successive rock slides and ravines. He eased the Sled higher, mounting the bouldered slope to the dry plateau above. The rugged flatland was seamed by old watercourses like wrinkles on an aged face, later softened into the barren hills footing the northernmost of the mountain ranges that made up the Grigar, Lagri's Wall.

Once they had left the level ground of the Dop Arek, Danforth kept to the lowlands, grazing the wide sand-bottomed mountain valleys where russet tufts of shrubbery still clung to the shadeside of the hills and canyons. Ghirra pointed out the dark cliffside cave openings and dry terraced fields of scattered settlements. Clumps of dust-colored succulents dotted the softer slopes. The sky's white glow was disorientingly diffuse. It bleached out the shadows and flattened the geography until the landscape seemed caught in a flash of strobe light.

As the terrain roughened, signs of habitation vanished. Stavros unbuckled and got up to stretch. The Sled hustled along smoothly in the calm air, occasionally rising like a gliding hawk in the thermals beside a particularly precipitous edge. Ghirra followed suit, but stood cautiously, testing the faintly shifting floor while steadying himself on the back of his bench. Aguidran threw off her flight harness and rose to join Stavros in the cargo hold.

"Go easy on the moving around," Danforth complained as the vehicle wavered with the shifting of weight.

Susannah watched Aguidran adapt to the unsettled footing as naturally as a sailor to a rolling deck and recalled the narrow unstable creshin of Ogo Dul. This brother and sister had spent their early childhood on the water. Little wonder they were faring well. But Liphar looked less happy, a little airsick. Susannah left her seat to retrieve her medikit.

Stavros was filling a canteen from the refrigerated water tank. She knelt beside him to refresh her own. Aguidran wandered uneasily among the lashed crates at the back of the hold, then accepted a long drink from Stavros' canteen and returned to her seat. Ghirra joined Susannah on the rear bench as she fed Liphar a pill to ease his stomach.

"To Ogo Dul, we go like this maybe for one cycle only!" he marvelled with boyish excitement.

"Less," said Susannah. "I think you could fly from DulElesi to the ocean in an hour or two . . . ah, one thirty-part of a cycle."

Ghirra's face lengthened thoughtfully. "This make trade more easy, ah? Go more far with this Sledd."

"You could visit settlements all over your world."

"But Sleds are even more dangerous in bad weather than being on the ground," Stavros reminded them as he leaned over to offer the canteen.

As if to reinforce his point, the Sled veered suddenly over a broad canyon that sliced across the plateau. Caught in a thermal, it lifted sickeningly, soared and then dropped. Susannah was made sharply aware of the boulders speeding by beneath the fans before the craft settled again into a comfortable forward motion. Danforth waved a mute apology without looking around. Liphar moaned weakly and clutched his stomach, but Ghirra watched Danforth's hand on the stick with a faintly envious eye.

The long rocky miles slid past without serious incident. They left the desert foothills and climbed into the mountains. The ravines deepened into breathless chasms choked with rockfall. The crags towered more steeply. The valleys narrowed into canyons. The barrenness of the landscape caught like sand in Danforth's throat. His cautious low-altitude flight plan did not offer the comforting objectivity of a bird's eye view. The poignancy of a single cluster of brush wedged among the rocks, even the bare dead skeleton of a tree brought near tears to his eyes. He could not help but identify with any living thing left to shrivel away in such a wasteland, abandoned by the climate that had sired it in the first place. Desolation surrounded him, towered over him, caused him to stare at the sheer peaks of pale bright stone and the endless corrugated vistas of ridge and canyon and ridge as if they were singing a chorus to his human insignificance.

I used to rejoice in the majesty, the purity even, of such emptiness, he mused with some surprise as he guided the Sled between two monstrous crags. *Used to think it cleansing. But then, I didn't used to think so much about what I was thinking, either.* He wondered if this new habit of introspection would prove to be permanent. Though it had its uses and even its pleasures, it was not, he decided, an altogether pleasant compulsion. It nagged at him, like doubt or a sore tooth, teasing at his belief not so much in himself or in his skill and knowledge, but in the final authority of that knowledge to answer all questions put to it.

He decided that it did not do to be too introspective in the wasteland. So frail a commodity as human hope had less chance than the dying vegetation to flourish in such primal desolation.

Danforth shook his head like a dog and took the Sled up higher, skimming just below the lowering white veil of clouds, concentrating on the comfortingly physical act of flying.

But by the time he began to feel some confidence in his piloting, he was tiring fast. *Pretty dumb, to think I could manage a four-day flight single-handed when we can't afford the time for a real rest stop.*

His eyes hurt from staring into the white sky. On the benches, his passengers dozed.

"Christ, my butt aches," he muttered into the thin comwire curling from his ear to his jaw.

"Surprised it took so long," came a quiet reply over the com.

Danforth started. "Didn't know you were awake, Ibiá."

Stavros leaned forward, rotating the stiffness out of his injured shoulder. "CRI, what's the word on our quarry?"

"Proceeding due south at the moment, Mr. Ibiá, at a mean distance of one thousand thirty-seven kilometers. Mr. Clausen and Lieutenant McPherson have exchanged seats."

"She shouldn't have gone with him," Stavros growled.

"You think she had a choice?" Danforth returned testily.

"The Lieutenant is piloting," CRI reminded them. "Shall I connect you?"

"NO!"

"Jesus, CRI! What are you thinking?" Danforth fumed.

"Mr. Clausen is well aware of your pursuit," CRI answered.

"How?" Danforth was irritated by the computer's self-righteous tone.

"He has asked for periodic reports, as you have."

Danforth glanced at his copilot. "Great. Not only has he got someone to spell him but he knows we're after him. I did notice his speed picked up just after we took off."

Stavros shrugged. "We never had much chance of surprise with Emil."

"Shit, what do we have a chance of?"

Stavros offered a look opaque with mystery. "Knowing who to talk to once we get there."

"Ah. And I take it you're not referring to a local population."

"Not exactly. The main problem will be getting Her attention."

Danforth nodded sagely. "You still believe this living goddess stuff?"

"Did you think I didn't?"

"Well, I figure, you see, that fifty percent of what anyone says in public is for effect, politics and the like. I figure your hidden agenda requires you to believe, or seem to . . . ?" But Danforth could find no guile in the faint frown that creased the

284

younger man's angular profile. "Even with the lithium angle suggesting itself? I mean, with your Sawl power plant and all?"

"The lithium is key, yes, but a guess at the energy source doesn't explain the implications of consciousness. That's why I have Megan putting CRI through the First Contact procedures."

Stavros stared ahead into the white glare, then settled back into his seat with an air of decision.

"Tay, if you can manage to keep this thing in the air a little longer without cramping up, I'll tell you a story . . . no, two." He murmured into the comset as if offering secrets. "Not to convince you—you can believe what you like—but to put you in possession of all the facts as I see them. And to warn you. Things may get a little . . . strange where we're going. I may get a little . . ."

He paused. His voice whispering through the wire was ironic and throaty, compelling in its intimate hush. "Look, I know what you think of me, Tay, but what do you say? Will you listen for a while to the ravings of a madman?"

Danforth's flesh tingled. "If it'll keep me awake, I'll listen," he replied, trying not to sound too eager.

As Stavros unfolded his story yet again, the guar-fire burned hot in the soft inside centers of his hands. He watched the whitened dessicated landscape scud by and kept his voice calm, matter-of-fact, a cool murmur over the com to woo Danforth's rationality with the merest hint of miracle.

What does it matter if he believes me?

It didn't. They would both be faced with the same truth, whatever it was, once they got there. Danforth's belief or lack thereof would be irrelevant to the final outcome. Stavros was sure that rested in his hands alone.

Mine and Lagri's.

He wanted Danforth to believe him for more personal reasons, reasons he was surprised still mattered to him. It still mattered that the expedition's Chief Scientist accept him as an equal. It was a vestige of the life that had gone before, perhaps the last, of the ambitions that had brought him to Fiix to discover a very different destiny.

Stavros doubted CRI's broadcast messages would meet with any response. He had ordered it because he wanted no stone left unturned. His own confidence rested in the pull he felt southward, as strong and direct as a rope around his neck, or more accurately, issuing from the centers of his palms. He was sure he could have plotted the course to Nolagri without benefit of a compass. This he did not tell Danforth. There was no way he could think to express it that would sound vaguely rational.

When Stavros had finished his tale of voids and apprentices and a release from dying, Danforth was silent for a long stretch of difficult climbing terrain. He wound the Sled through a forest of wind-devoured spindles broken by long sheeting grades of sheer rock. The grades sharpened eventually into a wall of snowless crags and dry hard-faced peaks, the summits of the first range of the Grigar. The white cloud veil pressed in from above, suffocatingly close. Danforth checked windspeeds and altitude, then banked west to find a pass that cut south sooner than Clausen's reported route.

"Might pick up some time," he commented neutrally into the com.

Stavros grunted.

"You'd think there'd be more wind at this height," said Danforth.

Stavros made another, less distinct sound of assent.

"Or snow at least."

"Not when Lagri has the upper hand," insisted Stavros at last, and then understood that he needed Danforth's vote of confidence as he needed Susannah's love, to counteract the guar-fire's pull toward the total isolation of a mystic. He might joke about madness, but it no longer held any romance for him.

"Stav." Danforth used his Christian name for the first time in Stavros' memory. "Just like you need to suspect me of ulterior motives, I need to reserve judgment on all this. You dig?"

"Yeah, I dig." Stavros savored the ancient colloquialism as Danforth gained altitude to slip the Sled over the top of a long, smooth ridge between two shattered peaks. He knew an offer of friendship when he heard one.

On the far side of the range, Danforth managed a jolted landing in a gravelled wash on the floor of a wide yellow valley. He dropped the force field's protective dome and heat engulfed them, pressing them into their seats. Nobody moved.

"Should have found some shade," Danforth apologized.

"Where?" Susannah waved a languid, heat-heavy arm at the unbroken waste sloping away for endless miles to either side of them.

Their voices seemed overloud and brittle, discouraging to chatter. The small clink of unbuckled seat harness rang through the hot silence like an off-tune carillon. Aguidran rose first, stretching elaborately, surveying the distance with eyes narrowed against the glare. Danforth hauled his legs out from beneath the control panel and tried to pull himself up against the back of his chair. His right leg gave as he shifted weight onto it, but Aguidran was there to steady him while Ghirra jumped up to hand him his crutches.

Danforth nodded his thanks, making light of his exhaustion, but when the hatch has been opened in the floor of the hold, and they were resting in the shade of the Sled's blunt delta wings, he quietly asked Susannah what she could give him to keep him alert and functioning.

"Not as strong as I thought yet," he grumbled.

"I can keep you going for a while," she said, "but what you really need is a relief pilot."

"You offering?" Stavros retorted, annoyed by his own uselessness.

"It doesn't look so hard," ventured Susannah lightly.

"Depends on the weather and the terrain," said Danforth. "Right now, windless as it is, thermals are the only issue. You ever flown before?"

"Small conventional craft, a few hours here and there in the air. No take off or landing, though."

Danforth looked to Stavros. "It could be the edge we need."

Stavros frowned.

"I think you ought to try me out," Susannah urged gamely.

"Makes sense to me." Danforth lay back in the pebbled sand, folding one arm over his eyes and the other over the laser stuck into his belt. "Now just give me a few quick winks here, a couple of pills, and I'll be raring to go."

While Danforth slept, Susannah put together a cold meal from ship's rations.

"Not very appetizing, I'm afraid," she told Ghirra. But the three Sawls ate without complaint, long used to the idea that food must often be no more than necessary nourishment. Stavros chewed at a bar of dried fruit, shoveled the rest of his share onto Liphar's plate, and wandered off to sit alone behind the tail fin.

Ghirra brushed soy crumbs from his borrowed therm-suit and asked Susannah about its workings. He marvelled at the protection it provided, that from the neck down, he could feel cool and dry in such deadly heat. He made jocular but pointed reference to his sister's refusal to wear the suit they had brought for her. Aguidran grunted and resumed her reflex study of the countryside. Ghirra fingered the smooth resilient fabric of his sleeve, then flicked a covert glance at Stavros behind the tail. He kept his voice low, almost a whisper.

"I think, sometime, Suzhannah, maybe it is better say yes, Clauzen, bring all this here to us. How do you say to this?"

Susannah had been expecting something like this from the Master Healer. His self-image was to be unafraid of new ideas. Technology excited him and he understood enough to see its advantages. But he was hardly in possession of the whole picture.

"If therm-suits and Sleds and medicine were all Emil would bring," she replied after some consideration, "then I'd welcome him with open arms. If we could offer the lifesaving benefits of our tech without all the accompanying dangers . . . but technology has a history of running away with itself, particularly in the hands of megacorporations like CONPLEX. Imagine a guild that disregarded all the other guilds' interests for the sake of its own enrichment and power."

Ghirra spread his hands as if the outcome were obvious. "This guild will not survive. The FoodGuild will not feed it. The Weavers will give it no cloth."

"This guild I speak of provides for all its own needs, through physical and economic intimidation."

Ghirra floundered. "In-tim . . . ?"

"What Clausen does with his laser," said Danforth from the ground. "You don't give me what I want, I'll shoot you." He raised himself on one elbow, patting the gun nestled against his belly. "Oh, he tries to buy you first, but that's just because it's less trouble. He'll try to buy you, doc, if he gets half a chance."

"Buy me?"

"Sure. Your talk of weather machines suggests you might be interested in a trade: your planet in exchange for whatever techy trinkets he has to offer. And, doc, your brain working overtime like it is, you're vulnerable. Take it from one who knows."

"Clauzen tried this to you?"

Danforth laughed bitterly. "He fucking *owned* me, man. Lock, stock and barrel. He just let me think it was a mutually beneficial arrangement. Which is how he'll put it to you, doc. It's called colonialism."

Aguidran lunged forward suddenly with a sharp cry of warning. Plates and food and water mugs went flying. She shoved Susannah aside with a sweep of her arm, whipped the long blade from her boot and flung it into the sand a scant meter past where Susannah had been sitting. Fine grit and gravel erupted as the knife struck home, its carved handle humming wildly. A six legged lizard, two feet long from head to tail, thrashed to the surface, coiling back on itself, its needle fangs slashing furiously at the invading blade. Aguidran scrambled to her feet and pinned the creature's long neck under her heel, then jerked the knife free and cut off the head with a single clean slice.

"Jesus!" Danforth exhaled. "Is everything trying to kill us on this planet?" It had not occurred to him to draw the laser.

"It looked for our water," said Ghirra with something akin to sympathy.

"Guess we take our breaks inside the Sled from now on."

Susannah began immediate negotiations with Aguidran for the dead reptile's remains. Stavros was drawn out of his solitary contemplation to stare down at the bloodied sand.

Danforth gathered scattered cups and plate. "What're you up to back there, Ibiá?"

"Listening," Stavros replied abstractedly.

"What do you hear?"

"So far, nothing."

Danforth marvelled at his new-found patience. "What do you expect to hear?"

"I don't know," Stavros regarded him earnestly. "One of the many things I needed the old man to tell me before he died . . ."

They continued south, winding from pass to pass, scaling the second range of the Grigar, Under Danforth's initially nervous eye, Susannah took the stick for an easy hour of low-altitude flying as they crossed a high barren plateau. He allowed her to negotiate a gentle slope or two, and when she proved equal to both the milder terrain and his impatient teaching, he talked her across a stretch of rugged canyon land before resuming the chair to push the Sled over the more perilous heights of the range.

On the far side, the mountains fell away into high, flat desert dotted with strange wind-smoothed rock formations reminiscent of a giant topiary garden. Danforth flew onward until Susannah's drug no longer vibrated in his veins. When his eyelids drooped long enough that she leaned over from the copilot's seat to shake him awake, he set the Sled down on a ledge in the shade of a rising peak.

The passengers unbuckled slowly but made no move to venture outside the craft. Susannah promised a cooked meal and hustled Liphar to the rear to set up the portable stove. Stavros woke from his doze on the rear bench and came forward to talk to CRI.

"Anything on those test updates?"

"I am currently mapping anomalous magnetic field variations in an area centered approximately forty-five degrees off the southern pole. Remote sensing shows no indication so far of refined metal masses . . ."

"Just call them machines, CRI," drawled Danforth.

". . . but high-res imaging of the area is proceeding." CRI

supplied coordinates for the magnetic field, still over two days travel to the south.

Stavros asked Clausen's position.

"We've gained another seventy-five kilometers on him," offered Danforth. "He's still not exactly proceeding as the crow flies. I suspect he's doing a little prospecting along the way."

"Fine. Let him."

"Do you wish an update on the Contact procedures, Mr. Ibiá?"

"Oh. Yeah, sure."

Danforth chuckled. "You're drifting, Stav. Still listening for your voices?"

Stavros nodded, more seriously than Danforth had meant the question.

"There has been no indication of response to sixteen hours of continuous broadcast on the standard twenty-five frequencies," CRI reported dutifully.

"Both a binary and a decimal code?"

"That is the procedure," returned the computer stiffly.

Stavros grimaced. "She's humoring me." He paced away, around the back of the empty benches, his hands fisting. "Up there in that goddamn orbiter where all this is nothing but a string of data to them! Christ! I don't need this. I need help!"

Danforth turned in his seat. "Easy, man . . . "

"It's about language, not just some damn procedure! Don't they see? It's always about language! How you find the right words, the right *kind* of words to bridge the gap between one consciousness and another!"

Danforth remembered this passionate anger, how it used to rile him. He realized that he had wanted no rival to his own intensity. "Consciousness seems to be the thing in question, though," he said mildly.

At the sudden floating glaze in Ibia's eyes, he amended himself hastily. "For them in the Orbiter, I mean, and CRI, who has enough trouble of her own being considered a consciousness. Hey, what do you care what they think up there? CRI's doing what you asked—it's just part of her own little campaign for recognition that she questions your judgment."

Stavros slowed his pacing and returned forward to slump into his seat. He dragged both palms down across his face with a collecting sigh. "Okay, CRI. Then maybe we should try something that *isn't* the procedure."

CRI waited, a mere hiss of disapproving static.

Stavros turned to Danforth. "Any ideas?"

Danforth tried to look committed to the inquiry. "Not my

field, really. The machines I talk to already know I'm here. What tactics do you guys usually use beside numerical code?"

"Math, geometry, pictures, patterns in the color and duration of light pulses, um . . ." Stavros let his head fall back, eyes lidded. "Patterns of sound . . ."

To Danforth's surprise, an idea surfaced "Ever try music?"

"Sometimes. Usually a long shot."

"Why not send them some of Weng's?"

He could sense Ibiá replaying his words to ferret out the mockery the linguist was sure must be there. He found himself liking his long shot even more. It had a kind of wild mathematical elegance about it.

"Stav, I'm serious. Despite all her protests to the contrary, her game theory analysis seems to me the best, in a way the most concrete evidence you have for consciousness. The whole concept of a game implies intention to me, I don't care what the mathematicians say, and intention implies consciousness. Weng's music is constructed around the same set of algorithms."

Stavros buried his chin in his chest with a faint, pensive glower.

Danforth hazarded blunt honesty. "Look, you always used to be throwing the superiority of insight and instinct in my face like so much wet shit, right? 'Cause you didn't think I had the intellectual balls for it. A straight numbers man all the way, right?"

"Tay, I never . . ."

"Sure you did. Forget it. But grant me this one, okay? My personal gesture to the irrational. Don't reject it just 'cause it ain't yours."

Stavros chewed his lip for a moment, then leaned forward. "You get all that, CRI?"

"Yes, Mr. Ibiá."

"Then I suggest you give it a try." He rose tiredly, grasping Danforth's shoulder for support against the pain in his own, but letting his hand linger briefly as he gained his feet. "Get some sleep, Tay. We'll keep the food warm for you."

Danforth was dreaming of machines made of cloud and ice when Susannah shook him awake. Her eyes were wide.

Not fear, he thought, *but something close to it.*

"I think you might want a look at this, Tay."

He glanced around the cockpit, slit-eyed against the brightness, but Susannah was pointing straight up. Danforth studied the sky without comment until she demanded impatiently, "What is it?"

He shook his head slowly. The flat, unyielding white was quivering like a curtain in a wind. Waves of cooler white or dirty gray chased each other from horizon to horizon. He was reminded of the ripples of shadow that race across the ground prior to a solar eclipse, but he'd never seen anything like it in the sky.

"What do you think, Tay?" Stavros came up from the rear of the hold, trailing Ghirra and Liphar. The young apprentice priest wore a doom-struck knowing look and would not stray a half step from Stavros' side.

"I, ah . . . I'd guess some sort of instability along the interface between the dry heat down here and the cooler, moister air above that's creating the cloud." He noted the direction of movement: north-northeast.

The ripples broadened, like an ocean flowing slowly northward. The hot white landscape throbbed beneath the undulating sky.

"Valla's death throes, Lifa says." Stavros was struggling for some measure of calm. "Apparently it's due to get fairly spectacular when Lagri calls in the heavy artillery . . . fire falling from the sky, the like . . . Devastation."

"I remember," said Danforth. "He sang us the song—about the little children. But I don't think it's . . ."

"Lifa says it's all going according to schedule."

A wave of color surged past, a shell-pink gust across the pale surface of the sky. The long ends of Susannah's hair lifted freely away from her body and crackled with tiny blue fire when she swept them back to bundle into a tight coil.

Danforth saw terror bloom behind Stavros' steady gaze, but because it was not fear of anything he could accept or understand, he could not imagine how to ease it. He looked at the pulsing sky and shrugged. "Best we be moving along, then. . ."

39

Megan stopped along the path to rest, pulling her broad-brimmed ranger hat low over her eyes. She thought this would have to be her last trip to the Caves until nightfall brought some relief from the crushing heat. She sat on a raised earthwork edging a terrace, where the mud and stone had dried as hard as fired ceramic. Dust clung to the legs of Megan's therm-suit and to her hands as she tried to brush it away.

In the fields, nothing stirred. Not a hint of breeze to rattle the dessicated stalks. The Sawls had salvaged what they could of their meager harvest. The rest had been left to shrivel as the irrigation pipes ran dry. After the departure of the Sleds, the population withdrew completely into the Caves. Only Ampiar ventured out into the white heat, dutifully, until Weng assured her that it was unnecessary for her to come unless needed.

When the heat of sitting still became less bearable than the heat of moving, Megan roused herself onward, feeling helpless and profoundly depressed. The Lander glimmered like a white mirage, a mocking image of technological impotence.

Clausen will not have to lift a finger, Megan mourned. *Nature herself is delivering the planet right into his hands.*

The hard bright path wavered in front of her. Megan halted, blinking at nonexistent tears. Her eyes were dry but her vision oddly blurring. She swayed dizzily, convinced she was about to faint. When she did not, and the light continued to fluctuate, she peered out from under her hat brim, then cautiously up at the sky.

She watched open-mouthed as long as her eyes could bear the dancing glare, then hurried on through the heat to tell Weng.

Crossing the deserted clearing, she heard strange sounds echoing through the cylinder. In the deep cool of the inside, she found Weng in a folding recliner, her feet up, her head thrown back in an uncharacteristic position of repose. The sounds reverberated from the computer terminal, and though Megan had never heard Weng's music before, she knew instinctively that this was it.

Her immediate impression was of the monumental scale of the composer's intentions. CRI's tiny speaker could not possibly be doing justice to either tone or volume. She did not disturb Weng with news of the rippling sky, but sat down to cool off and to listen, wondering if coming into the middle of the composition would inhibit her understanding of it.

At first, she heard only confusion, vast randomness, long squeaks chittering against sharp burps of percussion, loosely bound by an underscoring hum.

But as she relaxed into concentration, vague patterns of rhythm suggested themselves. Hints of melody sparkled in bell-pure sequences like wind-driven rain on the surface of a lake. The rhythm strummed deeply. There was a bass drone almost below the range of hearing that pulled her into the spaces between the notes, as if time slowed and left her suspended, her breath imprisoned within her ribs, awaiting the next stroke of sound to release it. And the space that she lingered in was infinite, black, utterly still. Megan closed her eyes, thrilled and impressed.

Huge! Like being sucked into a void. This is spacer music, all right.

But there was something edgy as well. Something that disallowed true relaxation. Something stubborn, striving, contentious in the unrelenting percussion and the relationship of melodic themes.

How unlike Weng, Megan thought, and then, upon reconsideration, *but perhaps not. You don't win a command and keep it without being competitive.* She reminded herself that competition can be variously expressed, as well as repressed. *Into impulses such as using Game Theory as a basis for musical composition.*

Considering this, her perception of the tonal and rhythmic patterning shifted. She heard the music as a concrete expression of a mathematical abstraction, a bridge between two realms. She sensed the pure logic of numbers as it both constrained and freed the music, forming it to suit a human ear, yet setting it beyond emotion of any sort.

Beyond intention?

Strains as distinct and compelling as overhead whispers emerged out of the randomness, in many possible voices that she resolved at last into two. *Not melodies,* she decided, *not even themes.* Two sensibilities, rather, chasing each other through the fluid medium of surrounding sound, lunging, shoving, twining around one another like fish fighting in deep water.

Megan assumed the vibrato rumbling that shook her chair to be part of the composition. She recognized the push and pull of the Game, not just Weng's theoretical one, but the mythic one as well. It occurred to her that if she listened long enough, the music would reveal the rules to her.

But Weng started up from her near-trance in the recliner and slapped the switch to cut off the audio.

The rumbling continued, not loud but disturbingly deep, as if the very earth was groaning in pain. Megan swung her feet to the floor and felt the vibrations translate upward to her knees.

"Earthquake?"

"Mr. Clausen did not expect noticeable seismic activity in this old a planet." Weng's hands wobbled in tandem with the arms of her chair. The tremor crested in a broken growl like the clatter of falling rocks, then tapered off and died into silence.

Weng touched the keypad, reactivated the speaker. "CRI?"

"I am reading some sort of local disturbance, Commander, rather close to the surface. I am checking further."

Megan went to the cylinder mouth. A few distant dark forms had appeared on the cliff. She could see arms raised in the direction of the plain.

"I'm going out to take a look."

From the highest point of the clearing, the full expanse of plain was visible over the crumbled stalks. Megan gaped at what she saw.

A vast ragged hole had swallowed several tens of acres of burned fields and the uncultivated land beyond. A haze of dust drifted lazily away from the crater, captured by the slow dance of rising heat.

"Sinkhole," said Weng beside her. "The acquifers are drying out underneath the plain."

"You mean, it just collapsed?"

Weng nodded. "The water left a vacuum to be filled."

"My god, Weng, that could happen under the Lander!" As Megan stared at the hole, a protruding chunk of dry earth gave way and crumbled into the abyss. She had a sudden image of the planet devouring itself in a mad heat of rage. "Maybe your abort idea isn't so ridiculous after all."

The exhilaration of departure and the chase was fading behind a haze of exhaustion and noise and the constant vibrations of the straining engines. Stavros routed the cycling broadcast of Weng's compositions into the copilot's comset, then shut out all external considerations and lay back to listen, praying secretely for a revelation.

Susannah sat at the controls, her lower lip sucked in, her eyes flitting nervously between the instrument read-outs and the terrain ahead. Liphar curled at Stavros' feet, crammed into the narrow space between the seat and the exposed ribbing of the hull. Danforth slept on the floor behind, his big body too long for the bench. Ghirra claimed the bench, stretched out on his back but wide awake, watching Susannah's hand on the stick. Aguidran paced in the rear of the hold.

The third and final range of the Grigar was still a distant crenelation at the end of a blasted moonscape of desert, dunes rolling into wind-scoured hardpan dotted with spherical boulders. Stavros was glad for the easy flying over the endless sand. It allowed Danforth a much-needed rest, and himself a quiet time to pursue concentration, a state that was increasingly elusive as his goal, the source of his compulsion and terror, drew nearer.

The music, if it could be called such, also frightened him. It expressed his dying slide into the Void far better than he could have in words.

So close, as if she'd been right there with me!

He wondered if Weng had made a Connection similar to his but was unaware of it. *Should she be here in my place?*

But Kav Daven had not chosen Weng. *Did the old man choose wrong?*

The guar-fire was a growing agony in his palms, the symbol of his Connection but a further barrier to his concentration. It heightened his awareness of other distractions, the relentless rush of the fans, or the wind sighing along the force shield, or the constant questioning eyes of his companions, waiting for him to say, do or be something decisive.

His body sang with energy, but he knew it was not his own. He felt it as a surge from outside. It forced passage through him as if he were plugged in, light searing through an optical filament but delivering no message, only raw nerve endings, overfired synapses, pain.

Stavros sank into the music for escape, and idly tried to match the pulsing of the sky to the snarling rhythm of the bass drone. The sky had discovered color, a subtle range of glowing pinks and blues and lavender, pale electric hues. In the music, there was no color, only the darkness of the Void. Stavros remembered that all too well. The darkness flowed into him with the music and fanned the fire in his palms into a hungry blaze. Yet there was comfort in the familiarity. He gave in to the push and pull of the rhythm, let himself drift in the music as he had in the dark river of his dying.

A touch on his knee pulled him back. Susannah, glancing away from the instruments and the speeding vista of sand dunes, frowning with concern, pointing emphatically at her ear. He became aware of the tinny voice nagging at his own, repeating his name. The guar-fire eased as he shook off the music's spell.

"Yes, CRI?" he mumbled, trying to sound alert.

"Dr. James refused to wake Dr. Danforth," the computer began in peevish apology.

"By Dr. Danforth's request, and mine. What've you got?"

"Nothing to cause interest normally, but under the circumstances . . ."

Stavros had never known CRI to pause with such human hesitation in the middle of a thought. "Yes?"

"A slight correlation, Mr. Ibiá. Or rather a brief moment of complete correlation."

"Spill it, CRI. What are you talking about?"

"The Commander's music. And the patterns of atmospheric energy flux. A moment ago, their separate graphs matched completely, a very complicated rhythm, for exactly forty-one seconds."

"What happened?"

"Based on current data, I cannot offer an explanation . . ."

"I mean, when did it cut off? This correlation."

"Just now, as you answered my call."

Stavros squeezed his eyes shut against the chill rush of vertigo. *Raellil.*

Apprentice . . . messenger . . . the message was inside him, like the music.

Was *the music, this time?*

A strand of wire. More like a circuit.

He thought he understood suddenly and what he understood renewed his terror.

She'll burn me to a goddamn crisp.

"Thank you, CRI," he managed. "Let me know if it happens again."

But it would not happen again, not until he let it. He understood that as well, and wondered where he would find the courage.

He had seen himself thus far as the chosen victim of forces visiting from without. Not as a collaborator, whose willingness was essential to the connection.

But I WAS willing, from the very beginning. Willing to give over his self for the sake of understanding, willing to adopt a Sawl mindset to better his translations, willing to surrender to Kav Daven's call to mysticism.

That's it. That's what he saw in me. Willingness. Not some special strength or power. Stavros waited for disappointment but found relief and excitement instead. The explanation was so simple, it had to be right.

But surely there were Sawls *who were equally willing, willing enough to carry the guar uncomplaining in their hands. Mine was a Willingness, then, to do something else. What?*

He pictured the old man lost in the spiraling fury of his dance. He tore off the comset and struggled up, stiff and aching, fired by sudden need. Brusquely, he shook Liphar awake.

The young Sawl crawled blinking from his burrow beside the hull and stood shifting his weight and swinging his arms in response to this unexplained burst of energy. Stavros woke Ghirra, and astonished and delighted him by drawing him into the copilot's chair and placing the comwire in his ear with a quick explanation of its use. Then he wrapped his good arm around Liphar's back and urged him toward the rear of the hold. Aguidran paced irritably away, back to the front and her brother's company. Stavros settled cross-legged on the grated floor, a crate hard against his back. With a certain unconscious formality, he motioned Liphar to sit opposite him.

"Lifa, you said you could teach me about being a priest."

Liphar did not respond with the same bravado that had inspired his bid to win a seat on the Sled. His fingers twined nervously.

"There are a few things I need to know right now," said Stavros.

Liphar waited solemnly, very much the willing but unsure apprentice.

"What is it like when you contemplate the Flame?"

The apprentice smiled with relief, expecting a sterner interrogation. "This is a joining, Ibi. Very peace, and dark, like in water."

Stavros wet his lips, gone instantly dry. "Like swimming, in a river?"

Liphar's nod accepted an imperfect but viable description.

"Do you hear anything?"

Liphar hunched his shoulders, conspiratorial. "You see, Ibi? You know this already."

"No. Tell me."

"I listen this singing of the world and the Sisters."

Stavros shut his eyes, opened them. "Lifa, what did Kav Daven *really* mean when he told me to dance?"

Liphar's thin lips twitched into a doubting grin. It occurred to Stavros that the young man preferred to think he was joking.

"I mean, how does a priest learn to dance? Who teaches this? Who taught you the dances to celebrate the Planting, or the Birth dances?"

"I learn this in the guild."

"From your journeymen? From the master priests?"

"Anyone teach this, Ibi." Liphar's grin wavered.

"Anyone? Can you teach me?"

The young Sawl looked mildly shocked. "Ibi, this dances is not same dances." He frowned as if scolding Stavros for playing lightly with a serious matter. "I teach to you about the signs and the First Books, yes. I teach about all the chant and the story. But my dances is not to you."

Stavros felt twisted about a circular reasoning. "But he never . . . Kav Daven died before he could teach me his." He pressed his fist against his teeth. *Lured me to his purpose and deserted me . . .*

"Why didn't he choose an apprentice earlier, Lifa?"

The priest-to-be spread his hands as if it were obvious. "He find no one to know the dances."

"To know? No one who *knew* the dances?"

Liphar nodded. "He does not teach this dances, Ibi." He gestured from the pit of his stomach. "This is here, like the child inside, in you he calls 'raellil'." His expression mixed admiration with compassion for those whose gifts rule them instead of the other way around. "You know this, Ibi," he chided with a self-reassuring smile. "If you not know this, Kav Daven no say, this is my raellil."

"Lifa, if I know it, I don't know I know it."

Liphar offered in return the unflinching gaze of the faithful.

Stavros backed his spine against the crate. The lashing cords nudged the tender skin below his shoulder blade, pushed at the pad of bandages higher up. He was abruptly tired of mystery. Like wandering lost in a jungle, he might eventually get where he was going, but the many false starts and wrong turns were frustratingly inefficient. Unlike Clausen. Clausen was so sure of where he was going and what to do when he got there, he wasn't even in much of a hurry.

Willingness alone was not enough. Willingness to wander in the jungle did not tell you the right path to take.

Willingness, in this case, to wander in the Void.

The vibrations of the Sled sang through his palms, flattened against the plastic floor grate. Stavros reconsidered that place he called the Void: the dark windswept plane that the Sisters' consciousnesses inhabited. Though he must sink deep within himself to enter it, it existed elsewhere, outside, he was sure. *Not some trance state, not some waking dream.*

What then? Where? Do the priests go there when they meditate?

The old priest's dying order confounded him. Stavros pictured himself as a locked door. The Kav had carried the key in his withered brown hands. The Kav had opened him at will and, dying, had taken the key with him.

It's give up or find a new key.

Having processed his confusion as rationally as he could, Stavros allowed himself to contemplate the surprise of Weng's music.

Shall a Terran music lead my Sawlish dance?

He jumped up, startling Liphar out of a heat-doze. He paced forward, edged past Aguidran who watched her brother with disapproval as he tried to involve CRI in conversation over the shining strand of comwire. Ghirra was hunched in concentration.

Stavros crouched between the two forward seats. His stomach knotted in anticipation, fear of what he was about to attempt. He weighed the wisdom of waking Danforth to tell him about the correlation of weather and music, but the slack exhaustion in the planetologist's sleeping face deterred him. Instead, he leaned over to brush a quick kiss across Susannah's cheek. The soft warmth of her skin reassured him. She smiled but did not look away from the windscreen.

Stavros touched Ghirra's shoulder, requesting the comset. Ghirra removed it regretfully and handed it over, vacating the chair.

Stavros slipped into the seat and hooked the wire around his jaw, trying not to feel imprisoned by it. "CRI, patch me through to Weng."

"The Commander is currently in her sleep period, Mr. Ibiá."

"No matter, you tell me: what's her most recent composition? Can you play it for me?"

CRI paused like a secretary over an open file drawer. "There are a number of unfinished works in storage, some studies, many notes."

"Her newest completed work."

"That would be the piece she finished last month during the flood, while I was out of contact. Her *Dies Irae*."

"Her what?"

"The title of the piece is *Dies Irae*. Archaic perhaps, but thematically appropriate under the circumstances, wouldn't you agree?"

Something in the computer's tone rang harshly familiar. "Is that what Emil said about it?"

"Yes," CRI admitted. "How did you know?"

"Never mind. Play it for me. And send it out simultaneously, direct beam to Nolagri."

"Ready, Mr. Ibiá."

The violence of it astonished him, laid him flat against the back of his seat as if it were physical, like a blow to the jaw, like a cathedral door thrown open on an explosion of wind and rain. The sound hissed and spat at him, music only by the broadest definition, but vast enough in scale to encompass the chaos of galaxies. It yowled like a blizzard gale, raked his brain and eardrums with razored claws. Stavros recoiled, forseeing its dangers, and circled around it, listening from a mental distance in a last gesture of self-preservation.

"Lifa!" Instinct prompted the call.

Liphar wriggled in next to him, reclaiming the narrow slot between seat and hull. The young Sawl pressed against his side without need of explanation and laid a hand across his wrist where it rested limp along his thigh.

The knot of fear in Stavros' stomach dropped like a stone into the well of his spine as an image of Kav Daven flashed to mind, the old man sitting so still among the leaping flames of the

StoryHall, the tawny girl's hand resting on his knee, so lightly, so like the feather touch of Liphar's fingers on his wrist.

But it was too late to resist. He had offered himself to the music just as he used to do with his panic and fantasies, and it drew him inward. The sound burned into his ears. His teeth buzzed with its ravening drone. But the light pressure of Liphar's hand remained in his awareness, a faint but steady beacon pointing the direction home to reality, as the roar of the waters rose around him.

The dark river was a torrent, a flood of raw aggression. Stavros tumbled in the current, coughing up bile sucked like water into drowning lungs. Pain folded his chest in a vise. He could not gasp, so let the reflex go, gave himself once more to the darkness, and sank.

Willing . . . .

He sank through the black water, his lungs filling, expanding, himself expanding, heavy with water, heavier than the current. Sank into the shock of enveloping mud, cold as death, and still. The still, cold mud wrapped the current with arms as wide as a river of stars.

His arms.

Power seared his veins with fire. He raised his arms of mud to cradle the torrent.

Raellil

Circuit.

Carrier?

Susannah signalled Ghirra to wake Danforth when the pulsating sky began to spit showers of static spark. Stavros was immobile in the next chair, Liphar curled close beside him.

Asleep, she presumed, preoccupied with keeping the Sled in the air.

The Sled bucked and dropped. The far whine deepened briefly. The aft engines stuttered. Over the cockpit com, CRI reported a momentary disruption in the power beam.

"Jesus! Not now!" Danforth struggled groggily into the pilot's chair, dragging his rigid leg behind him. "We've got another whole mountain range to get over. What's Clausen's position?"

Susannah helped him strap in, then crouched at his shoulder, kneading cramp from her forearm. She had been gripping the stick as if their lives depended on the strength of her hands. The cloud ripples blinked electric blue sparkles far to the east where the sky was faintly darkening.

"Nearing forty degrees," CRI replied. "Slowing. He has

asked me to plot gravitometric measurements and complete detailed mapping of a discrete magnetic field detected at forty-seven degrees.''

''He'll be looking for its center of symmetry,'' remarked Danforth, ''where the source is most likely located.''

''So he is looking for more than his lithium.''

''Oh,. yes. That power surge'll have him worried, though.'' He patted the plastic encasing his thigh. ''That's what happened to us last time we went for a spin.''

''So maybe he'll stick closer to the ground,'' Susannah said. ''Slow him down a bit.'' Beyond the windscreen, the final range rose without the polite preliminary of foothills, as if a giant fist had sheared the forward half away with a cleaver the size of a small planet. The white cloud veil seemed balanced on the very tip of the peaks.

''Distance, CRI?''

''Eight hundred and eighty-seven kilometers.''

Danforth flashed Susannah a wan smile of approval. ''Kept right up, didn't you, girl? He's only three, four hours ahead now.'' He glanced at the copilot's chair. ''How long's Ibiá been out?''

''Don't know. Not long. Should I wake him?''

Something in Stavros' slump made her look more closely, something in his loose-curled upturned palms. His bowed head and his long eyelashes had camouflaged his half-lidded stare. His eyes were focussed somewhere far beyond the silvered metal of his belt buckle. But as Susannah reached to shake him, Liphar's hand shot out to catch her wrist.

''No!'' he hissed.

Susannah stared. ''What's the matter? What's happened to him?''

The Sled dropped again sickeningly as a shell-burst of tiny fire lit the white cloud ceiling above. The force field flickered, the fans coughed and whined back up to speed.

''Shit,'' Danforth muttered at the approaching blank wall of mountain. ''What now?''

''Ghirra?'' called Susannah shakily. Liphar, raised up on his haunches like a cobra over Stavros' knees, still gripped her arm without apology, as if holding her back from an unwitting blasphemy. The weirdness of it fueled her panic. ''Ghirra!''

The Sled shuddered. Light broke around them like a wave cresting into sunlit foam. The white landscape pulsed rainbows of color. Instant black shadows bloomed like inky smoke behind boulders, inside crevices, then faded as instantly.

Ghirra forsook the safety of his seat and struggled forward to

302

crouch unsteadily beside Susannah. His long jaw was tight from resisting fear. He took in the frozen tableau: Liphar the hovering accolyte, Susannah incomprehending, Stavros in the grip of his mystery, lit by prismatic flashes from a sky gone mad. He gasped a question at Liphar.

The younger Sawl answered with fervent conviction, his determination temporarily overriding his fear of the seesawing Sled and his awe of the Master Healer's authority.

Ghirra hesitated.

"What *is* it?" Susannah demanded.

The healer's voice was flat with ambivalence. "He says 'TavrosIbia looks for his dance."

"His *what*?"

His reply was lost in his own intake of breath as the Sled swayed side to side with the casual floating violence of a leaf in a hurricane. The polished vertical face of the mountain loomed like a speeding nightmare.

"Get everyone strapped in!" Danforth yelled. "We're going over!"

The Sled tilted wildly as he rammed the stick forward. Ghirra clung to the back of Danforth's seat, his nails scrabbling against the hard plastic as he fought to keep from sliding down the sloping deck. He searched desperately for Aguidran. Liphar cringed back against the gray hull in terror, wedging himself between the ribs. Freed from his grasp, Susannah forgot Stavros for a breathless moment.

"Tay, what can I do? Is there anything I can do?"

Danforth was snarling at CRI over his comset. "Just hold tight," he roared between clenched teeth. "Damn boat is like a wild animal all of a sudden!"

Aguidran battled her way uphill from the rear of the hold, and tumbled into the bench behind her brother. She wrapped a loose strap across her chest, then hauled Ghirra back against the padding beside her, shoving his own harness into his hands.

The Sled banked crazily as Danforth swerved to clear the rock face. It cut sharp right and rose, fans and engines screaming, struggling for enough altitude to clear the unfathomable cliff. The sky glowed pink, then salmon, then gold.

"We lose power now, we ain't got a prayer!" he swore, louder than he had intended. "These piss-poor emergency batteries hold enough for about thirty seconds at this weight!"

"Thanks, I really needed to know that!" Susannah yelled back.

The bright sheer rock fell past the windscreens meter by meter as they rose, ripple-scorched with color. Danforth searched for a break, a pass, even a ledge with space enough to allow him to land and sit out the sky's latest inventive malice. Nothing. He circled out, away from the cliff's rough-edged proximity, and headed west, still rising along the faceless wall. The white clouds loomed above, too close. From two thousand dizzy meters below, the rocky desert plateau stared back at him unrelentingly.

"Motherfucker's not built for this!" muttered Danforth. "Come ON!" His whole body jerked and swayed as if to amplify the frustratingly slight motions of the stick. Susannah leaned hard against his seatback and prayed.

Suddenly the sky exploded. Danforth bellowed a useless warning. Atop the mountain wall, the white clouds tore and gaped open.

The glowing rent belched fire. Flaming spheres fell like a torrent of giant hailstones, consuming themselves in trailing smoke before they hit the distant ground. The rent closed over as another appeared directly above the Sled. Danforth fought an onslaught of turbulence, yelling directions to himself like curses. St. Elmo's fire danced across the delta wings. Bright tongues sparked against the force field.

Stavros' cry rang out over the straining roar of the engines as the Sled sank in a downdraft. Distracted by her own battle against panic, Susannah heard the cry as a summons, and lurched to his aid.

His eyes were open but unseeing. His fingers twitched, curling and uncurling around his upturned palms. His lips worked convulsively, and Susannah cringed away revolted, as her mind overlaid on her lover's youthful beauty the remembered image of a muttering, dessicated priest.

Liphar's head jerked out of the protective shield of his arms. In his cramped burrow against the hull, he gathered his legs beneath him, watching Stavros intently. A devout hopeful joy softened the rictus of fear twisting his narrow face.

The sky exploded again. The Sled veered, slicing past the mountain face. Fire cascaded around the windscreens and fought with the force field. The cockpit glowed orange. The muscles of Danforth's neck bunched against the strain as he struggled to guide the bucking craft away from the rock. His eyes stared with concentration. Susannah held her scream like a needle of ice in the back of her throat, physical enough to choke on.

Stavros cried out again, but this time it was a yowl of terror. His back arched. His hands flew up to shield his face. He fought the restraints of the flight harness as if desperate to escape.

Liphar sprang instantly from his crouch, his terror of the flight

304

submerged in a greater panic. He screamed for Ghirra, straddling
Stavros' thighs, throwing all his slight weight against Stavros'
arms to press him back against the padding. The Master Healer
whipped off his half-fastened straps and balancing against the
Sled's lurch and rock, he swayed forward like a sailor in a gale
and flattened himself against the back of the seat. He unhooked
the comwire from Stavros' ear, then pinned the resisting head
between strong hands, his long fingers curling around Stavros'
jaw. Stavros' struggling eased. Ghirra's fingers slid up to work
at his temples.

The Sled leaped abruptly as if catapulted. It coasted upward to
sail high and wide over a break in the sheer mountain wall.
Danforth cheered incredulously.

A sharp cut lay before them, the snowless summit peaks
crowding to either side like stained, misshapen teeth. Danforth
eased off the throttle and slipped the still-swaying craft into the
narrow pass. Sparks ran off the wings like rain water and vanished. The sky closed over, whiter and hotter than before. The
Sled steadied and flew straight.

Ghirra relaxed his hold on Stavros' head and slumped against
the back of the seat. Stavros' eyes sagged closed, then opened
listlessly. He did not move.

Liphar slid back into his crouch against the hull. His fingers
fluttered around Stavros' knee, suddenly unsure.

Susannah leaned in. "Stav? Are you all right?"

Stavros stared dully. "Yeah." Flexing his palms, he reached to
still Liphar's nervous hands. He gazed at the young man solemnly, then whispered, "I'm sorry, Lifa. I couldn't do it."

Liphar shivered with negation. "Give good strength, you, to
Valla, so she send back Her Sister's fire soldier this time." He
gestured at the sky's solid lowering white.

"I did nothing."

"This is not learn one time, Ibi."

"You don't understand." Stavros shook his head slowly, as if
its weight were an unbearable burden. "I couldn't face Them. I
was scared shitless. Kev Daven was wrong. I am not the one he
hoped I was."

He shook his head again and would not speak again or move
until Danforth had cleared the heights of the Grigar and set the
Sled down on a descending plateau in the southern slope.

"Quite a view." Danforth stumped to the edge of the drop,
balancing on his crutches at Stavros' side. At their feet, eroded
pink rock fell away into a twisted landscape of deep ravines and

flat-topped pink and white mesas that stretched as far as they could see, blurring into sooty gray on a distant curved horizon.

"Not a bush, not a twig, not even a dried-up thorny old cactus," Danforth remarked companionably. "I've seen uninhabitable worlds nicer than this."

Stavros stared silently southward.

"Lot of water here once, though. All that channel erosion." Danforth nosed in the dust with the toes of his cast-bound right leg. "Sky's starting to pulse again, you notice?"

Stavros' eyes flicked across the glowing white and back to the horizon without comment.

Danforth uncovered a stone with his toes and pushed it around with awkward stiff-legged little kicks. "CRI was just babbling about some ninety-second phase correlation with Weng's music being twice as long as the one before. What one before?"

Stavros swayed slightly, moving away.

Danforth grabbed his arm and jerked him back. "Listen, if you're gonna crap out on me, I gotta know it. Fast. What's going on?"

Unresisting in his grasp, Stavros turned dead eyes on him. "Crap out on *you*? I just crapped out on the whole goddamn thing."

The bitter tone reminded Danforth of his own. He let the limp arm go. "Care to explain?"

"Weng's music. It was a great bit of insight, but dangerous, as it turned out. I mean, They *did* hear it. I brought it to Them and They listened, sort of. Actually, They absorbed it. Played with it like a toy. Incorporated its violence right into the Arrah until the weather was expressing it, instead of the other way around." His mouth began a smile that quickly died. "They made Weng's game music a part of the Game."

"They."

"Lagri, mostly. This being Her turf."

Danforth ran his tongue around the inside of his cheek, kicked his stone toward the edge and saved it from death at the last minute. "Hunh."

"The music was a key—your instinct was right. It brought me to Them. The problem is, it only encouraged further violence. It's too much like Them. Their struggle inspired it in the first place."

"You're saying Weng's music made fire rain from the sky? You mean, like some kind of signal to the machine?"

Stavros turned back to the smooth southern horizon, held out a raised palm and curled it slowly into a fist. "I could feel Her, fire-eyed Lagri, like it was myself, feel Her joining with the

306

music as it flowed through me, out of me, to Her, She making it Hers, warping it to Her abiding obsession, the Game, the game, the one becoming the other as seamless as an interface . . ." He dropped his hand. "And I was a flood-tossed mote, the infinitesimal messenger, She no more aware of me than of that rock. Or of the millions of Sawls who have been murdered by Her blind passion to annihilate Her Sister.

"So I thought, if I manipulate the music, if I play little tweaking games with a signal She has already internalized, might She not notice? Might that not get Her attention? And that is where my courage failed . . . failed in the face of a Power vaster than . . . ah, that old man! My Christ! He had Their fire boiling through him for decades! How did he stand it?"

Danforth had no answer for that. "Tell me, Ibiá. What would you do with their attention if you had it?"

Stavros's laugh was like a sob. "That's the problem! It's sort of like sailing into the middle of an air war, broadcasting on all channels. Unless you know the right code, you're likely to get blown out of the sky. The old man didn't leave me his signals." He paused, regarding Danforth quizically. "This is hard for you, isn't it?" he murmured. "I can hear you being patient with me at the top of your voice."

Danforth smiled, liking him in earnest. "The madman's ravings?"

"Just so. You still think I'm imagining all this?"

"You got me, Ibiá." He glanced down, rolling the stone under the ball of his foot. "There's *something* down there, though, at forty-seven degrees. CRI has just completed mapping a magnetic field two thousand kilometers in diameter, plopped right on a highland exactly opposite the middle of the northern ocean. Clausen's got her determining a center of symmetry. He's asked for high-res as well, plus she's been able to link the pattern of gravitational variations with the peaks of weather activity." Danforth shrugged. "So no, I don't think you're imagining *every*thing. And while Emil fumbles around down there with this test and that test, he's showing us where to go and we're gaining on him, slowly but surely."

"We don't need him to show us," said Stavros quietly. "I can take us right there."

Danforth raised an eyebrow at his stone as if it had misbehaved.

"Tay, I swear. I don't know how, but it's true." He held up his palms in offering. "I'm keyed into that magnetic field. I'm . . . aligned. Like the little iron filings. I know exactly where my poles are. I can feel the pull." Stavros raised his arm and pointed, slightly south of due southwest. "There."

Danforth chuckled, shifting his crutches, and kicked his stone off the ledge. "Well, you'll be happy to know CRI agrees with you on that score. But if you're done with your magic tricks for the moment, can I convince you to come back to the Sled and eat something?"

"My thought precisely," said Susannah, coming up behind them and taking both their arms.

Stavros shook his head, but pressed Susannah's hand close to his side.

"Talk to this boy," Danforth told her gruffly. "Tell him some of those sweet things you women are so good at. We're due back in the air in twenty minutes and I want him fed and watered by then."

He disengaged his arm with a crooked smile, and swung uphill over the crumbly rock toward the Sled and a cold trail breakfast.

40

The pink and white desert slid past tediously. Danforth flew for a long stretch, surrendered the stick to Susannah for several hours, then resumed the seat when at last the smooth arc of the southwestern horizon broke into a jagged line. The sky shuddered with chasing waves of color, but the cloud veil was thinning, its glowing white tinged with pink.

After a long silence, Danforth cleared his throat over the com, calling up satellite photos on the tiny cockpit monitor. "No cloud at all over the area of the magnetic field."

Stavros leaned in to look. The central darkish area was like a hole punched into the middle of a hot white waste of cloud.

"Looks like another distant mountain range from down here, but the radar imaging shows a near perfect two-thousand-kilometer circle of violently upthrust terrain." Danforth jabbed at the screen with an eager finger. "Good place to hide a complex machine, also the best evidence for CRI's suggestion of the ocean as an impact basin. The shock waves from the impact travel through the planet's crust to collide at an exactly opposing point, and presto! Crustal chaos. Stop me if I'm boring you, Ibiá."

"Nolagri means 'Lagri's Fortress,' more literally, Lagri's Rock. Lagri's father built it for Her with a giant bolt of lightning."

Stavros found the precise roundness of the hole in the cloud uncanny. "Stop *me* if I'm boring *you*."

Danforth grinned. "Increase resolution, CRI."

The darker circle swelled like a balloon, became a grainy pattern of greys, a hot white arc hugging one hemisphere, a darker shadow line the other.

Danforth traced the white highlight. "Interesting terrain. Nice sharp rise all around off the surrounding plateau, cleanly delineated. From there, the max altitude levels off, but you can see how broken up it is—all those fissures and cracking. Easy prospecting."

"Looks like a giant's sand castle," offered Stavros. "The drip kind, all dried out by the sun."

"Very scientific," Danforth drawled.

But Stavros was eying the borderline between cloud and clear. Instinct told him he would not cross it unawares.

"Clausen's already in there," reported Danforth. "Doing the usual preclaim survey, by the book. He's got CRI scanning the upland kilometer by kilometer. The terrain is unusual as I said, but so far, there's nothing more to catch the eye."

Stavros frowned distractedly. "You want smoke plumes, Tay? The flash of solar collectors? Something you can easily recognize?"

"Whoa, back off, man," warned Danforth. "I'm just looking for a signpost. Take anything I can get."

"I'm all the signpost you need," Stavros returned stubbornly. "I'll get you there." He removed the comwire from his ear, letting it hang on his shoulder like an offbeat necklace. Danforth glared at him briefly, then shrugged and returned his full attention to the Sled.

The direction of the pull was the one thing Stavros was sure of.

The guar-fire had burned in quiet embers since his last tumble in the black torrent. But the spark was rekindling. Stavros ground his thumb into the center of his palm. Incredible that the sensitive thumbpad could feel no heat. Mortal flesh and bones. No more than that. Idly, Stavros plotted the rise and fall of the guar-fire's flame: always low after a brush with the Power, then rebuilding to a peak at the next encounter, like water collecting inside a lock, or potential energy, agitating for release.

Liphar stirred beside him, asleep against his knee.

My faithful sheepdog, or is he really my shepherd?

The young man's unswerving devotion had been flattering when Stavros had a less clear idea of what was expected of him. Now such adoration made him nervous and pressured, sensitive as he was to failure, past and future. He admitted to relief that the potential of violent climatic side effects excused him from further attempts at contact through Weng's music.

Once again, he questioned the wisdom of the old priest's choice.

Why not a Sawl, after all? How can I succeed, with my offworld thoughts and ways? Or is it my alienness itself that makes me eligible?

The willing stranger? The uninvolved messenger?

The neutral current?

Kav, tell me!

He kept his plea from voicing itself and shaming him further. He was more grateful than he would ever say aloud for Danforth's new tolerance and restraint. Though he could not keep himself from pushing at it on occasion, testing it like a naughty child, he had no real wish to abuse it.

Danforth tapped his knee and gestured to the abandoned comset. Reluctantly, Stavros slipped it back in his ear. Danforth was monitoring Clausen's communications with CRI.

". . . find no detectable center to the field, Mr. Clausen. It appears to be extremely diffuse. Shifting movements within the field itself are making accurate mapping difficult."

"Has to be a source somewhere," Clausen snapped. "Keep looking."

The prospector's voice, like raked gravel even at a distance, made Stavros shiver.

"Surface compositional analysis is showing a remarkable percentage of lithium oxides."

"Register exact coordinates of all locations at or above standard field percentages and prepare claim forms. I expect it will be a nice long list."

Danforth closed the channel on Clausen's satisfied chuckle, then flew wrapped in total concentration for a while. Stavros stayed on the com, sensing in the big man's abrupt silence an unvoiced concern.

Finally, Danforth commented casually, "Haven't heard Ronnie on the wire at all."

"Long as he needs her," said Stavros, "he'll keep her healthy."

Danforth nodded glumly. "Then I guess she better stay useful, eh?"

Susannah took her shift at the stick while the sky's pink tinge deepened into amber. When Danforth woke to resume his seat, Nolagri was in clear view. An arc of hot green sky cut into the thinning white cloud with a broad horizon-to-horizon sweep. From the Sled, the sun was still a bright patch of amber burning through the cloud cover, but the looming upland was already stained orange by late afternoon light.

Danforth urged the Sled higher, riding the thermals coiling up from the desert plateau. Rising, they skimmed the first sharp slopes of Nolagri's rubbled flank.

"Hardly any erosion softening at all here," he noted. "Looks like the impact could have happened yesterday."

Stavros watched the edge of green sky zoom toward him like the blade of a knife. "Lagri's idea of local climate control," he joked tightly. "No weather at all."

The three Sawls bunched along one windscreen until Danforth made them spread out to disperse their weight. Liphar's stunned awe said he had never expected to visit the dwelling place of a Goddess in his lifetime. He grasped the blue-green bead on his wrist and muttered a luck-chant.

At the top of the slope, the air was still, the sky a clear, hard green. Stavros stifled a gasp as the Sled passed out from under the faint remnant of cloud and white heat flared suddenly in his palms. Resisting the impulse to curl inward around the pain, he fought to breathe evenly and deeply, determined this time to control it and the swimming disconnection that accompanied it.

"Lifa?" he called thickly.

Liphar was enrapt in his chant at the windscreen, clutching his bead. A torn and silent wilderness stretched before him, an eruption of raw pink rock, the private strata of the planet's crust sundered and ripped open, entrails of mineral and crystal and stone strewn without ceremony. The low sun etched the rough waste with a web of hard shadow, cracks, fissure lines, the shade-sides of vast rift systems whose bottoms were lost in darkness.

The roar of the Void built inside Stavros' brain. "Lifa!"

Liphar started, flicking worried eyes at him, and was beside him in the space of a breath. Stavros hovered half in, half out of a space far removed from the cockpit of the Sled, struggling to explain his summons. But Liphar murmured at him soothingly and slipped back into his cramped spot against the hull, offering him the light anchor of a hand on his knee. Stavros' dizziness ebbed, though the black torrent still echoed in the distance and the pain remained.

"No taboos about trespassing on sacred ground?" Susannah asked Ghirra.

Ghirra did not seem to understand the concept.

Stavros strove for a semblance of normal speech. "How can we be trespassing when our very existence isn't even recognized?"

Danforth rechecked Clausen's position. "Heading straight for the center. Two hours away, maybe three. At least he's on the scope now. All the easier for us to tag along.''

"No." Stavros massaged his palms fitfully, but it did nothing to relieve the exploding heat. "Don't need him anymore."

"Stav, we came out here to try to stop him."

"Can, if we get there first."

"Okay, then." Danforth eyed him neutrally. "Where to?"

Without a moment's doubt, Stavros pointed off to the right.

Danforth banked the Sled gently. "CRI, let me see your map of the field." An abstracted contour diagram filled the little monitor. "Uh-hunh. Okay, Stav. A slight spike in the graph, off in your direction. Not as high as these others, but . . ." His finger circled several contour values, then one nearly at the geographic center of the field. "This one here's the one Emil's going for. You sure of your head?"

"Yes."

"Okay. CRI, give me high-res again, the terrain ahead."

"Maybe the real hot spots are decoys," ventured Susannah.

Danforth snorted. "For what against whom? Pictures, CRI."

A grainy black-and-white image replaced the field map: the white, the pockmarked ground; the black, the jagged diagonal slice of a huge sheer-sided canyon.

Gazing into that bottomless black, Stavros heard the far off whisper of flood waters.

"Decrease resolution," said Danforth.

The canyon dwindled to a mere side branch among many side branches of a vaster, blacker chasm.

"Again, CRI."

The chasm shrank into a minor offshoot of a stupendous rift that split the ravaged upland in a ragged serpentine grin. Its hundred lesser canyons with their thousand tributaries and subtributaries fanned out to the four points of the compass, writhing through the bedrock like the roots of an ancient tree.

"Well, damn, look at that," said Danforth. "That main crack's got to be six hundred long and a good twelve across."

"And straight down," breathed Susannah.

"Looks like someone pried the rock apart with a goddamn crowbar. Is that where we're headed?"

Dizzy again, Stavros looked away from the screen and nodded.

"Excuse me, Dr. Danforth. You asked to be informed when Mr. Clausen landed."

"Yeah. What's it look like where he is, CRI?"

The image showed a finely shattered terrain shaped by a series of concentric uplifts rising toward a central broken peak.

"Check that out, Ibiá. *That* I'd believe was some giant's

312

castle. Dead center in the magnetic field, I'll bet." Danforth could not hide his enthusiasm. "Oh, he'll love it in there—lots of deep layers nicely exposed. Prospector Heaven."

"The surface presence of lithium oxide is highly indicative of additional subsurface deposits in this area," offered CRI helpfully.

"I should be proud of myself," Danforth said mordantly. "I found this bloody planet for him!"

Clausen's mocking laugh suddenly flooded the cockpit. "A little off the beaten track, aren't you, Taylor?"

Liphar stared at the control panel as if it had grown teeth. Ghirra and Aguidran turned from the windscreen with identical narrow-eyed frowns.

"Well, now we're going to get down to business," the disembodied voice declared. "Start turning the ground a little. CRI, register this site as C-9, priority one."

"Here we go," Danforth muttered.

"Charge A, serial number 57460-U867.46, activated," CRI reported.

The silence in the cockpit held for the length of a heartbeat.

"Shit, that sonofabitch doesn't waste a second!" growled Danforth.

"He's really going to do it," Susannah murmured unbelievingly. "How powerful are those charges?"

"Make a nice crater out of a small city when tuned to full strength, though the point is to plant them real deep, to shatter the bedrock for the machines to pick through. Standard preliminary procedures, though legally he's supposed to wait until the claim is validated. They rarely do. If the claim is contested, the Courts are more likely to accept a fait-accompli . . . it's an old strategy. He probably dropped the charge at the bottom of a likely canyon and kept going."

"Won't work, Clausen," swore Stavros under his breath.

"You listening, Ibiá?" Clausen's voice goaded. "If you were hoping for the hand of God to reach out and snatch me from the sky, forget it. And the honored doctor's weather machines are a fiction as well. There's nothing here, boy. Not a damned thing, living or dead, except all this lovely money lying all over the ground, free for the taking. The richest lithium strike I've ever had the privilege to . . ."

Stavros reached to cut the connection. "If he's so sure there's nothing there, why'd he make a beeline for the center of the field?"

"Hedging his bets," Danforth replied. "If there was anything, he'd be killing two birds with one stone."

Susannah leaned forward. "CRI, do you have control of that device? Can you disarm it?"

"Under normal circumstances, yes, Dr. James. But Mr. Clausen has . . ."

"He's fenced it," supplied Danforth. "Damn. He must have done it ahead of time. Couldn't have managed it through the terminal on his Sled."

"That means we can't . . ."

Danforth shook his head. "These terminals aren't smart enough to give us access to mainframe programming. Not much more than a grown-up radio."

"Then we have to close down the com," said Stavros suddenly, slapping at the switches nearest him.

"What? Wait! Hold it!" Danforth swatted his hand away.

"We've got to shut down everything we can!" insisted Stavros. "Com black out, so he can't follow us!"

"He can home in on our power beam," Danforth objected.

"Not as accurately as the telemetry."

"How the hell do I fly without navigation fixes?"

"Seat of your pants. You'll still have the cockpit instruments. I'll be your navigation."

"No. We've got to keep CRI on line . . ."

"Taylor, please!"

"It's not the worst idea, Tay," Susannah interjected.

"Dr. Danforth," the computer broke in blandly. "Mr. Clausen asks me to say that it was unsporting of you to cut him off so brusquely."

"Tell him he can go . . ."

Stavros overrode him. "Tell him we're having trouble with the com."

"Trouble? I can detect no problem from here, Mr. Ibiá."

"Tell him anyway. Just say to him . . . for Christ's sake, CRI, *lie* to the sonofabitch."

"Mr. Ibiá, you know I cannot." The computer sounded vaguely regretful, as if her inability to produce deliberate falsehood were a machine failing that cast doubt on her claim to full sentience.

"Tay, listen to me." The agony in Stavros' palms leaked more desperation into his tone than he wanted. The planetologist had always responded negatively to being shoved too hard. "Either we go in as invisibly as we can, or we turn around now. We can't just lead him in with a big brass band!"

"In where? In where?" Danforth stared back at him. "Jesus! I don't know why I give you the time of day, you crazy motherfucker!"

314

"Because you *know* I'm right, by the same instinct that pulled Weng's music out of the hat!"

Danforth's jaw clapped shut. He glanced away, chewing his lip. "CRI, what's the detonation time on that charge?"

"One hour, twenty-eight minutes, forty seconds."

"Why so long?" asked Susannah.

"He's probably setting a string of them to go off at once. He's registered that whole central uplift as a primary claim." Danforth consulted his chronometer, his lower lip caught hard between his teeth. "Okay. We run in blackout for an hour and twenty eight. Then we try to listen in quietly, see what goes. I mean, what if he's right about the center of the field being where it's at, Stav?"

"He's not."

"Even so. You want to know, don't you?"

Stavros nodded faintly. "Every ounce of speed you can, Tay," he pleaded.

Susannah noticed his clenched fists and jaw. "Is the shoulder hurting, Stav? I could give you something."

"No!" he blurted, jerking away from her touch. Seeing he had hurt her, he added, "I mean, I have to keep alert," and gave her his hand, while invisible fire burned at its center with the heat of a star.

Stavros held Susannah's hand for the entire hour and a quarter that brought them to the center of the rift system. His inner senses had gone into overdrive. Like being in a noisy crowd, with everyone yelling at him at once, he was exhausted from the effort of staying coherent enough to guide Danforth across the miles of unmarked wilderness, where one twisting canyon looked much the same as a hundred others, winding through the broken rock, slicing deep into the crust.

He floated in a bubble of strange internal pressures. The reality of Susannah's quiet murmur at his side barely held its own against the noises of the Void. When Danforth spoke, Stavros heard him as if through water, or second-hand, through some other mind's apparatus. Liphar's hand on his knee retained the most reality, the light steadying tug of a sea anchor.

"Now that is a major hole in the ground," commented Danforth. He stretched forward to peer over the nose of the Sled. "And we've got twelve minutes to detonation."

Stavros pointed into the vast shadows of the rift. "Down."

"You got it." The Sled banked and dropped through the hot late sun like a white-gold stone, dipping below the bright scarred edge of the eastern rim, past smoothly undulating walls of sunlit amber rock toward the realm of unplumbed darkness far below.

Danforth flicked an eye at the altimeter. "One kilometer," and later, as he revved the fans to slow their rate of drop, "Two." The rift hardly narrowed. The western rim remained a distant shade-darkened wall, every crevice a sharp-etched detail in the clear, motionless air.

"Three," intoned Danforth as they sped south, still dropping along the eastern wall. "What the hell are we looking for?" He slowed their descent again as they passed into the shadow of a western peak, then out again. "We go down too far, we'll lose line of sight to the power beam."

"There," said Stavros suddenly.

Five pairs of eyes swung in the direction of his gaze.

A ledge far below, bathed in hard amber light; two, three kilometers wide, enough to build a small town on. The eastern wall of the rift rose up sheer from the ledge for at least a kilometer. Stavros pointed toward the southmost narrow end.

Aguidran gave a harsh cry of surprise and grabbed her brother's arm.

"Look!" Susannah exclaimed.

Black dots broke the bright, smooth rock face, enlarging into perfect round holes as the Sled descended, hundreds, thousands, laid out in even parallel tiers, spaced as neatly as the windows of a skyscraper.

Danforth swore in delighted disbelief. "Now that's something I can relate to! Christ, maybe there *are* people left!"

"No," said Stavros.

Danforth damped the Sled's forward thrust and steered it closer to the wall to skim the highest level of openings. The holes, so rivetingly precise in curve and placement, dwarfed the Sled, tunnelling straight into the rock and darkness.

"Look at the size of them!" he marvelled. "I could fly this thing right in there if I could see where I was going."

"No," Stavros insisted hoarsely.

Danforth eyed him, wonder mixing with lingering doubt. "Sure, sure. Okay."

The Sled dropped in a powered glide past tier after tier of circular tunnels, picking up another kilometer in depth before Danforth lifted the nose and revved the fans a final time to settle the craft on the ledge with improving skill. He cut fans, engines and force field, waiting for the weight of the exterior heat to descend like dirt into the grave. But the dustless air was temperate, almost cool. The surface of the ledge was oddly unreflective, dark and as finely granular as emery paper.

"Well, well, well." Danforth stretched but made no further move.

The three Sawls stared into the amber silence with varying degrees of awe. Aguidran studied the towering wall and its precise pattern of holes, then paced to the rear of the hold to unlatch the cargo hatch. Liphar shifted his attention back to Stavros, who seemed to be listening with every ounce of concentration he could muster.

"It's like . . . like a real city," Susannah murmured. "And look how oddly flat this ledge is, as if someone sanded it smooth."

"Perfect landing site," Danforth commented speculatively. "You could hide one hell of a lot of machinery in there . . . and the people to run them."

"You think someone still lives here?"

"Isn't that what we came all this way to find out? Oh, shit!" Danforth snapped his fingers, then cringed at the cascading ricochet of echo. "The charges!" he whispered, and leaned to reconnect the com.

Stavros tried to stop him but couldn't manage a simple no. It had not occurred to him that the Sled's small force field might be damping his own reception. He had not thought of his connection to the Sisters' dark plane as having any reality in the physical world. But with the dropping of the shield, he was overwhelmed.

He heard Danforth, then Susannah call his name through a fog of noise, roaring wind and water, their voices fading in and out like a dying radio signal. Only Liphar's steady touch told him up from down as the waters closed around him once again and he began to tumble.

Danforth opened a channel to hail CRI in the orbiter.

"Dr. Danforth!"

Susannah imagined she heard relief in the computer's flat voice.

"You were able to repair the malfunction Mr. Ibiá spoke of?" It was not quite a lie, but it did employ the language of their attempted deception. "Mr. Clausen has been most concerned as to your welfare."

"Our whereabouts, more likely."

"Make it quick, Tay," Susannah urged.

"The charges, CRI. How many has he laid?"

"Four, Dr. Danforth. Due to detonate in twenty-two seconds."

317

"Tay, cut her off before he can get a good fix on us. Maybe he'll assume we're still moving."

"CRI can tell him otherwise." But Danforth shut down the connection and all telltale power in the Sled. "Four charges. You want to know the combined megatonnage?"

"No." Susannah stared at her chronometer. Ghirra moved closer, feeling the tension, not understanding it.

"Susannah, we're hardly going to feel it this far away. What's the point of sitting here blind? We should be on the com."

"If anything bad happens, Stav will know," she replied, surprised by her own conviction.

"I'm reopening the line in another six seconds."

"Tay, I don't think . . ."

"Four, three . . ." His hand went for the com switches. "One."

In the silence, Stavros gasped once and shuddered. Liphar pressed close, whimpering softly.

Danforth hit the switch. "CRI? Results?"

Static replied for several seconds. Then, "I am recording surges in the field flux."

"The map, CRI! Update the map!"

The contour map of the magnetic field flashed onto the cockpit monitor, changing the moment it appeared and then again. The numerical values were unable to stabilize at a given figure. The high spike at the geographical center of the field diffused into a neat circle of four hot spots.

Danforth touched the screen thoughtfully. "Just where I'd have planted my charges if I were Clausen."

"The new centers of activity formed almost instantly after ignition of the charges," supplied CRI, "at precisely the four points of detonation. I lack appropriate information with which to attempt an explanation."

The map flickered, mutating again as new data flowed in. The contour shapes shifted amoebalike, drawing up around the four points like a quatrefoil noose. Abruptly, the four points vanished from the graph. The higher values along the upland's perimeter pulled inward.

Ghirra watched intently over Susannah's shoulder. "What does this picture tell?"

"The field's withdrawing," said Danforth, a lilt of astonishment in his deep voice. He offered no further explanation, riveted to the map. The contour lines gained regularity, shrinking into a tightening pattern of concentric circles. "No, wait." The planetologist let out a low whistle. "Well, the true center of symmetry has just declared itself, and guess what, it's right on top of us. Or more precisely . . ." He glanced up at the strangely smooth east wall and its neat diagram of holes. "Somewhere in there."

"Ah, no . . ." whispered Stavros, as if in pain.

Liphar hunched beside him, no longer calm.

"No . . ." Stavros repeated, staring at his empty palms with an expression of profound loss. Slowly, he turned shocked and sorrowing eyes to Ghirra, his mouth working soundlessly as if the words he must say would not come.

Liphar whimpered softly. Ghirra waited.

"GuildMaster, he . . ." Stavros began, then stopped, laying his cheek disconsolately against the seat back. "We."

"What is it now, Ibiá?" Danforth rumbled.

Stavros straightened suddenly. His head swiveled toward the towering rift wall. "Wait! You hear that? Ghirra, Lifa, do you hear it?"

Alert, confused, Liphar shook his head.

"He *didn't*!" Stavros exclaimed. And then he was tearing at the buckles of his flight harness, throwing off the straps, muttering to himself in rapid Sawlish. Liphar backed out of the way in hopeful astonishment as Stavros bolted from his seat, shoving past Susannah and Ghirra. He rushed to the back of the hold and swung down through the open cargo hatch. Outside, he collided with Aguidran as he ducked up from beneath the wing. She reached to steady him, but he took it for an attempt at restraint and pulled free of her with a shout of warning. Aguidran backed off as if burned. Stavros swerved aside, then broke into an awkward run, favoring his injured left side. He raced across the ledge, bright fleeting white against the sunlit amber of the rock.

Liphar collected himself and scrambled out of the Sled and after him across the flat granular ground. Stavros reached the nearest yawning tunnel mouth and swerved past it without hesitation. He ran determinedly along the long line of tunnels, then suddenly, at the eighteenth or twentieth opening, turned in and was swallowed by darkness.

Aguidran called to her brother, her eyes pursuing Stavros, marking his route. Ghirra stood at a loss in the open cockpit. Danforth levered his stiff legs into the space between the front seats.

"Better go after him, eh, doc? I'll stay here and guard the fort."

"Watch the Sled," Susannah translated.

Danforth patted the laser gun in his belt.

"Okay, light, food, water . . . and my kit." Susannah muttered, retreating into the hold to root among her lashed-down

319

gear. Ghirra hurried to fill the Terran canteens he had appropriated for himself and his sister.

They helped Danforth down onto the sandpapery ground and set up a quick base camp under the wings. The planetologist accompanied them across the ledge as far as the tunnel mouth. Inside the massive circular opening, the floor turned glossy. Danforth craned his neck at the smooth vault overhead. The hard sun slicing down the sides showed up a delicate pattern of light and shadow, fine parallel grooving like the thread on a screw. He tapped a crutch on the glassy curving floor. A resounding crash of echoes answered him. Every sound was hugely magnified, their careful footsteps, the creak of Aguidran's leathers, the faint clink of the pack hardware. Intimidated, they whispered, and resorted to gesture whenever possible.

Susannah showed Aguidran the workings of the searchbeam she had brought, and gave Ghirra the spare. The Master Ranger flashed the piercing ray into the velvet darkness ahead and nodded approvingly, impatient to proceed. She hushed them and they heard Liphar calling after Stavros, further in.

"Take notes," said Danforth enviously.

"Pictures," Susannah promised.

"Damn, damn, damn these legs!" Danforth gazed into the tunnel with a grimace of acute longing. "Well, hell. Get going!" He swung fiercely around and stumped back toward the sunlight, chased by a clatter of echoes.

Aguidran was already a hundred paces ahead, her beam searching the long upward curve of the walls. Ghirra called softly to her to wait while he and Susannah hurried to catch up.

Running in darkness, Stavros heard Liphar's tremulous cry behind him and slowed to a breathless walk. The tunnel dove straight as a ruled line into the rock. The curve of its unnaturally smooth surface kept him centered in the huge space like a bearing in a groove. He had no need of light except to ease the imagined terrors of the dark.

But he sensed no menace. He sensed nothing but the sound, the music that was not music, summoning him as irresistibly as the shriek of a siren.

Nothing . . .

He clenched his fists desperately, willing his guar-fire to respond. A moment after the mining charges had detonated, a deadly cold had invaded his palms, his precious flame snuffed like a mere candle.

With the guar-fire gone, the pain in his shoulder was once

again something to contend with. With the fire gone, he felt weak, dulled, as if he had lost a part of his senses as well.

At least there was the sound.

He wondered that the others could not hear it. It vibrated not in his mind but in his ears, like a true sound. It was not really a single sound at all, but complex, like music, with a simple core. It was both high-pitched and low, bell-clear and diffuse, steady as a drone yet intermittent. It evoked images of natural violence: the dry earth tearing, rocks cracking open, tree trunks blasted by lightning, underscored by smaller, gentler tragedies, a fish in mud gasping for air, an orphaned cub digging out of a landslide.

Stavros heard it as a call for help and followed unquestioningly.

Danforth struggled to hoist his sturdy weight through the cargo hatch by the strength of his arms alone. He was sweating and nauseous by the time he lay face down on the floor of the hold. He strained awkwardly for his crutches, which he had managed to kick out of reach. He rolled onto his side and pulled himself along the grating until he had them in hand, then hauled himself to his feet, setting the crutches gratefully under his arms.

He stood a moment, considering. Something felt wrong. He ran a head-to-toe mental check, searched around the hold, then looked down through the open hatch and froze.

The little laser pistol lay on the sandpaper rock beneath the Sled. His desperate acrobatics had knocked it out of his belt.

He glanced at the cockpit, his goal, then around at the empty silent ledge slumbering under the vast wall of the rift. He knew he lacked the strength to clamber down, retrieve the gun and haul himself into the Sled again.

First things first, he decided, and headed forward to the controls. He powered up the com and prepared to call the orbiter. Before he could tap in his code, CRI's voice blared forth, startling him.

"Dr. Danforth! I have been attempting to reply to your signal!"

"Signal? I hadn't even entered it." Danforth held to a near whisper, a gesture to the pressing silence rather than any instinctive caution. The utter stillness made him jumpy. A canyon this deep should have winds.

"The signal you've been broadcasting since the detonation?" CRI paused, sounding rather crestfallen. "Or perhaps this is the communications difficulty Mr. Ibiá mentioned that I was unable to detect before?"

"CRI, you've lost me. Listen, what's the weather doing out there? Did it show any response at all to the detonations?"

"I will transfer those figures." The usual run of satellite data blinked onto the cockpit monitor. Danforth bent close to study them. The computer's terseness surprised him.

"No summary observations, CRI?"

"Not at this time, Dr. Danforth. I would appreciate your input."

He read through it rapidly at first, then more carefully, his dark face drawing into a frown. "CRI, is this your machine idea of a joke?"

"Absolutely not."

"These figures are accurate?"

"I have been rechecking them over and over myself, Dr. Danforth."

Danforth squeezed his temples between thumb and forefinger. The familiar northeast-to-southwest diagonal movement was gone. "CRI, are you asking me to believe that the entire circulation of the planet has actually come to a *standstill?*"

"It would appear to be the case. Heat is rising in the habitable zone in response."

"Moving from here to there," said Danforth faintly. "Heading for equilibrium. Shit, maybe he did blow them up. Maybe Ibiá was right about machines and wrong about the location."

"There are some signs that a new circulatory pattern is asserting itself. Did you notice the hints of west-to-east zonal movement? The potential pattern is closer, I might point out, to what your original model had projected for this planet."

"Umm. Great. Are they all right, there in the Lander?"

"They are safe as long as the power link is maintained. The Commander has promised to retreat to the Caves if for some reason the link is broken."

"I wonder how long even the Caves'll be livable," he muttered. *My god, what have we done?* He lowered himself into the pilot's seat, stunned, then remembered and asked automatically, "You said something about a signal?"

"I am picking up an omni-directional, broad-band transmission from the area of your coordinates."

Danforth was startled out of his guilty mope. "You are? Take a clear fix, CRI. *Exactly* my coordinates?"

"A little to the east, perhaps three kilometers."

"CRI, I'm down inside a canyon. Three klicks east of here is solid rock." But he caught himself staring at the black tunnel openings. "What kind of signal is it? Steady? Pulsed?"

"Fluctuating is a better description, Dr. Danforth, both in power and frequency."

"Any pattern to it?"

"I am checking now for code, of course. But if I may venture an opinion, the nature of the fluctuations are reminiscent of Commander Weng's music. For this reason, I assumed someone of our party to be the source."

Danforth remembered the feeling from childhood reading, that wild surge of last-minute hope, just when you feared that the hero had had it for sure. He swallowed. "Play it for me."

"Yes, Dr. Danforth."

A low wail floated from the speaker, with a background growl like the rattle of pebbles in an undertow. The wail rose and shattered into squeaks and cracking groans, like rent wood. The growl escalated into the choked roar of falling rock. Danforth's shoulders hunched. Warily, he eyed the four-kilometer stone rampart between himself and the safety of open sky. He slumped into the padded chair, resisting an impulse he could not make good on anyway, to leap up and rush off into the tunnels as Ibiá had done.

Right after the charges blew, as if . . .

"CRI, this is without doubt an artificially generated signal?"

"Without doubt, Dr. Danforth. There is a long pattern of repeating with slight changes, not unlike thematic variations in musical composition."

He tried to think what Ibiá's response would be to this information. His own no longer seemed adequate. He was rather proud to have thought of using Weng's music, but knew it had been a random instinct and not based on a consistent pattern of thought with which he could continue to interpret events that refused to be governed by standard logic.

Finally, he said, "I think you should try to answer it, CRI. Meanwhile, there seems to be a tunnel complex down here. They may be too deep for your instruments to read, but try for a density mapping. Let's see if we can get some idea of how extensive they are . . . and where they go."

41

Aguidran set a stiff pace, dauntless in the fore as they proceeded single file into the dark. Susannah followed close behind her. Ghirra took up the rear. The travel was easy. The air in the tunnel was stale but comfortable. The curved floor was unobstructed, glassy smooth but astonishingly unslippery. No turns or branching corridors forced them to make a choice.

Susannah's apprehension was a distraction at first. Expecting sudden surprises, she listened too hard to the echoes, watched the blackness too intently, until her eyes created their own dancing phantoms in response to the strain.

She relaxed as they penetrated deeper, finding nothing and no one, but then she began to worry that Stavros' quest was soon to end in failure, that there was nothing in the tunnels, nothing but the unyielding darkness and cool musty air. What if they did find nothing? Would a report be taken back to DulElesi that the Goddesses did not exist?

She began to look more carefully. As the searchbeam slid up along the curving wall, she was struck by the amber beauty of the rock, glowing warmly even under the harsh light of the lamp.

Agate? She wondered what other stone possessed this striated translucence so reminiscent of gem-quality tortoiseshell. The deeper into the tunnel they went, the thicker the translucent layer became. The lamplight was caught and diffracted, softening as it passed through the surface layers. A mild glow pervaded the floor around the focus of the beam and crept up the curve of the walls. As the lucid material thickened, it developed undulations, gentle distortions. The precise arc of the tunnel relaxed into an oval.

The patter of their footsteps sharpened abruptly. Aguidran stopped, listening into the darkness. She flashed the lamp around, then traced the arc of the walls. The curving floor had flattened. The tunnel was widening. She aimed the lamp straight up. The top of the arc was suddenly no longer within range of the beam. She moved forward more cautiously. After a few hundred paces, the beam of light sliding along the wall met a sharp edge, and beyond, darkness. Aguidran halted again, and glanced back at her brother.

"Shouldn't we go straight ahead?" whispered Susannah. "Isn't that what he'd do? He should be tiring by now. I haven't heard Liphar calling for a while. You think he found him?"

Ghirra frowned into the darkness as if it were consciously trying to confound him, then motioned his sister onward. Aguidran focused the beam a short pace in front of her, wary of the floor dropping away as suddenly as the walls had done. But it did not. The hard lamplight diffused through its amber clarity like honey flowing through denser molasses. Susannah thought of black and amber ice. She stooped and found the floor warm to the touch. It did not feel like rock.

"Ghirra. Feel this."

The Master Healer crouched, put his palm to the floor. The lamp proceeded ahead with Aguidran, leaving them in increasing darkness. But the floor continued to glow faintly. Ghirra called to his sister to wait, but Susannah laid a hand on his arm, turning her back to the lamp beam.

"Ask her to turn it off."

Puzzled, he complied.

Aguidran growled about speed and their lack of progress, but snapped off the beam. Profound night closed in on them.

"Let your eyes adjust, then look around you," said Susannah. She heard Ghirra's soft exclamation before she could fully make out his silhouette against the weak but steady luminescence. The details of a giant cavern ghosted into view.

A golden glow surrounded them, as if they had been plunged inside the black and amber ice. The floor undulated away from a flat central axis which they had been following like a path. Several hundred meters in either direction, it rose into curving walls of lucent gold and apricot and saffron chased with madder and umber like wisps of cloud in sunset. Sturdy ribs of opaque material punctuated the glow with receding parentheses of darkness. Walls and ribs curled up and met seamlessly high above.

"How lovely," Susannah murmured.

Aguidran's silhouette retreated toward them, her leathers creaking as she knelt beside her brother. Ghirra ticked a fingernail against the smooth floor with a pensive grunt.

"Let's have the light again." Susannah swung her pack down, unlacing a side pocket. She dug out a small stainless penknife, and pried open a blade to pick experimentally at the floor while Aguidran held the light. The sharp point left whitish scars far more easily than Susannah had expected. She flattened the edge against the floor and drew it carefully towards her. Several pale shreds of material spiraled up before the blade. She gathered them carefully into a plastic sample bag.

"Ghirra, this is weird, but if you put a chunk of this stuff in my hand and asked me what it was, I'd guess at something organic, like elkhorn."

Patiently, Ghirra awaited clarification. Aguidran doused the beam again and hunkered down to scrutinize the cavern more thoroughly.

"Keratins," supplied Susannah, whispering again as if the cavern itself might be listening. "Fibrous proteins, like the material of our fingernails or our hair. On Earth, we have many herbivores with keratin-based growths called horns. Their feet are also protected by thick pads of keratin called hooves. But

325

mostly, horn is more opaque than this. This is more like tortoise shell. The point is, it takes something living to produce it.''

"But the light . . . ?''

"Bioluminescence," she replied impulsively, "like your fish in the deep-caves. It's a guess, Ghirra. Only a guess." She held the sample bag up to the cavern's glow, stemming the rush to conclusions, forcing herself to maintain some objective calm. "We'll know when I power up the analyzer. There could be rocks this soft, I'm sure."

"Living? All this big cave?" Ghirra let out a breath and looked around, absorbing the idea. The glow was too dim for her to read his expression but the awe in his voice was clear. "Ibi must know this thing!" he whispered fiercely.

He stood and shouted Stavros' name once into the silence. The echoes multiplied his call into an urgent phrase of summons and carried it inward.

Stavros hurried through the building glow, an unprotesting Liphar close on his heels. The siren fugue still rose and fell in his ears, though more gently now, as if calmed by his steady approach. But he had been pushing too hard. His shoulder protested every step, his chest ached when he breathed. He was stumbling so often that Liphar guarded his footing more carefully than he did his own.

Ghirra's shout chased after them, mixing with the clattering echoes of their own passage. Liphar slowed and glanced behind, but Stavros urged him onward. He was not avoiding the others. He merely did not wish to stop and wait. They would catch up on their own, not being weakened and in pain as he was.

Ahead, the tunnel walls dropped away again. Stavros was well into the sudden space before its enormity penetrated his awareness. It brought him to a slow, astonished halt.

A long rectangular cavern confronted him, five times the size of the shuttle bay on an FTL starship. The floor was once again cleanly flat, with the same oddly granular surface as the ledge outside. A distant ribbed vault arched overhead. Walls met and descended at right angles, supporting tier upon tier of narrow railed galleries. Gazing upward, Stavros stopped counting after twenty-five. The galleries were linked by spiraling columns of stair and empty cylindrical shaftways, cut from a translucent substance that reminded Stavros of the polished agate marbles he had coveted as a child, their swirling clouds of russet, black and sienna caught in a matrix of topaz and honey.

"Lord!" he breathed, moving out into the vast space. Liphar clung to him like a shadow.

The railings were carved from the same lovely substance, their simple but elegantly geometric lines creating an intriguing tension with the mutable quality of the material. There was no surface embellishment, no decorative frieze-work, no Tales being told in the architecture. The aesthetic of the space was the space itself: its proportions and the beauty of the material it was made from.

"Tastes have sure changed since then," Stavros murmured, wanting to linger, though the music called him inward.

"It is like the duld, this," ventured Liphar, eyes huge with awe.

"A dwelling, yes, it was. Your ancestors lived here, Lifa, when the planet could still support life this far south."

Behind the many storeys of pierce-work railings were rows of doorways, modest man-sized openings, small and dark against the luminous walls. Stavros looked back the way he had come, weighing the issue of proportion vs. function: the giant round tunnel so reminiscent of the underground rail tubes of Earth; the vast glowing courtyard, the ordinary doors.

I could fly this thing right in . . . ' he recalled Danforth saying, and realized that he stood in the middle of an ancient parking lot.

"Lifa," he whispered, spreading his arms wide, "just imagine . . . !"

Danforth jerked awake, wondering what, in the solitude of an empty landscape of sunlight and rock, could have summoned him from his doze so urgently. He tried to recall if he'd been dreaming.

The unidentified signal still issued at low volume from the cockpit speaker, bizarre background music to suit the surreal landscape.

On the monitor, a new diagram was forming, CRI's density map of the surrounding hundred kilometers. Danforth stood up, shaking out his stiff legs, uncramping his spine. He surveyed the deserted ledge, the vacant green sky, the distant shadowed western rim. Doubt nagged at him subliminally.

He shrugged and bent to the screen. The graphic was an awkward one, overly grainy like a photograph blown up too far. CRI was working at the upper limit of her instruments' resolution, within an area smaller than the instruments had been designed to cover. Still, a picture of sorts was taking shape out of a chaos of individual values: a pattern of dark markings against a lighter ground; the wide black grin of the rift, a hint of hair-fine parallel lines joining many darkish areas of a soft but undeniably regular geometry.

Danforth touched the dark spots wonderingly, traced the fine connecting lines. Empty spaces deep within the rock, tunnels large enough for CRI's imperfect sensors to detect.

"Christ, they're big!"

A slight shudder of the Sled's body alerted him. He straightened away from the screen and turned.

Clausen grinned at him from the rear of the hold, the laser pistol lolling in his open hand. "I'm not sure I approve of the way you leave my property lying around."

McPherson stood to one side ahead of him, significantly within an easy swing of the laser's snub nose. She smiled wanly and shrugged. Danforth thought she looked a little frightened, mostly angry, trying to hide both.

Clausen sauntered forward. "It was kind of you to send up the flares, Tay. Does this mean you're coming to your senses?"

He let the gun drift casually toward McPherson as he passed her, then leaned against the back of the copilot's chair and jerked his head toward the sounds issuing from the console.

"Does Ibiá think he's fooling anyone with this purported signal?"

Danforth regarded him neutrally. "If it's him doing it, he's got CRI well fooled."

"Nothing easier. Take some of Weng's music and doctor it a little." Clausen leaned into the monitor. "And what have we here?"

Danforth searched for a lie the prospector might believe and failed to find it.

"The tunnelling goes deep, then," commented Clausen, bending closer to read the scale indicator. "A hundred meters to the centimeter? Well. Rather impressively extensive. What's your thinking on those darker areas?"

"You read these pictures better than I do, Emil. They're your instruments."

"Tut, Taylor. This sounds like recalcitrance. Ibiá must be catching." He stretched luxuriously, squinting along the wide ledge, then up at the towering wall and its neat rows of holes. "Lovely spot, this must have been once, when the planet was still alive . . . where are the others?"

Danforth nodded at the map. "Inside."

"What do you think's in there, Tay?"

"You're good, Emil, I'll grant you . . . even when you're sure there's nothing, you keep on looking." The planetologist lifted his broad shoulders in an attempt at elegant disdain.

"Well, it doesn't matter, really." Clausen turned away. "If you're in communication with them, you'd better let them know they have an hour or so to clear out of there."

"I'm not in communication . . ."

"Emil, let me go bring them out," McPherson begged.

"No, my dear, you must stay with our good friend Taylor and convince him to behave." Clausen levelled the laser at the aft fuselage. A quick bright burst melted through the plastic com bubble forward of the tail fin. A thin line of smoke rose out of the charred hole.

"SONOFABITCH!" Danforth snatched for his crutches.

"Tay, no! He'll . . . !"

McPherson rushed to restrain him, but he whirled back to the controls, desperately punching switches. "CRI? CRI? Damn!"

Clausen sucked his teeth, studying the damage regretfully. "All those hours in the broiling sun, gone for naught."

McPherson glowered helplessly. "You're out of your fucking mind!"

"Tut, McP. I prefer to think, efficient and unemotional."

"Gone," she snarled. "Out there."

Clausen flashed a rueful grimace at Danforth's back. "Don't we all wish it was that easy? Profitable adherence to the status quo has never been considered a sign of insanity, my dear pilot. I thought we were in agreement on that issue."

"There are limits," she spat.

"Are there?" He went back into the cargo hold and picked up a longish steel cylinder from the floor near the open hatch. It was bound in a canvas sling with a wide strap which he tossed over one shoulder. He patted the cylinder's blunt gleaming head as it nestled beside his thigh.

"Now, Tay," he continued pleasantly. "Perhaps you will inform me which of these myriad and mysterious entries our colleagues used, or I shall have to choose at random and plant my charge without being able to warn them that the place is about to blow sky-high."

"You have no goddamn right!" Danforth fumed.

Clausen cocked his bullet head. "Have you seen the local ore count?"

"Yeah, but . . ."

"Then don't waste my time with right or wrong, Tay. We are talking wet-dream-level returns here! You'll be able to fund your own damn research and I can stay home for a change and see to my horses! Where are they?"

Raging inwardly, Danforth told him.

"Excellent. I'm glad you see it my way. With luck, we will

329

all rejoin you soon." Clausen saluted them jauntily, then vaulted to the ground and loped across the ledge toward the caves.

McPherson watched him go uneasily. "Anyone in there but our guys?"

Danforth turned away with an angry shrug.

"Tay, I'm sorry. Please understand. Maybe I coulda put up a bigger fight at first, but I thought if I went with him, I could, you know . . ." She shook her head, defeated. "He don't listen to reason."

Relenting, Danforth pulled her into the crook of his arm, dwarfing her. "Where's the other Sled?"

McPherson leaned into him happily. "The next ledge down. He's got the ignition sequence and stabilizer chip in his pocket."

Danforth glanced at the dash behind him. "Are they interchangeable?"

"No."

"Think you could follow him, maybe? Sneak that damn bomb out of there once he's planted it?"

"What would I do with it?"

"Throw it over the edge?"

"So it can take us and the Sleds out instead of them? I never saw either of us as martyr material, Tay."

"What, then? We can't just goddamn sit here."

Restored by his presence, she patted his big hand on her shoulder, then slipped out from under. "Well, for one thing, I'm gonna try fixing this boat. Again. Maybe we can get the com back at least."

Cursing Clausen cheerfully under her breath, she trudged into the hold. As she bent to rummage for tools, she looked back at Danforth and smiled into his brooding frown. "Hey. Come keep me company."

While Stavros stood in the ancient courtyard, eagerly reading the ancient Sawl history written in its size and shape, his inner music increased in volume, making clear thinking impossible. He gave in, and it drew him down the long axis of the hall to an archway centered in the end wall.

The arch was tall and graceful, without decoration to hint at purpose, only a broad casing band of the same opaque materials as the ribs, tracing the arch darkly against the glowing walls. Translating from the language of proportion, Stavros guessed a ceremonial intent. Though it was tall enough to split the first three tiers of galleries, it was not much wider than the full span of his arms. It did not look casual. Yet he thought he detected a whiff of engineering whimsey in this exaggeration of height, a see-what-I-can-do playfulness.

He urged Liphar through into a corridor of similar proportions that curved to the left in continuous and stately fashion for a full half-circle before reversing abruptly to curl off to the right. The unvarying dim glow of the walls was enough to light their way and nothing more. There was nothing to look at that required brighter illumination.

Tay will be disappointed. No plant, no machinery. The only sign of tech is the miraculous achievement of the space itself.

Stavros paced along the tall narrow tunnel, feeling smaller than he had in the far grander spaces behind them.

When the corridor reversed direction a third time, curling back on itself briefly only to reverse again, Stavros sensed that like pacing out the subtle geometry of a formal garden or wandering between the high hedges of a maze, the purpose of this tunnel was the pattern of walking it: the pleasures of smoothly flowing curves contrasted with the frisson of abrupt change of direction. It was like a dance, with his partner the architecture itself, or its long dead builder, enabled by his creation to reach out through time with a bodiless hand to lead a stranger through the steps.

Is this art, he wondered. *A sculpture? A game?*

Three staccato curves were followed by a long lazy one. The amber glow deepened to burnt orange. Then suddenly the corridor straightened and angled sharply right. A ruddier brightness crept along the walls, not this time a light from within. Stavros picked up his pace.

They emerged into a long, irregularly shaped hallway bathed in red-amber. It had no visible end, but disappeared around a distant snaking curve. The left-hand wall was tall and smooth and blank. The right wall slanted to meet it high above, slanting to the floor in broad panels of the same lucent agate-colored material, divided by stout vertical ribs.

Light spilled onto the floor like a shower of liquid embers. It had the angle and intensity of late afternoon sunlight. Stavros approached one fiery panel. He could feel its radiant heat from a distance.

It is sunlight! he decided.

He leaned as close to the heat as he could bear. He noticed a delicate internal structure not unlike a honeycomb. Its crystalline regularity seemed at odds with the free play of color, light and darkness across and through the surfaces. Stavros thought of practical objects crafted from materials chosen for their integral beauty rather than some appropriate relation to function. The ribs were as wide as two hand spans, and seemed to flow out of the panel in a thickening and darkening of the material itself. He could detect no fastenings, no joints. The entire translucent stretch seemed to be made of a single seamless piece.

Still the siren fugue beckoned. A single relentless tone began to override the subtler complexities.

He wanted to run directly to the source, but the hall meandered left and right, confounding his urgency. The heat soon became unbearable, and he switched on the tiny battery pack clipped to the belt of his therm-suit, showing Liphar how to do likewise. The young Sawl sighed with relief as he felt the surface cooling inside the suit begin to return his body temperature to a more comfortable range.

"How much far, Ibi?"

"Won't know till I get there."

Liphar gazed ahead dubiously.

"Don't look so discouraged, Lifa."

"Where live this Sister, ah?"

Stavros smiled. "Did you expect to find something familiar? Something like Eles-Nol?"

Liphar shrugged negatively, which meant to Stavros that he had, but thought he shouldn't admit it. He turned and started forward again, to prove his willingness, but his energy was flagging. Without thought for the length of the journey, they had both entered the tunnels without water. Stavros trudged alongside, ignoring his increasing thirst, trying to set an encouraging pace.

And suddenly, Liphar grabbed his sleeve.

"Listen! Ibi!"

In Stavros' ears, the siren fused into a single scream as it developed stronger directionality, like a diffuse light beam irising into focus. "You can hear it now?"

Liphar nodded frantically. "This is it, what you follow?"

The quality of the sound changed as it moved outside Stavros' head and into the range of ordinary hearing. It steadied into a high-pitched tone, like a machine alarm, anticlimactic and mundane compared to the symphonies of desperation that had filled his head since Clausen's charges had blown. But it was real, undeniably so. Liphar pointed down the twisting corridor, and eagerly they both broke into a run.

Several turns of red-lit corridor later, they pulled to a halt in the same breath.

"We've passed it," panted Stavros.

He retraced the last turn and discovered a small arched opening missed in his haste. He ducked into a narrow conical chamber, barely large enough for one man to stand with his arms extended. It was like an agate-colored bell jar, smooth bright walls swirled with striations of amber and gold and brown. The flat insistent tone surrounded Stavros as if he were within it.

By sheer instinct he put his hand to the luminous curve. Fine vibrations sang through his fingertips. The full symphony of sound blossomed once more inside his head.

He dropped his hand as if burned. The internal noise died, but the high tone continued. Stavros searched the entire surface of the chamber, his fingers hovering, reluctant to touch the singing walls.

"There's got to be something somewhere, a switch, a speaker, something?" But he found no sign of controls or mechanics. Somehow, the vibration of the chamber itself was creating the tone, like a giant tuning fork.

"Ibi?" Liphar waited outside, mystified.

Stavros dragged him in and flattened his palm to the wall. "What do you hear now?"

"The same thing, ah? Very big noise."

"No . . . music?"

Liphar shook his head slowly. "This music is for you, Ibi."

Stavros spread his palms in frustration. He had found the source of the sound but not its cause or its purpose. The guar-fire was still cold in his palms and he had no idea what to do next.

Hesitantly, he put his fingers to the wall, to seek a clue from the inner music. Listening to the chorus of creaks and squeals and groans was like balancing on the edge of a windy precipice, surrounded by space and sound. Stavros pondered its similarity to Weng's compositions, particularly her *Dies Irae*.

Have I imposed this likeness, or was it always there?

And then, his confusion shifted, and the way became self-evident. He stretched his arms and put his hands to opposite walls.

The alarm ceased.

He jerked his hands away. The alarm started up again. He stared wildly around the glowing chamber as if it were closing in on him. With a groan, he pushed past Liphar into the red outer corridor and sat down against the wall to gather his courage.

They found him there several minutes later, his arms folded on bent knees, staring across the wide hallway into the ruddy glow of the slanting panels.

Liphar ran to meet them anxiously. "Bring this water!" he begged, his hands fluttering around the canteen on Susannah's belt until she stripped it off and gave it to him. He gulped at it noisily as he paced alongside.

Ahead of the others, Aguidran halted beside Stavros. When he did not respond, she grunted and moved away, inspecting the inner chamber, nosing around restlessly as if the steady high-pitched hum made it impossible to stand still.

"Have you found anything?" Susannah called excitedly. "What is that sound? This place is amazing, but it does look like everyone left eons ago."

When Stavros said nothing, she took the canteen back from Liphar and knelt at his side. "Stav?"

He looked up slowly. "At last," he murmured, as if from a distance.

She offered him the canteen. "I mean, it's even more amazing than amazing! Do you know, I think it's all made from organic material!" She glanced around restlessly. "What *is* that noise? Sounds like an alarm."

"Organic." Stavros' eyes narrowed as if trying to place the word within the right context. He did not seem to see the canteen. "Organic?"

"Yes! Yet, if our timetable is correct, it's survived tens of thousands of years without decay, I guess because it's so dry here. Or . . . phew, wait a minute." Susannah stopped, glanced at Ghirra.

"Or?" urged Stavros softly.

Susannah's smirk rejected her statement before she made it. "Or it's still alive."

"Yes," Stavros whispered. "Alive . . ." He gazed around the fiery corridor as if seeing it for the first time, then looked up at Ghirra. "Alive. Ah, GuildMaster, here is your answer!"

He stood slowly, then drew Susannah up into his arms and held her close. When he let her go, he solemnly placed her hand in Ghirra's, like a father giving away his favorite child.

"Stav, what is this?" The implied melodrama made Susannah nervous.

But Ghirra nodded and folded her hand between both his own. Stavros turned away toward the inner chamber and the siren's shrilling, calling Liphar to him.

"Ghirra, what . . . ?" Annoyed, Susannah tried to pull free and found herself gently restrained. She felt unspoken ritual closing around her like a velvet blind. "Stav . . . !"

Aguidran followed Stavros to the little archway and placed herself in front of it protectively after he had entered. He sat cross-legged on the floor and spread his arms until his palms touched opposite walls.

Again, the alarm fell silent.

Liphar sat down facing Stavros, resting a thin hand on his knee.

Stavros sighed once, deeply, and his eyes closed as he settled into a posture of profound listening.

42

"There!" exclaimed McPherson. She brushed sweat-damp curls from her eyes. "Emils's getting cocky."

"*Getting*?"

"He didn't do so good a job messing this up as he thought. Go try her."

Danforth stumped back to the cockpit to tap in his call code. Silence.

He entered it again, and though the quiet remained unbroken, the little monitor began to read out a message.

"All right! You did it!" he cried eagerly. "Voice is still out, but we're getting something!"

The screen read: CHARGE E, SERIAL NUMBER 7582-9583BO-NL. ACTIVATED.

"Christ," said Danforth.

He tapped in: CRI, can you disable?

The answer came more slowly than it should: NO.

Are you still receiving unidentified signal?

YES.

Are you attempting answer?

YES.

Any response?

NONE.

Time to detonation of Charge E?

88 MINUTES, 29 SECONDS.

"Ronnie!" he called. "Keep working!"

Flattening his palms to the walls, he felt himself open to the music.

Not every priest's Dance will be the same.

The misunderstanding had been to picture himself dancing as Kav Daven had done. Another sort of Dance was needed now.

Stavros sank into the river of sound, toward the black torrent. He thought once of Susannah, in blazing images, the heat of passion, then let his last resistance slip away, his human clinging to love and normalcy, to survival, let it slip away like a final breath.

Some will find their Dance inside themselves.

He felt his outstretched arms like gulls' wings breaking his fall.

Some will dance without dancing.

He drifted down like a feather in evening air. He touched the black river as lightly as a leaf. The waters were still. He dropped through them as inexorably as stone. The cold mud embraced him, became him, he it, as his arms curled upward, outward, inward to embrace the silent water.

Raellil.

Carrier.

Channel?

The dark plane was windless, frigid, empty, a moonless night. The black river was a pool of still ink.

Still as death.

Is this it? Is this the end? He sensed finality in the mindscape that stretched vastly before him, but a dim spot of warmth disturbed its icy uniformity, distracting him.

His hand on my knee, he thought, without knowing what he meant.

Channel.

Connector?

He remembered sound, and sound returned to him. A background music of wind and soft rain falling, pebbles grinding in surf, a rattle of thunder, and beyond, a drawn-out animal wail of anguish echoing through the darkness.

The siren core of the music.

And then, an answer. Faint, unsure, not quite in kind, but nearly, like a clever child mimicking a hard-voiced adult.

The siren cried its aloneness unheeding.

Listen! he told it.

It would not or could not, revolving in a closed loop of hysteria, replaying its own anguish, endless variations on an unvarying theme.

The answer was distant, patient, steady, but weak. It was blind, a stranger calling out in fog for guidance through a dark unfamiliar land.

His outstretched hands remembered their heat.

Into the renewing fire of one palm, he sucked the siren wail. The other he opened to the patient stranger.

The Dancer joins hands to complete the circle, the circuit.

Connector.

Conduit.

His veins flowed heat and light. Wind sang through his bones. Ecstasy blossomed as pure and primal as the seething dance inside a newborn star. Elemental orgasm. Hot. White. Eternal.

Raellil.

Danforth's monitor blinked at him frantically: REPLY! REPLY! REPLY!

"To what?" he shouted, frustrated.

"What?" McPherson yelled from the tail.

"It's CRI." He typed: Reply to what?

TO MY ANSWER.

Make sense, CRI.

YOU INSTRUCTED ME TO ANSWER THE SIGNAL. HAVE DETECTED A POSSIBLE RESPONSE.

"Holy shit."

"*What?*" McPherson demanded again, looking up from her work.

"CRI's getting an answer!" Steadying his fingers, he typed: Transmit?

CONTENT OF SIGNAL UNCHANGED. NATURE OF "RESPONSE" IS ABRUPT SWITCHOVER FROM OMNIDIRECTIONAL TRANSMISSION TO TIGHT BEAM. DECTECTED AT SAME TIME NEW HIGH-ENERGY SOURCE, SAME LOCUS AS SIGNAL.

McPherson appeared at Danforth's elbow. "What's up?"

He scratched his jaw, indicating the screen. He felt foolish, overreactive. "It's a kind of reply, I guess."

"You mean it just zeroed right in on her?"

"So she claims."

"I'd call that a reply, all right."

He stared at the screen, pensive. "Are you going to get us voice back?"

"Don't think so, Tay. The damn gun was tuned real narrow, but what he did hit, he pretty much fried "

"How about power?"

"Don't know yet."

Nodding, Danforth typed: Are you still analyzing signal for code?

I FIND NO DISCERNABLE PATTERN AT THIS TIME, OTHER THAN WHAT YOU HEARD AS "MUSIC."

Keep trying. And keep answering.

YES, DR. DANFORTH.

* * *

The first unbearable rush of ecstasy lifted him to the brink of unconsciousness and held him swooning on the crest of the hot wave, refusing him the release of oblivion. His physical sensors, reacting with the clean logic of reflexes, balked at further input and shut down. The energies from without flowed in and through him unabsorbed, unheeded.

Conduit.

Anaesthetized by overstimulation, a strange floating kind of consciousness returned to him, an awareness of himself as process, of a responsibility to monitor. The Dancer sensed a lack of balance within, an inequality between the two sources his Dance sought to join, one not moving in time with the other. The Dance would be clumsy. The Dancer would fail. The Connection would not be made.

But it was in his Dance to shape the rhythm.

Conduit.

Transformer.

In the image of the throat, shaping incoherent air into reasoned sound, he was plumbing, arteries, organic valves. Drawing this identity into himself, he learned the steps he needed.

He stopped down one valve, his white-hot palm, to modulate the flow. The frantic siren eased. Its rhythm steadied. The second valve he opened wide, to suck in the weaker signal hungrily.

In the glassy-slick void-space inside him, the newly tuned signals raced past one another at matched speeds, slid through him and out, each on its way to meet the other's source.

No one offered Susannah an explanation.

She peered at Stavros across the barrier of Aguidran's arm, as the Ranger blocked the narrow doorway of the conical room. Liphar's slight body hid most of him from view. She saw only his white-clad arms, stretched from wall to wall, trembling as if shot through with current, and over the top of Liphar's curls, a dark head thrown back, neck arched as if to the sacrificial blade.

Her impulse was to fling herself against the Master Ranger's restraint and rescue Stavros from his trance, with drugs, with physical blows, whatever means available. But she recognized his open-eyed stare of ecstasy and knew what his choice would be, were it offered him. And it was his choice to make, not hers.

She turned away, embarrassed as if by public eroticism, but sensing also the totality of his sensing transport, and envying him just a little.

She retreated several paces down the hot red-lit corridor and unslung her pack. She dug out her penknife, scraped a whitish

338

sample shaving from wall and rib and floor, then unpacked the battery powered analyzer.

Most of her samples she would save for CRI's more sophisticated equipment. But she was eager to test her theory about the organic nature of the ancient Sawls' building material. She cut a small darker ringlet from the rib shaving and fed it into the slot.

As she waited, she caught Ghirra regarding her with a sympathetic concern. Susannah glanced away. She felt lately that he read her better than she could read him. She bent her head to the analyzer's tiny screen.

The preliminary results brought forth an audible groan of annoyance. She aborted the analysis, flushed the sample cavity and the sensors, and prepared to start over with a new sample.

Ghirra padded over to crouch at her side. "Something is wrong, Suzhanna?"

She did not look up, hating his patient tone. She would rather an explanation than his sympathy. She would rather it were Stavros kneeling beside her, awake and not lost in an alien trance. She pulled on a plastic glove with an emphatic snap.

"Must have handled this last sample too much," she grumbled.

"You do what with this?" he asked dutifully, though his real attention was with the goings-on in the conical room.

"You remember this thing." She pressed the boxy little instrument into his hands. "Tells me roughly what a thing is made of and in what proportions. It can be a little more accurate when programmed with a specific range of material. Right now, I'm doing a general scan."

Ghirra examined the box with interest, though he had done so before. Susannah got up to take a clean sample from a new location, using a sterilized scalpel blade. She returned to reclaim the analyzer, and fed in a pristine curl of material.

New results began to appear. "'Damn!"

Ghirra offered his usual quiet grunt of inquiry.

"Well, look!" Susannah thrust the box at him again, knowing he could not read the symbols on the screen, then felt a quick rush of shame and took it back. Her real irritation was not with Ghirra. She should not take advantage of his patience by making him a target.

"It's either broken or it's more sensitive to contamination than I thought," she explained resignedly. "It's telling me these samples are organic, as I suspected, but it's also throwing me the signal markers for advanced genetic material." She made a wry face and tossed a gesture of ridicule around the vast red-gold hallway. "*Human* genetic material, at that. I'll flush it twice this time and try again."

339

Danforth turned his back to the empty tunnel openings out of lingering childhood superstition about watched pots.

Should really be concentrating on an analysis of that reply signal.

But at the keypad, though he already knew from his chronometer, he typed: CRI, time to detonation?

68 MINUTES, 4 SECONDS.

A vivid picture of row stacked upon row of perfect black holes pushed itself into his brain like an unwelcome caller.

Will Clausen really try to bring them out?

It would be good for the prospector's lagging public image if he did, but Danforth too easily imagined him losing Ibiá conveniently in the rubble.

Heroic rescue of xenobiologist and native companions accompanies tragic loss of . . . etc, etc.

He worried for Susannah, wondering how much Ibiá really meant to her. He would not bet two cents on the young man's continuing health as long as Clausen was around and armed.

Armed! Shit. You fucked this up real good, TD . . .

He glanced again at the tunnel entries, but they yawned as dark and silent in the latening sun as they had two moments before. He squinted up at the oblate vermilion sun hovering a hand span above the western rim. The hard black shadow would soon rise out of the depths of the rift to swallow ledge, Sled and all, like Jonah's whale. He shifted his burdened legs restlessly. He wanted to be away from this place by darkfall.

"Ron? How's it?" he called, to fill the silence.

Concentrating on her tiny soldering arc, McPherson shook her head mutely.

"Will we be able to fly her?"

She set the tool down, grinning bravado enough to travel the length of the cargo hold. "Is that you or me you're talking, hotshot?"

"Don't get smart. Anyone."

The bravado dimmed. "No flying so far."

"Damn."

CRI was blinking at him again when he returned his attention to the monitor. Hurriedly, he answered her summons.

CRI replied: NEW ENERGY SOURCE DOWNRATED DRASTICALLY 53 SECONDS AGO. NOW WITHIN SIGNAL RANGE. ANALYZING FOR PATTERN. DETECT SHORT REPEAT SEQUENCE ALTERNATING WITH STRINGS OF PRIME NUMBERS, ALSO REPEATING. TRANSMISSION OF "MUSIC" CONTINUING ALONG WITH.

Primes! For Danforth, this was the final convincing link in the evidence chain. Primes surely meant sentience, either past or present.

He typed: Transmit short repeat.

CRI replied: 0101010101010101010101. . . . COMMENCING PRIME SEQUENCE: 2,3,5 . . .

Danforth froze the screen and stared. "Ron? Come take a look at this."

He typed: Comment, CRI?

IT IS NOT MUSIC.

"Great. Now we know one thing it isn't."

DUE TO CONTINUOUS UNVARYING REPEAT, AN AUTOMATIC RECYCLING SEQUENCE SEEMS A PROBABLE EXPLANATION.

"A blind loop? For what purpose?"

McPherson clattered up behind him. "What is it this time?"

He pointed at the monitor. "What do you make of it?"

She studied it closely, sucking her lip. "A neutral signal and a bunch of primes. So?"

"*Neutral*," he repeated musingly. "Hadn't thought of it that way." He typed: *neutral* signal between identifying prime sequences.

CRI replied: YES. A LOCATOR, PERHAPS.

"Yeah, some kinda 'I'm here' signal without the detailed data," McPherson suggested. "Like our homing beacons."

Danforth repressed an urge to scan the green-and-amber sky. He recalled Clausen's snide remark about repair crews. He gave an inch to his imagination and a vision burst behind his eyes like a colored flare: the planet fertile, teeming with life, the airwaves choked with signal, clear green skies busy with big and little traffic. He saw the empty ledge around them bathed in the golden light of dreams, crowded with shining aircraft, lightweight ceramic and spun-glass creations as delicate as the bodies of their Sawl builders, winged with fantasy.

The deep pulsing ache in his chest he knew to be longing.

They held the wind and clouds in their hands . . .

He marvelled that Ibiá was so entranced by the goddess mythos when it seemed to him so much more wondrous that mere men could make such miracles.

"Tay?"

He was staring at his own broad-fingered ebony hands. Never had they seemed to him so powerless. Danforth blinked, shook his head.

McPherson eyed him with unvoiced concern, then nodded at

the screen. "Now CRI's suggesting Emil's bombs might've tripped some kind of alarm reflex."

"An alarm . . ." Danforth reviewed the recent sequence of events. He pictured the magnetic field map, how the elaborate field contours had collapsed into a single weak focal point right after the detonations, how planetary circulation had ceased soon after.

Is all this actually possible?

His golden dream-image told him it was, and he was astonished at the depth of his sense of loss.

"He's done it, goddamn his eyes! There *were* machines and he's wrecked them, just like he hoped!"

"Hey, Tay, there's gotta be something still working in there," McPherson soothed logically. "To broadcast the alarm loop."

"And whatever it is," Danforth raged, "that sonofabitch is gonna blow it to smithereens in sixty-five minutes, along with a few of our colleagues, and maybe ourselves!"

He pounded his fist against the dash, and then repeatedly against the rigid plastic binding his thighs. "Damn, damn, damn these legs!"

When the energies within passed in equilibrium, hot plasma in a straight-line run, the Dancer could allow himself some further awareness. Not of his physical body or where he was, his material surroundings: the Dance was the only 'place'; the physical, only the two points of white heat and the howling space between that was himself, the link.

Yet other Identity still lurked, with its companions Meaning and Memory, elusive as shadows but nagging, insistent.

He listened to the dual music coursing through him. Something in the weaker signal nudged at his notice, a familiar syllable breaking repeatedly out of a sequence of nonsense.

A memory. Whose? The young man's memory. His.

His.

Could he be himself and be the Dancer still?

Memory prodded. The familiar pricked, echoed in the music. *Remember.*

Remember another dance. Excited particles leaping within endless microscopic circuitry. A different dance, and yet not so different.

Remember. Memory sharpened. The familiar was a knife point in his flesh.

Flesh

and not flesh . . .

Ahhhh. . . .

CRI.

Memory flooded the opened sluice. The Dancer staggered, stumbled, nearly fell.

CRI.

The weaker stranger-signal was suddenly the known. More than tone and pulse and energy. Identity.

CRI!

Rescind the automatic sensor shutdown. Absorb the siren's burning energies. As much ecstasy of matter as the human mind can bear . . .

and still compute.

CRI! Can you hear me?

Repattern those energies, in the impulsive skittish language of electrons. Sing the tale-chant of your Dance. Identity and meaning in the interplay of charge, the dance of positive and negative.

Ah, glorious!

Raellil.

Transformer.

Transmitter.

The monitor screen blanked abruptly.

"Hey!" McPherson rapped uselessly on the plastic housing. "Shit."

Danforth unclenched his fists, distracted from his fury of self-recrimination. "Huh?"

"She's gone dead!" McPherson scrambled up, heading for the tail.

But Danforth caught her arm. "No. Not yet. Look."

Together, they stared at the monitor, which now read, flashing for the expected reply: YES, MR. IBIÁ?

Danforth frowned. He typed: Ibiá not here, CRI.

WHERE, THEN? I AM RECEIVING . . .

The screen blanked again.

"What the . . . ?"

"Weird," McPherson agreed.

Danforth typed: What's going on, CRI?

There was no response. The screen stared back like a dead eye.

Danforth drummed his fingers fitfully. "Sixty-two minutes," he muttered. "Any luck with the power beam?" He flipped a random switch. The idiot light did not respond. "We're dead men," he muttered.

And then without preliminaries, the screen filled with rapid machine chatter: APOLOGIES, DR. DANFORTH. DIFFICULTY

FIXING MR. IBIÁ'S LOCATION RESOLVED. RECEIVING DATA TRANSFER NOW.

"What the hell's she talking about?"

SOURCE OF LOOPED SIGNAL COULD BE INTERPRETED AS COMPUTERLIKE MECHANISM IN RESPONSE FAILURE-MODE. "MUSIC" AS YET UNEXPLAINED.

Danforth typed: You're getting all this from Ibiá?

SECONDARY DATA RATE SIGNAL, SAME SOURCE, IDENTIFYING CALL CODE 175IBIÁ. INTERPRETATION OF DATA IS MINE.

"I don't get it." He typed: What kind of data?

The computer paused, as if pondering the proper descriptive: SENSORY DATA.

Where or what is he sending from?

THAT INFORMATION IS NOT INCLUDED, DR. DANFORTH. The computer made a rare excursion into the gray area of surmise. IT IS AS IF A COMPLEX SET OF NEW SENSORS HAVE BEEN TIED DIRECTLY INTO MY SYSTEM. THE CIRCUMSTANCES ARE SOMEWHAT UNPRECEDENTED.

"I'll say."

IF FAILURE MODE IS THE PROPER INTERPRETATION OF THIS DATA, THE MECHANISM INDICATED MAY YET BE REACTIVATED. I HAVE SUGGESTED THAT MR. IBIÁ SEARCH FOR A RESET INDICATOR.

You mean he's actually found *machinery* in there?

"He's obviously transmitting from *something*," put in McPherson.

NO MENTION OF MACHINERY AS SUCH. MY INSTRUMENTS REGISTER NO CONCENTRATION OF REFINED METALS TO INDICATE CENTRALIZED CIRCUITRY MASS. BUT GIVEN NATURE OF SIGNAL, ARTIFICIAL INTELLIGENCE ONLY PLAUSIBLE EXPLANATION.

"Even weirder," McPherson commented.

Danforth typed: You better tell Ibiá to get his ass out of there before he gets blown up, CRI. Ask him can he bring this AI with him?

Again, CRI paused. Then: I BELIEVE THE RESPONSE IS NO.

You're not sure?

THE REPLY WAS UNUSUAL. I AM INTERPRETING IT AS LAUGHTER.

A third and fourth sample produced the same unlikely results. A prickle of instinct woke along Susannah's spine. She flushed the instrument once again, doggedly, then sat with it in her lap, letting the prickle spread to a full-body tingle.

Ghirra waited with her patiently, casting an occasional quick eye at his sister guarding the narrow glowing doorway.

As if it were a casual adjustment, Susannah reprogrammed the little analyzer for greater accuracy within a very tight range: if the box claimed the presence of human DNA in the samples, she wanted more specific figures. If contamination was the problem, she would recognize her own genetic signature, even in the rough mapping allowed by an unsophisticated instrument.

She ran the next sample.

A human signature, with its familiar sequences of nucleotides, appeared on the screen, but a detailed reading showed no sign of contamination by her own genetic material. She looked again. It was human, yet subtly altered. Some of the differences she thought she recognized but couldn't place.

She stored the analysis, cleaned the cavity, then searched among her supplies for a disposable syringe. Pressing the thumb of her ungloved hand hard against the tip of her middle finger, she jabbed quickly and cleanly, drawing a few cc's of blood for her next sample run. She fed it into the machine, stuck her bleeding finger into her mouth and waited.

The DNA signature was clear and complete, indubitably hers.

She found another syringe, then looked up at Ghirra, whose full attention she had finally gathered. She held out her plastic-gloved hand.

He reached instead for the syringe. "I will do this."

Ghirra's blood produced the same basic human signature, as Susannah knew it would. She had run this comparision of Sawl and Terran genetic structure in detail with CRI, but then had been concentrating on the similarities, for likeness had been what she most wanted to see.

This time she focused on the differences, slight as they were.

That's what's familiar!

She called up the stored figures from the rib sample analysis and displayed them side by side with Ghirra's. Except for the hypervariable regions where genetic structure varies between individuals, the signatures were nearly identical.

Susannah nodded with the slow concentration of an old man at prayer. She turned to the wall beside her, touched it hesitantly.

"Ghirra," she said unsteadily, "I'll know better when I can run more accurate tests and a full protein analysis, but it would appear that, genetically, you are more closely related to this wall than you are to me."

* * *

345

The Dancer felt urgency enter his Dance.

The signal called CRI spoke to him.

As he led her through his steps, chanting his tale for her, she returned him data that helped to focus and identify his purpose.

And data that was problematical.

Memory stirred again, like silt in clear water.

The data showed that destruction was imminent. The signal called CRI advised escape.

But the other, still-steady siren wail. He was bound by its repetitive blind insistence.

The signal called CRI named it a loop, and offered the opinion that if the loop could be broken, proper functioning might be restored.

The Dancer knew it was his purpose to join loops, not undo them. But connections sundered may be remade, a large circle engendered.

Join all in the symmetry of the Dance.

Ghirra cocked his head, smiled uncertainly. "This is amusement, Suzhannah?"

"A joke? No. Look at the data. You may not be able to read the words but you can see the figures are very nearly the same."

He tapped the luminous wall with a delicate knuckle. "But I am not like this."

"Nor is your toenail like your eyes or your bones. They're made of specialized cells, but DNA from each will match exactly."

She ran her eyes up the long slant of the glowing panels across the wide hallway. Her theory was as audacious as this strange ancient construction itself. "I think the material to build these tunnels was grown by your ancestors from their own genetic material."

Ghirra's look was pure bewilderment.

"Maybe it was simply what they had the most of and the technology was in place. Maybe this structure needed support and they hadn't the strong metals for it. Perhaps this polar location was once frigid and needed a special insulation. Or perhaps they did it for the sheer beauty of it."

She leaned toward him eagerly. "They cloned the most resilient but workable substance their bodies had to offer. Ghirra, isn't it a marvelous possibility? Bioengineering on the grandest scale imaginable! This is the really conclusive proof that you *are* descendants of the old race of technocrats!"

Her voice rang down the hall, camouflaging the approaching quiet footsteps. But Aguidran sensed movement out of the corner of her eye. Her head jerked away from the bright doorway of the inner room. She bent swiftly for her knife.

Susannah heard her guttural oath and glanced up in time to see the wall flare and sizzle beside the Ranger's head.

Ghirra yelled a quick warning command. Aguidran froze, her hands instinctively spread wide.

"That's right, honored doctor," Clausen drawled, easing around the corner of the hall, laser in hand. "Keep your tiger leashed and we'll all get out of here alive." He advanced on them confidently, gesturing with the laser at the narrow doorway. "What's she got in there?"

Susannah's concern was for Stavros, so vulnerable in the tiny room. She leaped to her feet. "There's no lithium here to blow up, Emil."

"On the contrary, my dear Susannah. The place is lousy with it."

He stopped in front of her, shoved Ghirra against the wall and directed Aguidran to follow. "Which is what brings me here. I've got a full-strength standard charge detonating in fifty-eight minutes, more or less, which just gives us time to retrace our steps and be airborne."

She snatched at his arm, not for the laser but to pull at him pleadingly. "Turn it off! Emil, please, look around you! You can't destroy such an incredible artifact! Do you know what these tunnels are made of?"

"I heard," he said, shaking her off tiredly. "But it's too late, Susannah. You cannot say I didn't offer. The opportunities for deal-making have long since passed unexploited."

"But what if it's still alive?"

"Don't be ridiculous." He waved brusquely at the analyzer, abandoned on the floor. "You have your samples: proof enough to write your papers. Now I assume you would rather live to write them than not, so gather up your gear and your companions and be off."

He backed toward the doorway, the laser trained at Aguidran's gut. Ghirra flattened his palm against his sister's chest as she gathered herself to lunge forward. She growled in protest.

"Raellil . . . !" Susannah heard her mutter.

Ghirra moved closer, blocking her path, murmuring urgently, his hands pressing her back, desperate to convince.

Clausen halted at the doorway. One eyebrow arched in mild surprise. The laser's snub nose sank perceptibly. "Well, I was just going to ask where, but . . ." He glanced back at Susannah. "What the hell is he doing?"

She answered with an honest shrug. "Only Stav knows what he does these days."

Clausen frowned. The spectacle of Stavros made him even more uncomfortable. "Get him out of there," he snapped, and moved aside.

The Dancer wove into his tale-chant a dream of unison. He sang the glories of the circle. He sought to draw the signal called CRI deeper into the Dance.

But she would not rise and soar with him.

She had her own imperative, her warning: GET OUT GET OUT.

She sent him quantities to express her urgency. Straight-line measurements of time in response to the sinuous leapings of the Dance.

58 . . . 57 . . . 56 . . .

The Dance was not linear.

To the Dancer, Time was meaningless except as rhythm.

His purpose was to join.

To complete the circle.

The circuit.

What goes out must come back.

What goes out must come back.

Susannah prevaricated. "I'm afraid to break him out of it too suddenly. I don't know what it'll do to him."

"It'll keep him alive," Clausen returned tartly. "Fifty-six minutes, Susannah."

She slipped into the conical room and knelt on the blood-warm floor at Liphar's side. The young Sawl seemed as oblivious as his charge, his eyes intent on Stavros' upturned face, his hand steady on Stavros' knee. Susannah searched for sense or tone appropriate to this alien ritual, but Liphar spoke first.

"Clauzen," he murmured, so low she must lean closer to hear.

"He's set another bomb. We have to leave."

He has no idea what a bomb is, she worried, but Liphar heard the tightly reined fear behind her quiet words.

"His Dance is not finish," he whispered.

"We'll die in here if we don't leave now."

"Ibi is talk this angry Sister," Liphar insisted. "Talk now, make life for all Sawl. You go okay. We stay finish this Dance."

"Liphar, you can't make that decision for him."

"Ibi know this already to be Kav."

Susannah's whisper strained to keep back tears. "He's *not* a kav, damn it! He's a man, a Terran man and you can't just let him die because . . ."

"He is raellil," declared Liphar with fervent pride.

"I don't care!" She reached for Stavros and as he had before, Liphar snatched her hand in an iron grip before it could make contact.

"Fifty-five," Clausen intoned from the doorway.

The Dancer was tiring.

Burning through him, the signal energies consumed his own.

Awareness intervened now in flashes, like sun through deep water as the swimmer strokes surfaceward, running out of air.

Awareness of a hand upon his knee.

Awareness and memory. Other sensors reawakening.

He remembered an old man, a Dancer himself.

Songs he remembered, and language. A ritual of burning.

Language.

What goes out must come back.

Language . . .

Identity.

Ahhh . . .

"Liphar! You've got to bring him out of it!" Susannah stared fiercely at the young Sawl, preparing to shake off his restraining hand with all the desperate strength she could muster. Liphar stared back implacably.

"For Christ's sake, get on with it!" growled Clausen, crowding into the doorway.

Identity!

The swimmer surfaced.

Bright light and air and sound.

CRI! Stavros called through the circuit. Pain seared his palms. A woman and a young man knelt before him in a hot amber room. He knew where he was and remembered where he'd been.

The circuit. He was the Dancer and himself, could be both. Could both live and Dance.

GET OUT GET OUT GET OUT, sent CRI.

The Dance was not dying. It was a part of life, had been for all, so long ago. Until the meaning of the connection it forged was forgotten, submerged in ritual, lost to all but a few with an instinct for . . .

Connection. There was no guar. There never was. The miracle was Their fire burning through me. The me *willing* to believe that a man could speak to a Goddess.

Connection. Language.

GET OUT GET OUT GET OUT

No, I must talk to Her.

NO USE. SYSTEM IN FAILURE. GET OUT. YOU ARE IN DANGER.

What goes out must return . . .

She must be told of her danger.

GET OUT GET OUT GET OUT

Complete the circuit, CRI. Send the signal back. Send it back, CRI. I am the conduit, CRI. Send it back through me. NOW!

Awareness showed the bullet-headed man swooping down on him, hand outstretched to grapple. But Stavros was the Dancer, and Time only a rhythm that he could move within or without.

Send it, CRI!

I DO NOT UNDERSTAND THE CONTEXT OF THIS REQUEST.

His mind recalled the machine's man-made parameters, and a way that human will, his own, might be imposed on her circuitry. He, Stavros, framed the demand in human numbers and he the Dancer sang it into signal, weaving it into the siren pulse as it streamed through him, palm to burning palm, on its way to the source called CRI.

Raellil.

Transmitter.

Translator.

The grappling hand soared timelessly toward his shoulder.

Stavros waited.

GET OUT GET OUT GET OUT

                    and then . . .

What went out, returned.

The siren signal was answered by its returning self.

The Dance revolved in perfect harmony.

The circuit was complete.

Clausen's fist closed hard on his arm.

In your hands now, Sister-Goddess, Stavros prayed.

He was jerked upward to his knees, head flung back, arms flailing, ripped from the living walls as if from a socket.

Liphar screeched and launched himself at the prospector like a demon, then gasped and fell back wheezing as Susannah's arm swung hard against his chest to keep him from the laser's hungry beam.

"OUT!" Clausen roared. "Or I'll drill him and leave him!"

With a vicious wrench, he slammed Stavros against the doorway, then grabbed him up again and flung him out into the hall.

Stavros crashed unresisting to the floor and lay still. Susannah wrapped the hysterical, raging Liphar in a desperate bear hug.

At the door, Clausen threw them a look of disgust. "And shut that kid off!" He moved out into the hall, ordering Ghirra and Aguidran toward the crumpled body on the floor. "Get him up!"

The two Sawls heaved Stavros to his feet with effort. He was not quite dead weight but his knees buckled and his head lolled forward limply. Blood from his fall smeared his mouth and jaw. His lips fluttered soundlessly.

"Move!" said Clausen into the conical room.

Susannah wrestled Liphar past the prospector and his ready laser, then released him. They rushed to help with Stavros. Sticky red seeped from beneath the open collar of his therm-suit.

"The wound's opened up. At least give me a chance to look at him."

"Later," snapped Clausen. "He'll survive."

Aguidran hooked Stavros' left arm behind her back as gently as she could. From the other side, Ghirra grasped him firmly around the waist. Liphar hovered, patting at Stavros with feathery helpless hands and weeping.

Stavros began to mutter faint incoherence.

As Aguidran and her brother started down the hall, the Ranger flashed the prospector a look of hatred that washed past Susannah like ice water. She stepped hastily aside to gather up her pack and equipment. Clausen had robbed them of the chance to know if there were or had ever been machines within this strange complex, but she was determined not to lose her samples.

Catching up with her, Clausen complained, "You might show a little gratitude. I'm saving their goddamn miserable lives!"

"Oh, we're grateful, Emil," Susannah hissed. "Real grateful."

"My dear Susannah." He traced the profile of the slanting glowing walls with the laser's stubby nose. "When you're away from here and home again, all this will seem like a silly dream. You'll wonder what you got so worked up about."

Susannah stared at him with dull incredulity, then moved ahead to comfort Liphar as he stumbled along behind his battered, muttering hero, sobbing uncontrollably.

Danforth's chronometer felt like a lead weight on his wrist, one he did not want to keep staring at. He stared at the monitor instead.

RELAYING ALARM SIGNAL BACK TO SOURCE AS PER MR. IBIÁ'S ORDER.

McPherson chewed the tip of a thumbnail. "I've heard of that done in First Contact procedures, you know? When nothing else is working.''

Is that really what this is? Danforth wondered. *Are we talking about machines here or the men behind them?*

He did not notice CRI's next message until the computer flashed it impatiently.

THE ALARM HAS CEASED.

Hurriedly, he typed: Clarify.

ALARM LOOP CEASED TRANSMISSION FORTY SECONDS AGO. MR. IBIÁ HAS CEASED TRANSMISSION. SILENCE ON ALL FREQUENCIES BUT OUR OWN.

To Danforth, this did not sound like positive news. He caught himself listening to the vast rock-lined hush of the rift, musing that silence too is a relative quantity, able to become quite suddenly more profound than it was a moment before.

CRI, he typed. Time to detonation?

52 MINUTES, 21 SECONDS.

43

The sun balanced on the western rim like a fat salmon melon. Hard-edged shadow crawled out of the lower rift and advanced across the ledge. At eight minutes until detonation, Danforth slid heavily into the pilot's seat.

"Ron, strap in. Might as well be tied down to something when she blows.''

"Wait!'' she called out eagerly, "Here they come!''

Danforth stared across the ledge. The gaunt Master Ranger and her brother struggled out of the tunnels supporting Ibiá between them. Danforth saw blood on his therm-suit.

What's the sonofabitch done to him this time?

Liphar followed close behind with Susannah. Clausen appeared last of all. He paused in the giant opening, unseen by the others, looked upward toward the high perfect arch and touched the nose of his pistol to his brow in grim, smiling salute.

McPherson dropped through the hatch and took off across the ledge to help the exhausted Sawls with their burden. "Come on, we gotta take cover!''

Clausen caught her arm, pulled her away. He flipped her a small bit of metal and plastic. "Go bring up A-Sled.''

McPherson gripped the encased ignition sequence. "I might just take off without you."

"Sacrifice Taylor to get at me? You don't hate me that much, McP. Now get on it, eh?"

McPherson glared, as if she might leap for his throat, then whirled and raced off toward the edge of the ledge. She glanced back once, then disappeared down a hidden trail over the side.

Clausen strode toward the Sled. "On your feet, Tay. I want you down here on the ground where I can see you!"

Danforth did not move. The others dragged Stavros to the Sled and laid him on the ground beside the wing. Ghirra knelt immediately, unstoppering a canteen. Susannah went to the hatch for a blanket to use as a stretcher. Aguidran crouched with her back to Clausen as he shouldered past the wimpering Liphar.

"Taylor, get your ass moving!"

Danforth watched him approach the cockpit. Some instinct for rebellion kept him still, and over the prospector's shoulder, he saw Aguidran slide a hand down her leather-wrapped leg to her boot, her eyes steely on Clausen's back. Danforth felt the moment of decision come and go without surprise, understanding that this decision had been made weeks ago, as he lay on another wilderness ledge, wet, shivering, every breath an agony, praying for delirium to wrap him in its merciful cocoon, to end the humiliation of having to beg medicine against the pain, of having to suffer his grinning companion's lash of mockery.

He kept himself as still as he could. He forced his eyes not to glide past Clausen to the lithe brown hand grasping the handle of the knife, nor to seek out Susannah, who rustled around beneath the hatch, unawares.

His eyes locked with Clausen's instead, and too late he knew this to be an equal giveaway.

Clausen's blue eyes narrowed warily.

As the blade slipped out of its sheath, he spun, ducking, whipping the laser up and around. Aguidran lunged for him over Stavros' legs. Clausen sighted by instinct as he dropped to one knee and fired, twice.

Aguidran shuddered mid-flight but kept coming, her blood spattering Stavros and the grainy ledge and the white skin of the Sled. She fell to meet Clausen's sidelong dodge. Her strong arm arced and thrust in a fierce underhand jab that caught the prospector in the groin. The eight-inch blade rammed into his gut and he swore in pain and surprise, twisting away from the Ranger as she tumbled and collapsed, her momentum spent.

Liphar threw himself down to shield Stavros' blood-stained body, but the laser clattered loose as Clausen staggered against the wing. He slipped to his knees, hands wrapped around the protruding knife hilt, shiny hot red leaking between his clutching fingers.

Liphar screamed. Danforth struggled out of his seat. Susannah turned, wide-eyed, and ran to Clausen as he struggled to pull the blade himself. Ghirra stumbled to his fallen sister's side, calling for Susannah's help.

"A real deep breath, Emil." Gritting her teeth, Susannah grasped the knife and yanked it free, more roughly than she needed to. Ghirra's pleas for help pulled at her. She pressed Clausen's own hands to the wound. "She got you low. You're lucky this time."

He swore again, his breathing tight, but worked at staunching his bleeding knowledgeably. "I've been gut-cut before," he offered grimly. "Always hurts like a sonofabitch."

"But you were probably somewhere near a hospital that time. Don't move!" Susannah scrambled up and met Danforth on his crutches at the hatch, already holding out her medikit.

"The gun . . ." he reminded her urgently.

Hurrying to Aguidran, she bent and scooped up the little pistol, still lying within Clausen's reach. She tossed it into her kit with a grunt of loathing.

Clausen eyed her darkly. "Don't let this go too long, doc. We're losing minutes and I'm losing blood."

Susannah ignored him. Aguidran had fallen face down, arms splayed. Susannah helped Ghirra turn her over. The dark ranger leathers were slick with blood that welled up too fast from tiny double holes in the precise area of her heart. Susannah fumbled for one wrist, Ghirra for the other, their heads bent at the same intent listening angle. Leaning over the side of the open hold, Danforth watched their heads lift, their eyes meet with the kind of awful knowing that doctors share. He watched them put that knowing immediately aside and go diligently to work to save a life that had already slipped from their grasp.

He remembered the priority of the clock. "Susannah, we've got to scram the minute Ronnie brings up A-Sled!"

Susannah nodded distractedly, helping Ghirra to slice away thin layers of resilient leather, exposing Aguidran's wounds. "Tell Emil to disarm the charge."

Danforth went to the hatch. "Give me the release code," he called down to the prospector.

Propped against the left wing wheel, Clausen stared up at him, pale and sweating. "You sat there while she pulled a fucking knife on me . . . !" His pain-narrowed eyes flicked away from

Danforth's unremorseful gaze to search the ledge. "Jesus, where's McPherson?"

"Let me disarm the charge, Emil."

"Can't. It's a no-interrupt sequence."

"Will it take us out for sure when it blows?"

Clausen closed his eyes wearily. "I set it at full power."

"So even if we did get out alive, we'd never know what was in there." Danforth shook his head. "You really are unhinged."

He thought he heard the hum of A-Sled approaching. He reset the access ladder and lowered himself and his crutches clumsily through the hatch. He limped over to Clausen. "Can you walk?"

"He'd better not," Susannah warned over her shoulder.

"Let *him* work on me, then," said Clausen caustically. "Even untrained help is better than none."

"We'll get to you," she snapped.

"Susannah, we've got six minutes . . . !" Danforth protested.

She continued working on Aguidran. "See how Stav is doing."

"Give it up," Clausen rasped. "She was dead when she went down."

Danforth moved over to check on Stavros.

Still weeping, Liphar was hunched over his knees, palming blood from Stavros' face with bare hands and water from a canteen. Apart from superficial facial cuts and ugly leakage from the shoulder wound, the linguist seemed physically unharmed. But his hands clenched and unclenched. His lips moved purposefully. Occasional random syllables escaped as voice.

Danforth stood over them, his cast-bound legs preventing him from offering real help. "Liphar, can you get him on his feet?"

Liphar did not respond. He rocked gently and wept, continuing to bathe Stavros' face even after it was clean.

Four minutes. Danforth heard the whine of A-Sled's fans. Across the ledge, the white craft rose gracefully above the edge and swooped toward them.

Clausen coughed and winced. "Phew. Jesus. Damn, Susannah, get over here! A doctor's duty is to the living!"

Susannah gathered herself and her medikit. Her eyes begged Ghirra's understanding. "There's nothing we can do."

Ghirra's urgent efforts slowed.

"We won't leave her," Susannah assured him. "We'll put her in the other Sled as soon as it lands."

He nodded dully.

Susannah laid a gentle finger on his wrist, wet with his twin's blood, then turned away as the gusts from the descending craft whipped loose hair against her tear-streaked cheeks. She dragged her medikit over to Clausen and went to work sewing him up.

McPherson landed the Sled and left the fans cycling. She raced across the ledge, then pulled up in shock at the sight of bodies and spattered red. She stared down at Aguidran. "What the . . . ?"

"Later," Danforth ordered. "Get Ibiá into the hold. We've got three minutes and about zero chance of being airborne in time!"

They dragged Stavros to A-Sled. McPherson left Danforth and Liphar to struggle him up the ladder. She ran back to help Susannah maneuver Clausen onto the makeshift blanket stretcher.

"You don't deserve it but you're going to make it," Susannah told the prospector.

He attempted a grin, but McPherson's ungentle handling froze it into a grimace.

"Killing people's a real habit with you, eh?" she spat.

"Self-defense," he replied predictably.

Danforth stumped up, breathing hard. "Got him in. All ready here?"

"Ask Taylor. He saw all of it," Clausen insisted. "All of it."

"Easy does it," Susannah advised, gathering up her equipment. "The internal bleeding's controlled for now, but he's only stapled together."

Clausen was hauled to the Sled and hoisted into the hold with Liphar's unwilling assistance. McPherson raced to the cockpit to strap in. "We're out of here in sixty seconds!"

Danforth hovered by the open hatch. Susannah ran back for Ghirra.

He sat unmoving at his sister's side.

"We have to go," she urged, beginning to fold Aguidran's limp arms across her blood-soaked chest.

But Ghirra stilled her hands firmly. "You go, Suzhannah."

"Ghirra . . ."

"I will be with my sister."

"COME ON!" yelled McPherson from the Sled.

"Ghirra, don't you understand? This whole place is going to explode!"

"I understand this."

"She wouldn't want this. You can mourn her better by staying alive."

Danforth's imperative shout reinforced McPherson's.

Susannah tugged pleadingly on Ghirra's arm.

"My sister dies but Clauzen will live," he observed quietly. "Go, Suzhannah. They call for you."

"Ghirra, I'm a doctor! I had to do what I could for him!"

He nodded slowly.

"Damn it, I'm not leaving unless you come with me!"

Her declaration brought the first hint of pain to his impassive face. His shoulders sagged. He threw his head back and let out a howl of grief that rose above the whine of the fans like a roll of thunder.

"Twenty seconds, Susannah! Get him the fuck over here!"

Susannah grabbed him then, with the strength of desperation, and yanked him to his feet. She dragged him unresisting half the distance to the Sled, but suddenly, he stiffened and jerked away from her, then stumbled back to where Aguidran lay in her darkening blood.

"For the love of God!" Danforth bellowed over the fan noise. "We can't wait any longer!"

Desperate eyes watched her from the Sled.

Susannah looked back at Ghirra, struggling now to haul away his sister's body, too heavy in death for him to manage alone. Before she was aware of it, she was rushing to help him.

"Tay, hold tight!" McPherson screamed. "We're outa here!" The Sled lifted with a burst of wind, the hatch gaping open, the ladder dangling furiously. Danforth clung to the lashings of a crate, yelling unheard protests into the roar of the engines.

Susannah caught up with Ghirra and grabbed Aguidran's legs. "Under here!" she shouted.

The disabled B-Sled was the only possibility for shelter from the coming blast. They dragged the body under the belly of the craft. Susannah rammed the hatch shut above their heads. The hum of the escaping Sled receded into the green-amber sky above the rift like a fading dream. Aguidran's knife lay beside the thick tread of the wing wheel, Clausen's blood drying on its blade. A mental countdown blared in Susannah's mind. She huddled close to Ghirra and tried to block its second-by-second yammer with a memory of Stavros, stretched languidly on the river rock where they had first made love. She waited.

Five seconds after the rift wall was due to erupt and rain destruction on their heads, the ledge shook with a single violent jolt, like a deep shudder of fear or cold. Susannah pressed her face to Ghirra's back, waiting for the ground to crack and yawn beneath them. She felt his body, expecting death, relax in welcome.

But stillness returned, descending like a gift of rain in the desert.

Minutes later it was broken by the hum of the distant Sled, growing louder as McPherson circled cautiously back. Susannah dared to lift her head. The Sled approached.

She left Ghirra sitting stunned and motionless. She moved out into the open to gaze up uncomprehending as the returning craft dropped slowly past the undisturbed four-kilometer rise of amber rock drilled with its neat black holes.

A-Sled settled with a more sedate rush and roar than it had departed with. White-clad legs appeared in the open hatch, and Stavros dropped heavily to the ground. He staggered weakly and recovered his balance.

With a cry, Susannah ran to meet him.

He caught her unsteadily in his arms, leaning into her for support.

"Stav, are you all right . . . ?"

His only response was to hold her closer.

The access ladder clanged into place. Liphar tumbled down and sped past to fling himself down before Aguidran's body. McPherson followed, shamefaced.

"You know, Susannah, eh? I had to think of the others." She shrugged defensively and moved on.

Susannah eased out of Stavros' tight embrace. His sustained silence unnerved her. "What happened? Why didn't it . . . ?"

"It did," he said. "Not as powerful as we expected, but enough to do the work." He let her go, slumped with defeat. "It's over, Suze. We failed."

"Failed? You mean . . . ?"

Stavros nodded, staring at the ground. Tears glistened unshed in his half-lidded eyes. "I can't hear Her anymore, there's nothing on the com, no signal, nothing. It's all gone dead." He spread his hands, palm up, his familiar gesture now weighted with tragedy. "Even my guar-fire's gone. He killed Her. And I had almost . . . I tried to warn Her!" The tears spilled over and he pulled her close again. "Ah, my people!"

McPherson and Liphar passed, returning with Aguidran's body in the blanket sling. Ghirra paced numbly behind, the bloodied knife dangling in his hand.

Over Stavros' shoulder, Susannah watched him pause beside the hatch as the others lifted his dead sister into the hold. With almost formal deliberation, he raised his arm and wiped the knife blade on the white sleeve of his borrowed therm-suit. He studied the dark, lustrous metal thoughtfully, spat on it and wiped it again.

Danforth called to him from above. The hatch was clear. The Master Healer pressed the knife blade briefly to his cheek, then slipped it between his belt and the small of his back. His characteristic stoop reclaimed him for a moment. Then he lifted his head and started up the ladder.

Intuition struck home. Susannah gasped and struggled against Stavros's suddenly restraining grasp. He held her fast. His tears wetting her cheek, he murmured gently, implacably, "No, my love. Not this time."

Danforth limped forward to the cockpit as the Master Healer climbed through the hatch. A fleeting look passed between them, a nod, and Danforth beckoned Liphar and McPherson away from laying out Aguidran on the floor of the hold. McPherson covered the dead Ranger with a silverfilm tarp and went to join him.

Clausen lay on a blanket at the rear. His chest rose and fell in shallow gasps, but his head was turned, his eyes alert. They widened faintly as the Master Healer approached, but Ghirra's hands were empty and his handsome face serene. Clausen's breathing quickened as he felt the healer's cool fingers surround his jaw, but he did not cry out. He stared up at Ghirra warily.

"You have much pain?" Ghirra inquired.

"Hell, no. I feel just great."

The long fingers probed gently. "I can help this pain."

Clausen twisted his head to throw off the Master Healer's touch.

"You must lie quiet, Clauzen." Ghirra's hands worked and soothed. A disbelieving sigh escaped the prospector as numbness seeped through him. Slowly, he relaxed.

"This is better, Clauzen?"

Clausen's eyes were heavy-lidded with relief. "Inspired hands," he murmured.

Ghirra smiled his da Vinci angel smile, light seeming to suffuse his brown face from within. He eased one hand away from its healing work and reached around his back to draw the knife from his belt.

As the prospector lapsed into sleep, the Master Healer brought the eight-inch blade around and calmly slit his throat.

When Ghirra descended the ladder again, Stavros let Susannah go and did not try to stop her as she snatched up her kit and bolted for the Sled.

She accosted the Master Healer as he stood methodically cleaning the blade of his sister's knife. His white therm-suit looked like a butcher's apron.

She almost screamed, *How could you?*, but his blank calm stopped her. His movements were slow and mechanical, his eyes like dark glass. She could see nothing of him in them, only her own apalled reflection.

She pushed by him and scrambled up the ladder.

Blood pooled in the floor grating. Clausen's eyes were closed. He had died quickly and without a struggle.

Danforth waited wrapped in the silence of the cockpit, his arms folded over the tops of his crutches. Beside him, McPherson shared his look of grim relief. Liphar shivered against the padding of a bench. In answer to Susannah's accusing stare, Danforth shrugged faintly and shook his head.

"We had to!" McPherson blurted. "No other way he'd ever stop hurting people!"

Susannah had no response. It appalled her that what they had done might just be defensible in the larger scheme of things, that her doctor's reflex to sew Clausen up had disregarded the future for the sake of present moral self-image. *A doctor saves lives* . . .

In the end, Clausen's executioners had acted as pragmatically as he, lured at last into his Machiavellian universe where any means could be justified if the end was great enough.

Even Ghirra . . . Emil would surely approve.

Clausen's still, waxy face, furred with sandy three-day stubble, made Susannah infinitely sad.

The smartest and ablest, she mused. He had died for the sake of greed and in the service of a faceless entity that would mourn him briefly if at all. She shook open a silverfilm tarp and crouched to spread it over him, touching his cheek in farewell.

When she rose again, she stood for a moment gazing vacantly at the swollen vermilion sun, beginning its descent, huge and clumsy, its belly flattened by the western rim of the rift. Darkness approached with the march of shadow across the flat, granular ground. Four kilometers higher, at ground level, it would still be late afternoon.

She saw Ghirra drift a distance across the ledge to kneel at the edge of the shadow. He settled himself cross-legged and something flashed dull amber sunlight in his hand.

Susannah squinted, then stared in horror. "O my god . . ."

She had thought the worst was over, but it was not.

She nearly fell down the ladder, yelling for Stavros, charging across the ledge at a dead run with her medikit banging at her side, screaming now to Ghirra, pleading, begging him to stop.

Unheeding, the Master Healer raised his sister's blade. With a surgeon's precision, he drew its needle point down one wrist and then the other, laying open his veins.

Susannah knocked the knife from his hand. "NO! I WON'T LET YOU!"

She grabbed his blood-slick wrists. Stavros caught up, breathless. He wrapped his good arm around Ghirra's chest as he fought to shake off Susannah's restraint. Even in the fury of his determination, Ghirra could not overcome their equal determination to deny him the death he desired. Stavros wrestled him to the ground while Susannah wrapped his wrists tightly, then knocked him out with a shot of tranquilizer. When he lay limp in Stavros' lap, she began a desperate attempt to stitch him back together.

Liphar ran up behind them, then knelt in dumb shock. Danforth and McPherson gathered in a silent anxious circle. Susannah glared up at them once, then bent back to her work.

"You let him do it," she muttered. "You let a man committed to saving lives be the first of his kind in who knows how many centuries to take one intentionally! You let him be Executioner without a thought of what it would do to him!"

Stavros began, "He was the only one of us with the guts to actually . . ."

"You *used* him! *You*, Stav, who claim to love the Sawls so well!" Susannah bit her lip. A quick brush of her hand left a smudge of blood across her cheek. She whispered, "We are worse than the Goddesses could ever be. They wreaked their havoc without a thought for human life, but *us* . . . we knowingly took a man of saintly brilliance, a healer, and made him into a murderer!"

44

A-Sled sped homeward over the silent desert planet.

"The dead and the living dead," McPherson remarked as she powered the craft for its final departure from the shadowed ledge. "Can't even get damn CRI to talk to me."

"If you can suggest a cause for celebration," returned Danforth darkly, "I'm all ears."

"We made it out, how 'bout that?"

"Some of us did," murmured Susannah.

Stavros wrapped himself in a fog of self-recrimination and failure. Letting exhaustion be his excuse, he retreated into constant sleep, under Liphar's worried and watchful eye. He stirred occasionally to eat in a desultory fashion, but that only, Susannah thought, to set a positive example for the Master Healer, who would eat or drink nothing at all.

Ghirra sat unmoving beside his sister's silver-wrapped corpse. Susannah kept him under mild sedation as a precaution. She had done her best to sponge away the blood that had spattered him,

Aguidran's, Clausen's, his own. Still, he passed the long hours staring in horror at his hands, which lay heavily in his lap as if weighed down by the bandaging on his wrists, or by some less material burden. He would not speak, would not acknowledge Susannah's presence as she sat vigil with him for long patient hours, offering him endless reasoned arguments for continuing his existence.

"Damn crew of zombies," complained McPherson a day into the return, taking her next turn at the stick. But there was no heart to her complaint. Her tone was disconsolate, and she moved about as sluggishly as Danforth, retiring to the benches to brood or sleep when not active in the cockpit.

Susannah left her vigil at Ghirra's side to catch Danforth as he came off his shift. They shared a cold meal and a subdued discussion about how Clausen's murder should be reported. CRI's silence since the detonation, though still unexplained, had saved them from the need for a quick decision.

"We can't let Ghirra be made the scapegoat," Susannah insisted.

"Two bodies, two murders. It's easy," McPherson offered over her shoulder from the pilot's chair. "They had a fight and killed each other."

"One look at his throat and the forensics will know better."

"Can't we just lose him someplace in this godforsaken desert? Say he got blown up by his own charges?"

"That's sure what he'd do if it was one of us," Danforth declared quietly.

McPherson flew at the upper limit of the Sled's altitude range, seeking the fastest possible straight-line return. The mountain ranges were hard sweeps of serrated shadow. The cracked yellow planet rolled by beneath them, its barren monotony echoed by the dimming, empty sky. They took no rest stops, racing to reach DulElesi before darkfall yet dreading the news they carried with them.

"Stav's still talking as if Lagri 'died' in the explosion. Wonder how the Sawl myths cover the death of a goddess," Susannah mused.

Danforth was grim. "Probably don't, but those weather priests are sure to have figured out something bad's occurred. Must be getting really unlivable back there about now."

"What are their chances, Tay?"

He shook his head. "Goddess or machine, whatever it was Emil blew up, the climate is reverting to what it 'should' be in the presence of the Coal Sack. Survival for the Sawls is measured now by how long their supplies of food and water hold out. They'll never harvest another crop on this world. They'll never see another rainfall, I doubt even so much as a cloud. It's what Emil intended, I'm sure: that if there were machines and he destroyed them, our only recourse would be to encourage the CONPLEX claim, in order to effect an emergency evacuation of the population, which only CONPLEX has the resources to carry out.''

The second silver-shrouded bundle drew their simultaneous gaze. It lay at the back of the hold, unattended.

Susannah said musingly, "So he wins in the end anyway."

"Yeah. But at least we don't have him around to gloat."

Later, Susannah tried to interest Danforth in her theories about the building of the Nolagri tunnels. He nosed casually through her data, yawning, depressed, weary from his turn at the controls.

"Organic, huh? All of it."

She was not sure he believed her. She showed him a curl of the horn-like material. "Even the big slanting walls where the sun was shining in.''

He grunted politely. "Interesting."

But after several hours of sleep and a few more in the cockpit, sunk deep in a pensive, dusky silence, Danforth called to her suddenly.

The edge in his voice and the brief veer and drop of the Sled sent Susannah scurrying forward, scattering the cup of water she had been unsuccessfully urging on Ghirra.

"What? What is it?"

The Sled flew steadily again, but Danforth looked as if he'd been struck by an attack of vertigo. "Wake up Ibiá," he demanded. "Get him up here!"

"Tay, are you . . . ?"

"Just get him up here!"

Stavros had no stake in dire emergencies, survival being low on his current priority list. But to please Susannah, he got up and shuffled to the cockpit like an old man routed out of bed in the middle of the night.

"Sit there." Danforth brusquely indicated the copilot's seat. "Tell me again about that Sawl genesis myth, about the king and his daughters.''

Stavros blinked at him dully and backed away from his vehemence as if from a blinding light. The Sled began a slow, sickening slide to starboard as Danforth grabbed him.

"No, you don't, Ibiá! This is important!"

Stavros let himself be dragged forward. While Danforth lev-

363

eled the veering craft, he settled heavily into the empty chair. He began the Tale of Origins in chanted Sawlish, then caught himself in confusion as Danforth turned to stare. Images of his Dance haunted him. He began again in English, stumbling at first but gaining confidence as the two languages merged in his brain and he could sing his translation with the grace and rhythm of the original.

"Raellil," Liphar murmured in admiration, and squeezed into his chosen burrow between Stavros' knee and the hull.

Danforth interrupted the recitation mid-sentence. "That's it, right there! There's no other explanation, given the data. It says *three* daughters: the two goddesses and the third is the Sawls. The two stronger sisters were charged with the protection of the weaker middle child.

"But it's not quite like the story says, that the Darkness came afterward, or it did, but the king *knew* it was coming, because this king was the old race, the ancient Sawls who made the *two* goddess-machines, designed them to protect their descendants during the planet's lethal passage through the Coal Sack."

"But we never found any machines," Susannah reminded him.

Danforth laughed exultantly. "Machine! Not plural. The other would be up north, I'd guess somewhere in the ocean."

Stavros ceased his chant to listen.

"Organic, you said?" Danforth prompted. "A Sawl genetic match? Susannah, you were standing right inside it! What the ancients grew from their own flesh and blood were the goddess-machines themselves: actual daughters, actual sisters!"

"Grew machines . . . ?" An organic bias clogged Susannah's understanding.

"Every creature is a living machine, right? The brain most of all. A clump of biomechanical circuitry. An organic computer. Instead of building their AI, they *grew* it."

"Oh yes," said Stavros, as the vision swelled in his mind.

Susannah let the data shuffle and reshuffle. "But why go to all that trouble?"

"Like you said, lack of sufficient mineral resource. We tend to think technology begins with metallurgy. But the Sawls' genius was biological. You saw that but even you didn't follow it out far enough."

"And even if théy'd had the metals . . ." she pursued. "Because of the vast span of time involved, they needed a machine to last a near eternity without wearing out. They needed a self-repairing, self-replicating organism. Wow. Oh wow." She gazed at him wide-eyed. "Have you figured out a food supply?"

"Fuel, not food," he warned. "This was not a life as we know it. CRI would have felt more akin to it than we, despite its human genetic background. I think it was solar-powered."

Stavros glanced at him. "Not . . . ?"

"Your lithium connection I'm still pondering, but those miles of slanting translucent walls Susannah described sure sound like collectors to me. I'm guessing that's what the whole vast weblike rift system was about. Whether the original impact that created it was man-made or not, I won't venture to guess, but it provided thousands of square kilometers of convenient surface for solar collectors, to feed a gigantic mechano-organism that used magetism and field mechanics to manipulate the climate, and tunnelled the rock down there like the roots of a vast tree. The old dwelling area you saw probably housed the builders originally, the geneticists and AI experts, the lab techs and the maintenance crew." He sat back, arm stretched to the stick as if piloting a racer. "Phew! Can you imagine?"

Susannah could, and did for a while, in awed silence.

"Lagri, Fire-Sister . . ." Stavros mourned, as the living, breathing nature the Sawls had always claimed for their goddesses moved closer to scientific reality. "I heard her too late."

"But wait," Susannah remembered with a start. "If there were two machines, the other may still be functioning."

Stavros shook his head disconsolately.

Danforth sighed. "I'll give you the rest of my theory: climate has two basic components, heat and moisture. Lagri handled the heat, Valla Ired the moisture. Without Lagri to gather and redistribute the overheating from this now-lethal sun, there won't be any moisture much longer. It'll all be evaporated off by a thirsty atmosphere and then . . ."

Stavros pressed his head against the back of his seat with a soft moan as he squeezed his eyes shut against the grief that cut him as deeply as the Master Ranger's knife had cut the prospector.

Susannah's shoulders drooped. "So it seems that CONPLEX does offer the only possibility of saving the Sawls. Oh, Taylor, I'm not sure I can bear the irony."

On the second day, coming off her shift, McPherson found Ghirra sitting untended. Susannah had given in to her own exhaustion and collapsed on one of the benches. McPherson heated a package of soup at the portable galley and brought it over to sit with the Master Healer, noisily spooning the thick reconstituted mush into her mouth, less with hunger than with a vain hope of arousing his appetite.

The shrouded corpse was a third presence between them.

McPherson stared at it for a while, chewing thoughtfully, then gestured with her mug.

"I ain't much good at speeches, but I just wanna say I don't blame you, missing her like this so much. She was a no-bullshit lady, Aguidran, and I learned a lot from her. She even had me thinking if I had to stay here forever, it wouldn't be so bad because, you know, at least I could work with her and be a ranger."

McPherson lowered her mug, suddenly sad and sober. "Yeah. I guess I admired her most of anyone I ever met."

Danforth tried his own hand at psychology. During Susannah's next surrender to sleep, he eased himself awkwardly to the grated floor at Ghirra's side and leaned against the hull, his bound legs stiff in front of him. He knocked the hard plastic enveloping his left thigh.

"A real pain in the ass, this is getting to be," he began conversationally, then fell silent. Later, he tried again:

"Look, I know this has been really hard on you, doc, but believe me, it's going to get even worse now with the machines gone. I mean, they may not have been working quite right, but at least they were doing *something*. The folks at home are going to need you, doc."

He listened to Ghirra's feather-light breathing, just audible within the field-damped huch of the cargo hold. It was unchanged. Danforth tried another tack.

"Doesn't it mean anything to you that you were the first to propose climate control here, and you appear to have been right? You're a good scientist, doc. Be proud of that."

Danforth paused, eying him speculatively, then plunged ahead. "Even if this planet *is* finished. Well, it may be. But so what? So you come with us. A man of your talents and imagination can't just give up. You've got to pull through this one, doc. Your home world may be finished but your work is not. There's a whole universe out there for people like you to discover. If nothing else, you owe it to your sister's memory. She was an explorer. I can't believe *she* wouldn't have jumped at the chance.

"So what do you say, doc? You coming with us? I know of at least one cabin that'll be empty on the trip home . . ."

McPherson called him for his shift then. He struggled upright and onto his crutches with difficulty, and did not notice the Master Healer's thin shoulders rise and fall in a sigh like a slow sea swell.

Later, when Susannah woke and brought him her usual patient offerings of soup and water, Ghirra had drifted into sleep, slumped against the hull. She laid him down gently and pillowed his head on a blanket, praying that sleep would be the restorative balm to his grief that all her well-meaning ministrations had failed to be.

At the end of the third day, nearing the northernmost range of the Grigar, McPherson piloted while the others slept. The rugged peaks saw-toothed the horizon, reflecting the bright pink-amber of the setting sun in slashes like the brush strokes of a painter in love with light. The sun was a red half-dome squatting in the west. North of the mountains, the sky was deep blue-green and streaked with glowing strands of salmon and orange.

McPherson had heard Danforth's negative pronouncements. She peered at the colored strands intently. "Clouds?" she muttered aloud. "Nah. Can't be."

But an hour later, she reached behind her seat to the bench where Danforth slept and shook him awake. She pointed ahead into the topaz dusk.

The strands had swelled into soft pink-edged billows, spread across the full northern horizon, mounting high into the blue-lavender sky like a final mountain range of cotton wool.

"Clouds!" Danforth exclaimed.

His arm shot out to point a little to the east, where the sky below the cloud range seemed to thicken in vertical lines and grow opaque. "And rain! Jesus, Ron, rain!" His big fist pounded McPherson's shoulder. "I don't get it at all, but that is goddamn *rain* out there!"

"No shit, rain? All right!"

Their whoopings woke Susannah, who woke Liphar, who blinked at the distant dusky mist as if he were sure he was dreaming.

"ValEmbriha!" he breathed, then bolted into the hold to wake Stavros, laughing and crying, unable to keep his frantic hands from dancing midair.

"Han khem, Ibi! Han khem!"

Stavros stumbled forward, staring, half asleep. "What does it mean?" he whispered.

"It means *life*, Ibiá," Danforth replied excitedly, "It means the possibility that it's not over yet!"

45

They flew into DulElesi through a warm lavender dusk.

The clear evening sky was dotted with puffy clouds that wandered the arching violet expanse like pink sheep grazing a meadow. The sheer white cliff caught the sun's last rays. It seemed carved of pure, brilliant gold, and the cliff stairs, long flights of gold ascending to purple-shadowed archways. The Lander's tilted nose shone with the same magical light, like the gilded spire of some rich, exotic temple. A golden mist hung low over the fields. Golden rivulets, bright water reflecting the sinking sun, laced the amber contours of the plain.

McPherson skimmed the golden fields and set the Sled down in the Lander clearing. She cut the power and sat back. As the force field dissolved, the evening eased in to replace stale, machined air with breezes indolent with heat and moisture. The stunned passengers were wrapped with damp earthy fragrances and the music of running water. They gazed at each other dumbstruck.

"Something truly remarkable has occurred" Susannah whispered, as if the jewel-like landscape might vanish with the quiet opalescent pop of a soap bubble.

"Looks like Valla's been hard at work," Danforth murmured.

Stavros stood up, swaying like a dreamer. High up on the glowing cliff, a PriestGuild relay's call rang out, a clear trill of welcome.

Liphar broke from his wondering daze and answered impulsively, joyously, then raced alongside McPherson to undog the hatch and slide it open. Dancing impatiently aside while she set the ladder, he found himself facing Aguidran's shrouded corpse and her brother's mild, blank stare. His eager joy faded and he edged back to Stavros' side. From the cliff came the chatter and rumble of a gathering throng as word spread of the Sled's return. Weng and Megan appeared at the mouth of the entry cylinder, smiling.

Danforth went first down the ladder. The clearing was spread with a velvet carpet of young plant growth. The tips of his crutches sank into the spongy ground as he swung to meet Weng.

"There's been a death," he told her. "Two, in fact."

Weng's eyes flicked past him, seeking a head count as the others descended the ladder.

"Clausen and Aguidran," he supplied.

"Ah," said Weng, unsurprised.

Behind her, Megan's shoulders heaved, with relief, Danforth thought, then sadness for the loss of the Master Ranger. "The guild must be informed," she murmured. "How's Ghirra taking it?"

Danforth's mouth tightened. "Not well."

McPherson strode up with a crisp salute, which Weng returned with equal formality. At the bottom of the ladder, Stavros sank to one knee, Liphar beside him. Dazedly, he fingered a handful of earth rich with vegetation.

Danforth said, "We thought . . . we were sure . . ." He spread his arms in amazement. "What's happened here? Do you know?"

Weng patted his arm, an oddly maternal gesture. "Yes. And it was a very close call indeed, Dr. Danforth." She moved past him to stand before the kneeling linguist. "Congratulations, Mr. Ibiá. It worked."

He stared up at her, the thick earth clotting moistly in his palm.

"It?"

"You."

Cautious hope surfaced slowly. Stavros rose, one hand grasping Liphar's shoulder. "You mean They're not . . . ?"

Weng smiled. "If you will come inside, CRI has finally come out of her own little spell and can explain to you what your instincts already knew."

As eager as she was to hear the story, Susannah stayed with Ghirra in the hold, too afraid of what he might do if he woke and found himself alone.

Aguidran's knife was hidden at the bottom of her medikit, along with Clausen's laser pistol, but the cargo hold was rich with potential weapons of self-destruction, even for one who would probably be too weak to move when he did awaken. Susannah decided to keep him in the Underbelly for treatment, where he could be fed intravenously if needed.

Megan stuck her head through the hatch, then plodded up the ladder. "There you are."

"Oh, Meg. A sight for sore eyes." Susannah hugged her gratefully.

"Looks like the last act of a Jacobean tragedy in here." She nodded at the nearer bundle of silverfilm. "Aguidran?"

"Umm."

Megan bent to lay a palm to the Ranger's body. "What a waste."

Suddenly, Susannah could not bear any more mourning. "What's important now is getting Ghirra the hell out of here. See if you could hunt up some help, maybe a stretcher?"

Megan nodded but she was gazing at the other shrouded bundle lying alone at the back. "Killed each other off, did they?"

Susannah hesitated the merest fraction. "Yes. They did."

"Natural adversaries." Megan sighed, heading for the ladder. "A stretcher, humm. Well, there should be plenty of help along in a moment—the whole population's on its way down here to welcome him."

"Him?"

Megan grinned back at her crookedly. "Stavros. Or as they call him now, Kav Ibiá."

"But he's not . . . ." Susannah could not make herself repeat the syllables.

"Funny how things work out," Megan continued. "The Sawls say the weather changed because Stav talked the Sisters into settling their arguments with gentler games. CRI's story has a somewhat more technical emphasis, but the results are the same: perfect balmy weather for the last three ship's days, with a lovely rainshower every fifteen hours. The vegetation's running riot and the FoodGuild's planting a new crop already. The Goddesses have remembered their sibling duty."

As Megan disappeared down the ladder, Susannah turned to find Ghirra awake. His breathing was fuller and his eyes more focused than they had been since she had ripped his sister's knife from his blood-slick hand. He stared up at the lavender sky and its docile herd of pastel-tinted cloud. His attention drifted toward her, then away again, but his lips parted and he seemed to be trying to move.

Susannah ran for water and brought back a brimming mug. She eased Ghirra into a sitting position and cradled his head against her shoulder. She offered the mug as she had nearly every hour for three long days, expecting him to refuse it again. Instead he allowed a trickle of water into his mouth and swallowed awkwardly, as if he had forgotten how. Then he willingly drank all she would allow him.

When she set the mug aside, he shuddered faintly and turned his face into her chest. Susannah folded her arms around him and rocked him, while he wept against her like a child.

46

The ranger honor guard who came for Aguidran's body helped Susannah settle Ghirra into a cot in a quiet corner of the Underbelly. The force field was down, and though it was not yet dark, Weng had set out oil lanterns that glowed and flickered in the faint, fragrant evening breeze. Ampiar and Phea joined them quietly, and stationed themselves beside their guildmaster to wait and watch.

Susannah took the senior ranger aside and surrendered Aguidran's knife, as a treasure of the guild and a precious relic of her leadership. He took it gratefully but sheathed it quickly in his boot. Susannah was relieved to have it out of her possession.

As the rangers were leaving, Ghirra roused briefly. In a whisper like the dry rustle of leaves, he begged them to delay his sister's funeral until he had strength enough to attend. Though the guild and not the family held precedence in matters of a member's death, the four rangers showed the grieving Master Healer great deference and promised to plead his case before the elder guildsmen. This calmed him sufficiently for Susannah to persuade him to take a few swallows of soup before he retreated again into sleep. Convinced that he had decided to live after all, she left him with Ampiar in the lavender shadows and went to listen in on CRI's debriefing.

The expedition members were gathered around the computer terminal as if around a dinner table. An oil lamp burned beside the keypad. Megan and Weng stood a bit aside, already privy to the story. Danforth leaned forward eagerly to study the flash of figures across the glowing monitor. McPherson pressed against his back, reading over his shoulder. Stavros sat beside him, frowning slightly but constrained, for a moment again the overly intense young man he had been only short months before. But Liphar, his priestly familiar, the material evidence of his transformation, curled against him, sound asleep.

". . . Lagri's alarm loop," CRI was explaining to augment her visuals, "was set off by the first series of exploratory charges, but it carried an inbuilt reset signal."

Susannah could not recall having heard the computer refer to the Goddesses so familiarly before.

"When Mr. Ibiá's priority program ordered me to relay that signal back to its source, the failure mode was interrupted and the reloading of Lagri's initial programming began automatically. The first thing she did was interpret Mr. Ibiá's warning correctly and absorb the second, larger charge when it detonated."

Reading the figures, Danforth let out a low whistle. "She ate up the energy from that explosion like it was candy."

"Through the link that Mr. Ibiá established," CRI continued, "I have been monitoring the reload, which required giving over more of my sectors to that effort than might have seemed preferable. I hope I have not seriously inconvenienced anyone by remaining out of communications for so long. I judged it important enough to do so, and was careful to maintain all other functions."

Danforth shifted impatiently. "Yes, yes, CRI; you're forgiven. Go on."

"It was the re-IPL that brought climate operations back to what they should have been all along," Weng interposed, like a proud war correspondent reporting a victory. "A balanced, nonlethal environment; the life-support system that the ancients had intended for their descendants. They designed in a simple way to stop and restart the system if anything went wrong, which of course, it did. What never occurred to them was that the very idea of the reset itself might be forgotten."

"They were human after all," said Megan dreamily. "Like us, they could imagine almost anything being lost to the ravages of time, except the memory of their own existence."

"And as the eons passed," Weng continued, "the program degenerated. But the climate worsened so gradually that succeeding generations had nothing but legend to suggest that it had ever been better. Their own technical language became priestly gibberish to them. They lost the knowledge that they had ever had control over their weather."

"They lost the memory of the Connection," murmured Stavros. "Though the old man must have understood something of it . . ."

The others turned to him expectantly.

"Connection?" Danforth finally prompted.

Stavros shrugged. "I don't know what it is, just that it *is*, or was."

CRI spoke up briskly. "The Goddesses were designed to use field manipulation of human sensors, whose biochemistry they shared. Information such as sense perceptions could be digitized and transmitted. Specific parts of a willing human brain could be activated like switches, offering a kind of long-distance awareness of the functioning of the machines, for the purpose of monitoring and maintenance."

"It is my belief," offered Weng, "that such maintenance personnel were the origin of the PriestGuild. With further study, I'm sure the relevant technical information will be unearthed from the oldest guild records."

"The Toph-leta," said Megan. "Life-gifts, indeed. The story of how a planet's life was being preserved. They did the best they could to keep their memory alive, those old Sawls."

Danforth leaned back against McPherson to stretch his legs. "And damned if we don't have Emil to thank for knocking Lagri into failure mode in the first place, so that the re-IPL could be initiated. Otherwise her program would have kept on degenerating, beyond the point of ever being able to reestablish any kind of livable climate."

"No." Stavros spoke as if from the bottom of a well. "The Sisters' struggle has always resumed after a Devastation."

Liphar stirred beside him and woke, rubbing reddened eyes.

Danforth said, "Not this time, I don't think. I'd say Fiix was doomed."

"The Sawls, yes, maybe the entire population this time. But not Fiix. The Arrah would continue."

"You're saying there's another reset trigger we haven't found yet?"

Weng said, "The basic philosophy of the system was the balance of contentious opposites—wet and dry, hot and cold—with the assumption that the tension natural to such an arrangement was better suited to living organisms over the very long term than static equilibrium."

"Shit, yeah," McPherson remarked. "Don't want them machines getting bored . . ."

"Over the time span we are dealing with here, Lieutenant," said CRI icily, "boredom is a valid consideration, even for a machine."

"Hey, don't take it personal."

"So all this insane battling was built into the initial program," Danforth guessed.

"The Game, Dr. Danforth." Weng smiled, the Cheshire cat in all her glory. "The intricacies of play can be as simple as a child's gambling amusement or as complex as a symphony. The Game was meant to provide the needed climatic variation, but more importantly, to offer the Sisters a very long-term reason to live, a meaning for their existence that could be expressed not in emphemerally emotional human terms but in hard numbers that a

373

circuit could process. I believe it was this very element of Chance, inserted to keep things lively, that proved nearly fatal."

Weng paused, looked down. "Interestingly enough, despite the Sisters' remarkable power and complexity, true consciousness does not seem to have been achieved or even intended by their creators. The Goddesses are not aware in their play."

Stavros offered a quick murmur of protest.

CRI said, "This is not totally accurate, Commander."

Weng raised an eyebrow at the monitor. "As you are currently demonstrating, you possess a greater independent conciousness than the constructs in question."

Undaunted, CRI replied, "I would prefer to say that the nature of their awareness is as yet undetermined, and unexplored by all except Mr. Ibiá and myself."

Cheeky. Susannah was amused and intrigued. *CRI will be as changed by this as any of us. As Megan says, funny how things work out.*

"I can't believe they weren't aware of trying to massacre each other all the time," announced Megan.

"Newton's Third Law of Motion does not imply consciousness in the reaction," returned Weng stiffly.

"Yeah, but that's opposite and *equal*," McPherson pointed out. "Somehow things must've gotten out of hand."

"A variability of reaction is inherent in the nature of the organic circuit, I believe," said CRI.

"You would," said McPherson.

"As I said, the element of Chance in the program. The pendulum of conflict swung a little too far one time," Weng pursued. "Is it possible, Mr. Ibiá, that 'chance' is the original meaning of the word 'khem'? One Sister played too hard. The balance slipped, and in order to right it, the other compensated appropriately. The conflict was perforce escalated."

McPherson made a soft exploding noise.

"No longer a game," said Danforth.

"Sounds like world history," Megan commented.

Weng nodded, her good humor restored. "Indeed. If you are willing to see our Terran population as a similarly vast machine, organic in nature . . ."

"And inherently contentious," put in Danforth.

"Unbalanced," added Megan.

"Unaware," said Susannah.

McPherson giggled and nudged Stavros across Danforth's back. "Hey, Stav, I think they've got another reprogramming job for you . . ."

The others gladly accepted the excuse for a laugh, for a

release of the tension that lingered as habit after so many weeks of constant crisis. Even Stavros allowed an abashed half-grin.

McPherson pushed away from the terminal. "So I guess it's really all over, then. I mean, things are gonna be okay here." She tousled Liphar's curls as if his Little League home team had just scored the winning run. "That's great. That's really great! In fact, that's really amazing!"

But Megan glanced up at the darkening tilted belly of the Lander. "Now all we have to do is find out if we can get ourselves off the damn planet."

When dusk became night, and the Cluster glowed hugely in the eastern sky, the Sawls came down from the Caves with torches. They filled the clearing quietly. Serpentine double rows of light lined the long curving path to the bottom of the cliff and snaked up the zigzag stair to the third level entry closest to the PriestHall. The cliff face glittered with a necklace of tiny fires.

Stavros' attention wandered from the debriefing. Liphar was restless with anticipation. A waiting host of torches flickered in the clearing. Stavros felt their summons like a steady pull. A final threshold remained to be crossed. If he went out into that firelit darkness to accept the Sawls' acclaim, he would also be accepting the full measure of Kav Daven's dying wish.

He was aware of his silent palms as most are aware of their beating hearts. Their centers were the new centers of his being and he longed to waken their mystic fire again. He did not remember it as pain, but as Connection.

Weng's theory gave the Connection to the original PriestGuild alone. Stavros thought his own sensitivity to it belied such exclusion.

'I listen this singing of the world,' he recalled Liphar saying. *All Sawls knew it once. They will know it again.*

He thought of how he would explain it to Susannah. He would be eloquent about the good he would do, translating the Sawls' past and thereby assuring their future by bringing them a new understanding of themselves and their ancestors, of the nature of the Arrah, and what their real duties must be to the Goddesses who made their world habitable. The teaching must be offered slowly, in terms the Sawls could accept, in tale-chant and metaphor, by digging in the guild records for lost gems of history, approaching the truth gradually so that it was never imposed, but intuited and absorbed from within, to become an understanding profound enough to survive the next seventy-five centuries.

Stavros was glad he was young.

Such teaching would require a lifetime.

He glanced at Liphar, whose attention now hardly left him except in sleep. He nodded and the young man smiled beatifically. CRI was replying to questions and cheerfully supplying details like the chief scientist at a press conference. Stavros rose, diffident but firm. He indicated the expectant hush of torches in the clearing.

"Excuse me, Commander, but out of respect, I don't think we should keep them waiting any longer."

We? thought Susannah. *There's only one of us they're waiting for.* His tact was touching, being so new. Already he was learning something of the arts of leadership.

Weng agreed that the debriefing could continue at any time and buttoned up the collar of her spotless uniform. Danforth pleaded exhaustion and asked that his respects be conveyed. Susannah elected to remain with Ghirra until she was sure he was out of danger, from his wounds and from himself.

Stavros' smile approved her decision. He ducked into the shadows where the Master Healer was sleeping soundly and gazed down at him lingeringly.

"The many times he has eased my pain, here I am unable to do anything for him in return. Healing is *his* gift . . . and yours, Susannah."

He hugged her tightly and was gone, shrugging off his own weariness, striding through the entry cylinder with sudden energy. In the clearing, the bright torches came to attention like a dress regiment. The throng murmured in welcome.

Susannah went with Megan to the mouth of the cylinder. The council of guild elders, the Kethed, waited in a reduced semicircle, missing Ghirra and Aguidran. Plump TiNiamar of the FoodGuild stood slightly forward with Kav Ashimmel as Stavros approached.

Ashimmel was resplendent in her embroidered whites, her iron-gray curls stirred by faint breezes. She faced Stavros squarely, and he returned her stern regard, then took a short step back and bowed his head in respect. Ashimmel's taut mouth quirked, not quite a smile. Her rigid posture eased. She bowed her head briefly in return and stepped aside to allow Stavros to proceed her along the winding lines of torchlight. TiNiamar moved in smartly to accompany Weng, and at Liphar's urgings, Megan and McPherson filed along behind.

A chant was begun high up on the stair. It travelled swiftly down the lines to gather every one of the five thousand voices in a song of celebration. From the top of the cliff, the priest-horns boomed a joyous rhythm into a night alight with torchfire and in the east, the burning gleam of a billion stars.

Susannah wandered back into the Underbelly and dropped heavily into the nearest chair. The chanting and torches receded. She watched after the departing throng for a long time, musing in the depths of her chair, feeling it absurd that she wanted to cry now, over this, after all she had just lived through relatively dry-eyed. But the placid lamplit darkness of the Underbelly was comforting, and the breezy scents of new plants and damp earth soothed her expectations of sadness yet to come. She tried to recall when she had first known that she would leave this world and Stavros would stay behind.

At the console, Danforth gently cleared his throat. "You okay?"

She turned to smile at him wanly, then rose with determined energy and claimed the empty seat beside him. "So what about the specifics on the ecosystem? When the system had unbalanced so far in one direction, as during a Great Destruction, what made it swing back again at all?"

True delight warmed Danforth's ebony face. "You're going to like this one . . . I think I've found the inbuilt reset Ibiá was talking about. CRI, show off your biochemical model."

Susannah peered at the diagram that promptly appeared on the monitor.

"Neat, eh? Here's Valla Ired, here Lagri and in the middle, the Sawls." Danforth traced a structural line in the diagram. "It's Ibiá's lithium connection."

Susannah pointed. "And photosynthesis?"

"Yup. Let me lay it out for you: the creators needed to control water and heat distribution in order to get through the hot time of the passage through the Coal Sack. The whole planet couldn't be made habitable. They needed some place to put the excess heat.

"So they created an artificial habitable zone more or less at the planet's equator by pulling the heat to one side, the desert, then the water to an opposite position where it could be controlled and distributed as needed. And essentially, they split photosynthesis into two processes, using lithium as a sort of control substance, you see?

"Now, Valla Ired from her ocean controls the water distribution. She processes the CO_2 produced within the ecosystem, but lithium effects her uptake of CO_2 by controlling the alkalinity of water. Using sunlight to split LiO into lithium and oxygen, she increases the acidity of her water and can clear the atmosphere of more CO_2.

"Lagri also uses sunlight to split LiO, but she counters Valla's moisture disbursement by recombining free lithium with water, to control humidity and produce free hydrogen, some of which the Sawls use for necessary fuel, and energy which fuels her own metabolism. These processes had badly degenerated by the time we got here, but do you begin to see how this cycle acts as a needed population control within a system of very limited resources?"

Susannah nodded admiringly. "If the population grows too large, too much CO_2 is produced, which acidifies . . ."

"The ocean. This poisons Valla Ired's metabolism, her control weakens. Water vapor builds up in the atmosphere due to evaporation, which then poisons Lagri, breathable oxygen decreases and the Sawls die off."

"So it *is* culling, like I said, to keep the species tough and active during their eons of environmental crisis. The sick and the weak go first, plus a kill-off decreases the excess of CO_2 and restores the balance for a while, until the population grows too large again. There's your reset."

Danforth nodded. "Or on the other hand, if in her field manipulations of the climate, Lagri grows too strong, by heating up the system's water she can decrease CO_2 to a point which also weakens Valla. Conversely, if Valla can flood Lagri's heat with moisture . . ."

Susannah regarded the diagram musingly. "I only hope they meant it to be a gentler process originally, a gradual shifting of balances to control the ecosystem more subtly."

"When you're thinking of the long-term survival of a race, you may be willing to forego a certain concern for the individual," said Danforth. "The real point is, it worked for a long, long while before it got knocked out of whack. With this planet's astronomical situation, it has no business supporting life at all. It wasn't nice for the generations of Sawls around when the peak of a population boom brought on a Devastation, but at least there were some of them left to complain about it then, and will be still, when the system moves out of the Coal Sack in another seventy-five thousand years. Without the Sisters, the Sawls would have vanished long, long ago."

He withdrew for a while, bemused, clicking his fingers along the rim of the keypad. Then he exclaimed, "Damn, the sheer audacity of it! The utter genius! I would like to have known those old Sawls!"

Susannah grinned at his outburst. They sat in comfortable silence, each contemplating the profound elegance of the ancients' plan while adding to mental lists of questions yet to be answered.

"By the way," said Danforth finally. "I asked the doc to come with us."

"You did? When?"

"Some point during the return flight. But he was so out of it, he probably won't even remember."

"Ah." Susannah was sure she understood now why the Master Healer had decided to live. "Oh Taylor, that was brilliant. I wish I'd thought of it."

"Between us, I figure we can convince Weng. He may have a hard time fitting in again here, with all he's learned and been through. I thought we sort of owe him a new lease on life, that is, if he wants to come."

"Oh, I think he will." She smiled at him gratefully. "I think he'll jump at the chance."

"It's, I mean, *he's* gone, Commander." McPherson shifted uneasily.

Susannah clicked off her searchbeam. "None of us know anything about this, Weng. I promise you. He was still there when they took away Aguidran."

Weng folded her arms thoughtfully, gazing at the tall line of torches burning along the dark clifftop. Singing resounded from the cave mouths.

"Spirited him away, they did," said Megan. "For whatever reason."

"Gotta admit, they're saving us a lot of trouble," McPherson offered. "Not having to bring him back in cold storage 'n all."

"Not having to explain certain details . . ." added Megan.

Weng rocked gently on her heels.

"CONPLEX is used to losing men in the field, but it will complicate the invalidation of the claim if there's any whiff of suspicion that it wasn't an accident," said Megan. "Going to be hard enough to convince them as it is, with all those charges he racked up against us."

Weng sucked in a deep breath of damp-scented night air, then sighed and shook her head. "Why did you even bother to bring him back?"

Susannah and McPherson said nothing, but Megan smiled, knowing the victory was won. "They didn't want your job getting too easy on you, Commander."

47

Stavros Maria Rafael Ibiá became Kav Ibiá a ship's week later before the towering glass cylinders of Eles-Nol.

The vast glowing hall was nearly empty. Most of the population was too busy preparing for the dawn Planting to attend the ceremony, but the PriestGuild had been temporarily excused from those duties and Susannah was there with Megan and the others, Danforth having laboriously negotiated the long spiral stairs for his first viewing of DulElesi's major monument to the ancient technology.

They watched Ashimmel robe the new priest in embroidered white as he swore loyalty to his guild. Then he knelt to receive from her scarred hands the silvery lump of guar, the pure lithium mined deep in the rock. His face tightened only slightly as the guar dropped into his palms. He rose and advanced the short, agonizing distance to the central cylinder. As a PriestGuild elder drew open a tiny square panel, Kav Ibiá deposited the guar within.

When he returned across the arched wooden bridgeway, his eyes alight, the Master Healer stepped forward with herbal salve for his burns.

"No miracle to worry you this time, GuildMaster." Stavros smiled through the pain in his damaged palms. "Clausen was right. The old man tricked us. There was no guar at the leavetaking. Only the Sisters."

Ghirra was gaunt from his mourning, but his long face was calm. His touch was a feather weight, spreading the cooling salve. He said with quiet disapproval, "These Sisters do not know you do this for them, Ibi."

"Not for Them, Ghirra." Stavros nodded behind him, into the waiting ranks of the PriestGuild. "For them. It may take some time," he promised, "but I will end the guar ritual. For now, it's a needed metaphor for a more natural connection to the Sisters which every Sawl once had, and someday, will have again. Science, Ghirra, to replace the miracle . . ."

Ghirra smiled gravely. "I will tell Xifa this promise, so she will know it when I am gone."

"Yes, and so she'll hold me to it."

When dawn came again, Kav Ibiá's first duty as Ritual Master was to welcome his own designated apprentice to full membership in the guild. As the guildsmen chanted, the newly elected Master Healer stood ready to ease with her skilled hands the young man's painful passage into priesthood.

But as the guar ate into his willing, virgin palm, Liphar showed little awareness of pain. He thought only of his Ritual Master's loving, encouraging touch, and of the solemn privilege that it was to feed the Goddesses.

48

They made love a final time. The weeks between had made her leaving harder for them both.

"Did it occur to you to stay?" he asked her.

"Did it occur to you to ask?" she replied.

Stavros ran smooth-scarred palms along her back, aching for her already. "I'm hoping that when you're done rediscovering the universe through Ghirra's eyes, you'll both be back."

Susannah calculated the years and distances involved. Given the explosive nature of the data they would bring to Earth, a return expedition was likely. Many of them, in fact. "Perhaps we will. Or perhaps *I* will."

And then she added, "We have yet to prove that we can even leave . . ."

But mere hours later, Stavros stood at the top of the cliff among his guildsmen and others to see the bright fire ignite at the Lander's base. The cliff rock shook as engines lain idle for four months coughed dry mud and woke. The tall russet stalks in the surrounding fields bent low in the heat gale. The tilted cone vibrated and lifted, so gradually that his every muscle tensed with the effort of urging the silver craft to flight.

The tilt righted. The cone did not fall back in a whiteout of flame. Slowly, stubbornly, it crawled up out of the gravity well, gaining speed until it was a shining bird-speck climbing the hard malachite sky.

And then it was gone.

Stavros fought the urge to cry out after it, after them, his departing colleagues, after her, whom he loved, but not so much as the new life that had claimed him.

Liphar touched his arm in concern, and Master Healer Xifa offered a face of gentle sympathy. But as the smoke billows cleared and the roar of engines faded into lonely silence, Kav Ashimmel rubbed her scarred hands together like a busy merchant and started briskly toward the cliff stair. On the wide top step, she glanced back at Stavros expectantly as if to say, "Well, my young upstart? Isn't there work to be done?"

TITLES AVAILABLE FROM
VGSF

The prices shown below were correct at the time
of going to press (July 1988)

☐ 04008 4	HEGIRA	*Greg Bear*	£2.95
☐ 04090 4	STRENGTH OF STONES	*Greg Bear*	£2.95
☐ 04009 2	ANGEL WITH THE SWORD	*C.J. Cherryh*	£2.95
☐ 04044 0	THE DREAMSTONE	*C.J. Cherryh*	£2.50
☐ 04032 2	THE TREE OF SWORDS AND JEWELS	*C. J. Cherryh*	£2.95
☐ 03988 4	THE OTHER SIDE OF THE SKY	*Arthur C. Clarke*	£2.95
☐ 04199 4	BUY JUPITER	*Isaac Asimov*	£2.95
☐ 03995 7	WITCH WORLD	*Andre Norton*	£2.50
☐ 03996 5	WEB OF THE WITCH WORLD	*Andre Norton*	£2.50
☐ 03999 X	YEAR OF THE UNICORN	*Andre Norton*	£2.50
☐ 03998 1	THREE AGAINST THE WITCH WORLD	*Andre Norton*	£2.50
☐ 03997 3	WARLOCK OF THE WITCH WORLD	*Andre Norton*	£2.50
☐ 04007 6	STAR GATE	*Andre Norton*	£2.50
☐ 04124 2	STAR MAN'S SON	*Andre Norton*	£2.50
☐ 03989 2	TO LIVE AGAIN	*Robert Silverberg*	£2.95
☐ 04038 6	UP THE LINE	*Robert Silverberg*	£2.95
☐ 04040 8	THE TIME HOPPERS	*Robert Silverberg*	£2.95
☐ 04032 7	THE FACELESS MAN	*Jack Vance*	£2.50
☐ 04053 X	THE BRAVE FREE MEN	*Jack Vance*	£2.50
☐ 04052 1	THE ASUTRA	*Jack Vance*	£2.50
☐ 04022 X	MISSION OF GRAVITY	*Hal Clement*	£2.50
☐ 04096 3	MEDUSA'S CHILDREN	*Bob Shaw*	£2.50
☐ 04090 4	WHO GOES HERE?	*Bob Shaw*	£2.95
☐ 04011 4	EARTHWIND	*Robert Holdstock*	£2.95
☐ 04023 8	IN THE VALLEY OF THE STATUES	*Robert Holdstock*	£2.95
☐ 04125 0	QUEST OF THE THREE WORLDS	*Cordwainer Smith*	£2.50

Also available: VGSF CLASSICS

☐ 03819 5	THE SIRENS OF TITAN	*Kurt Vonnegut*	£3.50
☐ 03821 7	MORE THAN HUMAN	*Theodore Sturgeon*	£3.50
☐ 03820 9	A TIME OF CHANGES	*Robert Silverberg*	£3.50

Continued overleaf

☐ 03849 7	THE CITY AND THE STARS	*Arthur C. Clarke*	£3.50
☐ 03850 0	THE DOOR INTO SUMMER	*Robert Heinlein*	£3.50
☐ 03851 9	THE REPRODUCTIVE SYSTEM	*John Sladek*	£3.50
☐ 03978 7	A FALL OF MOONDUST	*Arthur C. Clarke*	£3.50
☐ 03979 5	ROGUE MOON	*Algis Budrys*	£3.50
☐ 03981 7	MAN PLUS	*Frederik Pohl*	£3.50
☐ 03993 0	INVERTED WORLD	*Christopher Priest*	£3.50
☐ 04061 0	FLOWERS FOR ALGERNON	*Daniel Keyes*	£3.50
☐ 04122 6	JOURNEY BEYOND TOMORROW		
		Robert Sheckley	£3.50
☐ 04144 7	DANGEROUS VISIONS	*ed. by Harlan Ellison*	£6.95
☐ 04123 4	BABEL-17	*Samuel R. Delany*	£3.95
☐ 04127 7	GLADIATOR-AT-LAW		
		Frederik Pohl & C.M. Kornbluth	£3.95
☐ 04121 8	BRING THE JUBILEE	*Ward Moore*	£3.95
☐ 04134 X	BEASTS	*John Crowley*	£3.95
☐ 04195 1	RENDEZVOUS WITH RAMA	*Arthur C. Clarke*	£3.50
☐ 03994 9	THE SPACE MACHINE	*Christopher Priest*	£3.50

All these books are available at your shop or newsagent or can be ordered direct from the publisher. Just tick the titles you want and fill in the form below.

VGSF, Cash Sales Department, PO Box 11, Falmouth, Cornwall.

Please send cheque or postal order, no currency.

Please allow cost of book(s) plus the following for postage and packing:

UK customers – Allow 60p for the first book, 25p for the second book plus 15p for each additional book ordered, to a maximum charge of £1.90.

BFPO – Allow 60p for the first book, 25p for the second book plus 15p per copy for the next seven books, thereafter 9p per book.

Overseas customers including Eire – Allow £1.25 for the first book, 75p for the second book plus 28p for each additional book ordered.

NAME *(Block letters)* ....

ADDRESS ....

....

....